Sorrowblade

Untold ages ago the race of Elves were cast to the four winds, forced to dwell in the underworld within the veil of the Evermore to protect the Tree of Life. Split into separate clans, their dying race withdrew to the far reaches of the world. Among them existed a darker faction of Elves who had burrowed deep into the depths of the earth, evolving into the seven houses of the Drow.

From the seed of the Elders came the children of the Faerie with a dire legacy to fulfill; a generation of Elvenborn whose destiny was to save the Faerylands.

Almost forgotten among the Fey were the whispered legends of a warrior priestess from the Sisterhood of Blood; a young outcast trained in the forbidden sorcery of an accursed cult known as the Obsidian Order. These maidens skilled in both spell and blade were charged with battling the dark and terrible blight known as the Craven. Those few who might remember their saga know that without their noble sacrifice all hope would have been lost.

Titles by Michel Savage

Faerylands Series
The Grey Forest
Soulstorm Keep
Sorrowblade
Ivory

Shadoworld Series
Shadow of the Sun
Veil of Shadows
Shadows Gate

Outlaws of Europa
Rebels of Alpha Prime

Hellbot • Battle Planet

A Couple of Zeros

Forgotten Future

Broken Mirror

Project EVE

Witchwood

III

Faerylands
Sorrowblade

MICHEL SAVAGE

Mother Nature has a voice
one only needs to listen

*Artwork from the Faerylands series
available online*

Enter the Grey Forest
www.GreyForest.com

FAERYLANDS • Sorrowblade
Faerylands Trilogy ~ Book 3

The Grey Forest
P.O. Box 71494
Springfield, OR 97475

www.GreyForest.com

Cover art by Michel Savage

ISBN: 978-09719168-8-3

First Edition: March 2017

Printed in the United States of America

0 9 8 7 6 5 4 3 2 1

Sequel from Book 2
Soulstorm Keep

Wrath of the Drow

A once beautiful elvish maiden from the Eternal City, Medusa Sorrowblade earned her legend battling to free their world from the terrible blight known as the Craven.

Banished to the lone isle of Tyre, now an acolyte in the studies of forbidden sorcery as one of the Sisterhood of Blood; the cult of accursed and powerful priestesses known as the Obsidian Order, reside alone in a brooding structure christened as a tower of madness. A tall ghostly fortress of despair created by the woven tapestry of magic siphoned from the living essence of the Drow, whose Seven Houses dwell within the ruins of a shattered city, sunken deep beneath this mystic shrine.

Forbidden from stepping from these sacred grounds, the Order battles in the realms of the netherworld against the withering; lurking as a dark hunger awaiting its chance to consume what little is left of their fragile world.

The Elves had become a dying race, and if they failed in their task, their future would be lost and the race of Fey would be the last of their kind.

Table of Contents

Dawn

"You have told us the enchanting story of the Grey Forest and of Soulstorm keep, Mother Nyx, but what ever happened to the High Elves?" The tiny sprite inquired, for she was a bundle of curiosity and questions about the wide world she was so very eager to explore.

Nyx stood from her throne carved of living wood. Her feet were long roots that withdrew and replanted themselves upon every step, for the mother of the Fey was a tree sprite herself. Her skin was taught and marbled with rings of bark, green leaves sprouted from her hair, her emerald eyes were glazed with life as her very essence was one with the Evermore; the breathing spirit of the living earth. The warm morning light seeped in through the entry to the colossal timber hall as birds of every hue flitted about the high arches of the chamber. Mother Nyx was an ancient creature of the forest, born by nature, fathered by the Elves, the last of the Elvenborn.

The grand tree was her castle, its bloom and branches reaching out to the blue sky, towering above all others. It stood as a titan, a dominant icon at the center of a lush forest, its leaves glittering in the morning dew of the rising sun. Nyx had grown the tree from a tiny sapling, its roots set deep within the rich soil reached to the very edges of the valley; touching every living plant. The forest matron stood tall, towering over the little sprite before her, who sat innocently at the roots of her feet as she fiddled with her pale golden hair.

"Now Dawn, don't be impatient," Nyx spoke gently, her eyes curved with the soft smile of her cheeks, "for it is sunrise, and time for you to attend to your duties," she marked as her hand reached out to catch the rays of sunlight radiating into the throne room.

It seemed as if Dawn wanted to pout but was unable to make her lips form a frown, for she was the essence of sunlight herself, the smiling sun that caresses the land with its warm kiss. Though she was young and free as the morning light, Dawn had learned the importance of her task. The world was waiting for the coming of a new day.

Dawn tilted her head and opened her mouth with a wide yawn and stretched her thin arms. With the briefest note of hesitation, she fluttered her translucent wings and flew out the doorway in a shower of tiny lights that followed in her wake. There were many of her kind zipping through the forest leaves across the valley this glorious day. Nipping the dark crevices with illumination, seeds sprouted upon her touch, flowers bloomed and leaves turned and sleeping creatures blinked their eyes, turning towards the warmth of the shining sun. Young birds chirped, hungry for their morning meal, while nocturnal creatures squinted at the encroaching glare, and withdrew into the nearest crevice or hollow to slumber through the day.

One thing Nyx had learned over the centuries was that there was an equilibrium that must be maintained with all things. Too much of one or another shifted the balance. Too much light could leave her children blinded and burned, too much darkness, and they would wither away. There was no true good or evil in the world, only the extremes which would sway our choices. To help or to harm, it was the way of things forged by the perspective of those that exist in this realm. The Faerylands was an enchanting world of possibilities where one's potential could be unveiled and explored.

Nyx turned in thought as her bright green eyes darkened to a shade of moss, for things had not always been this way. There had been times of great struggle and strife that had suppressed her kind into the shadows, hidden from the rest of the world while the Evermore slumbered. It had been countless centuries of renewal to correct the discord their realm had suffered from the blight of the Craven. Thankfully, its taint no longer touched the lives of the forest fey, though the scars of its unpleasant memory still lingered. Nyx was one of the few true-blood Elvenborn, whose task it was to guide the children of the Fey after the patron Elves had faded from their world.

This hidden glade where she now rooted was but one of many such sanctuaries scattered across the darkened lands, reclaimed from the decay which a selfish and brutal species had left in ruin after their fall. These hollow beings were known to the fey as the race of Men, empty vessels that had shed themselves from the Evermore. They had poisoned Mother Nature with their taint, which had spread beyond the far reaches of the world to the doors of the Eternal City, where even the Elven Lords discovered they were not safe from its touch. But that was a long time ago, longer than most could remember. For only the Undying, the ancient spirits of the land, sea, and sky; could speak they're true name. These ancients were the lost race of the Dragons, mentors to the most High Elves.

The great dragons were all but a memory; for they no longer rumbled within the earth, churning the waters of the wide oceans, or stirred the winds as they flew among the limitless skies. Their spirits now resided as one with the Gaia, the very bloodline to the Evermore itself. It was the living energy that made us what we were, in every tree and leaf, in every foot and paw, in every scale of fish, and every feather of bird. It was the darkness and the light, and breathed through every part of the world. The Evermore was the purity of life itself.

Nyx had a burden to carry, for it was her responsibility to teach the faerie the ways of nature and to heal the earth as their ancestors had done since the dawn of time. It had been the beginning of a new age the day she had emerged from the underworld to unfold her limbs to the open sky. Nyx stood at the doorway, soaking in the morning light upon her face as tiny leaves sprouted in her hair with the kiss of each sunbeam. She turned and rooted herself upon the sculpted throne of the living wood and waited for the children of her forest to gather; for today was the day of stories, which the eager fey assembled in numbers to attend on every eve before each new moon.

One by one, creatures of the woods and brook, from hillside and grotto, high peaks or sunken caves, traveled from the far reaches of the valley to assemble within her court. They came to the great tree to learn of the past, and of their future. Beings of light and dark, of mud and straw, of bark and root, and of fur and fang, gathered as one. No matter their differences, within the great tree all were welcome and considered one another as family, and saw each other as equals. No matter how large or small, or thick, or thin, unyielding or ethereal; under the constant gaze of mother Nyx, all were recognized as one.

It took the entire day for the congregation to grow as the sun began to wane in the sky. Fireflies blinked softly to drift within the throne room as the shadow of night fell and the stars began to glitter in the evening sky. A cool night breeze sifted through the thick leaves, rustling high above in the cathedral of woven limbs that enveloped the audience in its protective embrace.

"Good eve, my children," Nyx began as the last of the fey straggled in; her green soothing eyes were alive with the flicker of life as she gazed down upon her audience resting at her feet.

"Good eve, Mother," issued from the wee folk who answered in joyous unison from those who had voices to do so. The crowd of playful fey quickly calmed their chatter to huddle together and snuggle amongst one another as the storytime began. All attention fell to Nyx, for she was their oracle, their soothsayer, and weaver of tales. The living Fey were always curious; for those who were not had minds of mush and rot.

Dawn was there with her sisters, aglow with their inner light, other fairy males and females, boys and girls, and all creatures in-between sat and crouched, crawled, and slithered into a position of rest, while those who had them, perked their ears of whatever shape to hear tonight's tale. Even the nocturnal creatures of forest and caverns gathered for this evening's story, their glowing eyes peering in through the dark crevices and tangled branches beyond the lattice walls. For this evening Nyx had promised a special story.

With a curl of her wooden hand, glowing seeds drifted from her palm to swirl about the room in a mesmerizing dance of light. With a delighted gasp of awe from the audience below, the shimmering seeds collected into a central orb above them and shattered into a shower of bright sparks, birthing laughter and excited glee from the younger fey.

"Tonight, my wildlings," Nyx began with a capricious glint in her eyes as the resounding tone of her voice soothed the crowd, "I will tell you the legend of Sorrowblade, who lived in a time not so long ago..."

ℰᏯᏇ

Every story has a beginning and an end, but the tale of Sorrowblade reaches far beyond the centuries; back to a single moment in time when there was nothing more than perfection. Many might imagine the Eternal City of the ancient High Elves as a palace of white marble and golden filigree glittering among lush gardens and blue waterfalls, with spires of bright silk flags uncurling upon a gentle breeze as their towers reached high into the clouds. Truth be told, it was anything but such a fanciful vision. Within the crevices of the earth wove a honeycomb of cathedral arches of gray stone. Flows of spring water cascaded over etched alcoves like liquid panes as they poured into the mist-filled voids deep below the surface. These were the burrows of the Elders, where stone and water met, containing the libraries of knowledge where the elven folk hid their immortal secrets from prying eyes.

They were concealed from the world above; even from the Undying themselves, for both the pride and the shame of the Elves was so profound that they forever sealed it away from those who might criticize their noble race for their misdeeds. It was a cold broth of fear and conceit that led them from the fields and forests and tall mountains, and down into the forbidden depths of the earth. For in their long years the Elves had unveiled hidden knowledge which they dare not reveal.

This world has changed hands with many other beings that have come and gone since the spark of creation itself. Creatures we will never know, and those that are yet to be. The time of the Faerylands was one of many that had been woven into the tapestry of life ...but there was once a time of grave concern among the living. Beings came into this world known as Man, who were similar in many ways to the Elves, thus they were once welcomed as brethren. Though what type of men they would prove to be was revealed in the centuries to come. For thousands of years, they mingled as the benevolent Elven folk accepted all life. However, in but a small span of time, the race of men began to swarm across the earth, suffocating it like a plague of locusts.

The wise elders of the elves approached mankind, concerned about their growing greed and rampant leeching of all that was nature; but their arrogance was too strong, for they seemed blind to their sins with their empty eyes and hollow hearts. They were void of conscience and seen but as depraved husks that became detached from the Evermore, the living essence of our world. It was the first time the High Elves had been so utterly deceived by another race to have misread them so. In the tense years that followed, the Elves learned to fear mankind, for these walking vermin were prone to poisoning everything they touched. They decimated mountains and rivers and darkened the oceans with their decay, and even the skies were tormented by the fetid breath of their vile creations.

They murdered beasts of scales and feather and hide, wiping them from existence; and there finally came the hour when they declared war against the Elves. Fearing their hidden knowledge of the Gaia would be discovered by these mindless brutes who would only exploit their secrets, the Elves withdrew into the Sidhe, the deep burrows of the earth as the very essence of the living world retreated below the land, forever shunning the race of Men that ravaged the surface above. Within these secluded vaults, the elven folk continued their sacred ways as the rest of the Faerie migrated to the protective embrace of the Evermore as mankind ravaged the world above.

There finally came a time to pass when humanity was no more, and their living existence was extinguished from the earth by their own hand. Even so, the Elves waited beyond the boundaries of their sanctuaries, for a new menace had filled their place. The blight of the Craven lingered in their wake, the corrupt shadow that the race of Men had left behind to darken the land. Sentient beings such as the Dwarves, also retreated back into the underworld, for they also feared the savagery of Men and had distanced themselves from their once enduring friendship with the Elves.

In their stout breasts and thick heads, they believed this curse was deserved as they had felt betrayed by the Elven Lords in their battle against the scourge of man and its ghostly wraith which had corrupted the land. The Elves, though, were no match for this strange enemy which began to consume their world. The Dwarves cared not, and they refused to listen to the reasons why the elven folk had abandoned the battlefield and left their bearded comrades behind to face their dire fate alone.

The Elves were dying you see, and they had but one duty that outshined all others, which was to protect the World Tree. Even among the countless races of fey, little did they know that the enormous Tree of Life, which stood like a symbol of strength at the center of their Eden, was actually but a mere sprig in its infancy. Powerful magics were woven to braid an illusion of strength and stability, using the faerie glamour as a mask against their enemies. For mankind saw power only in size and might, but they would stop at nothing to gain the living energy of Mother Nature to mold to their own ends.

Thus, through guile and deceit, the Elves spread rumors, gossip, and lies, that the Tree of Life was actually but a myth, a story told to children in the ancient past, and nothing more. As rogue knights and paladins and scribes from the courts and kingdoms of Men failed in their quests to find the hidden tree of this lost Eden, the stories of its existence began to wane. Soon the World Tree was but a legend and a forgotten tale, for the race of Men could no longer perceive the spirit of the Gaia which had abandoned them. It was the charge of the Elves to preserve the sacred tree and to protect this spark of life from all harm; though as powerful as the sacred tree was, compared to the eternal cosmos, it was still young and fragile.

The love of the Elves was returned to nature, and from this union was birthed the Elvenborn; the first blood faerie who would have the strength and fortitude to continue their legacy.

ഊ◌ഔ

"Venusa," the high priestess ordered with a spiteful glare towards the brooding girl who stood before her, "you are to be banished from the temple for your offenses, and are hereby instructed never to return to this sacred sanctuary!" The lean woman spat.

The young girl was robed in nothing but a sheer linen of white, her hands were not bound together but bore the two red cords of exile wrapped upon her wrists, which dangled like icons of shame beside her thighs; trailing back upon the wet stone floor behind her.

Venusa Viper was one of many recruits accepted into the folds of the High Elves who rose from the ancient island of the Vy, a primal world older than the sky itself. Many new disciples had a rough time learning their place and bending to the rules of the temple grounds, but rarely was there ordered a punishment quite so dreadful as to earn expulsion. The unbound twine, dyed in vivid red, was the Elves symbolic icon of the cut and severed umbilical to the Evermore, separating her from the very threads of life. It was the lowest emblem of dishonor, to be shunned so by the essence of life itself.

The discouraged girl shed but a single tear, for her eyes also held a seething glare of contempt. Venusa lifted herself from her knees and turned from the persecuting stare of the high priestess and her guards, to make her long walk out from the gates of the temple and beyond the labyrinth of narrow cliffs that led from their hidden sanctuary. Anger welled up within her upon every step, as did her reluctance to leave her home. It was times like these that tested her strength of spirit, even though they left her feeling infertile and alone.

The race of men emerged from the Vy, and built a vast fortress as a keep for their kind. They were barbaric savages that ate the flesh and bones of others and wore their skins to cover themselves. They wrapped themselves in these husks of flesh and fur and were named by their rough and unpleasant appearance. The Elves had embraced their kind and began to teach them of hearth and fire, and the weaving plants and silk to wean them from wearing the blood-stained vestments they adorned. It was a shocking sight for a High Elf to see such a creature to don the skin of another being as if it were their own.

With patience and poise, the race of elves aided men to become cultured so that they could rise to their own potential and discover a greater destiny. Little did the Elves realize in their ignorance and blind trust, that their gifts of knowledge would become their own undoing. The race of Men were curious creatures that showed promising skill with eye and hand, and learned from the elves the joys of poetry and music and art, but they seemed to lack the ability to tap the higher learning of philosophy of wisdom and inner peace; for the great majority of them became enamored by baubles and power, and could not perceive the true magic of the world around them.

Over the passage of time, Man became jealous of the Elves and suspicious as to why they would not share the divine secrets they so fiercely protected. The more these savages saw in the wonders of the Elven lands, the further they dared to hunger and take what they desired by force. The highborn Elves knew mankind was brutish but did not foresee just how dangerous and unpredictable they could be. This gluttony, this hunger, this craving that seethed through their veins seemed to consume them; and the season finally came when Man used these bitter talents against their kind.

Diplomacy was reached, and those few children bred between the two races were allowed to enter the Eternal City as a gesture of peace. Venusa had felt like a mongrel among the pure-blood elves, and the way they looked down their noses upon her reinforced that sentiment every day. Her ears were small and barely pointed, and were such an embarrassment that she covered them with a circlet worn beneath a shrouding hood.

She had never felt truly welcome here and felt strangely out of place in this alien atmosphere of cold twisting mazes and lofty corridors. She was raised near the Shale Mountains under the big sky near the valley of Soulstorm Keep. As mankind grew in numbers, they built boats to travel across the great waters and set foot upon distant lands; and took arms of wood, and metal, and fire, to loot and plunder wherever they roamed. Amid a treaty with the highborn Elves, scores of interbred children were accepted as scholars to learn of their peaceful ways; for it was mankind's obscure attempt to glean their hidden knowledge. With this agreement between their two races, men and elves held an unsteady truce.

For what seemed like countless days, Venusa made her way barefoot through the web of corridors, only to be shunned by any Elf whose path she crossed. The sight of the red cords bound upon her wrists would cause them to turn their backs to her as she passed. It wasn't the rejection she was given or the insulting whispers from their lips as she strolled past that scarred her so, it was the disdain she felt from this abandonment that poisoned her mind and began to germinate within her.

A part of her felt sadness, but an equal half felt the writhing fingers of spite clamp around her wounded heart that grew ever colder. Though she tried to understand the reasons for her punishment, her tears only fed the seeds of vengeance that began to sprout roots of hatred within her.

This was a dangerous combination for an Elf, but she was also half-human; an outcast that could never meet the approval of the lofty elves and their quest for purity. Among the chieftains of the Vy, the Elves were called egotistic and vain within their huddled chatter far beyond the perception of their pointy ears. Venusa was torn but not broken. Though she was deserted by her own kind for being a half-breed and shunned for her impurity by the guardians, she was now left as a lowly orphan of both worlds.

Instead of collapsing in despair, she saw it as a test. Upon the final gate that emerged as she left the Elven City, she stood in the pale light of day at the threshold of the cavern walls; pausing for but a moment, knowing she could never return. With a single step beyond its shimmering boundary, she appeared as a wisp within a circle of stones braced within the mossy ground. In a moment mixed of pain and ecstasy, the wisp of light unfolded to weave her physical form into being within this dark and misty realm; leaving her standing in the center of the ancient cairn. For a confusing moment, a shiver ran up her spine as a chilling wind touched her skin for the first time as she emerged from the Elven lands and the protective embrace of the Evermore.

Looking down at her hands, she tugged at the ruby cords in aggravation to remove them; but the Elven magic persisted and the bindings would not come undone. Though they did not pinch, they had a strange weight to them and she now saw that the scarlet dye of their color had begun to stain her pure white linens wherever they touched as if to further blemish her in disgrace.

The young half-breed girl huddled against the biting wind as the crimson hue began to seep through every strand of her thin mantle. For a moment, a sliver of fear shot through her, wondering how she would survive alone in this bleak landscape. She leaned against the nearest stone cairn as she stepped beyond the closing portal to get a glimpse of the world before her, for it was one she barely recognized.

Flitting through the sharp wind flickered a tiny speck of coal, tumbling through the breeze like a dark leaf. With effort, the ebony butterfly reached her as she held out her hand to catch this fragile creature. It fluttered there once and gently closed its obsidian black wings. Venusa closed her eyes and listened, for the tiny creature was a Sending; a message of mystical nature. Venusa heard the soft whispers that emanated from her cupped hands and learned that the Dark Elves had heard of her plight, and that the House of Wrath had answered. The Drow were few but their numbers grew as the disdain for their distant brethren, the High Elves, had mounted; soon to reach its crest.

A howl broke the eerie silence beyond the misty moors that swirled around the standing stones; the portal to the hidden world below. Venusa turned her attention to the fog for but a moment, then gritted her teeth as a sting of pain rippled up her arm. She grasped at her hand which had held the black butterfly and saw that it had merged to her wrist. Her salvation by the mystical darkness would now forever be a part of her being, which had marked her as one of their own.

Through the gloom strode a giant gray wolf, its eyes aglow with an inner fire. Atop this shaggy beast rode a dark hooded figure with a large bow strapped to its back. For a moment, the girl saw its eyes flash her way as the creature spoke while its mount panted through its ivory fangs.

"The order of the Drow calls you, show me your mark," the man instructed with a growl.

With a tear of pain, Venusa held up her wrist to show the scout as he held out a gloved hand to pluck her from the cold ground and onto the back of the furred beast. With a clench of its silver mane in his fist, the dire wolf jolted off into the haze with its new passenger. Venusa held on for dear life, finding herself clinging onto this strange chauffeur dressed in his black leather coated with a layer of fine sable fur. She lay with her head against his back, his dark coat felt soft and the scent earthy, and she found the soothing fragrance strangely familiar.

By leaps and bounds through the thick fog the giant wolf strode over broken stone and lichen, over crevice and cliff while guided by the howl of its master. She felt the lungs of the hound heave between her legs with every breath as it raced at impossible speed through the countryside. The haze of the sun above struggled to reach them through the gloom, its brightness left dull and sterile.

"Who are you...?" the girl finally dared to whisper from behind, fearing with every passing moment that she could be flung from the rear of the silverback mongrel in a heartbeat.

"I am known by many names, sister," he answered, noting the familiarity he offered to her over his shoulder, "but you may address me as, Ironbow," the shadowy figure replied, the chill of his breath billowing like a cloud from his lips within the folds of his hood as he tucked her arms securely around his waist. The gait of the beast was hypnotic as was the drum of its giant paws in its stride across the mossy fields; and within its rhythm, the exhausted girl clinging for her life on the back of the giant wolf fell into a slumber as they sped into the night among the choking darkness.

Venusa awoke from what felt like a strange dream and struggled to compose herself as her mind struggled to fill in the fragments of recent events. For but a moment she was lost, not knowing who or where she was as she squinted her eyes in the dim candlelight. Her body ached and she struggled to sit upright, noting the mounds of several thick furred skins lying beneath her delicate fingers.

She found herself in a cavern of the likes she had never seen, surrounded by groups of candles tucked away in carved niches. The stone walls glittered as her gaze was drawn to a large hearth across the room, where the fire within it was strangely ablaze in a slow dance as if time itself was caught in a prism of glass. Ironbow stepped out of the shadows next to the fireplace, a casual tone beset in his frozen voice.

"Calmly, sister," he advised while Venusa shed the grogginess from her mind, "your body was stressed from the shift."

"What do you mean," the girl inquired as she rubbed her eyes to clear her vision, feeling weaker than she had ever felt before, "and why do you keep calling me sister?"

"You are still feeling the effects of the transition from the Evermore to the outer world; the severing from it can be somewhat ...disorienting," the archer finished with a pause and promptly strolled to a shadowed alcove, where he poured a brown liquid from an ornate jar into a small glazed cup. With light steps, he brought it to the girl who accepted the mug with trembling hands and a measure of gratitude.

"What is this?" Venusa inquired, testing the aroma of the broth as its delicate scent weaved tendrils of steam like fine spider silk that escaped the curved lip of the vessel.

"It is called Solace," he breathed, "though in the elvish tongue it is known as *ambrosia*," he turned back towards the table, assuming she would know its reference as if it were common knowledge. The liquid smelt of smoked honey yet possessed the quaint bitterness of jasmine. Oddly, she felt a mixture of emotion twinge through her body when she inhaled its fragrance, coupled with flashes of lost memories she had long forgotten. The images recalled into her mind shocked her for a moment and she nearly dropped the cup shaking in her hands.

"What does it do?" She reeled away, though drawn back to its sweet aroma which she found alluring. The archer picked up the glass jar with his gloved hand and swirled its contents in the light; specs of leaves, and moss, and bits of other mysterious ingredients stuck to the glass as the dark film mixed within.

"It's a rough blend, I admit," Ironbow granted, "but it will help ebb the discomfort you will feel in the days to come."

Like a puzzle and all its broken pieces, she recalled what had happened. The exile, the arduous trek of shame as the Elves shunned her presence like a walking ghost among them. She recalled the envelope of the doorway that peeled away as she emerged from the portal to the underworld. There, she was greeted by the cold mist and a mysterious man astride a giant wolf ...and there was something else. Venusa grasped her wrist yet again, looking down to see the black butterfly etched within her skin. It had a strange ache to it, not quite painful but noticeably tender.

She tried to remember the words of the dark sending, but they somehow eluded her. Swept away into the misty moors, she had passed out from weariness by recent events and awoken here in this chamber. It was the first time she had withdrawn from the folds of the life force of the Evermore, and the trauma of it weakened her. The Eternal City dwelt within its essence, where time itself had slowed. She could see it in the creeping flames of the burning hearth, the Elfire as it was known; the living flame of the Elves.

Outside of the protective embrace of the Evermore, time on the surface world hastened, where all living things withered and died at an unnatural pace. The ambrosia she ingested would ebb its effects, acting as a temporary tincture to offset the recoil of its shedding for but a brief time. Still, there was the matter of where she was and the purpose of her host who had rescued her from the mist.

"Where are we?" Venusa inquired while she dared to stand on her shaky legs.

"This is Limbo, my humble refuge between the shifting grey," the archer answered, though Venusa was confused by this analogy.

"I'm not sure what you mean..." she conceded while trying to catch her thoughts.

"The realms of all living creatures is always unsteady and in a state of motion; like an ocean in a storm which is always trying to seek balance and regain the familiar rhythms of its own tide," he explained, "though they try to find their equilibrium, there are forces of nature that sway this unruly cradle between the darkness and the light."

His explanation upset her, for she had never quite become accustomed to the way the Elves spoke in their aggravating riddles, which unfortunately, was an irritating trait her host seemed to share.

"And who was it that sent you to gather me?" Venusa asked as her head started to clear from drinking the thick Solace tea, and was feeling herself once again. The archer glided to the mantle stationed above the hearth while his hand gently caressed the curve of the large bow that hung there. It was infused with iron that glinted darkly in the warm light. Iron was trouble for faeries and Elvin kind and was known as the handicraft of Men, who had learned of its forging from the Dwarves long ago.

Iron was the very essence of inertness, into which every ore and crystal would decay into this final lifeless element. Iron, itself, repelled magic, which is why it was the chosen metal for bars when men made traps and cages to capture mystical beings or beasts. Changelings could assume any form, as could elves and fey alike; their glamour was nullified by this most deadly substance that sapped their essence. It would resist elvish magic, but was especially deadly to the Faerie, and would drain their life force by even the slightest touch.

That bow of iron was an enigma in itself, though Venusa need not fear it for she was a mixture of both man and Elvin blood. It was presumed that mankind could touch this tainted metal only because they had no true living force within them to be drained. It was a disturbing detail that further distanced them from the race of Elves, who had learned to fear them.

"There are many races of the Elfin kind, young sister," the archer addressed her question at hand, "but it was the Houses of Seven that first answered your call; and thus, here I am to deliver you into their care."

"We have never met before, so why do you keep calling me by such a familiar term?" Venusa demanded.

Ironbow tilted his head in amusement at her inquiry, and pulled back his hood as a courtesy to his guest. His hair was sleek, peppered with streaks of dark gray. His features were noble, yet rugged but still refined. He graced her with his eyes, which were a color she could not clearly define. In his own way, he had a soft yet sinister bearing about his character that was both mildly alarming and warmly alluring.

"Though we are born of different times and different worlds, we are both orphans of the Grey; outcasts of the stormy seas between the races that reside in the lands of the Faery, to be left beached upon its broken shores," Wolf Ironbow answered.

It was beautiful the way he said it, and the inflection in his icy voice made Venusa wonder as to his personal history and how he came to be the solitary being that he now was. Little did she know that her life was about to change in ways she could have never imagined and would be walking a similar path as her curious host in the days to follow; for they were both castaways of the Faerylands, stripped of their heritage, and would never know a life of peace.

Ironbow

It was the race of Drow he had spoken of, a splintered dark faction from the domain of the High Elves. These Elven Lords were kindred, once whole and undivided, but discord bred internal feudalism and animosity until they were ultimately forced to split into separate clans during their flight from the race of Men. They escaped to places where man could not find them and within the eternal shadows of the caves is where the Dark Elves chose to reside. It was a deep division of principles that caused such a fissure between the elvish as to how to deal with the dilemma of man's destructive nature. War against men was once whispered under the breath of the Elven Council, though it was against their ethics to rule the genocide of an entire race of beings born of the world, for the ancient prophecies had told that mankind would one day follow in the footsteps of the Elves as their brethren, but they had instead betrayed their trust.

The original revelations were erased from the archives, but it was once told that in their adolescence that man had stolen a seed of awareness from the world tree, which was a profound degree of wisdom they were far too young to absorb. Unable to grasp its fundamental philosophies which they had prematurely obtained, a cruel and mysterious blight clouded their minds as they were unable to perceive the true nature of life. Tainted they had become from tasting this unripened fruit they had taken, not realizing such seeds from the tree of life were to be planted and nurtured and allowed to bloom in their own time; not consumed for mere instant gratification of insight.

Mankind had become jealous of their Elven brothers, but like impatient children, they wished to possess their magics before taking the path of learning and coming of age. Unsure of what measure of consciousness they had poached from the World Tree, the Elves chose to offer mankind a chance to mature so that the awareness which they had infused might one day blossom. Unfortunately for the Elves, this choice was a terrible miscalculation, for Mankind's newly acquired creativity knew no bounds and quickly melted into insanity. No matter what efforts the Elders took to influence mankind into abandoning their path of greed and destruction, they could not be swayed.

In the millennia that followed, the race of men became blind to the living world around them and the Evermore itself withdrew from the poison of their presence. Men soon became restless and thirsty to obtain secrets they were never meant to possess; eager for knowledge they were not meant to unravel, and the world suffered for their arrogance. In their impatience to outshine the Elves, they began to believe their own delusion and deceit. In their audacity, Mankind created their own creators in carved effigies and proclaimed that their race alone retained individual souls as if they were somehow separate from the spirit of creation.

When the Evermore receded from the taint of man and the venom of their abuse, the Elves and their mystical children had no other choice but to follow. They had split into separate tribes; many escaped to the ancient forests while others abandoned the land and took to the seas; becoming the merfolk. Still, others burrowed into the depths of the earth, the clan of Dark Elves known as the Drow, to which Venusa now found herself indebted.

It was a tale their Elders refused to speak of, and a subject of taboo among the ancient spirits of the earth. Mankind wove a different version of the tragedy from the threads of their past; one that erased the Elves and their kind from their own story of creation. The oracles and priests of men knew it was a lie but they told it nonetheless. So strong was their disdain towards the Elves who had refused to surrender their secrets to humanity which had proven themselves unworthy of such sacred gifts.

Here, Venusa sat at a crossroads between worlds; born by both races, accepted by none. She could foretell it was a lonely path ahead which she must tread, and the unease of what fate had befallen Ironbow might well become her own. The stories early men told of those blessed few who had first been invited to the Eternal City of the Elves had told of an Eden; a paradise of ivory marble crested with gilded gold. It was a place of lush gardens and unequal serenity; and as the story was retold among their people, they became envious.

Again, the race of men retold this tale, one which they warped and twisted in order to control their kindred with promises of an afterlife, the lie of a utopia they could never provide themselves and placed this realm within in the heavens to always be unreachable beyond their grasp. It was a facade the Elves found disturbing, that the minds of men would weave such deceit among their own kind. It was then that their Elders began to cut all ties with Mankind, and retrieved every last visage of Elven blood among their ranks.

Venusa was a half-elf, one who was flawed and tainted in the eyes of the Elders. She had been acquired like the other half-breeds of her kind, to deny the race of man the seed of their union. Of all the days she walked among the High Elves, she had never truly felt as if she belonged. Though, when she reflected upon that, the feeling of dejection which had weighed so heavily upon her shoulders seemed to fade in the presence of her mysterious host.

"Forgive my rudeness, as I mean no insult, young sister," Wolf began, as he took a sip of the ambrosia, "If I may ask what transgression you committed to earn your exile from the Eternal City?" The archer inquired respectfully.

Venusa gave a shrug of surrender amid the awkward silence as her host held his steady gaze upon her with the patience of a mountain.

"Apparently, having any measure of curiosity is an offense," she related with a tone of trepidation, "I was caught browsing the forbidden archives without their express permission and the Elders view any intrusion into the library as a dangerous breach of protocol; especially so from a lowly half-elf," she breathed.

"I have heard of the dark library of the Elven Lords, and that they are barred with intricate magics and shielded wards; how is it that you were able to gain access to their chambers unescorted?" The archer asked with an inflection that exposed his heightened interest. Venusa took but a moment to search for her words, not realizing that her host was reading every flinch and gesture she revealed.

"...I have my ways," she finally admitted.

"Hmm, such a feat is truly impressive; you must have a degree of talent," Ironbow grunted softly as he moved from the hearth to the far wall next to the open doorway where the howling wind had been kept at bay. He pressed upon a tiny catch and a hidden shelf exposed itself with a grinding of stone. From this shelf, he picked up a small object which he held hidden within his grasp.

Not knowing what he was doing, Venusa dared to stand and crossed the room to warm herself by the elfire, finding comfort within its slow hypnotic sway of light and flame. The archer came to stand beside her and gently took her hand in his leather gauntlet. She submitted as he opened her palm and placed something smooth and cylindrical within that pressed against her skin.

"And, if I may ask, what was it that you were searching for in the dark library of the high elves?" Wolf bid as he released her hand. Venusa carefully opened her fingers to see a small silver rod with a ringed end, strangely wrought with spiraled twists and curves. It looked old and unusual, but she was at a loss as to what it was for. She turned her confused gaze up towards Ironbow, who seemed to find a grade of amusement from the confusion resting in her puzzled eyes.

"Since my arrival in the Under-city of the Elves, I was met with an air of aversion," she noted with anguish, "and I became restless when constantly confronted by their calmness and smug contempt," the girl noted with a curl of her lip.

It was a different era when she had been accepted into the fold of the Elves, and it was easy to understand how she mistook their patience for a shade of disregard. Their riddles and philosophy only fueled her agitation and anxiety, for her perceptions of the world she had learned during her childhood in the company of Men had not changed. Within the protective embrace of the Evermore, the Elves acted as if they had all the time in the world; which apparently, they did. It was a concept Venusa found herself struggling with, for their doctrine of patience and restraint she merely read as wasteful idleness.

Truth be told, from the moment she had arrived within the Eternal City under their care, she had been bored to tears.

"So, you were merely ...bored?" The archer inquired with a bedeviled grin. Venusa knew this wasn't the case, and Ironbow read that in her nervous response.

"Yes ...and no," she hesitated, "I had asked around in an effort to inquire why the Elves were withdrawing their mediation with the race of Men, for I had left half of my family behind in the Vy," Venusa sauntered with her words, thinking back about how unkindly she had been treated by the human villagers because of her pointed ears. It was a stigma she had soon learned to cover from view because of the growing tensions between men and elves.

"But more to the point," Ironbow directed, "what was it you were seeking to discover among their vast archives, and most importantly of all, did you find your answers?" He challenged.

"After my initial appeals were brushed aside, I had heard of these so-called *forbidden* archive of theirs and decided to research the answers I sought myself. After being denied formal entry into the secret library by the custodians, I designed my own means of access," Venusa admitted; though Ironbow was a tinge intrigued that he couldn't interpret her usual gestures when she confessed to her trespass.

Venusa held up the silvery rod by the black hemp string tied to one end, which had been threaded through its loop. It's pitted metal gleamed in the candlelight that flickered within the chamber. It was the length of a long nail, though tapered slightly on its tip. She had tried to absorb the patient virtues of the Elves during her short stay in their presence, though she assumed Ironbow would eventually get around to telling her what exactly this small silver memento was for. The archer could see the question of it dancing within her wide eyes, but he let the enigma of its mystery simmer as it lingered upon her thoughts. He was testing her in his own way.

Ironbow knew of the Dark Library, as it was called by the Elven elders, buried deep within the recesses of the Eternal City. It was said to have the ability to move and shift from place to place in order to keep its location secured. This secret archive earned its strange name because no illumination was allowed within its chambers, so as to keep the scripts and tomes from being read or spied upon by the prying eyes of Oracles or the witchery of a Scry. It was an effective method to thwart unwelcome scrutiny from mages and channelers who might abuse the records for their own personal gain.

Powerful wards had been laminated upon the archive and kept the writings secure, yet this small half-elf girl had somehow circumvented those protocols. Ironbow was mildly impressed that she was capable of countering such measures but only to a point, for the end result was she had still been caught red-handed. He stepped forward for but a moment and lifted the tip of the silver rod as it dangled from the cord around her finger on her raised hand. Letting it go, it swung like a pendulum before her face where it glazed her eyes with a brilliant sheen. To her amazement, the small rod swayed back and forth, changing shape as it did so.

"I have held onto this artifact for quite some time, but admit I have no use for it here in the Grey, but perhaps this small keepsake may be of use to you on the path you are about to take in life," the archer granted.

"What is this?" Venusa asked while she was held mesmerized by the curious pin transforming before her as it swung from its delicate cord.

"It is a passkey to allow oneself through almost any door," Ironbow answered while motioning to its changing shape as it flickered in the light, though when she suddenly stopped its momentum to get a better look at the relic, it reverted back to its unremarkable form, "it alters itself to fit any lock or latch that has a keyhole, of course," the archer related.

With hesitation, Venusa recognized the value of such a tool and looped the thread it hung by over her head and to rest around her neck. Still, she fondled its cool touch as it lay upon her chest, wondering why he would offer her such a remarkable and priceless gift.

"Why would you...?" she began with a stuttered response, but Ironbow could see through her loss of words.

"It was but a remnant from a time long past, but please, do

keep it as a souvenir of our brief acquaintance," he offered as a gesture, "may it someday aid you in finding the answers you have sacrificed so much for."

Her host's words were deeply touching, for it resounded within her in that moment when she had lost everything, her new home with the elves and the human family that had abandoned her into their ward only to be disposed of as an outcast; and all for what? Venusa had failed to find anything in the archives before she was caught, for she had been stripped of her lineage and marked by these two binding ribbons as a symbol of dishonor for all to see. She was without a true home or a place of belonging, now shunned from the only two worlds in her life she had ever known.

"Thank you..." was the only words she could muster with a well of tears coming to her eyes as she clenched onto the small token. Ironbow could see the emotions stirring within her, for she was vulnerable like a boat in a storm and in danger of crashing upon the unforgiving rocks of a troubled shore.

"Our time here is short," Ironbow pressed while Venusa was collecting herself, "the Brood Mother awaits your arrival."

With mild shock, the girl turned as the shadows beyond the reach of the candlelight stirred behind her. The blink of two large glowing eyes appeared from the darkness where the giant wolf had lain dormant, silent as death itself. With one swift motion, the archer retrieved his bow from above the mantle and followed the silver hound outside beyond the mouth of the small cavern. The moment she breached the doorway, the comfort of the warm chamber was exchanged for a biting wind that pierced her to the bone. With a shiver, she took the dark archer's hand as he helped her upon his silver-furred mount.

The canine howled once as if in answer to the moaning wind of the moors and began its furious pace into the cold haze beyond. Venusa wrapped her hands around Ironbow's waist, clenching on for dear life and somehow feeling a faint sense of loss begin to knot itself tightly within her. Little did she know that the strange sensation she now felt would forever linger for the rest of her days.

In but a wink, the wolf leapt forward and crossed into an eerie darkness. The fog, the wind, even the stars above blinked out. There was but a strange nothingness. Not even the sound of the mongrel's paws touching the blurred ground could be sensed, all she heard was the faint heaving of her own breath. It was the in-between, the boundaries of the Greymoore they had pierced; the shadow between realms. Venusa blinked once and found herself surrounded by sunlight, still sitting on the silver mount high upon a grassy hill.

"Where are we?" She dared to ask, feeling a tremble of shock and astonishment.

"The same place we were before but in another time," Ironbow answered with sharp boldness.

"This almost looks like my homeland near the Vy," the girl declared, looking out across the open rolling hills that brushed upon jagged mountains capped with ice. The skies were a deep azure and stroked with mottled clouds that towered into the blue as if to challenge its limitations and constraints. A roar could be heard echoing from the valley near the mountain pass, carried to them upon a strong and fragrant breeze.

"Your time with the Elves came with a price," the archer issued gently, "everyone you knew from your human family and their clan are gone, their lives now long past," he conceded, "as for the Elves, time is their art to sculpt and we are but the audience."

With a pinch of his legs and a tug of the beast's mane, the great dire wolf jaunted across the fields toward the sound of the blasting horn echoing across the green tundra. Wisps of seeds dangled in the wind as poppies blushed underfoot. Venusa soon realized that this place was not the home she had known, it felt somehow different and displaced.

Writhing on the back of the giant hound, she was glad when its run finally ended at the tip of a deep ravine. Ironbow helped his passenger down, who felt wobbly on her own two feet after such a harrowing ride. Dismounting, the panting wolf glazed him with its molten eyes and turned to disappear over the broken landscape. Venusa felt confused, not knowing why they had abandoned their mount so readily.

"This place is where your journey begins," the archer noted

while gesturing with his gloved hand towards the mountain pass. Regardless, she saw no path nor bridge across the chasm before her that would allow passage to the narrow road that sprouted upon its distant fringe. Bewildered as to what she should do next, Venusa timidly approached the steep rim, taking a cautious step in reverse after tapping a few loose stones from its crumbling edge.

The rocks tumbled into the darkness below, clattering upon its shattered wall. There was no way to climb down, for any handhold would surely give way. At this predicament, Venusa turned, and for the first time began to suspect that Ironbow must be of elven blood, with pointed ears hiding beneath his black hood and thick hair, for all the riddles he spewed. If this were true, then she was not amused.

"And how am I to cross?" She replied, feeling the urge to chastise him for playing with her. Ironbow stood poised where he had dismounted, appearing to be unwilling to approach further. To her aggravation, he just shrugged at her.

"That is for you to decide..." he offered bluntly.

Venusa fondled the key around her neck, but there was no lock to use it on here. This was a test of some sort, for she saw all the signs, as the elves had an obsession for such games.

"You could just sit for a spell and wait for the chasm to wear away, but I promise you the ravine will only get wider," the archer remarked as he squatted to the ground, as if mocking her dilemma. A haughty grin was cast upon his face, which made her blood begin to steam. She felt he was being very unkind at her expense, but such trials would usually appear spiteful.

"Weren't you going to accompany me to meet the Drow?" She finally huffed with a fold of her arms, unable to hide the pout forming upon her lips. Ironbow stood upright for a moment as if to address her with a measure of respect, but merely adjusted the longbow slung across his back and plopped back down upon the grassy knoll.

"Yes, actually I was just waiting for you to lead the way," he shot back in reply to her utter dismay.

Aggravation began to blur her vision. Elves were fond of their riddles and trials, and she was certain that the High Council of the Drow were watching her at this very moment to see if she could prove she was worthy of their time. The chasm was very deep, so much so that the bottom faded into a murky void despite the bright sunlight grazing the meadows nearby. It was far too wide to jump, being many times as wide as her own height, and she doubted that even the enormous dire wolf could cross such a rift. Looking to either side, it appeared the fissure separated the entire mountain chain from the rolling plains as if some quake had made a statement that none shall pass this way. Venusa stood there and pondered for a moment.

With a hint of despair, she glanced back at Ironbow with casual frequency as if to read some hint from his posture. The archer kicked back as he waited patiently, chewing on a stem of long grass as if to further agitate her with his lack of cooperation to aid in her dilemma. He appeared content to sit there all day and through the night, for that matter.

"I don't understand why you won't help me?" Venusa began to whine, though her plea was sincere, "There is no way to get to the other side, either over or around this crevasse," she contended. Ironbow finally stood up and brushed off his leather chaps, and took a long glance at the path on the other side of the deep rift that snaked its way up the narrow trail past the cliffs.

"For one, you didn't bother to ask for my assistance; and furthermore, you seem to be obsessed with getting us to the other side of this ravine, rather than getting the other side to us," he tendered.

His words struck her like a slap to her logic, and she almost misread his wit for its brutal sarcasm. She turned back toward the gorge and tried to gain another perspective. After a few moments, she stomped past where the archer stood waiting beyond the shadow of the mountain, and stepped far enough away so that she could get a good look at her surroundings.

"Bring the other side to us ...what kind of snarky remark was that?" Venusa whispered under her breath with contempt; still befuddled as to what she wasn't seeing. She could try to walk around one way or the other, but the wide rift appeared to flow endlessly in both directions. Needless to say, there didn't appear to be a safe trail to the mountain pass along the far side of the rim even if she managed to find a narrow section to cross somewhere along the way. Wolf Ironbow waited calmly while his companion began to fume. She finally had to suggest the possibility of an alternative route.

"Are you sure that path over there is the only way to reach the Drow Council; is there another trail we could take?" She finally inquired while pointing towards the mountain pass on the opposite side of the rift, as she was lost for lack of any other suggestions. That was when the archer finally stepped forward.

"Actually, I never said *that* was the path we needed to take," Ironbow admitted as he gestured to the trail on the other side, "I merely said this is where your journey begins. The path and direction are up to you," he offered coolly.

"But you pointed towards that path across the ravine!" She spouted in defiance with an accusing glare.

"Did I?" He questioned lightly with a raised brow mocking his innocence, "Or did you assume that the trail yonder was the passage we needed to take to your destination?"

Venusa was feeling rife with outrage. Wondering why he had dropped her off here if this wasn't the right direction in the first place. He was supposed to be acting as her chaperone to deliver her to the Drow ...so she had assumed.

"What was your appointed task when you first retrieved me?" She finally asked with subtle despair. Ironbow could see that her demeanor had finally changed color, and thus, she could finally take the reigns of her own destiny.

"I am here to escort you safely, not to guide your way. Ideally, your journey in life should precede in the direction you decide for yourself," he granted.

His words reverberated within her and Venusa gave a gentle smile of mixed respite and consideration. He was testing her strength of character, to temper her resolve, and to be her own person. She would have to be more decisive if she was to survive the fate she had been dealt. To endure as an exile of both worlds, she would have to mold her own existence.

"But, how do we reach the Drow?" She finally pressed, looking into his pale glassy eyes. In the sunlight, she caught a glimpse to note his eyes were devoid of pupils and bleached as white as bone. The archer blinked once with a tilt of his head as he conceded that the half-elf girl was ready for her next step.

"This," he motioned to the surrounding landscape, "is the realm of Antilla, the Isle of the Seven Cities, realm of the Dark Elves; each run by a prominent house, separate but united under the rule of the Brood Mother, their royal queen."

Wolf Ironbow used the tip of his bow to draw a map of the island in the dirt at her feet. Venusa had seen many charts before but never of a land so strangely defined. Antilla's borders appeared quite peculiar, with three straight edges as if the land that rose out of the Eon Sea had been neatly cleaved with an axe, although the far the outer fringe of the stretched island appeared like a broken shard. Four inlets were positioned along one long edge, while the three left to the city ports were located on its opposite side. It was obvious to anyone that this was not a natural feature and its boundaries had been forged by magic, but the purpose for its unusual design was a mystery.

Each of the regions was separate but retained an equal allotment of land; however, the barbed edged, which stuck out like a thorn at its tip, was reserved for the court of their honored Queen. Adventurers and travelers from across the world would venture to this secluded isle to partake of its many forbidden pleasures. Explorers from the lands of men would weave tales of its wonders to their many tribes, while countless voyagers risked their lives to set foot upon its distant shores. Few ever survived the journey to this realm across the great and turbulent oceans, as most visitors to this realm were fated to find their final rest at the bottom of these dark and stormy seas.

Ironbow had placed them in the middle of the map where a long stretch of mountains formed a natural border between each province. It didn't take long for Venusa to realize that the deep chasm before them was not natural but likely fashioned by design to thwart trespassers.

"Which region are we in now?" Venusa asked the archer while she gazed intently at the crude map in the dirt.

"The Grey released us somewhere in the middle of the island, for I cannot see the waters from here," he answered while scanning the open fields that sloped towards a tangled forest, "it is never the same place that one arrives here from an ethereal shift, and I can vouch that the location is always random every time I arrive here on the island," Ironbow conceded.

There was always an air of struggle and conflict between the seven houses, for each sought favor with the Brood Mother. Like spoiled children, they contended in reverence of their Queen to recognize their strength. Unlike the peaceful High Elves, the Drow sought trial and contest as a brutal trait that tempered their character. For the more conniving, and backstabbing, and skilled in the art of betrayal, the more the Brood Mother admired their cunning and initiative.

In the minds of the dark elves, this competition kept them sharp and attentive to reshape their strengths and weaknesses; as any mother would wish to have her children to remain adept and able. It wasn't friendly banter but bloodshed they gifted one another, through skirmishes and assassinations, as one house falters, so another may rise. The one rule that rose above all others was; do not get caught.

"Let us cut to the chase and head to the court of the Drow Queen," Venusa dared to propose.

Ironbow appreciated her candor and nerve. The archer pulled a small clay flute from beneath his tunic that had been strapped around his neck. Blowing with effort into the small instrument, the girl was unimpressed, for it appeared to make no noise. Seemingly satisfied at his failure to make it sound, Ironbow tucked the flute away.

"Where to now, Sister?" The dark archer inquired.

"Well, we could certainly use that beast of yours, if it hadn't run off," she responded with a note of displeasure.

"I just summoned Ironclaw, she is on her way," he assured; though Venusa was a bit puzzled at his statement.

"Your flute must be broken, for it wasn't working as you could tell," she scoffed, while finding mild amusement at the hound's kindred name to its master.

"She will hear the call, just be patient," he noted whilst he scanned the horizon and adjusted his short quiver that contained peculiar transparent arrows synched within.

"How could it hear a silent whistle," she bade in disbelief, presuming he was testing her intellect once again, "is that instrument imbued with some sort of magic?" She inquired out of curiosity; though the archer just gave a quizzical glance at the simple clay device.

"*Hmm*, I suppose that it is," he shrugged while offering his curt response.

The giant wolf came trotting across the countryside, appearing from the edge of the rolling hills. Its run came to a sudden halt while Ironclaw's paws shifted in the broken shale near the rift as it came to a stop. The beast was panting, its large pink tongue hanging from one side between sharp ivory fangs, now stained red with blood from a recent kill of its hunted prey. Venusa was still puzzled by the enchantment of the summoning flute that called the wolf's return.

After mounting the beast once again, Ironbow took her arms and placed them securely around his waist as she clung to him in her position behind him.

"This mountain range will lead us directly to the coastal region at the extended cape of the island," he noted, "or would you prefer to take the scenic route?" The soft-spoken archer offered. Venusa took a moment to think about the answer, only to realize she was being far too analytical about her reply.

"Certainly, let's take the scenic path if you think it will be more fun!" She curled with a smile as she pressed herself into the embrace of his cape. With a bound, the dire wolf sprang off towards the forests that flowed away from the central mountain range and out towards the great ocean.

"It most certainly will be," the archer replied over his shoulder as they raced through the grassy fields towards the tall trees of these mysterious woods.

Treesong

The path through the wooded hills was thick with strange and wonderful vegetation, alive with a dimension of colors that melded between the undergrowth and the living trees. They were of the likes Venusa had never seen before; each bent and twisted with a defined grace of their own. In them, she thought she could see faces and wary eyes, but the stride of their wolf mount kept her from being sure of what she saw. The hum of birds met with the howl of the wind and curious groans from this vibrant woodland that stretched out beyond the shores of the cold blue ocean.

The forest floor was blanketed with moss of rich hues. Giant toadstools and blooming flowers sprouted from hidden cracks and hung from thick swaying vines. The island of the Drow had a magic of its own, competing with the lavish but sterile architecture of the Eternal City of the Elves. Antilla was a craftwork of earth and sky, resting between the stark and stormy horizon and the rolling seas. Long ago, the race of Elves achieved their own equilibrium with nature and weaved the Evermore itself into new creations. Left free to grow, this chaos of abundance explored the diversity of life in every spectrum of shape and color.

There was a rhythm present, which Venusa could almost feel; the elven side of her began touching gently upon a strange energy, which her human side failed to grasp. Ironbow guided their path alongside cascading waterfalls and high bluffs, where the girl could view the stark wildness of the island in all its grandeur. Without her guide, she could see how easy it would be to become lost within this maze of trees, and cliffs, and the open seas that beckoned them to explore their sandy lagoons and rocky shores.

The dark archer explained a few points which the girl already knew, having been drilled on studies on all elven lore when she had been drafted as a student in the walls of the Eternal City.

The Drow indulged themselves in quite the opposite manner as their High Elven Lords, whose articulate studies were prone to be more mannered and rational yet all-around stuffy with pompous ceremony. The dark elves, however, sated their time with more selfish pursuits; revering the desires of the one over the many. Needless to say, the two castes were constantly at odds.

At one time, all of Elvenkind were of one race but became divided when the essence of the Evermore began to ebb from the world above. They once thrived among islands in the sky, living upon floating temples and kingdoms in the clouds, whose elders would study the heavens and the stars above. Those lofty sanctuaries were long since abandoned after they fell and the living spirit of the Gaia began to wane.

At first, the Elves were confused as their world began to die around them and the magic of life decayed. It was the Human race, you see, who were the cause of this sorrow. Men once followed in the steps of the Elven folk but were prone to spreading their infectious hatred and destruction among themselves and to all other beings. The Elders tried to show them how to harness the living energy of our world, but they were greedy. In their pride, the race of men began to take magics that were not their own and manipulated and twisted its nature, abusing the Gaia for their own means; caring not whom they might harm. This fundamental lack of conscience soon became a clear separation between the clans of men and elves.

They were too capricious to care about the world they injured, for they failed to view the flora and fauna as a part of themselves. Their stubborn pride, their envy of the Elven race, their gluttony and insatiable lust for the sake of greed, their slothful minds slowly became blind to this world they shared and claimed it as their own. Humans became so estranged and arrogant that they began to create their own creators through idols and myth; forever turning their back on the World Tree and casting themselves adrift. They made up lies they told themselves about the true nature of the world and even denied the spirit of this realm which every living creature shared; in place of the collective spirit, they claimed to possess individual souls; as unique and separate from all other beings. Mankind became delusional in their conquest; and instead of being content with what they were, they wanted to know all and ownership of everything they beheld of the land, and sea, and sky.

This tension caused the Elven Lords to quarrel among themselves on how to address the Human threat. Over time, the elves splintered into factions to escape by land, mountain, and sea beyond the reach of this new menace. Humanity proved itself incapable of insight; they were thoughtless and hollow, nothing more than walking husks who cared not for, nor desired to share the very world that gave them life.

Venusa had known that many factions of Elves withdrew to the deep forests and snow-capped mountains, while others migrated to the blue oceans of the Mer. The Drow retreated to their islands and guarded the labyrinths of the underworld that connected these hidden realms. The Drow, themselves, chose to study the dark side of mankind and the sins they committed against one another in order to grasp a better understanding of their weaknesses. This was how the origin of the Seven Houses of the Drow was conceived. Not long thereafter, the Elders began to harvest all stray elven blood from the tribes of Men; for the shadow of war stretched its darkness over the lands.

"The Elves tried to teach them to be one with nature, but the race of Men refused to listen," the archer commented to his passenger as they strode through the thick green forests towards the court of the Drow Mother, "thus, the world was split asunder. Now the emptiness, the Grey between the realms, is widening and we are entering an age of change.

"I don't quite understand," Venusa voiced from where she sat mounted behind the Archer, "why do you reside within the Grey, that realm of nothingness?" She asked while noting there was ample room within the vast forests and plains of Antilla; for surely he would prefer life here than to live in such gloom.

"It is a choice not of my own, sister; as it was not yours," was his stark reply. Venusa tried to recognize what he might have meant by that tempered remark but finally concluded that she, like Ironbow, no longer belonged in the world that once was. If there had been a place for them at one time, it no longer existed.

Venusa fondled the silver key dangling around her neck and wondered what mysteries she might unlock and what direction her life might take. There was a brief sadness for what she had left behind and would be lying to herself if she didn't feel a twinge of anxiety and doubt about her future. She wondered what role the Drow had in mind for her; especially so since she was an outcast of the High Elves. What could they possibly want with a half-breed stray like herself?

Ironbow himself, also pondered this question, for on the surface Venusa was young and unexceptional in many ways; though he was slightly impressed that she had somehow managed to skulk her way into the secret library of the Elven Lords. He also noted how she had skillfully evaded his inquiry to reveal how she had managed such a difficult feat. Perhaps his patience would pay off someday should he choose not to press his curiosity upon her. Ironbow was wise enough to know that sometimes it is better not to ask such dangerous questions, as there are times when one may regret the answers they reveal.

They strolled into a wide grassy clearing surrounded by trees and Ironclaw laid down to rest. A small trickle from a spring allowed them to refresh themselves while they glanced at the thickening clouds through the window of branches swaying overhead. It appeared a storm was approaching so they couldn't linger for long, but the giant wolf needed to catch her breath as she sat panting, for carrying two riders at such a pace was a taxing feat for the she-wolf.

Seeing that his beast was exhausted, Wolf Ironbow took a knee and leaned back into the folds of the hound's thick silver fur. Venusa, on the other hand, chose to explore the boundary of the meadow. Isolated here among the thick forest, the tall trees weaved in a dance of twisted branches. From their depths issued an eerie sound, an unnerving shrill softly carried in the wind which caressed her face.

At the far edge of the clearing, she found an upturned tree whose roots were torn asunder from the earth, likely felled by a fierce storm which she presumed. Exploring further, she found that the hollow of its underside bore a tunnel that led into its heart. With hesitation, Venusa turned to glance back towards the hill where the giant hound and the archer slept, and she decided to take a peek within the strange hollow out of innocent curiosity. A few steps within and she was rewarded with the rich smells of damp soil and wood. Tiny glowing mushrooms that sprouted in clusters led the way inside, offering barely enough light for her to find her footing between the twisting rotted wood.

A faint rolling snore could be heard issuing from within, which became ever louder with every step she took. When the sound of it became almost deafening, she fell a shade hesitant and thought about turning back to the safety of the meadow. Though, with a stiffened posture, she grounded herself and Venusa realized she would never get anywhere in her new life if she didn't find a measure of self-confidence as the archer had affirmed. She chose to press onward and intoned a spell for a pinch of light; a small magic she had learned from her elven masters.

A tiny glow sprang into her palm and floated above her when she gently lifted the delicate light. To her surprise, as the light rose high above she could see that she was now deep underground. Moisture sparkled from the roots dangling from the rocky roof as the aroma of thick mud and dampness lingered gently in the air. The odd sound she had heard made its presence known as the light flickered once and suddenly shot across the small cavern as it was caught in an exhale of air.

Aghast as to what her eyes beheld, the image of a large creature of earth and stone many times her size, sitting upright against one wall, suddenly began to rouse. Its dark glassy eyes blinked slowly, awoken by the wisp of light. Venusa suddenly froze as she began to fill with the presence of mind to turn on her heels and run. The giant stretched out its enormous hand to catch its weight while it yawned, placing its arm directly in the path of her escape. A sense of worry began to well inside her and she feared being crushed by the movement of the behemoth as it shifted its girth within the confines of the tiny cave.

Seeing no other path of retreat, she fumbled through the muck of the floor to the farthest wall, attempting to evade certain death.   When the monster shifted its foot forward in her direction and came dangerously close to squashing her where she stood, Venusa gave out a yelp.

"Stop!" She cried aloud while covering her head, which would do little to protect her from being smashed to bits, "Please don't kill me..." she pleaded.

The leviathan blinked for a moment in confusion as it awoke from its slumber and looked about the cave, having been entirely unaware of his uninvited guest. Its large head turned from side to side, seeing nothing. Looking towards its two monstrous disjointed feet, it spied the young girl clad in her scarlet-stained dress.   What could be read as a look of bewilderment crossed its rocky face, wondering why this small visitor was lurking in his den.

"Huh ...where did you come from?" The giant breathed in a voice so deep it sounded like rolling thunder.   The half-elf scrambled around into the illumination of the floating orb as its light began to wane.   Seeing that the hulking beast was not displaying aggression, she bargained for an introduction.

"I came in from the hollow of a tree above in the clearing," she offered with a change of tone.

"What? What is that you say? Your voice is but a squeak," the leviathan barked back while turning a rocky ear toward the small girl.

"I came in through the hollow tree!" She shouted towards the giant while cupping her hands around her mouth. Realizing her voice was not up to the level of screaming for this goliath to hear her properly.

"A hollow tree you say?" It responded with a furrowed brow as thick slates of stone curled above its eyes. Venusa had read of such giants in the earth from the ancient scrolls and aged tomes during her studies; though honestly, she thought them to be nothing more than wild exaggerations until this moment. The grinding of stone echoed in the cramped grotto as the giant shifted its weight to get a better look at his tiny guest.

"Well, yes..." Venusa answered as she pointed towards the small passage behind its resting arm.   It didn't take but a moment for her to realize that the entrance of the tunnel was far too small to even come close to fitting the size of this giant's considerable size and girth.

"Well, I don't have a hollow tree," the giant sputtered in its own defense, seeming not to believe her words as it looked around the cavern in the dull light.

"Not down here, the one above that led into your ...home," Venusa replied with a slight pause as she searched for what she should call this dark muddy hole in the ground without offending her host.

"Home, you say? Bah! You must be flubberghasted, I don't have a home either!" It spat back as tiny bits of grit and gravel fell from its rocky lips. The half-elf girl was at a loss, realizing she was getting off on the wrong foot by assuming something she shouldn't have. She didn't know what *flubberghasted* meant, but she took a wild guess that it wasn't something nice.

"I didn't mean to offend you," she shouted back up at the giant, loud enough so that it could hear, "I was just looking inside a dead tree and it led me down into your..." she paused while catching her words, "led me down into this cave."

The giant seemed to glance around for a moment in a daze, appearing slightly bewildered as to where he was.

"Now how did I get down here?" The giant groaned with a squint of his stony eyes. The giant was obviously confused. Venusa thought it would be the best opportunity to get introduced so she could politely ask the creature to move its arm for her, and she could be on her merry way.

"I am Venusa Viper, what is your name?" She gathered herself with a gentle wave of her hand as if to greet the enormous stone giant and assure it that she was not a threat.

"Ah, *heh*," it huffed with a grating half-hearted laugh, "you silly flesh-beings and your addiction to *names*."

Venusa seemed righteously perturbed at its response, realizing in afterthought that she may have just been insulted, somehow.

"I don't understand?" she offered in return.

"There are things in this world that need not be named, for they have been around long before there were voices to speak them, tiny spec," it breathed aloud as it scanned the confines of the cavern, "Do I look like I need to own a name?" The giant proposed in retort.

"No, I guess not," Venusa mumbled back, having never considered that she would ever be party to such a bewildering comment, "but it helps to identify oneself among others," she presented with a shrug of her shoulders and a weak smile.

"Hah, I know who I am," the giant muttered back, "and I don't see any others around except you and me at the moment," it bargained with contempt. The monstrosity had a point but Venusa was becoming exhausted trying to understand its level of logic.

"Look, um, *Giant* – if I may call you that," she offered with a tilt of her head, "I'm very sorry for having woken you, but I do need to be on my way," Venusa stated firmly while she motioned once again to his stone arm that blocked the tunnel exit. With a moment's pause, as if it was slowly processing that its hand was in her way; it lifted its arm to free her passage with a measure of guilt washing across its stony face.

"Oh, I must have dozed off for quite some time," the giant argued as an excuse to shrug off the accusing glare of the little girl, who was but the size of its tiniest finger. It pressed a massive hand up towards the roots of the ceiling, testing its firmness. Chunks of rock and soil began to shower to the floor at its touch and Venusa was forced to dodge the falling debris, realizing she should take the opportunity to escape back up the tunnel the moment it presented itself.

"Thank you giant ...thing," she offered as a final farewell before she departed and vanished up the narrow passage.

She stepped out into the daylight from the tip of the sprawling roots of the hollow tree and frowning at her now muddy feet, Venusa groaned to herself that it be a lesson learned to not go wandering off into places unknown. She strode off back towards her companions; if that is what she could truly call the Archer and his giant pet. Once again, the strange whistling hum filled the air, a soft and gentle tune that was lost upon her. Feeling exhausted from her encounter, she sought to join Ironbow where he rested while wondering if perhaps the large wolf would mind her using its large fluffy tail as a blanket.

Upon reaching the sleeping pair, she poised for a moment as to where she might lay to make use of the canine's soft tail until the archer spoke aloud to her surprise, for he was sly enough to keep his eyes shut while he addressed her.

"And where might you have wandered off to?" He asked with a curious tone. Venusa turned and remarked to herself that she needn't make an excuse for her curious nature, but replied regardless.

"Oh, I made a new friend," she half-lied about her run-in with the slumbering giant. She waited for a moment for Ironbow to respond in jest or with some snarky remark but he just leaned there silently as if he was still asleep.

A rumble in the ground shook their feet, so strongly that the massive wolf lifted its head with a whine. Ironbow, himself, was also moved to respond as he patted the wolf's dander from his chaps and got to his feet.

"A friend you say ...are you sure about that?" The archer challenged as the rumbling rose with the violent shaking of the ground beneath their feet. The forest rustled, leaves fell, and branches swayed as the earth around the meadow began to quake. Looking out across the field at the source of the disturbance, a sudden spray of dirt and soil shot up into the air followed by a shower of chunks of sod and clumps of earth. The entire clearing began to convulse with cracks and fissures that split the soil as the stone giant fought to free itself from its chamber buried deep below.

"What did you do?" Ironbow grazed her with his tone, wondering what type of trouble she had rained down upon them as chunks of dirt sprayed across the once peaceful field.

"Perhaps we should go..." she offered in return, considering they might not have time for a long explanation in this given moment.

The dire wolf was promptly on its feet as the archer was to mount, and he held out his hand to help the half-elf girl to his side. Without delay, they departed from the grove erupting with churning soil and flying roots as the giant dug its way to the surface. The stone giant clawed its way one massive hand at a time, clasped upon the jagged brink of the deep chasm it had created. It lifted its colossal body with a knee on the rim of the rift as it breached the crumbling edge.

With a heave, the golem of stone gained its freedom from its earthen cage and gazed upward into the open sky and looked out upon the sea of treetops swaying below its knees. A soft hum could be heard in the forest and the giant took a seat for a moment to contemplate this unfamiliar terrain. Feeling taxed from his efforts, the hulking creature of earth and stone chose to take a short rest to recoup as compensation for gaining its freedom. The goliath found the sound of the wind and the sway of the blanket of green relaxing, and ever so slowly, it staggered and laid down as it spread across the open field, and with a final nod, it lowered its rocky head and shut its eyes to dream the long sleep once again.

Giants, you see, are very simple-minded; and their bumbling from place to place is very destructive to the plants of the forests which are brushed aside and crushed beneath their massive feet. It was the woodlands themselves that created a defense in the form of a Treesong, a chorus sung by the voices of the dryads. The gentle winds whistling through the trees were the song of slumber to such colossal creatures. The flutter of leaves and groan of the timbers is the call of the trees to pacify such elemental giants, sapping them of their strength and taming the mountains on which the flora grows like a blanket upon the living earth.

What was once an open meadow at dawn was now a rocky hill by sunset. The trees would continue their song in order to cover the sleeping giant in the quilt of their greenery over the course of many centuries to come, making a new home for their sprouts and seedlings. Even the forests here had secrets of their own and found a way to coexist with the ancients of the earth. Far past the field and through the twisting path, Venusa and her companions finally reached the edge of the forest and pushed through the grasslands that skirted the vast lakes and valleys that lay beyond. As evening fell the stormy skies parted for but a moment as the stars shone through, glittering like a thousand candles across the night sky.

She was told by one of the elven Elders that above the heavens there existed realms far beyond our reach but she had passed it off as just an elaborate exaggeration of an old crone who was prone to telling tall tales to test the ignorance of others. Sometimes she wondered though, for it was the stuff of dreams to believe in something you could not prove nor see. Magic was a strange substance, so she could not discount it entirely but for all the struggles of her new life, there was little time to dwell upon such fantasies.

With her thoughts in a jumble from the day's events, a faint spatter of rain began to fall to wash away her worries. Soon the drizzle began to shower across the dusky horizon and the strange trio found an outcropping of rock to shelter themselves from the encroaching storm. In his usual strength of character, Ironbow chose not to demand or pry but let Venusa admit of her own will the cause of the disturbing events they had witnessed.

The half-elf girl soon learned to appreciate the archer and his way of respecting her as an equal by not acting as though he were entitled to the point that she must answer to him upon his every whim. It was a change of pace for her that would take some effort to become accustomed to. Ironbow found peace in his solitude she realized, he was a lone wolf after all ...except for his large furry pet, that is. When the conversation arose, Ironbow was quick to correct her presumptions.

"I do not own Ironclaw in any fashion, nor does she answer to me as my servant or a beast of burden," the archer advised the young half-elf maiden. Venusa raised a thin brow upon realizing the dire wolf was female.

"She accompanies you by choice?" The girl offered to assume.

"I would have it no other way," Ironbow admitted as he pulled a stick from the small fire he had built in the stony alcove before the rain had saturated the sparse pile of wood they found in the underbrush nearby. He pulled out a wickedly curved blade and began whittling something that resembled a small flute as they spoke in the dancing firelight.

"It was just that your names were akin to one another, so I wasn't sure what to think," Venusa granted, while turning to glance at the large silver wolf sleeping in the back of the small cleft as sheets of rain fell like a curtain just outside the reach of the firelight. They were a strange pair. A dark archer astride a giant wolf made a formidable enemy; she was glad they were friends instead.

"Her given name is unpronounceable in my tongue, so I just called her that so she might consider herself more familiar," he shrugged while continuing to carve delicately at the small stick with his dagger.

"And what does her true name mean?" the half-elf asked with heightened curiosity, but Ironbow just stopped for a brief moment and gave her a strange glare.

"I have no idea," he declared with a mild condescending tone before he started back on his project, "I don't speak dog."

Venusa frowned, feeling like a dolt for asking. She glanced back at him for a second, wondering if he was merely joking with her but he was unreadable as a rock. She shrugged off the comment and chalked it up to his lack of social skills being the loner that he was.

"May I ask how you two met?" she pried in an attempt to usher some measure of momentum to the awkward turn of their conversation. With skilled finesse, the archer finished the fine points of the tiny flute and dusted off the stray flecks with a sharp breath. Admiring his handiwork for but a brief moment, he tossed the small instrument to the girl.

"She lost her pack to a string of hunters who butchered many of the animals of the forest by using trickery and traps. The wild beasts were no threat to them, but killed them merely for their skins; leaving their carcasses to rot," the dark archer spat with a venomous undertone in his breath.

"Humans?" She dared to allege, feeling suddenly conscience of her heritage as if that somehow made her share the blame.

"Mortals," Ironbow corrected, "we don't call them by any manner of honor within the elven lands," he stated coldly, "to slay a living creature for need or survival is one thing, but for mere profit is a transgression against nature itself."

As a young child, Venusa had grown up in the human villages where deer and elk had been hunted for food and clothing. Most every part of the animal was used to its extent, for it was the hunters and priests of their tribe who would honor the gift of these sacrifices, and did so with great ceremony. They showed a significant reverence for nature. Though over many years, such times had changed when strangers came to their lands and ravaged the wilderness and the creatures that lived there. Soon thereafter, conflict came between the tribes of men and their many hues of color. True or not, she suspected that their kind had derived from being labeled as the hue-men; the race of many shades.

Mankind, you see, feared the unknown; and would even spread hatred and disdain among their own breed based solely on the tint of their skins. Such conduct seemed absurd to the Elven people, who could not fathom the philosophy of their strange culture. Every leaf of a branch has a different shade between the seasons, yet they are all from the same tree, of course. The mannerisms of Mankind's ideology made no rational sense to the Elves, which is why they began to fear them so, and rightly questioned their sanity.

"So you two became friends and you took her in?" Venusa continued to query as she inspected the small flute he had given her. Ironbow took his time to answer while he oiled his bowstring and set his glass arrows aside.

"Only after I helped her dispatch those that had killed her family," the archer answered grimly, "and one might say we came to an unspoken understanding."

It was the cold casualness in his voice when he said that which made Venusa shiver. However, death in the Faerylands was regarded quite differently by Elves in the cycle of life, far more so than it was considered by humankind. It was a view of oneness with the Evermore and rebirth that was the base of their perception; and what mattered in one's life was what one did to learn and make the world a better place for all; whether it was achieved in life, or in death. Humans, however, feared death as an ultimate finality, and only cared about what they could gain for themselves. It was a selfish and petty way to live.

"Why does she let you ride her?" The half-elf had to ask, since it was unnatural for any sentient creature to allow themselves to be used in such a manner; especially so if they were of entirely different species. In a rare show of humor, Ironbow dropped a slight chuckle at her question.

"*Hmph* ...because obviously, we would hardly get anywhere if she had to wait for me to walk all the time," he offered bluntly as he grazed her with a cynical grin.

Venusa started to feel like she was making an idiot of herself by asking such rounded questions and being slapped with such conspicuous answers. She grasped the tiny flute and held it up in the flickering firelight to inquire about the purpose of the trinket. The archer pulled out a larger but similar one from the cord hanging around his neck.

"Is this for me to call the wolf?" She asked, "Don't you have to enchant it or some-such with a spell?" She presumed as she held it gently to her lips to test its tune. Ironbow held up his hand to stop her just a moment too late as Venusa blew with all her might into the small whistle. Hearing nothing, she seemed unimpressed about his skill at carving.

Ironclaw, however, perked her head up with a whine, startled from being roused so rudely from her rest. The giant wolf gave a questionable gaze towards the dark archer as to the nature of the rude awakening but he merely shrugged a measured apology towards the hound. Bidding the canine back to sleep, the large wolf whined again in clear discontent and laid its head back down with a few licks of her sharp fangs with mild annoyance.

"I think it's broken..." Venusa grimaced from where she sat.

"It works just fine the way it is," the archer advised to the girl who had her back to the large wolf and was entirely oblivious that she had startled the animal, "but only use it if we are separated, if you please," he pleaded. After the incident back at the meadow, he determined it would be prudent to give her the means to call for help; at least until she was conveyed to the care of the Drow as he had been chartered. Ironbow himself, also wondered why the Dark Elves had taken such interest in this unassuming girl.

He sat with his back within the folds of the wolf's paws and crossed his boots while tucking down his hood to cover his eyes. It would be a long journey to the far side of the island to the court of the Drow Queen. Antilla was a wild and untamed land with strange and treacherous shores. He had never lingered here for long, only coming and going when called; for he had committed to a pact of honor to serve the Queen Mother when hailed.

Venusa sat alone for some time, staring into the dwindling fire while her chaperone took rest in the sleek fur of his canine companion. She, too, wondered why the Drow would come to her aid, for she wasn't anyone special; quite the opposite actually. She was a misfit by nature, always getting herself into trouble in one way or another and she was certain her reputation would only serve to disappoint her royal caller. Life had been unkind to her lately and she didn't know where to begin to start over again. Perhaps this venture would prove to be her savior, or perhaps, her undoing.

She finally submitted to the chirp of the crickets and the quiet of the night, for the rain that had subsided to a gentle pelting upon the forest floor. She was tired and worn from travel and too much worrying over circumstances she could not control. Venusa crawled over and snuck her way under the thick fluffy tail of the dire wolf, finding warmth from the damp cold of the rain where she could sleep until the coming dawn. She had more apprehensions than she could count but realized that tormenting herself with self-doubt would serve nothing.

It was that insight that helped her finally close her eyes to dream just as the cloudy night skies opened to a blanket of stars that glittered overhead. Tomorrow would be a new day of freedom; although, little did she know that it would be the last she would ever see.

Bitterroot

The break of day colored the morning sky with a swash of orange and violet as the evening storms transformed into high towers of billowing clouds that caught the sunlight. All the little creatures that had sought shelter from the storm overnight sprung forth from their hiding and the forest and fields came alive with the song of birds and chirping bugs. Butterflies fluttered through the trees while glowing wisps raced among them with ribbons of light trailing in their wake. Tiny beings lifted their heads from leaf and root, from moss and mushroom, and everything in between, drinking the morning dew that covered the landscape like a blanket of glitter in the rising sun.

It seemed like a beautiful day, the likes Venusa had rarely seen in her short life. Even the giant wolf seemed to be in better spirits than her regular brooding self. The Archer, however, remained unreadable. It was as if he had spent too much time submerged in the Grey of limbo and was unable to appreciate a world of such vibrant colors. Whatever his perspective, he did not burden her with shadowed thoughts that might dampen her spirits on such a glorious day.

Breathing deep the cool brisk air, Venusa stretched her arms and gave a deep sigh. This place was certainly more agreeable to her than the formality of the Eternal City. It was a sad thought to dwell upon since the legendary kingdom of the Elves had once been woven from the very forests and bathed in sunlight. Awash with high waterfalls and unfathomable depths of green, their once-living palace was drawn into the underworld within the envelope of the Evermore where even the trees petrified into rock. Now stone and water replaced woodlands and rivers of light as the Elves withdrew from the reach of Men; forever hidden from their sight.

The Drow severed their ties and fled to this island retreat, keeping alive a splinter of what the Faerylands had once been. Here magic was still brimming in the land and all it touched.

The apprehension Venusa had felt the day before was now replaced by delight. If this island represented the world of the Drow, it couldn't possibly be as terrible as the rumors of their troubled history had implied.

The High Elves had looked down upon their dark brethren, the Drow, but she could not decipher why. She would soon meet the Drow Queen and could decide that for herself. This island bloomed with life and diversity, so the half-elf girl was confused as to why the ancient text described the dark elves as devious and malign? The legends she had heard did not match what her eyes beheld upon this beautiful isle of Antilla.

"Ironbow, why do the Elven Lords seem to have such disdain for the Drow?" Venusa asked of the archer as he retrieved his bow and quiver while snuffing out the last embers of the evening fire with his boot. Ironbow seemed cavalier in his answer.

"I wouldn't know, since I don't grace myself with the company of the High Elves, little sister," he offered as a curt reply of which he failed to elaborate further. Venusa was slowly beginning to realize it was a difficult venue to try to fish information out of him without being direct.

"During my short stay with the Elves, I had gathered that they were less than cordial with the Drow," she mentioned casually, though Ironbow just grunted as if that was an interesting observation on her part. Before meeting this royal Queen of the dark elves, Venusa desired an opportunity to size them up before placing herself at such a disadvantage. Mostly she was afraid of making a fool of herself as a first impression.

Ironbow realized, of course, that she was expressing an underlying desire to be prepared, which was a prudent if not admiral trait to possess. Such precautions would serve the girl well in her trials to come. The dark archer had seen many such outcasts as Venusa being taken in as guests of the Drow who arrived as rescues, only to disappear to a questionable fate. He was helping to prepare her for the tests she would soon face. The Dark Elves had a shady reputation, and more often than naught, they didn't disappoint.

Mounting the dire wolf, they made off over the countryside

toward the spire that snaked its way up a precarious path to the tip of the island. From such a distance, the size of the manor perched there was rivaled by the path that led to it. From both sides, high stone walls converged to mate with the regal gate at its center. From there, towers and buttresses jutted up like claws from the ocean cliffs which bordered their edges until the winding path melded into the spires of the central palace.

It was an impressive structure that dominated the horizon. Unlike the Eternal City, the castle of the queen mother was not adorned with intricate floral carvings graced with runes, but with statues and busts of nightmarish beasts. It had an organic, if not primal, appearance to it that befitted its location which resided at the precipice of the jagged cliffs poised above the violent sea. There, the ocean mists rose with a curtain of fog that plumed around its walls like an eerie wreath.

As they approached the central gate, soldiers in red armor appeared and accepted Ironbow's address.

"The Mother calls, and I answer the dark sending," was all he stated, and the guards with their sharp curved pikes withdrew to grant them entrance. The gate was formed like the fangs of a monstrous gargoyle, and Venusa noted it was made of iron as black as midnight. Such metal was used as a barrier against magical creatures, and especially deadly to the fey. In all respects, it kept out prying eyes and malicious spirits who might seek illicit entry.

The guards never turned to look at her, but merely returned to their post like crimson statues. Once beyond the gate, Venusa saw many elves traversing the hidden path that lay protected beyond the thick walls. They wore elegant clothing of embroidered velvet's and silk, some wore rare furs and exquisite jewelry of onyx and gold. Women bore tiaras of exotic feathers and barbed horns that once adorned strange and terrifying beasts. What struck her most was the elaborate makeup they wore on their faces and arms, depicting symbols and shocking colors to excite the eyes.

Such pomp was usually reserved for festivals or ceremonies in the human tribes, but here adorning such flashy garb appeared to be commonplace. Their painted masks made each individual unique to their own caste, yet also accomplished to obscure their identities from wandering eyes. She saw some elves carrying snakes around their throats and wrists as if they were living jewelry, while others left trails of fire in their steps. This was certainly a far stretch from the world of the High Elves who valued simplicity as a form of etiquette. She could now see why these two twins of the same race might clash.

Many of the patrons roaming the grounds of the Queens Court gazed upon Venusa with both mild curiosity and penetrating glares of contempt. She assumed it was because human side and her short pointed ears, which was a common symbol of embarrassment among her kind; her human scent was seen as a taint to that of the pure-blood elf within her. Upon their approach of a great door wreathed with gilded bronze, Ironbow came to a stop and they dismounted the dire wolf to make their way inside the great castle.

The interior was elaborate, etched with archaic runes and faces of strange beasts carved within each block of stone. A circular balcony lined the high walls surrounding the ornately tiled floor of the central court, where there hung a white sheet of silk draped before a spiked throne. Numerous candles set behind it displayed a figure whose shadow was cast upon the silk of a figure veiled from the audience within the chamber. Ironbow ushered Venusa into the central circle and introduced his guest.

"Queen Mother, I present to you Venusa Viper, who has accepted your invitation for asylum," he offered with a cordial bow towards the throne. Upon this introduction, the other members in the audience cleared the circle to its outer edges where they stood and watched with anticipation. Feeling a degree of unease, the half-elf girl stood in the middle of the court as all eyes fell upon her.

A thin hand from behind the ivory veil rose sharply in silent acknowledgment while the archer stepped away at this cue to depart and disappeared among the crowd. Venusa thought that she had prepared herself for this moment but came to realize that she had woefully misread herself. The Drow queen turned her hands to cup beneath her chin just as her silhouette displayed a second set of arms that rested upon the edge of the great throne.   Somehow, Venusa could feel the queen's eyes upon her, despite the opaque veil that masked the line of sight between them.

"Step closer, sister," the queen bade, her voice a breathy hiss the girl found quite unsettling. With but a brief moment of hesitation, the half-elf girl stepped forward. There was a still silence in the court, but ever so slightly, a mumble arose as members of the crowd noted her rounded facial features and the shortness of her ears. No half-human had ever been seen within the court of the dark elves before this day.

With a snap, the queen quieted the onlookers with her gesture. Venusa wasn't sure what the Queen mother was, for she was certainly something more than just a mere Elf.

"A little respect for our honored guest, if you please," the queen hissed aloud, and the murmured whispers subsided, "we must welcome a new member among our family and the houses of the Drow," she declared.

"I thank you for taking me in," Venusa offered with a pause, not knowing if she should curtsey, though expecting she would likely make a fool of herself if she tried.

"Your gratitude is appreciated in kind, young sister, but you will have your chance to repay the favor soon enough," the queen offered in her strung voice. Venusa realized she would have been indentured to some degree, for the Drow would not aid another without exacting some sort of payment. Venusa did wonder what would have become of her had she been left abandoned at the portal of standing stones on that barren plain within the Grey. Left to her own devices, she likely would have wandered into trouble and eventually yielded to the elements over a short period of time.

The queen rose from her throne and casually brushed aside the ivory drapery so that Venusa could see her clearly. Striding forward with unnerving grace, the queen stood before her. A smaller transparent veil pinned to her headdress cloaked the glint of red eyes that shone beneath. Her features were gaunt, and while in the queen's presence, Venusa felt a tremor of fear well up from within her that she could not explain. Though, she was successful at keeping the shudder from being too apparent under the penetrating gaze of the queen mother as she circled around her.

"Forgive the stares of the others, for our courtesans would have never dreamt that a half-mundane would ever be allowed within these walls," the queen advised as she motioned to the onlookers in all their pomp and lavish attire, "but you are an exception, an experiment I have chosen to stake at a most peculiar time in our kingdom."

"A kingdom without a king?" Venusa blubbered aloud out of turn, as if to question the queen mothers choice of words; to which the drow mother cackled with a strange hiss, as if in amusement at her salty comment.

"...And also quite astute I see. You will make a good student for the trials ahead," the tall queen ushered, but her tone turned to a harsher note at the girl's smart reply, "though do try to keep that shrewd tongue of yours on a tighter leash, young one. We wouldn't want to get the impression that you were impertinent or impolite," she offered sternly to her guest.

Venusa knew little of the Drow themselves, for what she had studied about them was sparse. It seemed the High Elves did not like to make information about their dark rivals readily available to new students. From what she had read, however, was that within the realm of the Dark Elves they had no male hierarchy within their rule, but that it was the females who held a higher rank within their social order.

"Not to be disrespectful, but why was I brought here and what are these trials you speak of?" The half-elf imposed to ask. Continuing to circle the girl as she stood poised within the center of the chamber, the Queen Mother offered an answer.

"I would ask that you gather some information for our Magi who seek to repel the growing scourge upon our world," the Drow Mother proposed.

Venusa was confused as to the point the queen was attempting to make, for she wasn't clear as to the adversary she spoke of. The staunch look of confusion must have been obvious, for a murmur once again rose within the crowd as the queen made a spectacle of the girl.

"I'm ...I'm not quite sure I understand," Venusa submitted with a stutter.

"You have lived among the tribes of men," the queen offered as she gently pricked the short tip of the girl's ear with her jeweled nails, as if to make a point of her mixed heritage, "and are privy to their secrets. The human mages and mystics steal and manipulate natural magic to pervert it, and we wish to thwart their abuse of this power."

At this disclosure, Venusa was at a loss; for she had no prior knowledge of how priests of men conducted such studies into the arcane. Growing up in the human realms, she knew most men feared magic but there where those few that sought to exploit it towards their own ends and others would even kill for such knowledge. Understandably, the Elves were reluctant to offer such powers so freely to a race that failed to use it responsibly. Humans had a reputation of being dangerous and unpredictable, and would frequently use such terrible skills as leverage against one another.

"But, don't you allow men into your cities here on Antilla?" The girl inquired, "Certainly, there must be others far more qualified than I for such a task," Venusa offered, "for I know nothing of the works of wizards and warlocks."

"Ah, but you will learn, young one..." the queen offered with a sly grin, which was ever more disquieting since her eyes were unreadable behind her thin veil. With a pause, the Queen returned to her throne as the servants replaced the silk drapery before her. Venusa didn't think her initial introduction would be easy but now she found herself being recruited to spy on her own kind. Whether it would be to repel the growing threat that mankind had proven to be, or if such knowledge might be garnered against the High Elves themselves, would eventually be revealed. She certainly wouldn't put such a scheme below the dark elves.

"I will try my best, if I only knew what it is that you ask of me?" The half-elf inquired while trying to gather the courage for such an endeavor. The only magic she had studied had been in the presence of the Elven sages. Minor spells of creating light or sprouting seedlings were trivial talents that were of little consequence, though she had heard of rumors of great battles between the conjurers of the Djinn and their bloody war with the Elves eons ago. A majority of those scripts and records were kept sealed within the dark library in an attempt to erase its past. Such hidden knowledge was tempting to her, but her elven side took the path of caution knowing that such history was likely kept secret for good reason. She was only half-elf, of course, so questioning the wisdom of the Elven Lords came with the territory in spite of her curious nature.

"Your assignment will be revealed in due time; meanwhile, you will be assigned a consort as a tutor to our coven who will instruct you in their ways, and perhaps cleanse you of the token you bear from our noble brethren," the queen granted with a hint of sarcasm while motioning to the deep rose-colored cords that bound the girl's wrists; their stain having bled into her gown in hues of cardinal red. They were a badge of dishonor that was a mark of shame upon her, though Venusa felt as if they had the opposite effect among her current company.

The Drow honored rebellion and defiance on a level she struggled to understand. Though the more the young girl saw of this strange culture of the dark elves, the more she felt at home. She didn't fully understand this new sensation but there was an innate sense of individuality and dignity that swelled from them that affected her. Venusa was escorted to a lower chamber were the priestesses of their coven practiced their arts.

Deep below in a central chamber sat an enormous vial of glass; glowing from within with the elfire as its drowsy flames flickered in their slow ballet of light. The women here wore white tunics and studied at archaic spells, the likes of which Venusa could only dream existed. Fundamentally, magic itself was the living energy of the Evermore, the power that bound all living things. Here she learned that even crystals could grow as would sprouting seeds, and the many forms that elements could take when coaxed into unique mixtures. For many moons she resided within their walls below the castle, and longed for the time when she would find relief from such labors to visit the forests once again or feel the wind of the ocean breeze upon her skin and be free to wander on her own beneath a blue sky.

The passing of day and night was only seen through the light of the colored panes of stained glass windows that lined the walls of the sanctum which had become her cage. Not long thereafter, Venusa began to dread the endless exams and studies of magic, and wondered what had become of her friend the archer and his giant wolf. One evening a new maiden appeared within the chambers, upon her head sat a wreath of horns woven from a young elk. She came to sit beside Venusa as she just laid down to rest, now wearing her red-stained tunic as there seemed to be no way to remove the cords from her wrists or rescind their curse to keep them from blemishing her clothing, no matter how many times she changed her attire. Though she wasn't shunned here among the dark elves, the stigma of the hex kept the other girls of her order from getting too close to her lest they share her taint.

"Good eve to you sister, I am Eden Whitetail, and you have been assigned as my apprentice, and I will try to help teach you the arts we practice under my watchful guidance," the maiden offered as an introduction.

Venusa could see she was quite exceptional in beauty, and her name fit her well for her fawn-like features, down to the cloven shape of her sandals. Her hair was a mixture of colors that glistened with a healthy glow and she had a delicacy about her that the girl found alluring if not enviable. Eden's voice was soft and carried a gentle tone like the wind through the forest on a spring day.

"I am still not understanding the purpose of learning these mystical arts, Eden," Venusa admitted to her new tutor, "the queen mother said she wanted me to somehow oppose men from their use of natural magic's, yet I've been locked up behind these walls for many, many moons..." the weary girl breathed in exasperation.

The priestess could sense the aggravation in her voice and that her patience had been growing short. If she was to make this young half-elf a willful disciple, it would only be fair that the source of her apprehension should be revealed for her to fully grasp. Eden herself, knew this was a difficult path to follow, one that was often fraught with dangers to mind and body.

"As a new member of our Order, Venusa, you must learn the

basic techniques of natural energies and understand why we study them. So I will reveal to you what the High Elves may have kept hidden from you during your short recess in the Eternal City," she offered respectfully, "The elven race may once again be drawn into a battle with a foe we have only faced once before in the days of the Djinn, which were elemental beings of great power that siphoned the energies from the Evermore to bear great destruction upon our world. The final clash ended with our triumph, but also came at a great cost. As elementals, their lives could not be wholly extinguished but were sealed away in enchanted containers to confine them. Bottled up as they were, their capture came at the expense of many lives of our most esteemed Elders. Many other races have come into our world over the centuries since, but now Mankind has proven to be an equal danger, and conflict has befallen us once again," the slender elf noted.

"I have lived among them, but fail to see the danger that humans might pose," Venusa countered, feeling as if their contention was being overly exaggerated.

"In one sense, you may be blinded to their method of thinking and how it affects the living world," Eden explained, "long ago we welcomed Men as family into our embrace, but they soon proved that their minds were unable to comprehend the sense of duty and obligation to exist in this world in equilibrium with all other living beings," she added with a sense of regret, "they soon became jealous of the Elves and their abilities to weave the Evermore or the natural balance they retained, and sought to abuse such powers for their own benefit at great expense to others. Any cautions we offered them on the dangerous path they were heading only amplified their rage, and as with the Genie race, we saw they were blind to the delicate essence of our realm. Once that harmony was broken, it split the race of Elves to the lands and seas, and to the far stretches of the Faerylands in our effort to escape the grasp of Mankind and their tainted minds in effort to protect our secret knowledge that they would only aim to misuse."

"But if you fear them so, why do you allow them into the cities of Antilla and the scattered ports on this remote island?"

Venusa imposed with an air of accusation.

"The society of the Drow took a darker path from the High Elves, for while the Elders entombed the Eternal City and hid from the blight of mankind, we instead chose to study their transgressions so we may use them to our advantage," Eden responded.   Her explanation made sense, for instead of cowering and fleeing from their human foe, the faction of Drow chose to know thy enemy in an effort to gain a tactical advantage against them.

"Why are there so many Houses of the Drow?" She inquired, for all her studies of alchemy and scrying and all the nuances of weaving spells failed to address these basic answers.   The priestess resolved herself to the fact that this half-elf girl was making every attempt not to be as naive as they expected her to be and only sought to understand her role in the coming conflict.

"Fundamentally, mankind has several flaws; ones which most races are guilty of inciting at any given time. However, only the race of Men seems to have the inherent ability to possess every blemished trait equally. Each house of the Drow has been given the task to indulge and study their mannerisms and reveal as to why they are so entirely consuming to the cultures of Men," Eden offered to explain, "Any elf-born can see that all living beings and the world are but one entity, but Men sully themselves and everything around them, becoming a parasite to our world. It was the same with the Djinn and a sparse few other races from our ancient past who destroyed more than they could ever create, and poisoned everything they touched."

Eden's analogy seemed a bit harsh to the half-elf, but she did note certain odd practices of the human villagers in her time among them. They thought nothing of the slavery of animals or of creating phantom stories of divine beings used as trickery by their clerics, and utilize such fantasies as a source of conflict among other human tribes. They razed the lands, rivers, and oceans without replacing what they took, and were reckless and indifferent when they burned and poisoned their own habitats; caring nothing for the other plants and creatures they harmed in their wake. Now that she thought about it, it did seem insane.

Michel Savage

Likely men could not find balance in the world because their own selfish mentality was so entirely delusional.

It was a stark realization that a fierce war between elves and men was imminent. With the Evermore withdrawing from the surface world, mankind compensated the shortening of their lifespan by breeding themselves into infinity. It seemed like every sunrise there were more and more of them, spreading like a plague of locusts across the horizon.

"I'm sorry Eden, but I still don't see how I can contribute anything towards this endeavor," Venusa admitted with a sigh of despair, "why does the Queen Mother think my paltry efforts can make any contribution in the grand scheme of things?"

Eden sat there looking into the churning glow of the elfire blazing at the center of the chamber. Outsiders thought it just a magical flame, slowly swirling like an icy broth; but it was something far more precious. It was the living energies of the countless elves who had sacrificed themselves towards this trial the Drow now faced. As magic had ebbed from their world, its source had to be replaced. Unknown to the half-elf, this very flame was why they practiced their craft in this chamber around this central hearth. The Elf-fire was the living substance of the Drow; whose dying essence was withdrawn and confined using techniques they had learned from their struggles against the race of the Genie many eons ago.

The Faerylands had been split asunder and the elves of every faction sought to survive. Never before had they faced a threat that Mankind had become; one so dangerous that even the Evermore had begun to withdraw to abandon them to their fate. It was a dilemma that imperiled all living things, both great and small. Mankind could not accept that they were not the center of the universe, and would willfully destroy everything in their path to prove it so. Now it was up to the Elves to right this wrong.

"As you know, there were but few among the manlings who listened to the wisdom of the Elves; cast into the sects of white witches and druids but even they were hunted down and destroyed by their own kind," the priestess revealed, "so we must resort to the use of subterfuge as a defense against the breed of Men, or face the reality of our lineage and way of life becoming extinguished by their hand. If that should happen, all beings will suffer under their tyranny," Eden added with solemn remorse.

Venusa understood now the true depth of the peril at hand. It was the mystifying and insatiable hunger of Men to possess far more than they could ever possibly need. It was this one creed that displaced them so far out of tune with nature. Venusa thought long and hard on Eden's words, soaking in their deeper meaning and consequence if she turned a blind eye; for doing so would make her no better than the race of Men who caused this plight. Mankind was a war-like species that refused to listen to reason and would continue to spread like an unstoppable pestilence to the far corners of the world, pushing out all other races, beasts, or creatures that crossed their path. Mankind wasn't inherently evil, it was merely uncivil and immature; but their childish mannerisms and reckless damage they caused upon the world were very real, regardless.

Slowly, Venusa was beginning to understand the burden expected of her during her training under her new tutor. Elves had once tried to breed with men to conceive descendants who could better help them envision their principles among their own social orders. However, within the hierarchy of those few men in power, they viewed this as a dilution to their sacred bloodlines. Venusa was familiar with this discrimination for she had suffered intimidation and bullying more often than naught, as her pointed ears and sharp features were considered a deformity among the human population of her village.

This cruel treatment was not overlooked by the High Elves, who sought to save the rare breed of half-elves from such pettiness or being exploited for their talents with natural magic. Their intentions were honorable, but the elven lords could not foresee the flawed and bias mentality it would eventually yield; further forging a rift between the two races. Though, unfortunately, Venusa failed to find peace with either.

Venusa longed to take a break from her studies and to return to the green forests, and frequently found herself fondling the small flute resting beside the silver key upon the cord that hung around her neck. She was allowed to the inner court and to explore the castle on occasion, but was always restricted from going outside into the open yards or balconies to watch the sunset or gaze upon the starry sky as were the other female disciples. This rule began to gnaw at the half-elf girl in ways that bled her patience. Though the other women seemed content in this edict, Venusa was not. When she questioned this policy to her instructor, Eden adamantly refused to clarify the purpose; contending only that it was a rule she must obey.

Blind obedience did not sit well with Venusa, so she searched for a way to escape her confines. She sought a way to secret herself outside without getting noticed. It wasn't long before she started counting the number of guards and the times of their shifts. She noted the cast of shadows from the glazed windows and where they fell to keep track of time. She even swiped a cloak of black velvet, assured that the mystical stain of her crimson cords could not spoil its sable color. At every opportunity, she explored unused avenues and corridors to seek out the length of each passage. She even went as far as to store scraps of food in the event her flight was permanent. She didn't know if she could escape the island itself, although such thoughts were not beyond consideration.

All the while she kept up her act of compliance and delved into her studies whenever she was under Eden's watchful eyes. She thought it strange, however, that the Drow Queen never once bothered to visit the coven or inquire upon her progress. Perhaps she was nothing more than a forgotten pet to the Queen Mother, Venusa imagined to herself, who had simply lost interest in the insignificant half-elf among all her royal duties. In several ways, she began to feel more alone here than she had in the Eternal City among the company of the prudish elves.

One late evening after a long day of academic work, Venusa dared her move. She just wanted time alone to sit under the broad sky and see the stars once again, if but for a moment should she be able to sneak away from this gilded cage. If circumstances allowed, she could always escape from the castle and try to find her way to one of the port townships of Antilla, and live incognito for a short spell to consider what direction fate might turn for her.

Slipping from her bed in the dorm where the other students slept, she tiptoed out into the silent shimmering light of the glowing furnace and beyond the edge of the doorway. There in the darkness, she donned her black cape to hide her crimson-washed tunic from prying eyes. She had a meager cache of food and a few sparse ingredients for spells she had learned that might be of use upon any wards she may encounter, or use to distract any errant guards that might cross her path. With as much stealth as she could muster, Venusa made her way from shadow to shadow until she reached the entrance to an antechamber where she had seen several of the royal servants pass. Certain she would find a way to an open balcony; she dove inside the door just as an armed sentry passed by.

Slinking her way through the darkness, she was forced to hide behind a buttress, pressing her back upon the cold stone as an attendant suddenly turned into her corridor and passed within an arm's length of where she hid. Releasing a sigh of relief, the half-elf crept down the hall towards a broad wooden door that creaked with the sound of the wind. It was a promising find, and the girl made note of its latch before approaching. Its lavish gilded hasp seemed decorative but unassuming at first, but Venusa had her suspicions.

She pulled out a tiny vial of ethereal dust she had sequestered during her studies, and tilted the container but once on the tip of her finger. Her lips pursed and she gently blew the glittering silt onto the handle. Slowly, a curved image began to weave its way around the latch, as its snaking glow pulsed with energy. It revealed an armed ward, designed to obstruct entry from the exterior as far as she could tell. Furnished with the skills she had learned from her tutor, Venusa pulled out a silver pin and unraveled the spell with the most delicate touch.

Her patience was rewarded with a click when the door unlocked without triggering the alarm. A brisk wind flooded through the crack, and she slowly swung it open as the creaking hinges argued ever so slightly. Peering beyond the opening, she was discouraged to find a long hallway lying beyond as the source of the draft. Hoping to find but an open window or exit to the outer walls, she stepped inside as strings of delicate mist curled their way over the smooth cobbled floor beneath her feet.

What struck her was the sight of several runes lining one wall of the corridor along her path. Each glowing blue upon her approach, but growing brighter the closer she drew. They were hard to read but she spelled them out as best she could of the cryptic language she had recently learned; though her studies in the field were still incomplete. Below every rune she could see a niche in the wall, each holding a delicate glass bottle of varying designs. Glancing back to make sure she wasn't being followed, Venusa took a brief moment to sound out the runes lest they be of some import as to the contents of the numerous elixirs lining the wall.

"Bit, Bitter – oot...?" The half-elf curled her brow in confusion as she tried to read one particular rune, not having a clue as to what manner of chamber she had stumbled upon.

"Bitterroot," a familiar voice echoed from behind the girl, whereupon she nearly jumped out of her skin in shock. Beside the doorway stood the Queen, one pair of arms folded casually across her chest as a second set leaned upon the doorframe. Her headdress was absent and her eyes unobscured. Venusa was caught trespassing by the one person whom she could not invent and excuse for.

"I'm, I was just..." Venusa began to stutter nervously with a sinking knot beginning to well within her stomach.

"Just skulking around. Yes, I know," the drow mother conceded offhandedly, "although you forgot to hide yourself from a common scry. A little sloppy, but mildly impressive that you got this far, at least," the queen snapped a finger with a free hand, and a row of towering candles which lined the hallway suddenly flared to life at her command.

Looking down at her cape, Venusa could now see that the black velvet was a useless escape from the cursed insignia she bore, for several strips of deep crimson had bleached through the dark cloak. With a huff of aggravation, she realized she had been caught; literally red-handed.

"I instructed several servants to use this corridor to bait you into coming here," the queen admitted with a tilt of her head, "though I concede it took you many moons longer than I had presumed for you to make your move, but I wished to see for myself how it was that you managed to gain entrance into the dark library of the Elven Lords," she acknowledged to the girl's astonishment. The queen had laid a trap, and she had fallen for it. Still, she had her wits about her enough to stand her ground. If it was a trap, what had been the purpose of it?

"Am I a prisoner here?" The half-elf asked bluntly. The glint in Venusa's eyes must have sparked a thought in the Drow Queen, for she gave a small grin of admiration in her response.

"That depends entirely on your perspective, I suppose," she breathed with little change of tone, "hoarding stocks of food is not the actions of one seeking a momentary respite but of permanent desertion," the queen professed, revealing the extent of her observations on the young half-elf.

"When I inquired, Eden refused to address my request to leave the castle, and being constantly turned away by the guards would only leave me to conclude that I'm being held hostage for whatever scheme you have in mind," Venusa charged in defiance. The Queen took a step into the room and brought her attention to the glowing runes lining the wall, all of which began to glow hotly with a reddish hue in her immediate presence as the brood mother approached.

"Ah, well, your tutor was not at liberty to discuss that precaution, for the reasons are far more complicated than you may have presumed," the drow mother confessed to the girl's mild surprise, "but what we have tested here is your instinctive guile and devious nature which you turned to as a solution to your unbearable dilemma.

Venusa couldn't read if that last statement was meant as praise or an insult, for the queen continued to mark her attention at the handful of glowing runes inset above the mysterious vials. The half-elf began to stutter a response of confusion as the cloak she bore continued to bleach away its ebony hue, leaving it marred it in a blood-red tone. The drow queen was quick to interrupt her in mid-thought, proving herself far more astute than the young half-breed could fathom.

"Your mind thinks in ways that pure elves cannot," the queen granted to the girls curiosity, "and shows the cunning that lies in the human half of you. Men are strange, you see, for they have a unique ability to lie to themselves and others as if it were second nature to them, this is where Elves fail in their ability to predict this troublesome foe," she revealed. Venusa thought for a moment on her words and the parallels were clear; which, in light of this revelation, was her shrewd elvish side recognizing the basic logic of her statement.

"Regardless, I don't enjoy being your ...your *plaything* for whatever reason you have me here and stalking my every move!" The girl contended, coming off slightly more defensive than she had intended. The queen only smiled back at her reaction and gave a snap of her fingers in front of her face.

"That is the fire I was hoping to see, a mixture of passion and constraint that you will need for your next trial," the queen spouted, revealing tiny fangs in her smile, which disturbed Venusa on an entirely different level. Here she was touting about tests and trials; these never-ending evaluations of the Elves were irksome, to say the least.

"When we first met, you never did answer my question as to what you wanted of me?" Venusa reminded the queen. The drow mother turned once more with a wave of her hand at the row of runes and their tiny glass vials.

"For now, I want you to choose," she offered casually.

"I don't understand," the young half-elf answered reluctantly.

"If you would have completed your studies, then you would know the true meaning of each of these runes," she presented as a bargain, "choose the right vial and drink, and I will release you of your pledge," the queen smiled. It was that unreadable grin of hers that bothered Venusa the most, as if she was somehow a source of amusement to the Queen.

The drow mother stepped aside as Venusa came forward, the angry red hue of the glowing runes subsided and returned to their previous blue radiance as the half-elf drew nearer in her stead. The marks were decipherable but strangely misaligned and hard to read, as would be the difference between crude chicken scratch and fine calligraphy. Many of the symbols were either sideways or turned and even mirrored from their correct origin. Realizing now that she should have paid more attention to her studies, Venusa chose to inspect each of the vials for some clue to solve this puzzle. Pick one, and go free; simple enough.

The first one was a dull green and filled with strings of moss, and one red with tiny rising bubbles within; another was blue and full of glittering ice, while another a murky white, and the last in a bottle of black glass, its contents concealed. Each of the tiny decanters was of different shapes which bore no relation to their purpose. What was this 'bitterroot' anyways, the queen had spoken of?

"Choose one and drink it, and I can go?" Venusa challenged with her royal host, and the queen affirmed her promise.

Reaching for each vial at random, the half-elf attempted to read the reaction of the queen out of the corner of her eye, but her charade did nothing to divulge any sign or hint she was hoping for. With feigned confidence, she finally chose the last vial frosted in black. The others, she suspected, were related to the four elements and Venusa concluded the hidden contents of the ebony vial was the most likely candidate to be free of whatever adverse magic's these strange elixirs might contain.

Taking it from the shelf, she popped the glass cork and took a testing sip. Tasting nothing, she assumed it was likely a placebo and that this game was nothing more than another test to see which primordial essence she would favor. Instead of Earth, Fire, Water, or Air, she chose the Void, the ether in which all energies exist; as the ancient texts taught. Neither tasting nor feeling anything at first, Venusa gulped down the last sip, showed it was empty to the Drow Mother and promptly set the bottle back within its nook. Shining a presumptuous smile back at the queen seemed to find a measure of entertainment in the girl's smug attitude. Having won her freedom, Venusa turned back towards the door to relieve herself of this horrid place.

Without warning, black spots and glowing orbs began to fill her vision as her feet began to sway beneath her. The very stones in the floor seemed to move under her feet and the weight of the air around her tightened like a vise, and she suddenly felt as though she couldn't breathe. She unfixed the red-stained cloak and shed it from her shoulders as she felt her frail heart began to beat ever wilder beneath her breast. She sensed a tinge in her throat and the tips of her fingers began to feel strangely hot as though they were on fire, and the unpleasant feeling raced up her extremities.

The world went sideways, and the half-elf collapsed as her vision faded into darkness as black as the empty vial sitting upon the ledge. The Queen watched with mild fascination while the girl weakened as she struggled to breathe and fainted onto the stone floor before her, only to react with an air of satisfaction in her voice.

"You chose poorly..." the Queen whispered before she turned and disappeared into the twisting labyrinth of the castle.

Frostfall

Venusa cringed from the pounding headache she felt throbbing in her skull as her eyes struggled to open upon a brightly bleached landscape. She reacted with a shiver to the biting cold she felt, while noticing she could see the warm vapor from her own breath plume before her face. A rising chatter distracted the young girl from her personal misery as she strained to right herself, only to find she was in familiar company.

"Ah, the crimson princess awakens," Cynder, one of her fellow students from the coven, remarked coldly. Beside her stood Eve, a woman of thinner stature who was also another sorceress in training. They didn't look the worse for wear as did their half-elf companion who was battling to regain her feet. The last thing Venusa remembered was the uncomfortable feeling of her blood beginning to boil and the stone floor rushing up to meet her. She sat up, entirely confused. How did she get here; wherever *here* might be?

Eve Elmwood applied a far more generous quota of concern than did Cynder; whose fiery red hair was currently stripped from her usual long braids she was fond to wearing bound in curls upon her head. Approaching Venusa to assist her, Eve helped fill her in on recent events. Apparently, all three girls were to share their next lesson together. Venusa couldn't believe her eyes as she regained her poise and surveyed their surroundings.

They were grouped together within a small ice cave lined with streaks of blue frost. Smooth tunnels burrowed through the glacier, leading off in several directions. It was a maze of frigid white that enveloped them in its faint shadows; stark and bare as a desert of ice. Venusa dared to speak even though the effort pained her throat as the poison she had swallowed still lingered.

"What is this place?" She managed to whisper with a hint of misery in her voice that didn't go unnoticed. Cynder stepped forward to glare at the half-breed girl and her tainted tunic, which stood out like a splash of wine in their ivory cell.

"We are here because of you, and we're not too happy about it either," the red-haired girl barked at Venusa who was still feeling queasy while Eve attempted to comfort her.

"What she means is that we were recruited to join you for this academic challenge, though we didn't have much choice in the matter," Eve informed her as she brushed back her vanilla white hair that matched well with the surrounding decor, "we were sent to this abyss, which occupies a space between realms."

"You mean like the Grey?" Venusa stuttered while rubbing her sore eyes and blinking to regain her vision as the toxin she had ingested began to subside.

"Yes ...and no, it is similar to the misty limbo known as Greymoore as you mentioned, but fundamentally different in many ways," Eve attempted to clarify, "and we must work together to survive this trial," she finished with a mark of worry as she looked around the ice cave and the countless corridors that snaked through this frozen tundra. Noticing that the half-elf was beginning to shudder, Eve covered the young girl with the red-stained cape lying beside her.

"Your human side won't help you here," Cynder Firestorm grunted back at the shivering girl whom she blamed for this unfortunate circumstance, "what did you do to antagonize the Drow Mother so badly to end us up in this mess?" She snapped as Venusa began to recover her senses.

"I must have failed one of her stupid tests," she assumed, "the trial with the five elemental vials; I must have picked the wrong one," she reiterated while noting that the other two girls didn't seem to mind the bitter cold as much as she was suffering. It was their pure elven heritage that was more tolerable to temperature extremes than humans could ever be. It was unpleasantly chilly but she would survive, though she was silently thankful for the cloak. Searching its inner pockets, she was glad to notice her scraps of food were still there, tucked away within its folds. In a moment of fright, she double-checked and was relieved to find the silver key and the flute which still hung around her neck. Regaining her composure, Venusa faced the matter at hand and got up to consider their current dilemma.

"You didn't choose the wrong one," Cynder remarked with a huff, as she was familiar with the Queen's trickery and bias sense of humor, "all the vials contained the same poison bitterroot," she admitted to the girl, who appeared shocked at this confession.

The test had been fixed! So that was why the protective runes flamed to a ruby red when the queen wandered into their presence, as a warning that they were dangerous. Venusa realized she had overlooked the one vital clue that the queen had offered so indirectly. The test wasn't reading the text of the runes, nor the color of the liquid, or shape of the vials; it was a trial of perception. Venusa kicked herself for having failed to notice what now seemed so obvious.

"So there wasn't a right one to pick..." the half-elf trailed off in a lost thought while pondering the mistake she had made.

"The right choice would have been to pick nothing," Cynder remarked as Eve concurred with a nod, "if she offered to let you leave, you should have known that would never happen; even if you were foolish enough to believe her ruse," the girl remarked.

Venusa felt like a dolt, now being aware of the deception she had faced. The Queen Mother liked to keep her subjects on their toes, and those that were too slow to realize that simple fact ended up suffering the consequences.

There was still the matter at hand as to why they had been left abandoned in this frozen abyss. Such places as the Greymoore acted as a border between realms. The elves used portals to safely transition from one domain to another but these purgatories were places where outcasts could become lost and where dangerous creatures were banished. It was a precarious place for them to be, for death here could come swiftly to those who weren't vigilant. Separated from the Evermore, the amateur spell weavers were at an acute disadvantage. This is where Venusa failed to grasp the severity of their situation.

"It's merely the cycle of life in the Faerylands, for when a living being expires their essence is returned to the Evermore and reborn into another form; however, in cursed regions such as this..." Eve remarked as she waved her hands to their bleak surroundings, "your life force would be consumed, or even worse, twisted into something dark and malign."

Cynder proposed that there must have been a reason both her and Eve had been chosen to accompany Venusa on this challenge now set before them. It was a rational conclusion to consider that they should pool their combined talents to make it through this trial with their lives.

"From what I've read, I would venture to guess this is a place called Frostfall," Eve whispered over the cracking of the ice echoing through the frozen corridors, "that does not bode well for us," she breathed.

"Why is that?" Venusa asked while clenching her sullied cloak to stave off the chill.

"It is said this place is swarming with ice wraiths, ghouls, and silt walkers," Eve forewarned, though Venusa had never heard of such creatures.

Cynder's specialty was attuned to her namesake, and weaved a fan of flame from her hand, lighting up the chamber. The magical fire also helped to keep the half-elf warm, for she was at a particular disadvantage among her two companions. Eve studied wind and water, which conformed to her application of caring for plants and trees. The half-elf girl quickly considered that her own talents might be lacking in such a place when faced against such monsters.

"So, what is it that we have to do?" Venusa finally dared to ask the two girls while hoping that they would take the lead on this venture.

"We have to find a way out and stay alive in the process," the red-haired girl shot back as if it was the only discernable response. Eve concurred as she produced a tiny pool of water that welled up within her cupped hands and she gently blew upon it with her lips, where it formed into a mist. The delicate fog drifted like incense off into the direction of a wayward tunnel while she followed its trail as it marked their path.

"There will be certain tests along the way we can't predict," Eve advised.

"Which are likely secondary to the main trial, but we need to find a way out and stay alive, regardless!" Cynder corrected with a snub of her nose towards the silver-haired woman. As they followed the route of the drifting mist issuing from Eve's hands, Venusa made short notice that they were an odd combination and that this would be more of a test of character if they were to get along.

They followed the stream of vapor through a maze of mirrored tunnels with twists and turns that were impossible to tell apart until the three girls finally came upon an outlet that opened into a massive caldera of ice, where they found themselves at the bottom lip of a crater enclosed by the steep jagged cliffs of a glacier. Within this frozen world, they looked upwards towards the heavens as several giant moons hung within the cold sky above. Before them in the center of the crater stood a towering spire of white stone; worn smooth with many openings speckled upon its surface. Between them and the tower, thick sheets of cracked ice filled the spaces between bridges of snow that led towards the base of the central obelisk.

"What am I seeing?" Venusa wondered aloud with a sense of awe. It was far beyond anything she could have imagined in her wildest dreams.

Her visit to the Grey had been a mist-filled valley which concealed its true landscape. Had Greymoore also been something like this, a land so unusual and exotic if the veil of its fog had been lifted? Her two companions seemed just as baffled and began to tremble, not from the biting cold, but from the creeping fear that made them shudder. An ice-quake shook the ground beneath their feet as they stumbled to catch their balance. Great sheets of ice fell from the lip of the frozen cliffs high above, crashing to the ground as they shattered the silence of this dreadful place. Debris from the quake and flakes of snow settled in the shimmering air as they turned to one another to decide what course they should take.

"Well, we should investigate that central structure and see what we find within," Cynder offered as she waved her flaming hand in the direction of the strange monolith.

With a swipe of her palms, the pool of fog disappeared from Eve's hands and she held her right hand sideways to squeeze a stream of water from her clenched fist like a spigot. With her left arm, she waved a spiral of wind that coiled down the stream of water and froze it in place just as it hit the floor at her feet. Venusa was impressed to watch Eve create a staff of ice out of thin air, and used the formed icicle as a walking stick.

"Showoff..." Cynder grumbled over her shoulder as she took the lead out of the tunnels and chose a path over the bridges of snow towards the strange fortress looming before them. The frost crunched beneath their feet, breaking tiny snow flowers from their fragile stems in their wake. Among the two girls in white, Venusa stood like a ruby stuck in a block of ice as they made their way across the fractured tundra.

Venusa knelt down, and could see that these frost-laden flowers were truly alive, like a glittering blossom bleached of all color. They shattered into shards upon her touch and she cut herself upon the sharp edges of the splintered petals. A drop of blood from her finger fell upon the ice, soaking into its scarred fissures. With a glance, she saw something dart away below the sheet of ice and she jumped back in alarm, grasping her injured hand.

"What is it?" Eve inquired as she turned back towards the half-elf who had strayed behind to look at the frozen flora. Venusa took several steps back in the crunching snow towards the company of her friends as she saw more movement in the icy depths beneath the frozen surface of the lake where the pools of ice between the bridges met like the spokes of a wheel around the central hub of the tower.

"It ...it might have been nothing," Venusa shuddered in the cold, "I thought I saw something move beneath the frozen ice."

"What did it look like?" Eve asked as Cynder continued ahead.

"I'm not quite sure," the half-elf stuttered with uncertainty as they quickened their pace to catch up with their fiery friend.

Walking beside the red-haired girl, the glow of her flaming hands held aloft like a torch, led their path in this frozen coliseum towards the pale citadel that loomed before them. The strange monument was bizarre and alien in shape, like nothing she had ever seen. Venusa began to wonder to the truth of the myths she had been told about these realms beyond the night skies that rested among the twinkling stars.

Even the air here felt strange and heavy. The pale moons poised above them like giants in the sky, causing her to feel small and insignificant. Within the silence, a strange tune could be heard, carried through the air from the direction of the structure that towered before them. Another crack of ice shook the walls beyond its thin shadow and the trio gathered together in each other's arms to brace themselves as the tremor passed. Looking for an entrance, they circled its base but found none.

"How do we get in?" Eve contended with shared bewilderment between her companions. The hollows within the structure were enormous and far larger than their own stature. They were decorated with what appeared to be carved glyphs around the entire perimeter of the open windows; if that was in fact what they were. Touching it with her hands, the monolith seemed to be made of a soft stone that had a bizarre texture to it, much like the skin of a reptile. Her bloodied finger left a small streak in the rock which soaked into its unusual surface.

The crimson mark Venusa had left began to slowly spread, marbleizing the strange mineral until the small blemish grew as it began to stretch across the entire structure. Noting this odd reaction, the girls stepped back, confused as to what it was they were witnessing. A high pitched cry could be heard shrieking in the wind high above the crevice as the air cracked again with the sound of breaking ice.

"Whatever this is ...it can't be good," Cynder remarked as she gave an accusing glare towards the half-elf. Venusa wondered herself as to the disturbing effect coursing through the skin of the mysterious tower.

With a violent burst, chunks of ice erupted from the far edge of the crater, showering frigid water and shards of ice spraying across the frozen lake. The same piercing shriek pinned the girls with needles of pain while they watched in horror as a colossal snake of alabaster surged forth from the hole in the broken ice. The creature had a giant circular mouth rimmed with sharp daggers that flowed into its gullet. If it had eyes, they couldn't be distinguished from its armored shell which clicked and rattled upon its interlocking plates of bone.

"A white wurm!" Eve struggled to spout between the stinging

shrills hitting them like an invisible wave. The percussion of it nearly knocked them from their feet. With nowhere else to find cover, they scurried behind the base of the tower as the monstrosity weaved its bulk over the broken ice; circling the crater and rearing its head to shriek in erratic intervals. The beast was blind and used its shrill to locate its living prey in this artic world. The snow bridges began to crack and shatter as they collapsed behind them, leaving the three acolytes no way to return to the safety of the caves from which they arrived.

"We have to find a way inside the pylon," Eve shouted to the others in desperation.

"Can you burn it, or scare that monstrosity away?" Venusa suggested towards the red-haired girl while motioning to her flaming hand. Cynder shook her head in doubt.

"This is just illusionary flame for light and it barely has any heat; to do that I would need something that is combustible," Cynder refuted as she motioned with her flaring fingers, and not failing to note how thickly armored the giant wurm was. The leviathan attempted to circle the tower as the girls maneuvered around it in their retreat, though Venusa was perceptive enough to note that the creature seemed to lose their position even when there were moments when they were in its line of sight.

"I think it is blind..." the half-elf dared to venture.

"I believe you're right," Eve concurred, trying to recall any details about this creature from the many scrolls and legends she had read in her studies. It dawned on them in that moment that all the images and drawings of the countless mythical beasts and strange abominations they had seen in the ancient Elven tomes were likely very real. It wasn't a matter they could afford to take lightly lest they meet their eternal rest in this forgotten world. Attempting to recall its weaknesses, Eve made a suggestion to her companions.

"If I remember correctly, it uses sound to find its way," she stuttered as they covered their ears for a brief instant while the beast reared up when a painful wail issued from its jagged maw. Venusa thought that a strange kind of magic for a creature to have, but that it must have evolved as a necessary advantage in this bare and desolate realm. The whitewashed landscape would blind any creature living here, so it found other means to compensate, and a thought came to mind to use her tiny flute.

She fumbled for the whistle hanging around her neck, fighting with the folds of the tarnished cape as her fingers shook in the bitter cold. Cynder shot forth a ball of flame at the creature, catching it once in its throat as it lurched in anger; the other blazing missiles combusting harmlessly on its outer armor. This infuriated the white horror even more as it thrashed its girth upon the fragile floe, shaking their footing and causing them to slip on the buckling shelf of ice.

Venusa sprawled across the bridge and onto the frozen lake, which was now cracked and broken like shattered glass. She lost her grip and began to slide into the icy waters beneath as the frozen slate broke free and began to tip from her added weight. Her eyes widened with fear as her numb fingers slipped from the broken edge and she waved her hands wildly; barely finding a handhold upon the icy staff secured by her fellow students who dashed to her rescue.

Eve struggled with all her strength to pull Venusa to the relative safety of the bridge while fighting to catch her balance as the clamoring beast slammed to the ground, which sent a shockwave through the crater. Cynder continued to spray the giant wurm with fireballs in vain as they burst harmlessly upon its bony shell. It was difficult to aim effectively at the thrashing beast as it writhed in agitation. Cynder was becoming exhausted with the energy she was expending staving off the creature in their defense while Eve was busy rescuing their crimson-stained companion.

The beast turned to shriek once again, noting the diminishing attack from its prey. After getting the half-elf to safety, Eve turned, and with a wave of her hands, she wove a whirling cyclone in the air before them, the ethereal strokes swirling like a tempest had created a shield to protect them; effectively deflecting the waves of sound issuing from the monstrous beast.

For a brief moment, the white snake seemed confused as its senses had failed it, now both deaf and blind to the aerial defense Eve had raised before them. This minor relief was only momentary, as all three disciples could tell that the spell was quickly beginning to fade.

"We won't stay invisible to it for much longer," Eve whispered to her companions behind the swirling current of air cast before them as it slowly began to wane. The two elven girls knew they had steep limitations to their abilities and wondered what the half-elf had to offer in their defense.

Gathering herself in the numbing cold to face this danger, Venusa fumbled with frozen fingers as she grasped for the small charm Ironbow had carved for her. All hope for what her life would become and her secret desires to be accepted by others meant nothing in this dire moment. If she died here trapped upon this frozen world, no one would mourn her, or even care. Her name and memory would be forgotten as just another failure in the Elven struggle by an inadequate half-breed who had acquired more doubts about herself than she could count.

Venusa was exhausted, tired of feeling useless and seen as a lesser among her piers. She grew up feeling awkward among others and treated as if her thoughts had no value as she coped with the bias from both her human and elven kin alike. It wasn't fair; life had only seemed to be mean and unjust to her, making her toil for her own self-identity. It was that pillar of inner strength she found within herself and belief that the Faerylands, in all its intricate wonder, owed her no apology. Here and now, facing death, she felt no fear, and that alone was her salvation.

With all her might, she exhaled through the small flute, hearing nothing but the shrill of the howling gales high above the crater walls. Her companions turned to her in bewilderment as a sudden silence erupted from the giant Wurm, while it poised itself like a statue as bits of snow and frost rained down from its underbelly onto the shattered ice below. Eve's spell gently dissipated in a flurry as they stood there exposed to the onslaught of the monstrosity and found themselves at its mercy. Curiously, that decisive fate withdrew, while the trio watched in shock as the wurm slunk away without another sound; slowly retreating as if it had lost its tastes for its warm meal that stood there dwarfed and helpless before its dreadful presence.

"Remarkable..." Eve sighed in relief as she turned towards

Cynder, who had caught herself holding her breath; wondering what had just happened.

The side of the ivory tower began to melt into itself before them, slowly revealing a doorway for them to enter. As the cracking of ice-quakes continued, they scurried themselves inside for protection from the elements and the dissolving walkway. Once within, they found a maze of skinny passages forcing them to follow one another in single file. The smooth walls gave no indication of composition or pattern and they lost all sense of direction. Finally coming upon an open window along one side, the trio gathered and looked outside in mild surprise to find they were now several stories higher up the obelisk, and were rightly confused, for they had kept level on their path and never set foot upon any step or incline.

Venusa wondered at the magic's involved in this strange stairless tower as they passed through several rooms and chambers far larger than the exterior circumference would have allowed. Eve tried to explain the mystery as a type of dimensional swelling, like the stretching of a spider web beyond its original design and could absorb such expanding, similar to a crystal ball that appears to alter and curve any reflection to fit within its sphere. Her studies into the magic elements of water also covered gazing and scrying into circular bowls, as she explained that its particular shape was used for a specific reason; giving the seer the ability to encompass all aspects of a vision into one viewable image like a lens.

Cynder seemed to understand the artful concept, although Eve completely lost Venusa on her analogy of such advanced and archaic studies. Pure elves could perceive the strings of nature and how they were woven. Venusa, being only half-elven, could barely understand the theory; which was much like trying to explain various colors to someone who was blind. However, she embraced her limitations with a measure of surrender but was also preserved with the knowledge that the Drow Queen had recognized her alternative and unique talents, and was forging her into a useful tool for the challenges ahead.

The three girls had not bargained for such a harrowing encounter, which had left them lightheaded and exhausted. The further they progressed through the pale Obelisk, the higher they ascended. Reaching the apex, they finally arrived at a strange platform with curved outer walls. The sky above them shone through a shimmering membrane glittering with streaks of electric plasma. At the center of this odd chamber, a blue oval crystal hung in mid-air. The egg-shape was one of the sacred icons of creation, so they made an educated guess as to what action they were supposed to take in this trial.

"I haven't studied as long as the other disciples in the coven, and I'm not sure what that object is," Venusa admitted in ignorance to her companions on this quest. Eve was content to help her understand.

"This realm is based on a unique structure of magic; or rules, per se, that everything within must abide by. Each domain and the space between these worlds possess a different natural order," she offered to explain to the half-elf and Cynder, who was following the conversation in turn, "Frostfall, itself, is like a tether that can bind one realm to another from which to travel; but this," she stated while pointing at the glowing turquoise crystal before them, "...this does not belong here."

"Why would you say that?" Cynder snapped in rebuttal, noting that the obelisk appeared to be specifically designed to hold this mystical object. Venusa was interested to know the answer.

"This is likely a living seed," she breathed with a mark of awe and admiration at its rare beauty. The egg itself was a marvel of translucent blue streaks that seemed to emanate from within its shell. It wasn't that great in size and was relatively small enough to hold in two hands, but as she took a few steps closer to gaze at it, the crystal pulsed angrily, as if sensing its vulnerability as they drew near.

"You mean like the Tree of Life of our own realm?" Cynder suggested, "If this sprouts, then wouldn't Frostfall become a true world of its own?" The red-haired elf dared to ask.

"I don't know the answer to such questions," Eve confessed, "but it was likely our mission to retrieve this sacred object and return it to the head Priestess of the Order," However, Eve's suggestion left the half-elf feeling uneasy.

"You mean they didn't tell you both what our objective

actually was?" Venusa inquired with an air of astonishment.

"We were brought here through a portal where we found you lying unconscious, and were left abandoned to seek our own course," Cynder touted with a hint of rage, "To our regret; we were expecting you would know the specifics of this quest."

Venusa understood Cynder's touch of anger, for both she and Eve had risked their lives to accompany her on this crusade against their will. They had merely been following the instructions of their head Priestess by order of their Queen Mother. Being banished here felt more like an undeserved punishment, though they had effectively combined their unique skills to get this far. But what was the true goal if not to obtain this mystical keepsake?

"Let's take this with us and bring it back to the Queen," Venusa suggested, daring to step forward even closer as the crystal seed pulsated furiously with an angry light.

Gently grasping the floating crystal, she noted how strangely smooth it was, with a texture as if it were covered in oil; but her hands held fast, almost as if they were partially absorbed into its glowing shell. It felt like cold fire; not an entirely unpleasant sensation but one that left her feeling an overwhelming desire to release it the first chance she could. The half-elf untied her sullied cape and wrapped the crystal egg in its folds as she removed it from its floating pedestal. The very moment she did so the tower shuddered and the walls of the monolith began to blacken; spreading like a dark poison.

The other two elves stepped forward and held Venusa's shoulders when the floor beneath them began to tremble while the murky stain seeped towards them at a frightening pace. With a tingle, Venusa saw that her hair began to rise and watched in fascinated horror as her skin began to peel away in shafts of light. The other two girls also shared looks of dread and dismay as they observed themselves disintegrating before their eyes while their very bodies trickled into rising pins of light, until the luminosity brightened to the point of blindness.

They felt no discomfort from the transformation, but suddenly found themselves standing within a hollow darkness; the shock of what had just unfolded beyond any words they could describe. A dim fire blinked into existence before them, its luster growing by the moment until the trio recognized the familiar dance of the entrancing flames. As if through a gloom of thick webs, the room around them began to blur into view as the fog dissipated and they found themselves standing within the central chamber of the coven; warm with the glow of the elfire hearth. Behind them stood Eden Whitetail, poised with a glare in her eyes as if to scrutinize the method of their arrival.

"How ...how did you do that?" Eve asked with a gleam of astonishment towards the half-elf girl, while both she and Cynder removed their hands from Venusa's shoulders.

"You've returned," the Priestess announced as the three girls turned in unison, "I will take that, sister," Eden remarked as she held out her slender hands to receive the bundled egg from Venusa's grasp, though being explicitly careful not to touch its exposed shell.

Holding it aloft in mild wonderment, Eden let the folds of the cape fall away under her cupped hands, exposing the seed from Frostfall; though now it was oddly dark and black as slate, as though it were dormant. Carefully, she balanced it, propped upon its pillow of the crumbled cape and placed it securely within a thick wooden box and walked out of the room without another word. The three students stood there boggled as to what it was they had just accomplished.

"How did I do what?" Venusa finally responded in a daze back towards Eve.

"How were you able to touch that living seed with your bare hands?" Eve contested, "I was going to try to encase it in ice, but you dared to merge with its essence," she stuttered. Venusa could see that Cynder was also in a state of dismay, while she took a step away from the half-elf with noted apprehension.

"I just did what needed to be done ...what does it matter?" The half-elf blabbered in response to their odd misgivings, while still feeling remnants of the strange tingle upon her fingers where she had touched the relic.

"A living seed must never be handled in its own realm, or it will devour your entire being into is own essence," Eve tried to explain, "You should have been absorbed into it, like the living

Evermore," she illustrated while motioning with her hands what she was trying to describe.

Venusa hadn't a clue as to what she had done wrong, nor of the dangers involved. It was then that she looked down in astonishment at her own hands. The red cords of shame she bore had melded into her wrists, and her hands were now blackened like coal with a stain that appeared to have writhed its way through the embedded crimson on her forearms like a poison weed. Though try as she might, she couldn't rub out the blemish; leaving her feeling disfigured.

"After coming in contact with that relic, you should be dead..." Cynder remarked with tension creeping into her voice as Eve gazed upon the half-elf's tarnished hands. Somehow, she felt suddenly unclean, and Venusa turned away from the others in humiliation. What had she done to herself?

Shatterstone

Many days passed as Venusa and the others recouped from their journey while feeling strangely drained and ill from the venture. Their head priestess, Eden, assured them the sickness would pass and they eventually recovered with the aid from their fellow students. Once they were well enough to continue their studies, Eden took the time to debrief the girls as to their experience in the abyss known as Frostfall. It was then they were told the reason for that particular endeavor and the true objectives of the Queen, for which Venusa found herself pardoned from her previous transgressions.

As the Evermore bound every living thing in its presence, there was an aura of natural magic woven between them and all inanimate objects. Eden described these veils between worlds as trying to imagine a fish flying in the air or exploring lands it would otherwise never know, but without the means to traverse therein, or possess the ability to survive for long outside of its natural element. These were the natural laws known in our own world, and they also applied on the opposite scale such as would say, a frail forest fawn attempting to visit the cold and pressing ocean depths. It would only die a quick and unpleasant death; as such a delicate creature did not belong in such realms. As such, what she drew was a broad illustration of natural separation of all creatures at their most extreme concepts, whether they be of fin, feet, or feathers.

Eden further delved into what the underlying secret purpose of their Coven, as they were not allowed to discuss their studies with the other dark elves in the castle sanctuary, and this rule was strictly enforced. Mankind had become a threat to all creatures of the Faerylands to a level only a few were truly aware. The race of Men had a strange ability to weave and manipulate forces they had no right to possess. Through their tinkering in these unnatural magic's they provoked an instability that imperiled the balance of the world.

This led to a secretive and uneasy alliance between the Elves and the Dwarves, which evolved in their efforts to stave off the humans and their hunger for power as they spread like a plague across the earthly realms. In the beginning, rogue factions of Dwarves forged arms and inventions for Mankind; however, they came to realize that the secrets of their skills would be stolen and abused as Man's descendants began to burrow into the earth, trespassing into the realms of the Dwarves. They also continued such offenses against the kingdom of the High Elves as they encroached upon their lands and plundered sacred sanctuaries, and in turn, they spawned occults that were an insult to the very fabric of nature. Even Dwarves knew greed, but never on the scale of which Mankind had portrayed, and they, too, had learned to fear them.

Understandably, the High Elves were upset with the Dwarves and their prior collaboration with Men, which only increased the virility of their war-like race. Over the years that followed, during secret meetings held in closed chambers and the cover of night, an alliance was forged to defend against the antagonists that Mankind had become towards all beings in their craving for dominance over the known world.

"We have heard of this in whispered conversations," Eve conceded to the head Priestess, "this ...this *Craving* as it was called, but wasn't it known by another name?"

"At first, the Elven Lords titled it thus, so as not to directly name their adversary to be overheard by hidden ears, for they did not wish to arouse suspicion by the race of Men in their midst as to this new alliance forming against them. Such dangerous rumors would only escalate to a premature war between man and elf," the priestess affirmed, "spies among the tribes of Men were many, and they proved to be crafty and shrewd in their dishonorable ways. They were backstabbers and thieves, they broke their word and commitments with their forked tongues; and in light of their deception, they displayed a lack of honor and cowardice, their secret name among us became the Kakaruka; *the Craven*, which the Elves used to christen Mankind's rotting and diseased psychology," Eden revealed as she drew a sharp swath of a rune in the air, denoting the symbol of their mortal enemy. The class of disciples gazed upon the glowing marks floating before them and it became an emblem that would forever be seared into their minds.

Calling them 'Craven' was designed as an insulting title towards their adversary, but not one of racism towards their species as a whole but only to their broken mentality. Not all men were corrupt, of course, but their societies allowed enough of them to exist that it bred discontent, which only served to germinate the poison in their minds among others. It was well known that in their social order, Men would refuse to stand up against such solitary tyrants out of fear, without reason as to why so many would bow beneath their whip. As such, in their wide almond-shaped Elven eyes, they saw them as spiritually weak and cowardly.

In the strange and twisted world of Men, the many suffered for the sake of the few. Their ethics and leadership were queerly backward and contradicted any sense of philosophy or rational logic. They were not only dangerous to every living entity in their world and beyond but also to themselves, which is why the Elves feared them so. As the Elven Lords were to those born of the Faerie, the Drow Queen herself, was seen as a symbol of strength to all of elvenkind, and dared not show a hint of trepidation in the face of this dilemma; for doing so would only sow despair among the populace and further splinter their race.

"Why were we sent to harvest the living seed of Frostfall?" Venusa dared to interrupt at one point in the lesson. The other disciples were also interested as to this purpose.

"The ability of our seers is limited, and fundamentally ineffective in such purgatory planes that have not bloomed into living realms; such as Frostfall and Greymoore, as you yourself have experienced," Eden nodded towards the half-elf girl before her, who had wrapped her blackened hands in cloth in an attempt to hide them, "those are neutral planes of creation in perfect balance, still tethered by a common vibration before they have taken root. In a living plane such as ours in full bloom, energy returns to its source; which we know as the Evermore," the priestess remarked. This academic knowledge was educational, even enlightening, but Cynder noted that the

Priestess had danced around the core of Venusa's inquiry. Why had the three of them been placed in such dire danger, or such a vital task not been performed by the Priestess herself or the other Elders, who were far more skilled and better qualified to face such perils.

"But why were we sent to uproot that world seed?" Cynder snapped back with a measure of impatience, though the Priestess and the others noted well her peculiar choice of words.

"A well defined summary," Eden offered to the temperamental red-haired elf, "but as mentioned, our oracles and channelers are impotent in such neutral and incohesive realms where they are left blind. The Queen felt you three had the skills to acquire that particular source of power, and sent you on the journey which would help further your education."

Still, Cynder was unsatisfied to the explanation as were the other two girls, along with the quizzical glares from each of the other students as to what their tutor had stated.

"From my studies, it reveals that the seed we had taken could have sprouted into a world of its own," Eve charged while rifling through several scrolls, finally finding one, and holding up an ancient symbol of the world tree for all to see, showing the inverse image of its roots below and leaved branches above in perfect balance with the trunk; all enclosed in a perfectly woven sphere representing the circle of life in synergy with itself. In Elven lore, it was known as the Tree of Life – one and the same as the World Tree, the most sacred artifact of the High Elves which they kept guarded within the Eternal City. What Eve was implying denounced a darker side of their actions.

"I understand your concerns, Eve," the priestess consoled and waved her hands to hush the rising murmurs of her students, "and yes, there is always the possibility that the seed might have eventually sprouted and grown into a world of its own one day, with its own unique vibration and spectrum of living creatures and sentient beings. However, to relieve you of the burden of guilt, you did not kill that world by recovering a seed which had failed to root. Your true purpose was to save it." Eden charged with a turned brow, declaring it as an act of responsibility.

"You mean to protect it from..." Cynder began but was interrupted as the Drow Queen glided into the room, unnoticed by the crowd of students.

"Yes sister, to safeguard it from the Craven," the queen mother remarked coldly as everyone in the chamber turned in dismay. Her words were direct and meant to justify the risk.

Under her stern gaze that swept across the young sisters of her brood, it was clear that they were being schooled in such forbidden sorcery far outside normal avenues to battle the terrible blight known as the Craven. The Queen paced the room to scrutinize the students of their coven, only to end up at the very foot of the unhappy half-elf, who had good reason to feel apprehensive in the Drow Mother's presence. She felt little guilt from her attempt to escape the castle but held a level of embarrassment, if not downright animosity against the queen, especially after being poisoned by the trickery of her previously rigged challenge.

She almost felt like bolting off and hiding when the Queen Mother stood before her and reached out to take her sullied hands, now stained black and grotesque. As Venusa sulked, the queen inspected her palms and the mark of dishonor from the High Elves which had infused upon her wrists. The half-elf girl felt ugly and marred from this disfigurement; however, the Drow Mother declared otherwise.

"Quite fascinating," she breathed as she turned the girl's soiled hands and her beastly clawed nails, which were a new addition to the scarring, "I found it hard to believe that you had touched that obsidian seed," the queen added while all three pairs of her arms gently traced the girl's tainted hands and the blackened stains that crept along her skin. The queen was referring to the living crystal artifact they had commandeered from that strange netherworld obelisk of Frostfall, which had turned raven black after it had been removed from its own realm. The seed was not dead, but now lay dormant once it had been detached from the vibrational energies of its own domain.

"Will she be okay?" Eve was considerate enough to inquire, "Can we do anything to heal her wounds?"

In response, the Queen herself turned for but a moment

75

88

8878888

8 towards the silver-haired girl with a cavalier glare from her red eyes, implying that the young student was somehow ignorant.

"You would rather fix her, and cleanse her of these marks?" The queen challenged with a questioning tone as she held up Venusa's tainted hands for all to see; much to the girl's embarrassment, "these hands," she cited while also bringing directed attention to her own altered disfigurement and her extra set of arms as a comparison, "...are tinged with the mark of power!"

Releasing her grip, the queen gently returned Venusa's hands to her lap while she moved a loose hair from the girl's face with a degree of affection. At that moment, the half-elf outcast felt a brief kinship and unspoken understanding with the Queen, and the anger that had welled up within her began to melt away. Venusa felt alarmed at the sudden turn of her inner emotions and felt strangely vulnerable to what the brood mother had just revealed. Had the queen herself, also ventured to the netherworlds to be forever distorted and changed; never to be the same? Was it a curse ...or something more?

"This sisterhood is being trained to hone your talents in an effort to counter the destructive influence of the Craven, in both our own natural world and those beyond," the queen proclaimed, "from this moment forward your lives will be dedicated to this coven and to protect the Drow and all of our Elven brethren from this scourge we now face!"

Though her words placed a heavy responsibility upon them, Venusa and a few others in the chamber exchanged glances of self-doubt, revealing they were not quite so confident that this was the direction they wished their lives to face. The queen was not blind to this wavering indecision left floating like a haze among the students and shared the concern that any weak link in this chain they forged could cause the sisterhood to unbuckle. Never before has there been such a pact in all of their history, even with their ancient war with the Djinn. The queen was asking them to give up their lives to this endeavor, which would likely come to a very unpleasant end for each and every one of them.

"Madam Queen," a male scribe appeared at the chamber door,

holding a sealed container, "the requested items from the vault of the Elders," he offered solemnly as he held out a clay vase riddled with runes; its surface awash with the patina of age.

The queen strolled over and took the large vase within her lower pair of hands, but the students noted that the scribe did not dare step foot into their chamber. Elven males were not allowed into the light of the elfire, for it was reserved for those sisters of the brood who possessed the power of creation. With her upper set of arms, the queen examined the unbroken wax seal upon the lip of the container and turned back towards the assembly of young disciples. With measured effort, she hefted the urn onto a corner worktable and placed all six of her hands around its rim, thumb to finger, where they met.

Closing her eyes, and with the tensing of her body, the students reared as the protective runes of the vessel suddenly expelled into a violent waft of black smoke, and after a silent moment, the Queen waved the acrid vapor away. With one heave, she lifted the jar and cracked it sharply upon the table, shattering its shell. From within oozed a milky-white gas that dissipated like an eerie mist as scrolls of all shapes and sizes spilled forth from the broken shards of pottery. Wiping her hands once, she turned back to the sisterhood of elves.

"These are the forbidden codex, one of many decanters of knowledge sealed before the birth of the elven lords," she waved with her hand towards the pile of parchments, "if you accept this appointment by choice, you will be of the privileged few Elves to ever view their contents, to learn of the forces that move the tides and forgotten wisdom of the primal," she offered to the students who gasped in awe, for most had believed these archives to be merely legends, exaggerated myths lost to antiquity, "choose now, though be cautioned that awareness of such teachings is both a gift and a curse, for you cannot unlearn them," she forewarned.

With hesitation, one by one, each disciple stood and stepped forward to take a single bound scroll or sealed parchment from the lot; accepting this royal covenant in doing so. Only a few of the disciples chose otherwise and remained seated with a measure of disgrace to their own weakness and concerns. The queen, however, stood glaring at the half-elf who did not wish to accept this pact. Stepping aside, she invited Venusa with a final gesture to come forward and choose her destiny.

Venusa sat there for many moments surrounded by the hum of silence while staring down at her blackened scarred hands. As of late, her existence had taken such a drastic turn, and she thought long and hard on how the path of fate had brought her to this moment. She reflected on the real reason she had snuck into the dark library in the Eternal City and placed so much at risk to breach their security in an attempt to learn one particular spell. Venusa had been torn between two worlds, the ones of Men and Elves.

Through rumor and whispers, whether by myth or lore, she sought to find a way to change who she was. The arcane knowledge she sought with such determination was to help turn her into a pure elf or be it human as the result, for she felt it was too tortuous an existence to live as both. She was never accepted as she was but always finding herself prejudged for what she was not. She believed she could finally find peace if she could somehow transform into one or the other. Now, here she was, forever changed in ways she could not reverse; knowing that dream of equality would never be.

Something indescribable shed from Venusa in that moment of reflection, an aura that the Queen herself could almost sense as the half-elf girl suddenly stood and retrieved a scroll from the pile; thereby accepting the contract as an eternal vassal to the Sisterhood. The drow mother gave a sigh, perceiving the conflict raging within the girl and the personal struggles that led her to her choice; be it from inner strength or submission, only time would tell.

A majority of the disciples adhered to the stringent rules of their new position without question. Shortly thereafter, the entire coven was removed from the sanctuary for an assembly to a private arena located deep within the heart of the castle. There they were introduced to a handful of instructors who would drill them on the use of weapons of war. They were women warriors, masters at the art of combat by bewitchment or blade; each of a different race that dwelled within the

Faerylands who possessed the refined skills of their trade.

There was a Dwarven female battle mage who instructed the cadets on the use of brute force and the value of armor. Another was a Satyress with cloven feet and massive curled horns who would teach the art of the summoner. Another tutor was a Naga matron with a long writhing tail of a snake, who would train them in archery and stealth. A tall dark Faerie with torn and tattered wings would educate them in the craft of illusion. Among them stood a beautiful Blood Elf, with braided hair filled with coins and bells, who possessed mastery in all manner of blades. An unlikely mentor was a tough little She-Gnome with hardened eyes, who would educate them in the spectrum of elements and their uses. Though, beyond the gnome stood poised a single silent figure that seemed oddly out of place. A glass knight armored in gleaming crystal who brandished a glazed shield; her long snow-white hair flowing across her polished armor, who would tutor them in the art of defense.

Their coven priestess, Eden, would also further their studies in alchemy and remedies. It was an unusual assembly of champions for an extraordinary circumstance, and the students were separated and assigned to groups. At the conclusion of the formal introductions with their new weapon masters, the pupils were released back to the central coven to prepare themselves for the trials ahead. Once they arrived, the girls could not help but notice that the elfire in the central hearth was fully ablaze, shining brighter than they had ever known; the slow dance of its pure flame lighting the circular chamber.

A quiet rumor swiftly spread through the sisterhood of young apprentices, that the sparse few students who had chosen not to join this secret order had been infused into the elfire itself. Upon hearing this, each of them turned to stare into the renewed pyre of the hearth with a creeping sense of horror. Their fellow scholars had been killed to feed its flames with their living essence. The dark elves had begun to draw upon their own energy to fuel their mystic powers as the Evermore ebbed from this realm. It was clear to them now, as the animated flames flared from the central bell radiating before them, that the Queen Mother would not take 'no' for an answer, and the bid of secrecy of this sisterhood would instill a high price for all those who opposed her. They were now indentured servants and would be forever bound to the Queen's covenant, or serve the sisterhood in another manner with their own life force. So was the way of the Drow.

Venusa recognized the offer for what it was, which was akin to the test with the poisoned vials. Once the Queen Mother made a request, it was a command not to be confused with an appeal, and there would be dire consequences to face if denied.

"So the magic that we are weaving here uses the elf-fire as its source?" The half-elf inquired to her tutor. Eden helped to ease her tension at the disclosure to the disturbing news, but it was her task to prepare her students for all eventualities, no matter how unpleasant.

"Currently, the state of the Evermore, the living energy of the entire Faerylands, is in steep decline," the Priestess revealed, "which is one of the core reasons the High Elves chose to submerge the Eternal City into the depths of the earth, for they were not only concealing the kingdom and the secrets it held but were obligated to preserve the sacred Tree within the veil of the Evermore, to remain protected in its folds and beyond the reach of all mankind."

This waning of the world's living energy was much more conspicuous in the lands of Men, where it appeared there were far less flora and fauna that roamed the wilds. There was once a time when lush forests and jungles had transformed vast mountain ranges of barren stone and empty deserts. Though now, wherever Mankind dwelled, the Evermore withdrew. Like any living entity, the Gaia would react and recoil to protect itself from their infection and the trauma they caused. If the Elves did nothing to stop this scourge, then they, too, could be entirely consumed by this foul miasma.

Their training was difficult and notably strenuous for the remaining pupils as they were being prepared for the battle to come. Venusa's first lessons were with the large female Satyr by the name of Kashnar. Though her face also presented goat-like features, she was incredibly beautiful in a wild and primal way. The goat-legged woman bore armor made of polished bone adorned with an array of large fangs gathered from several carnivorous creatures. Her eyes were as black as midnight, and she donned burnished tattoos upon her upper torso and breasts.

"Honored greetings, child of elf," the creature bowed with a formality that the half-elf did not recognize, "so you are to be my first victim," Kashnar smiled, more of a statement of fact than a question. Venusa was taken off balance by her comment but returned the salutation, while the Satyr examined the girl's extremities with her dark ebony eyes.

"Where shall we start?" Venusa responded, eager to begin her lessons.

"Hmm, I see you have a marking," the goat woman noted towards Venusa's blackened hands, "let us see if it obstructs your teachings."

Venusa came to learn that the blemish she bore was one of such import that she should be mindful and wary if she should ever identify a similar mark on an opponent. Such impressions came in all manner of strange and obscure forms, which most always revealed that such an individual delved in powers far beyond their usual nature and that she should take heed if ever faced with such a foe. It was a peculiar warning, for the half-elf did not know the face of the Craven or what it was capable of.

"Summoning is a delicate art, for you can call forth a great many natural energies that could either help or hinder," Kashnar warned, "for instance, if you were to conjure forth a swarm of razor wasps, you might be well advised to run for cover, yourself," the Satyr cautioned, "until your skill evolves to the point you can invoke a familiar that you can completely control. So, it is upon you to play upon whichever circumstance you are presented to forge a proper counter; savvy?" the goat woman petitioned with a tilt of her massive horns as she eyed the small girl standing before her.

"Perhaps I could if you would enlighten me?" Venusa offered in response, wishing to make sure she understood the instructions of her trainer.

The Satyress began by referring to the skill set of the small burly Gnome who could teach the girl all spectrum's regarding elemental powers. Armed with such knowledge, Venusa could then conjure earth or ice elementals to counter fire spells, or werecats to consume a nest of plague rats, and even hellhounds or werewolves if the summoned felines were to get out of control. Most every creature has a mortal enemy, and the trick was to use such knowledge to your tactical advantage.

"Thus, do you understand the fundamentals of this art before we begin?" Kashnar inquired.

"You mean, for instance, if we summoned a swarm of wasps, to say, deter an attacking beast, but if the wasps should become a danger to myself, then I could perhaps conjure up a whirlwind to blow them away?" Venusa proposed as an example to suggest countermoves she could make in such a circumstance.

"Exactly," Kashnar debated, "or conjure a flock of ash ravens to consume them, or a freezing rain to kill them. Just be aware that whatever you choose to channel could also pose a threat to yourself or your allies."

"Forgive me for asking, but I had read many ancient texts during my studies with the high elves, of stories where Demons were summoned and even the dead raised to walk again; is such a thing actually possible?" The half-elf inquired to her tutor. Kashnar gave a beastly grunt as she stroked her curled horn in deep thought before giving her response.

"A demon can be any creature from any plane of existence that is imbued with an unnatural level of power; though, take note that the art of Necromancy is strictly forbidden, and in all respects, has only been performed by human sorcerers," the goat maiden warned.

Kashnar lectured the young half-elf as to the nature of the undead and how they twist and dissolve the very fabric of the Evermore. Zombies were a creation of Mankind who practiced dark sorcery, spawning un-life from the flesh of the dead. This was a type of abomination in the eyes of all beings and races; even among most of humanity. Such reanimated creatures were turned into mindless stalkers and their only existence was to devour the spark of life from the living, which served to dull the overwhelming pain of their condition. Their state of insufferable discomfort was why they would roam listlessly and moan in perpetual agony, and was seen as the worst abuse of slavery that could be imposed upon another being. Truly, victims of such black arts were to be pitied, if not feared.

Venusa found it interesting that Elves were incapable of such foul magic, and unable to perform necromancy itself. Mankind, though, was another matter entirely. On rare occasions, their depraved wizardry was able to create such atrocities from the corpses of beings, including their own kind, through the use of vile poisons and corrupted incantations. The summoning of Demons, on the other hand, was not quite as uncommon as Venusa had once believed. Such creatures were usually called forth to perform specific tasks as a pressured duty, though payment was high and the pacts that bound them were always a risky matter for those involved.

Each student of the sisterhood was to spend at least three moon cycles studying the craft they were appointed with each master. Venusa learned a great deal from the Satyr and the precarious balance that had to be maintained as a Summoner. The following season, she was commissioned under the instruction of the Gnome who went by the name of Shandi. Gnomes love to tinker and were the lesser of the few brethren races to the Dwarves, who were well known as masters of the forge.

Shandi was to be her teacher in the art of elements, which Venusa thought she already knew; Earth, Water, Fire, Wind, and the all mysterious Void; however, she did not know of the force of lightning was also included in that field. What the half-elf found interesting was how each of the elements could be transformed within their own state, such as how water could flow, or be made solid, or evaporated into a gaseous form. Earth itself, had a myriad of materials that it could be shifted into on its own or mixed with the other elements to create entirely different forms. Venusa recalled her brief encounter with the Stone Giant that slumbered in the earth, and learned how each element responded differently to the flow of time.

Air could be thinned to suffocate, or compressed into the colossal power of a typhoon. She found lightning to be the most curious of all. It was such wild and chaotic energy, which had the ability to conduct itself through other objects, and could be finely-tuned to either stun a foe with a minor jolt or use its spark to ignite a flame. The half-elf zapped herself many times by mistake during her lessons, simply by trying to understand its baffling and mysterious nature. She found herself truly impressed with the Gnome's extensive knowledge.

"After seeing the versatility of the other elements, one might find fire quite predictable, but it can be manipulated in ways beyond your imagination," Shandi expressed to the tall half-elf who stood twice her height, "it is the one element that can either cure or consume entirely; and is commonly known that most every wild beast will instinctually fear it above all others."

"I have seen my fellow student, Cynder, use such flames, but they had no true heat to them. She only used it as a source of light and a form of diversion," Venusa exclaimed.

"Certainly, but once she learns the dynamics of this most primal of all elements, she will be able to master it entirely," the small gnome suggested.

With that assurance, Shandi removed five small crystals from a velvet pouch tied at her waist. Placing them upon the ground between the two of them, the gnome adjusted the gems to turn their points towards one another like the directional arms of a compass. With a flick of her stubby wrist, a spark ignited at their center and a wild flame arose before them, reaching towards the ceiling high above; causing the half-elf to lurch back a step.

With a roll of her hands, the flame spout reacted by forming into the coiled form of a dragon, sculpted within its flickering light. Venusa looked on with glee as it dissolved back down into an orb of blue flame. Daring to place her hand near the glowing sphere, she could feel the cold fire sucking the heat from the area around her, chilling the air. If she had not witnessed such arcane magics for herself, she would have never believed it possible.

With a snap of the instructor's fingers, the orb vanished and the gnome scooped up the tiny crystals, which were all of a different shade, and placed them in the girl's palm.

"Take these, each of these crystals represents the five elements," she offered as a gift.

Venusa was confused at first by the Gnome's cryptic words, but accepted the instructions to make rings out of the five tiny crystals to use as talismans for her incantations. Through her second season, the half-elf was put through her paces in studies of the elements and their place in the living world. Learning how they interacted and repelled were not easy tasks to remember, but she used the ring charms to help her focus her skills at sorcery. Once she satisfied Shandi by her intensive screening, the half-elf was allowed to progress into the care of the thick Dwarf woman to learn the discipline of strength.

On the first day with her new master, Venusa was directed to a separate area far from the other cadets. A circular sunken arena was where she met the Dwarven maiden, who was grunting war cries while swinging a heavy blade that consumed both of her sturdy hands. Seeing Venusa approach, she halted her swing towards her with a sharp blow that stopped a mere fingernails breadth from the girl's nose, to which the girl failed to flinch; not out of courage, but of frozen shock. Noting the half-elf girl failed to cringe; the Dwarven champion gave a wide grin with a gleam of her teeth beneath her hairy beard.

"Ah, they brought me one with courage this time ...even though you are a bit lanky," the dwarf remarked with a pinch of the girl's arm from her bronze gauntlet. Still wide-eyed from the close shave offered by the Dwarf's reception, Venusa uttered a reply to the stout soldier.

"Greetings, Milady, I am known as Venusa Viper," the half-elf uttered with a catch of her breath. The dwarf chuckled heartily as she firmly set the thick blade of her claymore under Venusa's chin to prevent the girl from bowing during her formal introduction, and raised her back to her full height. Still leery at the sharp blade at her throat, Venusa kept her eyes on the sword with her full attention given to the Dwarven warrior.

"Hah, ha, oh, don't mistake me for a 'lady' little one," the warrior huffed, "you may address me as Argona Shatterstone from Fellhammer keep," she finished while lowering her blade to allow the girl to take a gulp of air.

"...Fellhammer keep?" Venusa began, trying to regain her composure while keeping the appearance of polite conversation.

"Of course, little one; our kings seem to name everything hammer this, and hammer that, you know, considering their infatuation with forges and all. Its silliness if you ask me," Argona finished with a wide smirk, though her tone ended with a hint of genuine disappointment with their lack of originality.

The dwarf led her to the edge of the arena to view several combinations of armor and their styles of construction. Argona herself, wore a hardened set of golden-bronze plate that was padded with furs and woven leather. It appeared battle-worn with various nicks and cuts scarring its thick surface; proving it was not used for decoration. Looking through the diverse sets of mannequins, Venusa was advised on the benefits and disadvantages of the styles of armor. There was plate steel, scale, bone, chain mail, and several different species of leather from mammal to reptile skins, and some that were far more exotic in nature. However, Venusa found herself drawn to the furs, for they came in a variety of colors.

Next came strength training, to which the half-elf appeared scrawny next to the thickly built dwarf. For many following moons, she was taught the value of exercise to tone her muscles, healthy eating, and how to assemble her own armor, followed by even more exercise until she was sore through and through. Every morning she woke up, her muscles ached and screamed with agony while she donned different types of armor so as to learn of their strengths and weaknesses.

"Ah, we'll make a warrior of you yet, little whelp," Argona burped with the stench of ale that always seemed to be lingering on her breath.

"In what situations would I ever need armor when I can simply defend myself with sorcery?" Venusa dared to ask. The dwarf furrowed her brow while stroking her beard with her stubby fingers; grumbling to herself as if she found the question itself offensive.

"It seems like you're in need of a formal lesson in pain," the dwarf snapped, and the half-elf immediately regretted her question. Argona stomped over to the weapons rack and took a moment of contemplation while eyeing over the giant hammers and battle-axes, heavy bastard swords and thick bladed glaives;

and finally settled on a tiny dirk, which was nothing more than a glorified dagger. She also grabbed up a large axe with one hand as she walked back towards Venusa, who stood waiting in the arena. The Dwarven war maiden was in such a fury that she unceremoniously lopped off the head of one of the wooden target mannequins as she walked past it, with nary a flinch.

With a glare in her beady eyes, the dwarf turned to the last wood dummy wearing a vestment of plates of riveted steel and violently jabbed the thin dagger in-between the kinks of armor. The dirk stuck there like a giant nail impaled into its body of timber as it rocked back from the force, causing the helmet to fall and clatter to the ground. Turning back towards the stunned half-elf, Argona placed her hands on the trunk of her hips and gave a growl of criticism. Venusa was just glad she wasn't a replacement for the decapitated dummy which had stood within the sphere of her tutor's anger.

"I'm still a little confused as to the point you were making..." Venusa finally admitted with an innocent shrug while her teacher stood there tapping her foot upon the floor with a heated glare in her eyes.

"Oh, really now?" Argona mocked with measured sarcasm, "Cast a spell at me!" She demanded. The half-elf student was a little taken aback by the order, hesitating if she should try a note of diplomacy to quell the dwarf's temper.

"Perhaps I was wrong and maybe we should..." Venusa began to argue but her tutor interrupted her attempts to avoid the taunt.

"That was not a request, little elfling!" The dwarf snapped as she stepped back towards the weapons rack. Fearing the repercussions of failing her training in the midst of the angry dwarf's conniption, Venusa configured her hand with the crystal rings and chose a spell that wouldn't harm the burly warrior too much. Forming a large icicle she had learned to summon from combining the teachings of the Satyr and the Gnome, Venusa shot the frozen dagger at the warrior.

As quick as a whip, the Dwarven maiden grabbed a gleaming shield from the armor rack and deflected the icicle, which shattered into a million shards.

"Again!" her tutor demanded, "Something else this time," the dwarf ordered as she stomped slowly, but menacingly, toward the lone girl poised at the center of the arena. Venusa complied by quickly adjusting her fingers to combine balls of flame to shoot towards her moving target. The dwarf dropped the shield with one fluid motion and crossed her bronze gauntlets to protect her face. To the girl's surprise, the fireballs dissipated harmlessly upon the heavy vambraces she wore. Taking steady steps forward, her tutor addressed her again.

"Hah, fireproof! Try again!" Argona challenged.

This time Venusa considered the elements she was fighting against and chose to use electricity, to which the sheath of metal the dwarf wore would have a distinct weakness. Still new to her studies, the half-elf combined all elements in dispersion to create a weak lightning bolt; sending its glowing fingers out to strike at the advancing tank of steel and flesh. Once again, the dwarf lurched to the side and grabbed up a large war hammer and blocked the bolt, which it seemed to absorb. The half-elf sorceress was momentarily dismayed until she noticed that the thick handle was made of wood, which effectively nullified the shock of energy. Now merely a few steps away, Venusa was caught in the heat of the moment and sought to defend herself, and readied another spell in defense.

Before the girl could trigger another incantation, the rushing dwarf launched herself up into the air and slammed down with the giant hammer upon the stone floor. The concussion split the ground and knocked Venusa off her feet. Still in shock, the half-elf was left prone upon her back while struggling to get to her feet but above her stood the short dwarf, who now appeared like a giant towering over her, bearing an enormous hammer to crush open her skull. Sweating in fear, Venusa put up a frail hand to defend the final blow but the armored battle maiden lowered her weapon instead, and held out a gauntlet to help her up. Cautiously, Venusa took her tutor's hand to let her rise; now seeing that her point had been made, the Dwarven warrior had a look of delight gleaming in her eyes.

"Ah, exhilarating isn't it?" Argona smiled with a deep breath of delight, "It always gets the blood pumping to teach a lil' whippersnapper a lesson in manners!"

"I ...I see what you mean now," Venusa conceded as she brushed the dirt from her crimson-stained tunic.

"Oh, I'm sure you do!" the dwarf bounced back with a cynical howl as she put her arm around the half-elf and guided her back towards the armored mannequins, "Shields and weapons can be imbued with protections from certain types of magic," she began, "you will find silver plating and coated blades have many uses, and rare salts can be infused into armor to make them resistant or entirely thwart flames," Argona smiled as she tapped her gauntlets to her chest, "but of all things, you cannot simply rely on spells alone to win the day; especially if you cross an opponent that is protected against such wizardry; naturally or by design," the dwarf huffed to make sure Venusa got the point, "always be able to rely on your own strength and steel as a back-up plan, rather than simply prancing around like a dainty spell caster!"

Venusa began to understand why Argona was so passionate about retaining vigor and fortitude. Maintaining a healthy diet and constitution would aid in her overall fitness for the rigorous trials ahead.

While showing her the gouged mannequin, the dwarf needed to make it clear how important it was to seek out the weakness in any given armor at a glance; so as to know how they could be bypassed should the use of magical attacks be ineffective or impractical. The banded armor adorned by the impaled dummy was commonly worn by Orcs, Ogres and Goblins and their ilk. At the mention of these beings by her instructor, Venusa had to admit she had no idea as to what these creatures were.

Argona was a tad bewildered by this claim and tried as best she could to describe them to the naive elfling. Venusa had certainly heard of Faeries, for they were a race of the Elvenborn that had sprouted into every size and shape, with the sole purpose to aid the world to grow and heal. There existed, however, a darker side of the fey, twisted beings made of the unnatural and discarded; created in secrecy by the High Elves in their desperation to utilize them as an aggressive defense against the warring humans. Scorned and censored from their troubled history, the Elves spawned these wretched beings to match the savagery of Men, and to counter their invasive onslaught with these misshapen and fearsome creatures.

However, soon thereafter, the race of orcs and goblins and their breed had proved too difficult to control; for they were infused with the foulness of the earth, and were molded from the rot doused in bitterness and fury. Born of hatred, these ugly and grotesque abominations soon multiplied beyond the restraint of the Elves, who began to question the wisdom of their creation. These putrid and loathsome kin of the fey spread uncontrolled to terrorize the outer realms and sought release from their obedience to the Elves, and there came a day to pass when the Elven Lords learned to regret what they had wrought.

Scarlet

Venusa woke one morning to find that she had been reassigned to a new tutor with the half-snake woman. The head priestess personally escorted her to a subterranean cavern buried deep beneath the outermost section of the castle. Eden Whitetail appeared to be nervous, which was far out of character for her since she had always stood as the idol of composure for the rest of the pupils in the coven. After observing much fidgeting and shedding of her composure, the half-elf girl chose to address her mentor.

"I don't mean to intrude upon your thoughts, Mistress, but is there something on your mind?" Venusa asked as she followed the head priestess across a solitary bridge located deep within the catacombs. With noted hesitation, Eden finally broke her silence.

"The queen mother has personally ordered the suspension of your training with the Dwarven battle maiden, Shatterstone; and requested to have you transferred immediately in order to receive your current assignment under Kos, the Naga warrior," Eden managed to struggle with flustered breath, "...for an early initiation into certain mystic arts," the priestess added.

"This *initiation* you mentioned; if I may ask what that might entail?" Venusa inquired, though she was authentically curious to know why she was being rushed so through her training. Eden's behavior at the moment was becoming a little infectious and Venusa was starting to become concerned. The half-elf then lingered on the probable cause that Argona's mention of the Orcs and Goblins as the polluted fey, which the Elves had bred in secret, may have been a breach of protocol on some level. The worrisome look in Eden's almond-shaped eyes did not do much to sooth her growing anxiety as they continued their deep descent into the massive cavern. This natural chamber exposed a breach that revealed the violent ocean and the rhythm of the rolling tide striking the rocky cliffs.

The crashing of waves and the smell of the sea permeated the cave. The ocean salt had accumulated upon the stalactites, coating them with a pale patina. From them grew delicate crystal shards of ocean brine. No matter how sharp the aroma, Venusa soaked in the scent of the fresh and salty air, for she had been kept below the Drow Queen's castle far longer than she had desired. She imagined one day she would complete her training and be allowed her freedom, or at least an escape from this dreary atmosphere.

"The queen has selected you for a christening and you will not be allowed to return to the coven until the ceremony is complete ...if you survive, that is," the tall elf mentioned as though it were an afterthought. Venusa certainly did not like the sound of those last words and begged for the priestess to elaborate.

"I don't understand," the half-elf began as she gazed around the cavern, the slick stone glistening from the humidity of the ocean spray that swept through the grotto; there were no accommodations present, such as a place to sleep or anything to eat, nor was this new tutor of hers anywhere in sight, " is this christening a form of ritual?"

"That would be an adequate choice of words," the priestess stuttered back as if she had a chill, though the atmosphere in the room was brisk but not unpleasantly so, "it will be a naming to your formal title among the Drow," she advised. Venusa didn't think that could be so bad if it hadn't been for the mortal threat she had mentioned the moment before.

"Will the rest of the apprentices be...?" the half-elf girl began to ask before the Priestess snapped back to interrupt her inquiry.

"No, few if any sisters have ever trained with Kos," which Eden pronounced in two syllables as 'kay-os.

Venusa had learned that there was power in a name, and her new instructor was known as *Chaos*. This did not bode well for the rest of the day to come, Venusa thought to herself. Scanning the dark corners and gloomy shadows cast by the stalagmites that littered the room, Venusa could not see how this could be a proper arena for training and wished the head priestess would enlighten her about this bizarre ceremony she was to face. Eden only stated that never had an elf of impure blood ever faced this sacred rite. Honestly, the half-elf girl was confused as to the purpose of all the hype but her tutor appeared genuinely fearful for her safety.

"How long do I have to stay here?" Venusa petitioned as the priestess turned to take her leave. She spun back with noted reluctance and placed her hand tenderly upon the young girl's shoulder, and with a soft caress upon Venusa's cheek, Eden looked at the girl with a mark of pain chiseled upon her face.

"You will stay here as long as it takes, but be warned, do not attempt to return across the bridge," she cautioned towards the stone catwalk which breached the deep crevasse that separated the cavern in which they now stood, "Goodbye, Venusa Viper," Eden whispered softly as she withdrew her hand, and as she did so, Venusa noticed the glint of a tear in her gentle eyes.

The young sorceress stood there in a daze as she was left standing alone in the middle of the cave while she watched the priestess ascend the long flight of stairs as she disappeared into the darkness. Only the rhythm of the crashing waves broke the silence as the beating heart of the ocean quelled the pounding within her breast. A surge of emotions began to swell within her as the tainted and scarred half-elf girl felt that familiar cloud of being left discarded and abandoned. At that quiet and empty moment, Venusa had never felt so alone.

Hours dragged on as she waited there, taking but brief walks around the pillars of stone to explore the grotto; but there was still no sign of the Naga. The evening approached quickly as the sunlight cast through the fissure faded and the night fell like a blanket beyond the breach. The glow of moonlight glistened across the water outside of her rocky cell while the ever-constant waves hammered the cliffs. With surrender, the exhaustion of waiting overtook her and Venusa found a solitary nook in which she curled up to rest; keeping warm by surrounding herself with a ring of conjured flame.

That night she had dreams that weren't dreams. She found herself awakening inside the cave, though her summon flames had long since died. She was surprised to find thin strings of spider webs coating her arms and legs as she sat up to brush them away. The cavern itself seemed the same but she was shocked when she saw that a full section that led to the outer bank had entirely collapsed, which worried her since she hadn't heard a thing. Venusa stood there trying to weigh how she could have slept through such a violent event.

Eager to view the damage and beckoned by the open sky denied to her for so long, she picked her way through the broken columns of rubble until she reached the edge of the cleft. There she stopped suddenly, realizing all was not what it seemed. The air here seemed to waver and was oddly tinged with a sweet yet bitter scent. Most obvious of all was the pathway that floated in nothingness before her.

An open sky of clouds and sullen blue wrapped around her without earth nor ocean below. Bewildered by this revelation, she followed the path before her into the emptiness while the girl recalled she was forbidden to return past the upper bridge from whence she came. Portions of rocks hovered near and far; some as small as stepping stones, while others so large they appeared like floating islands. Some were adorned by growths like trees and moss hanging like vines from their edges, while others were surrounded with streaks of dancing light.

For a brief instant, Venusa considered that she might have been delivered through a portal into another realm. She explored further, whichever way was reasonably safe to keep from falling into the void below; pursuing a path in whichever direction allowed her to keep a measure of solid ground beneath her feet. From a distance arose a strange sound like a symphony of dying harp strings, slowly resonating as if their melody had been drawn while it drifted through the wind. It was an eerie tone that ushered a feeling more mournful than sinister.

This unnatural and broken world certainly fit into the context of a forgotten limbo; a space between realms where anything was possible. She slowed her pace in areas where thick clouds crossed the scattered trail, making it a treacherous obstacle should she slip from the narrow path and into the awaiting abyss to either side. Looming ahead was a tall statue, roughly shaped into the form of a griffon. The sculpture looked beyond ancient, as though its outer surface bore the weather of age from a thousand lifetimes.

The idol was strangely, carved while standing impossibly tall like an enormous pillar. Unremarkably colored in a shade of sandstone, it was the only rising landmark as far as the eye could see. She was drawn to it like a beacon; calling her ever closer. The strange anomaly sat on a wide broken plateau of cobblestones with a glint of light above its crest, shining like a midnight star. When she finally reached the strange monument the pathway behind her tumbled away, leaving her stranded like a castaway on some celestial reef.

With nowhere else to go, Venusa circled the enormous statue letting her blackened hand graze the rough surface with their gentle caress as she roamed, staring upward at its towering height. The stone itself had a vibration to it as it hummed with an inner energy. She didn't know what this place was or why she was here. Choosing a moment, Venusa stopped in her tracks and placed both palms against the idol and closed her eyes, feeling the endless tone that rippled through her from the depths of the stone; at that sinking moment, she felt a sense of peace like she had never experienced before.

Suddenly pulling her hands away in shock, she had lost all sense of time and had no idea how long she had been standing there. From somewhere, layers of dust had piled upon her feet and even her stained tunic seemed faded and her hair bore streaks of white. Unnerved as she was by this, she continued her tour to the rear of the pillar, where she found a woman sitting alone upon a throne carved of white marble.

The female was entirely nude, though graced with pure ivory skin, beautiful and perfect in every way as if she were the portrait of womanhood. Her long dark hair was bundled upon her head with a single loose wrap of furled hair hanging before her face as she stared down upon a single rose which spread in full bloom. The cut flower lay in her hand upon her thigh, though Venusa could not see if her eyes were truly open; for the woman herself sat as still as stone. Upon her back, Venusa could see a set of dark feathered wings as delicate as a touch of sunlight. However, it was her ears that drew Venusa's attention, for they were short yet pointed as a half-elf, much like her own.

Venusa approached warily, though drawn by overwhelming curiosity as to who she might be for the woman resembled herself in many ways. Her nose and the lift of her brow were similar, though her proportions were different as if they were far too perfect. Circling towards this strange woman, Venusa noticed that the ruby color of the rose was fading to white while streaks of crimson began to slowly drip from her hands as though she clenched a fresh wound. Venusa stepped forward with a note of concern but realized it was the hue of the rose itself that was draining away from the cut of its broken stem.

"Nomas tu?" The winged woman spoke with a whisper that filled the air. Her voice was otherworldly and chimed with a deep and primal power. Venusa was alarmed by the terrifying tone of her voice. Not understanding the language the woman spoke, she tried to decipher if they were words to some type of incantation but she was at a loss as to what was being asked.

"Nomas tu!" The dark angel demanded as she lifted her head, her eyes a silvery blue and chilling in their stare. Venusa felt an overwhelming sense of danger from this being and turned to see she had nowhere to run. She immediately spun back towards the supernatural creature only to find that she was gone! In her place sat the rose upon the throne, its soft petals now bleached white with but the faintest shade of blush at its bud. Cautiously, Venusa looked around and slowly slipped closer to the marbled chair; daring to reach out for this most unusual token the graceful creature had left as a souvenir.

Just as Venusa's hand grasped the thorny stem, the ivory woman was suddenly beside her and clenched her wrist to restrain the young sorceress from stealing her charm. The sharp thorns of the stem bit into her flesh as she turned to watch in horror as the beautiful maiden transformed before her. Her feathered wings extended into bent and tattered wisps, while her skin faded into a shade of darkness. Blotches surrounded those eerie eyes while her hair spun itself into a tangle, bearing claws and dead twigs woven into her locks like dark talismans.

Blackened veins crept across her body as a shawl of ethereal gauze enwrapped her form. Her image dissolved from one of perfection into a repulsive specter of death. Corrupted shadows seemed to melt from her into the surrounding cobblestone like a spring as the thick smoke fingered its way towards her. The creature's grip was cold and stiff, and the half-elf sorceress felt as though she was being clutched in the arms of a statue.

Venusa tried to control the wave of fear that crawled over her as the apparition spoke into her ear with that terrible voice.

"No-Mas-Tuuuuu..." it breathed a third time as if to assert its point, though the half-elf was lost in the meaning of the foreign words or what this creature wanted from her.

Suddenly, a look of surprise and utter shock crossed the specter's face as her darkened eyes shifted back and forth in confusion. Her body began to transform yet again as the ghastly features began to soften. The tangle of horns that had grown upon her head withered as her dreadful crooked wings eased back into their previous form. The blackish veins receded as her loathsome exterior faded away and the creature melted into a figure the sorceress thought she recognized. The dark faerie suddenly released Venusa's arm and quickly regained her sense of composure.

"I know you..." Venusa remarked in shock at the familiar figure. The ethereal phantom was the Dark Faerie who was one of the female instructors assigned to the coven.

"You may call me Scarlet," the naked fey submitted to the half-elf girl in a language she could understand. Shaking her head in confusion, Venusa inquired why she had attacked her and what this strange realm was.

"Where are we ...and what were those curious words you kept saying?" The young half-elf demanded with a note of ire in her tone. She did not appreciate being scared in such a manner and felt uncomfortably tense from the stressful encounter.

"It is a mystical incantation you must learn to use whenever you encounter strange beings you are unfamiliar with," Scarlet answered to the troubled girl, "it roughly translates to ask '*by what name are you called*' in certain iterations," she professed.

"I don't understand, why would anyone do such a thing; and why were you transformed into that ...that horrid beast?" Venusa charged while trying to calm down and vent her anger without seeming too childish about her reaction. The dark fey stooped and picked up the bleached rose from the ground between them where it had fallen, the half-elf's blood still glistening upon the tips of its sharp thorns.

To her bewilderment, the dark faerie noticed the spot of blood on the thorns and licked it off with her pink tongue right in front of the stunned girl. The look in Scarlet's eyes when she did so was a mixture of ecstasy and detachment as if she had entirely forgotten the girl was watching her every move. Without even a hint of modesty, she glared back at Venusa with a capricious smile, one which troubled the girl more than she allowed herself to reveal. Faeries came in all manner of forms and could be spiteful tricksters when provoked. Whatever manner of mysterious magic's that Scarlet was party to, she was treacherous and wicked.

Taken aback by the cannibalistic gesture, Venusa recalled that Scarlet was a master of illusion. This entire realm could either be real or just a mirage of her making.

With a wave of her hands across her body, trailing tendrils of light followed in their wake, and in a single swipe, she had changed into an indigo sprite with sapphire gems embedded within her illustrated skin. Large butterfly wings adorned with ornamental calligraphy that glowed with every color of the rainbow sprouted from her back. The enchantress took a faint step backward and lifted like a feather in a gentle wind, floating above the girl as a shower of bubbles and light glittered through the air around them. Still holding the white flower, she addressed the young disciple who looked up at her with awe.

"Glamour is a unique quality among the race of Fey," Scarlet revealed, who was now in the form of the blue nymph flitting above her with her mesmerizing rainbow wings, "and it can be a terrible curse," she hissed as her form suddenly turned green and scaly with clawed wings stretched with pocked skin. The hissing drake now before her spat venom at the girl from its needle-sharp fangs and lashed at her with its long forked tongue while the flapping of its horrid leathery wings drowned out its hideous screech.

Venusa threw up her arms to protect herself from the spray of poison and turned her head aside to shield her eyes; yielding to the hideous creature. The half-elf was caught off guard to how dangerous and unpredictable this malevolent being was. In but an instant, Venusa noticed that no bitter acid had splashed upon her and that the dragon-creature itself, had vanished. Turning back towards the monolith, she saw Scarlet there in her original form as a dark angel; ivory and perfect in every way, except for her raven black wings folded behind her.

The petals of the frosted rose now lay scattered at her feet as she sat reclined upon her marble throne. There was a look of amusement in her silvery eyes and their pearl-lined lids as she gazed upon the half-elf in her tattered stained dress. It was all an illusion, for she could make the girl see whatever she wanted and prompted a reaction at every turn.

"So, this isn't real?" Venusa finally gathered herself to contemplate what she was seeing and the art of deception that Scarlet had proved herself to be capable of. The dark faerie only looked at the girl's blackened hands, noting their sharp talons which Venusa had since become accustomed to.

"You are marked..." Scarlet responded with a wry smirk while entirely ignoring the girl's original question. The half-elf girl looked down at her hands, noticing for the first time that her silver-wrapped crystal rings were missing. Touching her neck for their cords, she was shocked to find her flute and mystic key were also gone. With a note of panic, she looked around the cobblestone floor, hoping she had not somehow dropped them. Noting her anxious reaction, Scarlet gave a malicious giggle and took her time revealing to the distressed girl that her talismans were quite safe.

"Yes ...I, I got this blemish when I touched something I shouldn't have," was all that Venusa could muster to say while she brought her attention back to her scarred hands, "forgive my confusion, but I was led to believe that my next tutor would be Kos, the snake woman," Venusa declared while trying to get a grip on the situation. She gazed around at the strange floating world around her and up at the enormous statue towering above while the curious hum of the music slowly flowed upon the breeze with an undeniable sense of foreboding. It all seemed so very real, which only added to her puzzlement.

"And so she is," Scarlet granted as she referred to the Naga, "for your next trial is special indeed," the brooding faerie conceded to the worried look in Venusa's wide and bewildered eyes, "it is a christening you now face, a blessing and a curse to which you will be forever tethered," she mentioned with a sprinkle of disdain. Venusa didn't absorb the purpose of talking in riddles, for it only served to make her feel more perplexed.

"Then why are you here, instead?" The half-elf stiffened to demand, and not appreciating the games this wild and feral faerie had played upon her. The dark fey only laughed in response, it was a baleful sound that made Venusa feel like she was nothing more than a source of amusement; and she didn't enjoy being used in such a malign manner.

"And where would you presume *here* is, exactly...?" Scarlet inquired with a casual wave of her hand. Venusa looked around at a loss, for she had never read nor heard of such an esoteric realm as the one now floating before her eyes. She could have never envisioned such a place could exist.

"I – I don't know," she finally admitted with defeat; somehow feeling as if she had failed this test and would be cast from the coven. To be banished from the sorority would mean certain death, for any misstep would grant the evicted student a lethal sentence of not only being expelled, but also drawn into the consuming flames of the Elfire.

"Don't trouble yourself so, sister elfling," the dark fey offered with compassion in her voice towards the girl, "as of this moment, you are asleep in a cavern far beneath the pinnacle of the castle that reaches forth into the cold and dreadful sea."

Scarlet's revelation stunned the girl, for was this all just a dream? Watching Venusa touch the giant pillar and test the air, Scarlet was bemused that the girl could distrust her senses so.

"We are in a dreamtime?" Venusa begged to presume.

"It's slightly more complicated than that," Scarlet responded with a wide glance around the strange ambiance and the aura of its perception, "we are within your mind, which I hope you will forgive me for noticing, is more than slightly shattered ...which in ways can be seen as a reflection of your emotional state," the dark fey revealed as she motioned towards the splintered backdrop of floating islands.

"Why have you invaded my dreams?" Venusa suddenly turned with an accusing glare, but the ivory woman merely brushed off her condemnation.

"I was so looking forward to meeting the Queen Mother's star pupil before Kos was done with you, that I thought it would be prudent to help you understand the importance of your next trial; for it is a rare and uncommon occasion for one so very young as yourself," the ivory-skinned woman admitted as she pressed aside the pearl glazed petals lying at her feet.

"Why, what is so special about this ritual ...this *christening*? Venusa petitioned, not fully understanding what it pertained to. The dark angel spun and looked upwards into the sky at the glowing orb of light that lit the very tip of the pillar high above, and Venusa noticed a hint of emotional pain wash across Scarlet's perfect face. She had never seen an emotion so deep and sincere, that it touched her so. Whatever demons haunted Scarlet's past, they still lingered within her.

"Nomas tu – there is power in a name," Scarlet began with a stern tone, "to know a name is to have power over it," she noted, "In the trial ahead you will be named by the Gaia and bound to this title by the Evermore. This is not a small thing, little elfling, you have become a new leaf upon the Tree of life, and you must fight for your place among the branches, or you will be shed from its bough."

The words that seeped from Scarlet's lips struck Venusa like a bolt. Somehow, the stigma curse from the High Elves and her contact with the living seed from the limbo of Frostfall had melded together. That encounter, which in all respects should have killed her, had instead, transformed her into something entirely new. Fundamentally so, it may have also been the ingredient of her human side that allowed the two unnatural magics to merge and were somehow fused by her elven blood.

Scarlet advised the girl that she would be viewed as either a menace to the natural order, or would become an asset. They would be looking into her being, her strength of spirit, and all the facets that made her who she was. Like a gemstone, she would be cut and polished; chiseled into something unique, and forged to become one of the Masters as a warrior priestess.

The unfortunate dilemma was that most candidates or viable successors did not know their own powers or strengths and would not, nor could not, allow others to see them the way they see themselves; and thus, they perpetually hid behind a disguise. This is where they failed. To show the Evermore who they truly were, and be recognized, was the highest honor in the Faerylands; one that was to be celebrated as a rare and extraordinary accomplishment. There was, however, a sinister side to such an achievement that exacted a dreadful cost; some fared worse than others, as Scarlet herself could attest.

Venusa would have to expose her inner self, in all her faults or be disposed of as a fraud, a canker that would be perceived as a danger to the natural order that fed off the lifeblood of the Evermore. She would have to choose her words and her thoughts wisely to survive this trial. As Scarlet was now, she forever will be. It was akin to being asked to choose a single mask that would forever define you and could never be removed. Venusa could see how this would be a climactic decision ...one she dreaded that she might fail.

Venusa stooped to pick up one of the bleached rose petals, and Scarlet observed with a raised brow how the white petal slowly bled red again, as if fed by the tips of the girl's fingertips. The stigma placed upon her was a powerful hex, one that fused with the living seed that should have devoured her entirely. The half-elf was transformed into something more than she could imagine. Not knowing who you are, or what you're truly capable of, is equally both a very wasteful and dangerous thing. Scarlet knew there was no illusion that could ever mask this young girl's destiny which would consume her if she didn't face it directly.

"Remember my words, little sister," Scarlet advised with a softness that flushed across her eyes, as she looked at the young sorceress to be, "for it is time for you to awaken," she breathed.

With that revelation, a dark storm began to swirl overhead as the sound of thunder rolled and shook the stones beneath her feet. Looking back towards Scarlet, the half-elf saw that her body had solidified into the very marble from whence she came, now nothing more than an ivory statue of innocence and sorrow. A black rain began to pelt upon her shoulders as the inky blots smudged all that it touched. The dream world around her darkened drop by drop, like a tsunami of wet ash that stole the color from her vision until the torrent blinded her. A voice could be heard echoing from the depths of the storm, in the words of the dark angel who had sought to aide her.

"There is neither good nor evil; only darkness and light. Those who sway too far to either side will be blinded. Always seek balance within the shades of grey," Scarlet's words were deep and terrible, and their message seeped into the girl's being.

Watching the world dissolve around her, Venusa found herself suddenly shuddering from a chill. Shivering and gripping her arms, her eyes fluttered open and she found herself on the cold stone floor of the Cavern once again. The sound of the crashing waves outside the fissure slowly rose in volume as the scent of the sea spray smelled far more pungent than usual. She had no idea how long she had been asleep but the amount of light seeping in told her it was now nearly midday.

The young half-elf was still suffering a lingering hum in her mind from her visit to the dreamtime, where Scarlet had invited herself to trespass into the girl's mind to offer her message. Her thoughts were in a trance as she tried to define what she had seen. It could very well be that the parallels to that shattered world and her emotions were connected, and the visual image of that place only served to define her state of mind. Venusa wondered to herself if that was so, then how could she make herself whole again?

Though only half as sensitive as a full-blood elf, her pointed ears were still as keen. Venusa could perceive an intermittent hiss that echoed between the stone pillars littered throughout the grotto. She stood to face this challenge, assured it was the Naga who was hiding amongst the shadows.

"You seee meee..." a bitter voice hissed through the darkness.

"I do not, but I can hear your presence," the red-robed disciple conceded to her hidden guest.

"Ah, but you do not need eyesss to seee," the voice rasped, "all of your senses are but a form of sight, are they not?"

Venusa thought diligently on the question and admitted to the logic behind the analogy. Stepping forward into the light from the rift where the spray of ocean mist lingered in the breeze, Venusa took her stand. From high above the Naga slithered from the darkness, her strange eyes glowing with glints of light whenever she passed into shadow. Coiling down a stone pillar, the large monstrosity of the snake woman glided across the wet floor to face the girl, towering twice above her meager height.

The creature had thick scales running down the length of her reptilian half that crept upwards above her hips. Upon her chest was strapped a rough leather pauldron adorned with curved metal plates; the gear was cleverly attached to a back quiver from which many long arrows bristled. She was a strange beast to look at, being partially half-human, as Venusa was half-elf. Upon her head, she wore a circlet of silver embedded with a single gemstone. The Naga's hair was painstakingly woven into tiny braids that were sewn into curtains which flowed upon her shoulders.

Venusa wondered how a creature so fantastic could ever come into being, though admitting she knew little of their race; only aware that their kind was of ancient blood, perhaps even older than the Elves.

"Greetings, Kos," The girl offered her formal salutations to the Naga woman while making sure she respectfully pronounced it as 'chaos' in its proper accent, despite its alternate spelling. The Naga looked over the girl once with her strange eyes that did not blink, accompanied by the constant slither of her forked tongue which slipped between her lips and gave a final nod of approval.

"Do you know why you are here?" Kos whispered with her darting tongue as she unstrapped a curved bow from her back.

"To choose a name," Venusa granted to the master of archery and stealth.

"Nomas-tu?" Kos hissed at the girl draped in red as if to challenge her with its riddle. However, the Naga was taken aback when Venusa proved to be prepared.

"I am now known as Venusa Viper, and I submit to you to

show me my real name," the half-elf offered with a formal bow in reverence. The Naga moved around her between the stones and the shadows, taking her time as if to contemplate her next words. The snake woman circled back to where she once had been to address her new apprentice.

"And how did you earn the name of *Viper*?" Kos inquired with a hint of irony hiding within the faint chuckle escaping her lips.

"I was raised among humans, and my peers found me to be quick-witted, astute, and possessing even a fair measure of shrewdness, I dare say," Venusa answered, "though that may have only been the elvish side of me," she granted. Kos smirked at her quip, which had been cleverly presented as both a compliment and an insult to her Elven blood, which the Naga didn't fail to see as a double-edged sword. Kos could see this girl was strong. That was for the best, for she would need every ounce of courage for the trial ahead.

Kos untied an unassuming sack from her belted waist and held the tattered bag before the girl as its contents squirmed within. She motioned the girl to hold out her hands as if to accept the oddly moving pouch. Venusa complied to take it with both cupped hands before her. However, with one smooth motion, the Naga pulled the knot and upturned its contents into the girl's open hands.

Upon her palms flopped a dozen small snakes, thin and sleek, which began to wrap around her hands and writhe their way up both her arms. Venusa almost shrieked but held her tongue, though her mouth fell open with shock. With her eyes wide, but not wishing to show fear to her tutor during this test, she couldn't help but scream in pain when several sets of needled fangs began to pierce her skin. Tried as she might to stay on her feet from the agonizing ordeal, she eventually fell to her knees with both hands outstretched before her as the serpents bit, again and again, administering their venom. Feeling her body weaken and knowing she mustn't pass out, but unable to help herself, Venusa fainted from the poison of a hundred bites and the world around her faded into blackness.

The Evermore

When Venusa returned to consciousness she found herself in a lush jungle surrounded by plants and colorful insects. Strewn throughout the undergrowth were ruins and remnants of ancient buildings, each carved with unreadable glyphs in a language she did not recognize. She checked her arms and the dozens of tiny pinholes that perforated her skin from the needle-like fangs of the vipers were now closed, though she winced with pain when she touched the tender wounds. Tearing strips from her red-stained dress, she wrapped her arms as best she could.

Moments later, after the nausea from the poison began to subside; she noticed a faint tightness around her forehead. Touching her temple, she felt several thin lumps that lay wrapped around her head like a crown. When she tried to remove this strange circlet, Venusa jumped when the strands moved beneath her grasp and she gave a girlish yelp.

"Do not try to remove them," a soft female voice trickled in the air like a forest spring, "for they are a part of you now."

Venusa was shocked when the tiara bound even tighter upon her head as she looked around for the source of the woman who had spoken. She assumed this was the second time she had fallen asleep in this accursed cavern, though this place had a far different feeling than the dreamtime she had experienced before. It was a lingering despair that seemed to sap her very strength, twisting her perceptions of every leaf, twig, and stone.

"Who are you?" the half-elf asked as she looked towards the sky only to see it was concealed by the thick layers of moss covering every branch as it hung like tangles of hair. Everything around her was saturated in shades of green, surrounded by plants which glistened in a surge of bloom that seemed to move before her eyes.

Through a vine-covered arch walked a maiden, the likes of which Venusa had never seen in all her years. Around her, a warm glow with a delicate swarm of butterflies enveloped her like an aura. She was entirely nude in form; though her body was covered in intricate runes. There were parts of her skin that resembled the texture of bark, while leaves and vines clung to her body. Most remarkable of all was the rack of elk horns that grew from her head, adorned with several talismans and ornaments in the form of mystic charms.

Cradled in each branch of her horns were glowing white candles that created an umbrella of light above her. Small dragonflies and colorful winged insects seemed to be drawn towards her as if she were a source of nectar. Her eyes were the most remarkable of all as they glowed like orbs of polished emerald with a deep inner light. Within her hands before her she carried a small twig of a tree, bare of leaf but adorned instead with tiny butterflies that gently flapped their delicate wings in mesmerizing synchronicity.

"That is the very question I would ask of you, sister," the nymph conceded to the speechless half-elf, whose mouth had fallen open in wonder at the sight of this strange spirit of nature.

Venusa didn't know how to respond, taken off guard by the venom in her veins and the displacement to this strange realm. She remembered this was a test, a naming of herself that the Naga had initiated with her nasty little bag of tricks. As it was self-evident that Kos was merely the messenger of this trial and that her christening was to be performed by this luminous sylph. Venusa stuttered for a moment, for she finally began to perceive what the magical creature, which now graced her presence, might actually be.

"Are you...?" Venusa trailed off, not believing her eyes, for she had studied many ancient scripts about the Evermore. Venusa looked closer at the small strange tree she held in her hands and could make out what appeared to be a small egg embraced within its twisted roots, held protectively in her grasp between her fingers that ended in long sharpened claws.

"I have many names and many faces," the nymph confessed, "I am all, I am one, I am you," she ended with a parting of her lips that concealed a tender smile. Venusa could tell this was not a dream but something far more than she dared imagine; nor was this a normal realm but one that was strangely all too familiar.

She was at the heart of the Evermore.

"That tree, this place...?" Venusa trailed off again, staring around in wonder. The woman moved forward, her crown of horns alight like a grand candelabra with its radiance. She tilted her glance once towards a cupped stone that rested upon a broken pillar. A spring of water slowly began to fill the shallow bowl, and she invited the half-elf to gaze into this chalice.

In the reflection, Venusa could see that the garland wrapped around her head was a living wreath of snakes, the ones from the bag that Kos had cast upon her. She could still feel their stings up through her arms and neck that were inflicted along their path to nest upon her head. In a moment of panic, she wanted to rip them from her hair and cast them to the ground but the voice of the forest nymph soothed her into a sense of calm.

"This," she lifted the fluttering shrub in her clawed hands towards the girl, "is your perception of the tree of life, grown from a living seed," the crowned nymph answered, "and this is the way you perceive the Evermore within the Gaia."

Venusa was still confused by that answer, for if this place wasn't its true image and just an impression in her mind, how could she trust anything she saw?

"Why have I been brought to this place?" The half-elf inquired to her host who could sense her lack of faith and understood how her sudden arrival here might be a bit overwhelming for the girl.

"You were once of both Elf and Man, but you have evolved into something ...more," the nymph asserted in the simplest terms to the confused girl, "I am your image of the Matron Mother, the essence of Nature itself to whom you can see, and speak with, and understand. I am the Evermore, I am one, I am you," she offered with a faint smile of gentle regard, while her strange hollow eyes seemed to pierce through the young girl.

"I'm not sure I quite understand what that means," Venusa admitted solemnly with a shrug of her shoulders. The matron understood her aggravation and helped to explain in plain words she could grasp without a lather of riddles to confuse her.

"The world you know, the oceans and sky, even the very land

you walk upon is alive in a way you fail to understand," she offered with a motion to the thick overgrowth around them, "every creature and beast, every blade of grass to the tallest tree, every river pebble to snow-capped mountains, are a part of this thing you call the Gaia; and so are you," she explained, "thus, I am all, I am one, I am you."

The half-elf girl took a long moment to soak in her words and felt her knees weaken at the notion of it all while she leaned against the large stone bowl. It made sense to her, and in a way, it was something she had always known throughout her youth but it was too wild and fantastic a thought to possibly be true, so she shoved the concept of it to the back of her mind to be buried and forgotten since her childhood. However, the race of Men taught a different form of divinity, for they held a strange and disturbing habit of creating their own creators. They made up stories, fabricated idols, and effigies on which to blame their ill behavior upon, rather than take due responsibility for their own personal inadequacies.

Exposed for what it was, they either refused or could not see that with every stroke they made in their unbridled rage that they were also harming themselves. The race of Elves learned long ago to strive towards balance, and recognized that they themselves, and nature, were one.

"Thank you," Venusa offered kindly in return for her host's eloquent words, "...I see it now."

"Actually, you have understood it all before, as most children do in their youth, but they become blind with maturity as they build fabrications around them to obscure their sight," the nature spirit acknowledged, "This is just a lifting of the veil so that you may see once again."

"And if I may ask, Milady, why is it that I need a new name, why is there a necessity for this change?" The half-elf inquired, regarding her abduction to this inner realm and the core purpose of this trial. The mother of nature looked upon the young girl with a shade of empathy in her demeanor, understanding that sometimes it was a fearful thing to face such transition.

"Your very being has been altered from what it was, and must either be revered and accepted, or entirely abolished," she began to explain as a small butterfly here and there would release and flutter away from the living tree she held, "All parts of the Gaia exist to experience the miracle of life in all its forms; every plant, every animal, every stone, are all part of the whole," she explained further, "when any part should have its consciousness subside, it is returned to the Evermore to be remade," the nymph presented.

"If so, then why do the race of Mankind quarrel thus, and bring tides of death to our realm?" Venusa demanded passionately, feeling angry that she was drawn into a conflict she did not condone.

"Even though the veil has been lifted for them, they have still chosen to close their eyes," she answered promptly without a hint of sympathy. The matron simply observed their choice and acknowledged it.

"I ...I'm at a loss," Venusa declared, "I have seen both worlds of Elf and Man, and I have longed to be rid of one or the other in myself," the half-elf admitted with pain and remorse, "and now I am cursed to never know the life I could have embraced," the girl sobbed while feeling a sense of repulsion at the sight of her own tainted hands as she wiped away her tears. Observing this painful state in the young sorceress, the Matron extended her counsel on the matter.

"The spark of your name, *Ven*, means perfection and beauty; if I may ask, is this how you truly feel at this point in your life?" the nymph inquired.

Venusa shook her head in obstinate disagreement accompanied by a glare of loathing at her scarred arms and the stigma that she bore.

"No ...I don't feel beautiful," she sniffled, trying to regain her composure, but somehow failing to take the first step.

"What would you like instead?" the green nymph implored.

"I feel broken and scarred ...I only want to be healed," the half-elf answered tearfully with anguish in her voice.

"And in doing so, will you dedicate yourself to healing the Gaia; and thus, yourself?" The woman asked while butterflies flitted around her. The warmth in her enveloping glow touched Venusa in a way that helped her to regain her emotional balance, and she began to see that the source of the pain she held was in her mourning of what she once was, and the loss of a normal life she might have had.   In response to this affirmation, she finally mustered an answer for the Matron to judge her virtue.

"Yes..." the girl answered.

"Then from this time forward your name will be *Med*, which means healing.   This will be your secret name among your Sisterhood and the champions who are sworn to protect the living seed from our sacred Tree of Life," the matron charged.

Her words touched the half-elf, who felt a sense of beauty in her new name, and her tears began to dry. She didn't know if it was a new hope or a turn in her destiny, but she could not help but perceive the sense of peace in this strange land and within the gentle eyes of this Mother of grace and nature.

"You will be allowed to continue, as you are in the realms of the Faerylands to aid in our struggle to regain balance for this world," the matron mother granted, "from here on you must choose your path wisely, for you are now separate from all other creatures of this world and your actions are your own, but remember that your race nor your scars are of consequence, and that the point of your ears or color of your skin does not define you," she delivered with severity, "to your fellow pupils of the Brood and those of mortal blood, from this day forward they will know you by your new name as Medusa."

The half-elf spoke her own name quietly to herself, for she knew there was power held within it. She was now reborn, a warrior priestess of the Gaia, the giver of life. Still, her heart was heavy, for there was much sacrifice yet to come. With a nod of reverence, the half-elf finally regained her composure.

"How will I know what to do?" The half-elf asked when the Matron Mother turned away towards the broken archway beyond the small glade.

"You may stay here as long as you wish, Medusa, to gather your thoughts as you will, for time has no grasp within this realm," the maiden replied with a pause as she peered over her shoulder back at the girl, "Once you find contentment, you only need to drink of the waters to return from whence you came.

Complete your training among the Sisterhood and remember to always seek balance and peace," the matron bade as she departed. In but a moment, the glow of the candles within her horns faded into the foliage and she was gone.

The young sorceress stood there for a long moment, looking about the lush grotto and back towards the basin of water. She could stay here forever and never grow old. She could explore this inner realm of the Evermore, to understand its blessing and seek a solitary life of fulfillment. Untold centuries could pass while she spent time in contemplation and be but consumed within the breadth of a single moment.

The half-elf gazed into the basin, finding a familiar rune carved within its bowl below the gleam of water. At its bottom was an etching of a tree, equal of both root and bloom. It's thick trunk, the center of balance to both worlds, seen and unseen. As above, so below; was the chant of the coven.

The girl once again stared into the glassy surface of the still waters, seeing herself in a different light. The garland of snakes coiled tightly upon her head gently eased and she no longer found them repulsive. Even the venom which they had left coursing through her blood, that too, was a part of her now. She looked at her blackened hands and no longer saw the monster but a sign of maturity and transformation. She looked into her own eyes within the watery mirror and did not recognize them. Cupping her hands into the stone chalice, she took a single sip, and within a blink, she found herself crumbled upon the cold stone floor of the Cavern once again.

Kos was there, and she lifted the weak girl with her powerful arms. The naga slithered to a stone altar and gently laid her limp body down. There she lay prone while the other six warrior women arrived, one by one, while the Naga painted the girl's body with exotic salts and symbolic runes. Each warrior brought a single candle which they placed around the girl. With great reverence they completed the ceremony by touching hands, closing the circle around her. There rose a hum of energy in the air, and at the climax of the ritual, the Evermore tethered itself to the girl to forever sustain her.

Never before had the seasoned warriors witnessed such a

christening for one so very young. From the darkness of the stairwell approached the Drow Queen herself, fitted in a dark robe of shimmering silk. Entering the circle, she stared down into the girl's glazed eyes as the aura of the Evermore subsided. Pulling a beaded scarf from her waist, she wrapped it around the girl's head into a tight turban that covered her eyes, for she would no longer need them.

"I am Medusa, the bringer of sorrow," the half-elf whispered weakly as she began to stir, though the glow of the candlelight was masked from her vision with a final knot tied by the hands of the Queen.

The Drow Mother turned and departed in silence, gliding her way back up the age-worn path. At the top, her tiny fangs glinted with the smallest hint of approval before she turned and disappeared into darkness back towards the Keep. The warrior sisters remained to observe the ancient ceremony known as the Night of Candles; a sacred celebration when one of their own would reawaken into this world.

ଦେ

Medusa awoke with a yawn, and with a rub of her arms, she noticed the bites she had suffered had miraculously healed. She sat up and looked around, noticing that the chamber she occupied possessed the glow of a strange light as if the air itself was the source of illumination. She felt wetness upon her cheeks, and with a pad of her fingers, was surprised to feel streaks of tears upon them as if she had been crying. Looking down in wonder, her hands and arms appeared normal once again but with a strange and unsettling shimmer that distracted her senses.

Touching her eyelids, she discovered a strange sensation, one of cloth instead of flesh. Remembering the wreath of snakes, she could feel their coils under the silk wrapping draped about her head. The girl froze in fright upon hearing the odd voice that spoke to her from behind.

"Do not remove the dressing," the woman ordered as the girl stopped her fiddling with the gauze, "tell me what you see," the voice inquired as the young half-elf spun around in her seat.

She was in a domed chamber, though still in the castle she presumed, and had been resting on a stone slab softened with blankets of furred pelts. Several tall candles lit the room but their flames appeared like pins of light with beams that fanned and swayed. The woman who had addressed her was the one who wore the glass armor. She stood there beside her alter like a sentinel, keeping a watchful eye upon their new recruit.

"I see you, and ...and that my scars have healed," the half-elf mentioned as she caressed her arms, "and this room glows with an inner light," Medusa noted.

"Tell me, do you see any shadows or other figures nearby?" The glass knight further pried, wishing to understand what Medusa saw through her minds eye. The sorceress looked around and saw no one else in the room but the two of them, but did notice something distinctly out of place, for the candlelight cast no shadows upon the walls. This left her perplexed.

"Only you and I are present," the girl answered, "but what is this upon my face?" She asked while gently touching the beaded scarf around her head. It was difficult to adjust her perception of it, for she could not see the invisible cloth that seemed to be covering her eyes.

"That is good," the glass warrior resolved, "for the time of the Christening is fraught with danger," she confessed, "you may call me Druanna, I am a Knight from the order of Druids; and will be your mentor during your recovery. You have survived the ritual of transformation and the Night of Candles, but now you must learn to defend yourself from the unseen," she stated, "The drow queen has covered your head to conceal the nature of your powers."

The knight's explanation completely boggled the young sorceress, leaving her with more questions than it answered. Had the queen wished to hide the fact that she had a wreath of snakes coiled around her head from the other students so as not to frighten them? But this did not explain why her eyes were also covered with a translucent material.

"I'm sorry, what nature of power do you speak of, and why does everything look so strange?" Medusa asked, not wishing to lose her composure over how nervous she felt at this moment.

"The unique tiara you wear is a talisman, as is this translucent armor I wear," Druanna mentioned while gesturing to her crystal breastplate, "Each of our warrior sisters retains such a token; a symbol of their internal power. As such, it also harbors their weakness and is a burden they must bear," the knight conceded while turning the corner of the alter with a clink of her delicate armor upon every step.

"But it appears that I am healed; what do you mean by a weakness?" The half-elf asked with heightened confusion.

"In fact, you are not," Druanna answered firmly; "it may only appear that you are so in your altered eyes, but I confess that your malady is still the same as I first saw you."

The Druid's statement worried her and the dazed girl touched her arms again, wondering if this was some type of illusion the likes of which the dark faerie, Scarlet, had displayed. She appeared to be her old self to others but this invisible mask she wore left her unsettled. What was its purpose?

"What is this place and why was I brought here?" Medusa demanded as she was expecting that the Naga was her current tutor for the next several moons, but apparently, those lessons had been postponed. Druanna's supervision was vital at this vulnerable time during her recovery from the transformation. Medusa was confused by this, for she was still not fully aware of what had happened to her.

"This chamber is known as the crucible, young Medusa," a familiar voice aired as the Drow Queen entered the room, approaching the confused half-elf. The queen mother unfolded her half-dozen arms from under her shawl and checked the snug headpiece wrapped around the girl's eyes. She then unpinned a chain from around her own neck and removed several small bells, charms, and talismans engraved with runes that she attached to the folds of the scarf around the girl's head.

"What are those for?" Medusa asked while she sat there patiently as the Queen finished fastening the ornaments; however, to Medusa, they appeared to glow like tiny stars.

"These will help protect and aid you in helping you focus your new powers," the queen granted as she finished attaching the last talisman, "Now I want you to do something, and try to follow my instructions precisely."

"Okay, I will try," Medusa answered with a tinge of doubt while she watched the queen step back from her, though noticing that the Drow Mother had a strange aura that appeared to float upon the surface of her exposed skin, one which seemed to drip away like a fine black mist.

"Stay seated there, facing me. Now I want you to look at both ends of the alter upon which you sit; then at Druanna who is standing behind you," the queen ordered as she took a step backward.

Medusa sat for a moment, contemplating the instructions and began to turn her head from either side to view the edges of the stone table.

"No, no!" the Queen snapped, "Stay perfectly still and keep your head facing me, and try again," she instructed with diligence.

The bewildered elfling straightened herself and with a deep sigh, she tried again, keeping her head straight and turning her eyes buried beneath the bandages but became frustrated when her vision remained static, only slightly wavering.

"I can't seem to turn my eyes in either direction," the half-elf responded in a mixture of aggravation and alarm.

"That is because you are blind, dear," the queen acknowledged to the girl's disbelief as she placed one pair of her hands across her face as if to mimic the condition, "your physical eyes have succumbed to the venom, but the living wreath you wear allows you to see from all directions within your mind; for they are your third eye," the Drow Mother explained.

Medusa had read about such topics within the numerous tomes of the Coven and the High Elves, but she assumed they were just theories used by seers and oracles, which is a subject she had failed to research. The half-elf girl felt a flush of momentary horror that she was further scarred, having been turned into a blind monstrosity; although she could not understand how she could still see.

"Why," the girl began to cry in anguish, "...why would Kos do this to me?" She wept with a singe of anger towards the Naga master. The Queen approached her once again, and embraced her head gently with a motion of unexpected compassion in an attempt to calm the young sorceress.

"Do not blame the Naga, young sister, for the contents of the bag she cast upon you would only materialize whichever bane that your mind could summon. In reality, it was a trial of your own creation to expose your inner self to the voice of the Evermore," the Queen mother whispered to the sobbing girl, who began to realize she was suffering a physical sacrifice that was of her own making.

"How could that be...?" The girl sniffled as she wiped away the tears drenching her cheeks, all the while trying to regain her composure and sense of dignity, "You are saying that I manifested these asps and changed my vision?" The half-elf pondered for a brief moment.

"Yes, for each disciple the transformations of the ritual are different, and usually quite unexpected. We must die in this body to be remade; it is a sacrifice that all the priestess warriors must make. You, Druanna, myself..." the Queen Mother granted while pointing to the young girl and the glass knight behind her, and eventually to herself with a pose of her six hands. Medusa understood now. The poison of the asps had only weakened her just enough to make her linger on the very brink of death, and now she was more that what she had been before, but it had not come without a price.

"Okay," the girl whimpered quietly as she relaxed from the Queen's grasp while she once again stood back, "I understand now," the elfling added with renewed fortitude.

"Now, Medusa, try again as before," the Drow Mother bade.

The half-elf sat there looking at the Queen with her wisp-like skin; then extended her vision out towards the ends of the table. It was a strange sensation as the world around her began to bubble and Medusa nearly fell as she lost her balance.

"Oh my..." the girl breathed aloud as she braced herself.

"Now, while facing me, look at Druanna standing behind you. Take your time, but focus not only on her but also on your own center," the queen instructed to the young sorceress who wavered unsteadily. With refreshed intensity, Medusa felt lightheaded as if her eyes could now encompass the entire room, floating above her. Her vision fully panned around and connected so she could see the glass knight in her glinting armor, her white hair cast upon their smooth surface like rivers of snow.

With a shudder of shock, the sorceress nearly fell over and hit her head having lost her orientation and balance. The warrior knight caught Medusa in her arms and gently laid the girl down upon the altar to rest while wiping away a stream of blood that had escaped from the girl's nose due to the strain.

"It will take a while to adjust to your new senses," Druanna offered coldly, "do not stress yourself grasping for their control too soon," she advised the girl with a quick accusing glance towards the queen while she put down the bloodied cloth, "it will take time to master these skills."

"Calm yourself," the queen ordered as she placed a gentle hand over the girl's head while she was struggling with the dressing about her face, "you must never remove the bandages to look at your fellow sisters, nor yourself in any mirror, for the way you remember yourself, and what you have become, you may find too distressing, sister Medusa," the queen decreed to the troubled half-elf, "they shelter your one weakness that your current tutor will help you to recognize and protect."

"You can see beyond normal sight, and given time, you will be able to attune this enhanced vision beyond what you might have ever thought possible," the glass knight consoled, "you will see things move that should not, and recognize hidden beings and other creatures for what they really are," Druanna confessed.

"You mean, like an Augur?" Medusa inquired as she stilled her head; referring to the seers she had heard of.

"In similar ways, but much different in others," the queen advised, I would assume your gift is much more profound," the tall drow mentioned as she folded her triple pair of arms back under her long ruffled shawl. Medusa laid there staring up at the domed ceiling, realizing she was unable to close her eyes and darken her vision and was troubled by this notion.

In the days to follow, the half-elf sorceress slowly regained her strength as her new tutor nursed her to recovery while teaching her the many forms of avoidance and defense. These skills she combined with stealth and subterfuge of woven illusions, learning that true defense was not merely a type of armor, or the parry of a shield, but was a tactical practice to guard oneself in all ways. Such was the skill Druanna had refined, for her defenses had to be of such perfection and efficiency as to never to allow herself to be struck, or her fragile armor would certainly shatter. Eventually, the girl was reunited with the Naga archer, whom Medusa acknowledged and she learned to surrender her initial unease which had been replaced with a renewed sense of admiration for each of these mystic warriors.

Many moons had passed as Medusa was left secluded to the Crucible, separate from the other female disciples who had continued their studies with the warrior women. One final lesson was required before she could graduate into their ranks. One evening, the masked half-elf sorceress was led into a grand chamber that opened into a vast cavern; one so colossal that it could fit the entire castle within its borders. When she arrived, the young sorceress was introduced to a tall Blood Elf that went by the name of Ravenwind.

"Good eve to you," the blind sorceress introduced herself to the tall elf, who in her altered eyes, possessed skin that glittered like gold. To others, she appeared to have reddish skin marked with archaic tattoos across her eyes and cheeks. Her armor was sleek and artistically forged, but so sparse as to leave her vulnerable on most of her body as though it were intentionally designed to display her physique. She was beautiful in ways rarely seen, both striking in her self composure and poise. Upon her perfect legs, she wore stockings of metal mesh affixed with embossed silver plates which matched the rest of her skimpy armor in their intricate design. She too wore a tiara of black smooth steel, though to Medusa's third eye; it appeared to bristle like a crown of thorns.

Ravenwind accepted her introduction with a formal bow, and then rested her hand on the long slender staff of her spear that ended in the eloquent curve of a sharpened sickle. It was a vicious and graceful weapon. Looking down at the smaller girl with her masked eyes, the blood elf began to wonder at the handicaps her new student might possess, considering her head was covered and she appeared quite blind. Spinning her spear staff with one hand, she made several loops around her body as the sound of the curved blade sliced through the air at terrifying speed; quite suddenly in the middle of the maneuver, Ravenwind flipped the lance at the young sorceress.

She was mildly surprised when the blind half-elf caught the staff at arms reach before it hit her, proving she could either see or that her senses were quite keen. Through her training in the Crucible, Medusa had made several strides in regaining her balance with the sight of a seer, to the point it became second nature. She could see the moon bladed spear, of course, but knew that this new master was merely testing her.

"I am a Blademaster, do you know what that is?" The blood elf spouted with a dull tone.

"A master of the blade, I would presume..." the elfling blurted back, considering it the most obvious answer, which was not much of a verbal test of her knowledge. With a glare sharper than the sword at her side, Ravenwind snapped back at the young student.

"Oh, a sassy one, are you?" The blood elf spat in response as more of a rhetorical statement than a question, "Your lessons will be twice as hard and rigors twice as long for that little quip," she threatened, then proceeded to assume a stiff stance like a stone pillar to study the girl's reaction.

Unfortunately, she would receive no satisfaction from this new recruit, for Medusa's eyes were covered. Druanna had taught the half-elf that the mask she wore actually helped her defense since she was not as easily readable as most opponents, which is where her handicap gave her a measure of leverage.

"No, Mistress of the blade; but I am yours to accept the teachings of your wisdom," the half-elf countered with a bow; although the forefront of respect she offered made her appear even more insolent. Medusa had already read Ravenwind's personality by her stance and ascertained she was a tad arrogant about her skills and wasn't about to let it go unnoticed. Vanity went both ways, as the half-elf used her apparent blindness as a tactical advantage to those who might underestimate her.

Regardless of her self centered sense of pride, Medusa realized this Blademaster had been assigned as her last tutor, for either reason that her teachings were the most important, or the least so; which of the two was still yet to be determined.

The little half-elf had changed greatly since she had first stepped foot onto the island of the Drow and experienced a surge in self-confidence despite her apparent faults. She had grown bold enough to begin testing her own tutors, to analyze their limitations in her attempt to surpass them. This was likely the same determination the Drow Queen had recognized within the unassuming half-elf, for she too, perceived far more than the average elf with her most terrible red eyes.

"The ultimate goal of this tutoring will be for you to be skilled in all weapons when the situation should arise, and you will learn to make do with what is at hand; but in the end, you must choose the one that feels like an extension of your own body and mind," the blood elf proposed.

Medusa understood the premise but had no true idea just how large of a variety of weapons she would need to be skilled at. Within the season that followed, she had practiced how to make swords, spears, and daggers from the elements. Eventually, mystical steel was placed before her so as to learn how she could lay enchantments upon them. Forging ice blades, fire swords, and wind arrows soon became mere child's play to the blind girl. Ravenwind dictated how important it was to know each weapon for its strengths and weaknesses in battle.

The young sorceress was excited by the new challenges placed before her by the blood elf until the day the Drow Mother came to visit her in the training arena. This was the first time she had seen the queen in armor, who wore chain mail adorned with plates of black obsidian. Layered upon her own dark skin, it made the Queen appear like a specter of death. In each of her six hands she bore a different weapon; a wickedly curved dagger, a flaming sword, a spiked mace, a serrated sickle and a trident with a wavering blade, and a lantern with a blazing flame that scorched the air.

"My secret name among the sisterhood, is Kali," the queen bowed to the young sorceress with her veil removed. Upon her head, she wore a crown of black feathers that appeared to be ablaze with a shimmering fire within the blind girl's mind.

"The final trials of the sisterhood require graduation from each of the Masters, but you, Medusa, must pass a contest of a higher bar than the other students shall face," Ravenwind advised from the central stage; the braids in her hair jingled with their many talismans as she strolled over to a large crescent-shaped table.

Upon this strange alter lay an assortment of weapons Medusa had learned to master, though she still had not felt a distinct affinity to any particular type. She knew the advantages of long and short blades and polearms, and appreciated the speed of flying knives and spikes. She found she had exceptional skill with the bow since her radius of awareness allowed her to pick targets with ease, although archery still lacked the versatility she sought. She was attracted to the crescent spear that the Blood Elf was fond of wielding, though it still didn't feel right for her size.

"Have you chosen a favorite among these tools of war?" Ravenwind inquired, having been testing the young pupil these past several moons on her prowess with the speed, weight, and balance of each weapon. Medusa slowly strolled past each of the exquisite weapons that urged her to choose but one.

"I ...I do not feel attuned to any of these," the half-elf faltered, feeling quite despaired to admit as much while fearing the disappointment of her piers. A warrior priestess who had no prime weapon was a sterile opponent. From the look of the queen, she was not pleased. It was vital to their continued progress that their star pupil should find herself a weapon she felt balance and attunement with.

"Young Medusa, there will be trials ahead in realms where the magic's you are familiar with will fail you, where illusion and trickery will lapse, and incantations will backfire. You must discover a physical device that will be of both your first and last resort and are willing to master above all others," Kali, the queen, affirmed, "such a weapon will be an extension of you in both mind and spirit ...can you not choose?"

Medusa stood for a long time and looked over the assortment of exotic weapons that lay before her, forged by the most skilled smiths and charged with remarkable charms. They were all truly wonderful yet dreadful, menacing yet beautiful in design; but still, the young half-elf could not decide. With a shrug of despair, Medusa spun back towards her tutors and remained empty-handed.

This was a sour turn indeed, as the warrior women knew it was imprudent to force a choice upon her. Medusa, herself, was turning out to be a test of the tutor's patience. Despite this unforeseen setback, the challenge ahead could not wait.

"It is ill-advised to face this next test unarmed, which has never been accomplished before in the long history of our Sisterhood, and there is always a chance you may be left defenseless," the blood elf cautioned to the young half-breed sorceress who appeared quite despondent, "however, you will be charged with this quest, nonetheless."

"What is this challenge you speak of?" Medusa inquired as the armored queen approached her.

"We need to travel to a distant realm to acquire a living seed from the hands of our sworn enemy," Kali answered with a stern glare towards the girl whose eyes were hidden from her.

"You mean the Humans ...but they have no powers, how were they able to travel to other realms?" Medusa inquired with a hint of shock, for in her time living among the tribes of men, their magic's were weak and inadequate. It was one of the main motivations for their distinct jealousy of the Elves, one which drove the race of Men to sew such hatred towards all Elvenkind for spurning their endless demands. It was an eternal point of conflict that Mankind refused to curtail any effort to sate their consuming greed for such powers.

"Sister Medusa, you still have not seen the true face of our enemy," Kali offered with gentle remorse, "for it is a torment to all beings that dwell in our world. It is a dark blight that we must extinguish, or all will be lost."

The Withering

Mankind was drunk with power and their endless pursuit of it. Not only were they out of balance with the world but they actually sought out ways to feed that imbalance. The selfish greed of their race favored the demands of the few at the plight of the many. Within their social order, there were always those few who demanded to possess more than they could possibly ever need. They cared not for peace or harmony with the Gaia or other creatures of this world. Such a mentality could only lead to strife and war.

Within the folds of the Evermore the Elven Lords withdrew as its life force receded from the surface world of men, who either enslaved or destroyed all other species in their path until they eventually began to struggle among themselves. Their rage became unbridled as Men ravaged and poisoned the earth, caring not for what they left behind for the generations to follow in their steps.

Within the protective veil of the Evermore, time itself took a different course while the realms of men faded, and thus, it was called *the Withering* among the elders who recorded their words on tattered scrolls stashed within the nooks and shelves of the dark library. Like any living creature, the Gaia recoiled from the harm and pain caused upon itself by the race of men, and the Elves and all the ancient beasts who wished to survive were forced to follow. The Undying, which were the venerable spirits of the world, fell dormant and slumbered until the passing of men, which left the High Elves alone and without an ally in these desperate times.

Combing the earth, the Elves split into factions to survive the onslaught as flora and fauna were consumed in mankind's deadly stampede that trampled everything underfoot. Men feared anything different than themselves, and when they exterminated every other race they eventually turned upon their own. In this time of darkness, an even darker decay arose.

"Their ancient name is the Anatari," Kali declared to Medusa who was standing beside her on a high cliff overlooking a vast primeval forest in a realm known as Trinity.

"What are these *Anatari*?" The half-elf inquired as she turned back towards the warrior queen. High above, three moons could be seen floating in the evening sky while a splash of unfamiliar stars glittered across the darkness behind them to touch the distant horizon.

"Any beast or animal, be they sentient or not, are forbidden to kill another of their own kind," the Drow Queen explained, "it is like taking a dagger in one hand, only to stab the other. It is an unnatural act that severs it from the Evermore."

Medusa could understand the premise, that a species would harm itself denoted a type of savagery that was repugnant in the eyes of the Elves. Killing for survival was accepted as a natural order; however, slaughtering for sport or mere pleasure was beyond taboo and considered distasteful. Most revolting of all was a species that murdered one another without reason, which is how they viewed the race of Men, for butchering their own for the sake of greed itself was not a viable reason.

"What happens to the essence of each man or woman who dies in such a way," Medusa inquired, "do they not return to the Evermore to be remade?" The blind girl asked, turning back towards the mystical forest spread out before them.

"Sadly, no," the armored drow answered with noted anguish in her voice, for those beings who faced such cruelty will only fade from this world, which is a loss beyond remorse, "once the Evermore ebbs from one of its own creations, it is left to wilt and decay. Worse yet, their spirit putrefies when they are consumed by their own bloodshed. The result is a corruption called the Anatari," Kali related with a look of disgust.

"What harm do these corruptions impose and why are they such a danger to us?" The young sorceress countered, still confused as to what peril they were facing.

"If they end by acts of such tragedy, they become the ghosts of war," the drow queen defined for her young half-elf companion, "these banished specters have no place to return, but instead, seek out any living energy to leech upon to sate their hunger."

Within those words, Medusa understood the source of their origin. Over time, this corruption had been known by many names throughout the world. To the High Elves, they were labeled as the Craven, but to the Drow, this blight was known as the time of the withering, for all they touched was laid to waste. With her enhanced vision, Medusa could now see the many blurred shadows of beings shuffling aimlessly among the thick forest below. They sucked the life force from anything animated by living energy, much like any faerie gripped by iron. It was a deadly combination.

"Eons ago, the ancient elves contended with a newly arrived race in our domain who called themselves the Djinn," Kali explained, "whether they were birthed from the Gaia itself, or another seed world remains unknown, but they too glorified war and power. They had abilities far beyond the meek talents of the Elves and could leech power from the elemental void to summon the impossible. Though in the rule of magic, to attempt to create something from nothing only bleeds from the Evermore, and though they were but few, their aggressive demeanor hemorrhaged the magic's embedded within our world and the Faerylands began to die."

"From what I was taught by the scholars in the Eternal City, the legendary war with the genies was fought long ago. Do the corruptions of mankind actually present the same danger?" Medusa asked solemnly.

"Oh ...they are far, far worse," the warrior queen snapped with a grievous tone as her weapons twitched in her hands while she clenched them with bridled anger, "The djinn merely leached from the living energies; however, the Withering turns it into rot. When a being ends without having been tethered to the Evermore it becomes trapped in a state of limbo, but if that same spark of energy is destroyed by itself, it putrefies into a shade once known as the Anatari."

"How do we fight them?" Medusa asked with hollow despair muffling her voice, for the half-elf looked down upon the drifting ghosts and noticed they appeared ethereal, merely wandering shadows of men, their hollowed features strangely twisted and faceless

"The challenges we find against this Withering, or the *Craven*, as they are known to the kin of the Faerylands, is that their numbers are vast beyond comprehension," the dark queen expressed as she waved one arm toward the countless shades streaming through the valley below, "their touch can be vampiric, draining your strength. They can merge into one another, condensing into horrific atrocities. One can never be too careful in their presence."

"So ...you can see them too?" The young sorceress inquired of her companion Queen. Kali turned her dreadful red eyes towards the blind girl who suddenly felt naive for asking such a foolish question.

"In this world and many others," she conceded, "but your mind's eye should reveal them in all realms; which is why you are accompanying me upon this quest so as to test you as my successor," the warrior queen breathed as she stared upon the scene below. Medusa was stunned by this revelation, for not until this moment did she grasp that her own unique talents might be comparable to the Brood Mother herself.

The half-elf then began to wonder with doubt if such a thought would even be possible; for surely, no true blood elf in their kingdom would ever accept a half-breed to such a station as their appointed queen. Kali settled the girl's hesitations, reminding Medusa that the Drow were not of the same vain and pretentious mindset as the noble Elves hiding behind the high walls of their Eternal City. In the clan of the Drow, one was judged by their actions rather than prejudging a person's limitations into locked assumptions. If that had been so, the Drow Queen herself would have never come into her position.

This made Medusa wonder what the true history of the Brood Mother was, and how this warrior queen came into being. Looking upon this alien landscape, Kali pointed out the destination of their quest within this netherworld. Soon there would be a conjunction of the three crescent moons hanging in the sky, where they must make their way through this countless swarm of Craven and into a hidden portal that would reveal itself during that period.

"We are here in this realm by invitation," Kali advised to the blind sorceress, "during the celestial alignment, a rift will open momentarily for us to gain passage from the valley below."

"Do you know where we need to be?" Medusa petitioned.

"The tendrils between worlds are alive, and thus, always in motion unless secured by markers of their specific frequencies," the queen answered.

"You mean like the standing stone circles?" The half-elf asked, pondering the true function of these ancient monuments.

"Yes, exactly," Kali granted, "but the foliage below hides the particular location from our current vantage point," she professed, "for this is the first time we have visited this realm," the queen granted.

This did not bode well for the young girl's confidence, for she was now caught within an unfamiliar world that she, nor the Queen, had toured herself. The forgotten lands of Trinity were infrequently mentioned in their ancient text, but the true scope of what they might encounter here edged on speculation. Medusa didn't like risking her life on mere tales and obscure myths. As she had chosen to come unarmed, she would have to rely solely on her talents at weaving spells to defend herself.

The lore she knew of this plane was that there were many ruins spread across this overgrown basin, hidden beneath the veil of the canopy and wild growth of flora that had reclaimed these ancient lands. They would have little time to enter the rift once the doorway had opened, so they must choose wisely where to venture. Making their way down the cliffside to the valley floor in their search for the temple ruins, they set down upon a small clearing that led into the primeval forest.

"I'm ...I'm having problems seeing," Medusa stuttered as she gripped her head, almost rubbing her blind eyes out of old habit but realized that doing so would do nothing to relieve the fog in her mind, "I can see the Craven, but the plants and trees are strangely blurred as if they're trying to resist being seen?" The half-elf surmised. This would lead to a tactical disadvantage if her vision was not focused, but she was in another realm where her frequency of magic was hindered and could only hope that her skills weren't impeded as well.

"The flora of this world attempt to obscure themselves from

your nether-vision, which might either mean that they are protecting themselves from predators or..." the dark queen suggested as she trailed off to gauge her suspicions, but the blind sorceress did not like the sound of her hesitation.

"Or what...?" Medusa extended, hoping the Queen would elaborate.

"Or they are camouflaging themselves from their prey," she hinted with caution.

The colors of this world seemed a little off to the young priestess, for everything had a shifted aura, like a shadow that was not it's own. She could only imagine it was her mind's eye and the way this world was reacting towards the two trespassers, but it did make her wonder how the Anatari from their own world could have reached this obscure realm.

Lumbering in from the thick undergrowth, one of the craven stumbled towards the two warriors. For the first time, Medusa got the opportunity to gaze upon one of these abominations up close. It was the mere shadow of a man, a miserable wisp with sunken hollow eyes and a gaping mouth that hung unnaturally low. It was hunched over and lumbered forward as if in pain and turned towards them with a measured excitement as if to scream in eerie silence. Medusa wanted to feel hate and contempt for this walking blight, but as she stood now looking upon this wretched phantom, all she could feel was pity.

It lurched forward with ever-increasing vigor, like a creature trapped in suffocating darkness might reach for a shaft of light as its only beacon of hope. While Medusa stood mesmerized, with a single stroke, Kali swung her sickle and cleaved the creature in two. It froze there for a second as if time itself had stopped while its halves dissipated into a fine wisp of smoke that quickly faded away.

"You need to be wary, sister. Do not let them touch you," the Drow Queen cautioned the young elfling who was without weapons or armor.

Through the canopy high above, they could see the moons closing in on a convergence; how long they had left was only a guess. Where Medusa had seen dozens of these withering shades from above, she now realized there might be countless more hidden among the blur of the foliage.

"You said we were invited, who is our expectant host?" The half-elf asked as they make their way deeper into the jungle of giant vines that crawled up enormous trunks of trees where there sprouted exotic flowers and cords of hanging moss.

"That, we will discover when we enter the rift," Kali confessed with a mark of mystery. As it turned out, Medusa's first initiation as a priestess would be a diplomatic rescue mission. The oracles of the Queen had received a calling, channeled by a being trapped here in the wilds of Trinity.

"Do we even know who we are looking for?" The half-elf questioned with a measure of worry, considering their only measure of escape would be to find this wayward portal.

"What the soothsayers can perceive is limited, but there is a guardian here who was in distress and we are here to collect the living seed of their domain," Kali offered to sate the girl's curiosity. However, the result only elected further questioning from the young sorceress.

"We are here to collect the living seed?" Medusa blurted with a shard of confusion, "But why send only the two of us and not take the rest of the warrior sisters?" The girl wondered at the logic of their few numbers against such an overwhelming force.

"There was a high chance we would fail, regardless, and the danger was too great to risk the rest of the Sisterhood who are entrusted to continue their mission against the Craven should either of us fall on this quest," the queen advised.

Medusa admitted she didn't like the sound of that. The queen mother did, however, clarify that those of the Craven that had wandered here would be forever trapped upon this world. The unfortunate result of that effect was that this realm was now cursed with their blight. The young half-elf now wanted even more to find this rift and the answers that may arrive with its discovery.

"So, these craven are a plague from our world which spreads to other domains?" The half-elf whispered to herself.

"Yes, and it is the conscious obligation of all elvenkind to keep this pestilence from infecting other realms," the drow queen affirmed to the young sorceress, "for if they consume the World

Trees that exist in such domains, so will they devour the entire grove," Kali stated with gravity as she fanned her hands across the darkening sky above, referring to the cosmos.

Medusa stared up with her blind eyes towards the heavens and the splash of strange stars that began to twinkle above. Now she understood the vast scope of their task, for her world within the Faerylands was but one tiny tree in an endless forest. Growing up as a child, she had never imagined such wonders, nor guessed on how life was so full of infinite possibilities. Here she stood on the soil of an ancient jungle far from her own lands, which respectively, was only one tiny branch among a forest of stars.

Most elves standing in her footsteps at this moment might feel insignificant and overwhelmed but young Medusa found it exhilarating, and it left her with a sense of fascination. As the race of the elves melded with nature they became honor-bound to care for the growth of not only their small world but of the entire forest as a whole. In a way, they were also curators as was the custodian of this foreign domain.

It was then that the young elfling appreciated the sense of duty that was instilled by her bond with the Queen. Her intent was to create the Sisterhood into guardians of this domain and cure the harm done by the contagion of the Craven. The blight of the Anatari existed among the far reaches of the universe but there were those who also stood as sentinels in these distant realms to help preserve the magic of life in all its forms.

Entering upon a grotto, the two women warriors stumbled upon a condensed horde of the Craven, where they were welling up from a pool of mist that cut through the ground like an open wound. Their forms were twisted and pulled in brutal ways as they climbed from the glowing rift. Those few that had faces were contorted in a grim stare of anguish and dread, as if they were in the midst of escaping from some nameless terror beyond the grave. Apparently, the Queen herself had witnessed such an ethereal breach many times before.

"They are emerging through a stem. What you are witnessing, young sister, is a piercing root connecting to our own realm through which these shadows bleed," the dark queen voiced.

The specters clung to the vapor as they loomed upward, their new arrivals failing to notice the two elves in their presence. A great quake shook the sky as the moons began to merge in their union. The blurred images of the foliage made it difficult for Medusa to keep her footing among the undergrowth, which hampered their progress. A lumped figure from the horde crept forward, and the young half-elf readied her crystal rings with the proper formation to cast a spell in her defense. She made the motion for a fan of fire to push the specters back but was rewarded with nothing more than a few sparks from her rings.

"The spell failed..." she mumbled to herself in shock, suddenly remembering the Queens words of caution that such situations could materialize in these alternate realms.

"Be careful what you do here, for some magic's can backfire upon you," Kali warned as she stepped forward with a thrust of her pronged spear and neutralized the threat, "It appears as if these wraiths are weakened by their journey to this place but we must find a way to close this rift!"

"It will have to wait," Medusa breathed as the first rays of the conjoined moons met in a triple-halo of light high above. The rumbling in the air was soon replaced by a dulled shriek that pierced through every corner of the jungle. At this, the Anatari stalled for but a moment, but promptly continued their pursuit of the trespassers; following them as they fled towards a large grotto filled with shattered remnants of a mysterious temple. There were many such abandoned sites among this valley floor; unfortunately, this wasn't the one they were looking for. Suddenly, a beam of light pierced the sky through the thick canopy, and they turned towards it as a beacon.

"Over there!" Medusa cried, hoping that her companion could also see the sky-borne signal. Noting the Queen's advice, the sorceress summoned a flock of glowing doves that lit the darkness enfolding before them, helping to illuminate their path towards the pillar of light. Their radiance distracted the Craven stumbling in their direction as their attention was drawn to the soaring wisps as they flew through the trees. Kali took the lead, cutting down any errant wraith that reared itself upon them along their route.

They stumbled upon a set of ruins that rose above a circled courtyard; the thin beam of luminance within its ring reached for the heavens above. Racing their way past giant statues of forgotten gods, they weaved their way through the broken rubble. Finally reaching its center of debris and fallen monuments, a central ring stood clear. From it rose two tendrils of light on either side of the opening, which entwined upon themselves as they met to create an archway of glowing burnished gold. This was the portal door which they sought.

Looking behind them, they could see the horde closing in on their position. They were either following them or were drawn towards this open portal. Stumbling in a ghastly black fog, the ghosts fused into one another like an unsettling tide of death. Cleaving a phantom that had lunged at her from atop a broken pillar, its essence dissipated around the queen as she readied her blades for the onslaught.

"Enter the doorway, there is no time!" She commanded.

"Where does it lead?" The blind half-elf hesitated, looking back at the armored drow slashing at the few Craven which had reached them in the advance of the horde.

"It doesn't matter at this point; we can't stay here," the dark elf countered as she retreated from the crushing swarm washing upon them. Her battle skills were a sight to behold, with six arms to make her a most formidable foe. A dagger to slash a neck and the vapor of the Craven would dissipate like a snuffed candle. Her spear would cleave them with its blades catching her opponents fast upon their wicked hooks as her serrated scythe dissected their malformed limbs. Upon another arm held aloft she kept the mystic lantern to illuminate her adversaries as they danced among the shadows. Stepping backward in retreat through the doorway together, it was as if the world was suddenly bleached an ashen white.

"Can they follow us?" Medusa inquired towards her companion with due concern but noting how her voice sounded as if she was speaking underwater. A fluid of sound wavered and distorted around them. Surveying what lay beyond the portal, they found themselves standing upon a high ledge in a world awash in ivory. The shimmering glare was almost too much as Medusa tried to shield her blind eyes; only to realize there was little she could do to shut out the light. Before them spread a vast forest of stone poking up through a sea of clouds that lay before them.

"Most interesting..." Kali breathed as she scanned the horizon.

Connected between several of the marble cliffs were bridges rimmed with leaves as if they were somehow grown between each pale mast. The sky, too, was shaded white like an overcast cloud; though dark wounds tainted their perfection like the black stars cast above. Before them, a white wisp suddenly appeared; it was a strange thing closely resembling a silver owl.

"Is this our messenger?" The half-elf inquired with conjecture. Beside her, the dark queen lowered her blades and stepped towards the nearest bridge in pursuit of the glowing owl which drifted off in a precise direction.

"I would presume this is merely our guide," the queen turned back towards the sorceress, whose vision in red linens made her appear like an open wound in this alabaster realm. Turning back towards the glowing gate, Medusa could see the Craven flash themselves upon the pane of the doorway; unable to breach its barrier. Medusa took a moment to step around it, but the illuminated arch hung there like a sheet of light. She looked up again into the sky above and saw three black moons joined in configuration, revealing that this realm was a mirror image of the world on the opposite side of the gateway.

Following in step, the elfling rushed to catch up with the Drow Queen while they followed their avian escort as it soared through the air. As they delved deeper into this odd maze of stones, they came upon a central monument that stood taller than the rest. What appeared to be an enormous white tree with a thousand branches reaching into the sky, stood within the center of a vast circular clearing. Before it, the bridge leading forward ended abruptly, leaving a wide chasm of emptiness between them and this strange but familiar formation.

At the end of the bridge sat a pair of standing stones set to either side, but the pathway beyond was no more. Overhead, the glowing bird circled once and promptly made its way straight for the base of the immense tree that stood beyond.

"Well, this is a dead-end," Medusa blurted, not seeing any hidden walkway in her altered vision, but the Queen was not so dissuaded. She took a moment to inspect the pair of stones with noted interest, then calmly slapped one of them with the side of her blade. Interestingly enough, it began to ring and resonate like a bell. Satisfied by this discovery, she struck the opposite stone which joined the frequencies as a bridge grew its way like living light, out towards the base of the stone tree.

With merely a glance over her shoulder at the young sorceress, the queen quickly stepped forward upon the illuminated path. This bridge of light was a clever measure of protection from anything unsavory that might breach the portal which brought them here. Making their way to the base, both companions now saw how massive this structure was and slowed their pace to admire the frosted glass archway they passed beneath, one so intricate and stunning in design that it could rival any cathedral.

Within stood a lone figure at the center of the great trunk. Surrounding them were countless stairways carved from veined marble that weaved into halls and passages above and below. The being before them stepped forward, its eyes as black as pitch, though covered in white robes and adorned with silver ornaments and jeweled chains. Its face, too, was owl-like, with a hooked nose and two sharp fangs that hugged either side of its lips. It took a moment for Medusa to see it, but it was merely a mask hiding a mysterious face beneath.

"I welcome you," the male voice spoke, deep and powerful, yet so soft the half-elf had to strain to hear him under her own bound mask which covered her ears.

"Nomas tu?" The small blind sorceress stepped forward and ordered with an air of authority, much to her elder companion's surprise. Though the pale man's eyes were darkened, she could tell he was taken aback by her boldness, only to reply in a curious tone.

"You may address me as Akara, my beauty," he began with a bow of formality with both hands before him. She could see that he was wearing many silver rings encrusted with stones and etched with symbols she did not recognize, "as such, I was just about to introduce myself, Milady," he finished as he stood, though it took a silent moment for Medusa to realize he had responded to her given birth name by its literate meaning. He turned towards the tall Drow to allow her audience, as he recognized Medusa as the lesser of his two guests and that Kali was her elder.

"We have been called here from the realm of the Faerylands," the queen mother began while lowering her weapons, though still at the ready, "was it your summons that we answered?"

The man nodded in affirmation, then turned with a motion for them to follow. In her mind's eye, Medusa could see a trail of dust floating from his being as he moved; this too, Kali saw the fine powder flowing from him like a delicate aura.

"Yes," he granted with a nod, "I see you made it through the moon gate and have observed the source of our plight."

"We have," the queen began with a shrug of guilt, "there is a rift from which they ebb that must be closed," she instructed to their host. Akara showed them to a room flanked with white furs, and pale flowers, and many silver lanterns; not unlike the one Kali herself possessed. In the middle of the open chamber sat a fountain with gleaming water that rolled off a central stand. Within this crescent-shaped spring stood a small tree, its bare twigs bleached white with age; it too was lightly coated with the same frosted powder that gently drifted from its branches as if it were coated with pale ash.

"You said *our* plight," the half-elf interjected as she cautiously approached the dead shrub, "is there someone else here?"

"Why of course," their masked host offered with a wave towards the small barren tree. Medusa was puzzled until she saw the small white stone embraced within the roots of the tree, having grown around this rare relic infused with living energy.

Though the tree itself appeared dead, Kali understood such cycles; for even on her own world it was not uncommon in the depths of winter for an entire forest to go leafless, yet still, be quite alive. The image of the empty canopy sheltering an immense trunk from the exterior was not its topmost branches, but instead, the inverted roots which writhed into the sky. This was a mirror realm, after all, a mere reflection of the world beyond the gate. Their pale host turned again to take up a crystal staff leaning upon the bank beside the seedling. The rod itself glowed with a soft blue light as he offered it to the fierce warrior queen.

"Is this the living seed of Trinity?" Kali inquired as she nodded towards the barren tree resting within the fountain, noting that Akara seemed resolved to tender it into their care.

"Dark shadows invade our realm, which sparks the end of this vibrant young world," the pale guardian confessed, "...and we have asked you here to save us."

Akara

"You are aware of what the Anatari are?" Medusa questioned their host with light suspicion, but the pale guardian only took a step closer to the girl in her crimson-stained gown and nodded towards her in recognition.

"You, my beauty, are not the only blind one who can see," he revealed to her surprise, as his eyes were also hidden. Medusa's mouth opened in slight shock but came to terms that there might be those like herself among the other countless domains; each of them scarred by forms of raw magic they either protected or possessed.

Kali took a keen interest in viewing the seed in its natural state, which in itself, was much smaller than the relic from Frostfall. This one had rooted itself long enough to grow into a living world and this bleached mirror-realm acted as a sanctuary from the invading Craven beyond the Moon Gate.

"If we were able to close the corrupt rift to this domain, you would not need to relinquish this seed, which you must realize, that to do so, would cause this world to die," the drow advised their host as the half-elf approached him to accept the crystal staff in her stead. However, Akara stood to correct her mistaken assumption.

"The seed itself directs me to make this offer to you, and this place we now inhabit is its domain of influence," their masked host commanded, "This world is a realm of flora, left over from its primal age and now long-deceased civilization. The plants now rule this domain and they have been contaminated from the poisoned roots of your world, which now touches our own. From such a malady there is little hope of recovery," Akara conceded as he placed the ivory staff into the elfling's blackened hands.

"This mirror realm beyond the Moon Gate, as you call it, is the sanctuary of the seed?" Medusa lingered in her thoughts of its strange complexity.

"Much like the Evermore is to our own Mother Gaia," Kali granted. This revelation helped the young half-elf to consider a plan on how they might be able to help the pale guardian.

The two were quite opposite of one another, for unlike the Evermore, this spirit realm where they stood was sterile of plant life. The elements here were imbalanced in ways that were unfamiliar but they recognized that the dangers were related.

If the wraiths of the Anatari should breach the gate and enter this sanctuary they would drain the seed of its life entirely. So was the predicament back in the Faerylands if the Craven breached the Evermore, and why its aura recoils from the withering. The two companions had to cure the injury committed upon this world done by their own by cauterizing the rift and cleansing it of the invading blight.

What made this dilemma so alarming was that even the Queen had never faced these specters in such numbers. To keep them from bleeding into this realm they had to return back to the surface world and crimp the offending fissure from contacting this region. However, as the Queen warned her young priestess, that if they should succeed in this task that there was also the chance they may not be able to return to their own realm. This was the sacrifice she had mentioned to Medusa upon their arrival; one they very well might have to make.

The red-draped priestess did not know of what powers her Queen might possess besides her obvious skill in battle. Medusa asked why she would take such a risk to discard her esteemed title among the Drow and elected not to send another warrior in her place. With great humility, Kali apprised the half-elf that hers was not a heightened position above other Elves, and was far different, if not entirely contrasted, from what the half-elf had been taught about royalty amongst her human kin. The Queen Mother's title among the Drow was one of burden and selfless responsibility; not of privilege.

True leaders should always take the first step towards the front lines in harsh times, for it was an inherent obligation to protect their subjects. To be a Queen among the Dark Elves required a measure of sacrifice, not entitlement. All decisions she made that affected others would apply to her equally as well. When

Medusa spoke of human Kings and Queens and such seats of power and how they abused such position for personal gain, the Drow Mother laughed at the thought; for power meant nothing without honor and wisdom in the eyes of the Elves.

Medusa admired that the Drow Mother was willing to die here upon this foreign shore to correct this wrong and prevent this blight from spreading. Personally, she would prefer to avoid that possibility if they were able but it was assuring to have the Queen of the Drow by her side. They had only two choices at the moment; to either take the seed now for safekeeping to their own world or deal with this scourge here and now.

Removing the seed would draw them back to their own realm instantaneously, but would leave a flourishing world to perish while the decay of the Craven lingered unchecked. That left the risk of any further tendrils from other realms that might grow along its path to become infected with the Anatari, and further spreading its corruption.

Medusa examined the crystal staff given to her by their host, pondering what she was to use it for.

"This tool will allow you to focus the power of the living tree beyond this sanctuary, as an extension of its inner energies," Akara instructed.

"How does it work?" The crimson priestess inquired as she inspected the staff, seeing nothing of significance within its design.

"A valid question," the queen offered to the white-robed guardian, "we observed that the element of fire is weak within this domain, which leaves us at a tactical disadvantage."

"It only employs power outside of this sanctum where you may utilize the flora as an ally," Akara advised his guests, "it is the plants of this world that dictate the conditions of life, and understandably, have a strong aversion to flames," he noted while pointing towards the burning lantern the Queen held in one of her many arms, its glimmer now blue and dull.

With the staff they could communicate with the plants and use them to their advantage. Akara agreed to keep the gateway open for them as long as he could but warned that they must hurry once they breach the portal. Taking the bridge of ether back to the glowing archway, Akara offered the pair of warriors a final word of advice.

"I must stay here and protect the tree but there is only one rift that needs to be sealed," the guardian professed, "the people who once lived here long ago eventually lost their civilization to the foliage which consumes this domain. The vegetation has no natural defense against these specters, but perhaps you may find something of use in the remnants of their lost past to further aid you in this endeavor," Akara offered.

With a nod, the two warriors stepped through the archway below the black moons and into the world of shadows. While carrying the white crystal staff, Medusa noted that the jungle growth was no longer blurred to her vision within a measured sphere. The staff revealed a globe of energy surrounding them as the plants reacted to their presence. The crystal rod camouflaged the foreign guests as if they belonged within this realm and were not to be harmed by the carnivorous plant life.

Scanning the vestiges of the ancient temple, they discovered a familiar design revering the triple moons as a common symbol among the glyphs and sculptures they found. The plants covered most of the engravings that had become buried over time, which made it difficult to search for hidden clues. While keeping a wary eye out for wandering wraiths, Medusa ventured to test the staff on the plants in an effort to help explore the hidden shrine. With little notion as to how to operate the crystal-tipped rod, she wondered if there were incantations that Akara might have forgotten to mention.

"It would be helpful if we could remove this overgrowth from the shrine..." she whispered aloud just under her breath. To her surprise, the tip of the staff lit up brightly and the plants within the sphere of light responded. Every leaf and vine around them began to rise upwards as the vines shed themselves from the stone statues and pillars. They both stood there in awe as each plant stretched upward, as if being pulled into the sky. Vines became ropes that slipped straight up into the air as massive trees lifted their canopies like a protective umbrella to the ancient site beneath their bows. It was a spectacle to behold.

With the landscape of the temple revealed before them, they

made their way towards a central shrine through a doorway which lay beneath the bust of a long-forgotten god. Its face seemed almost human, wide and stark with bold tattoos engraved upon its forehead. The light from the staff lit their way within the dark corridors beyond, revealing rows of statuary lining their path.

Deep within the temple, they stumbled upon a lone circular chamber which appeared much more mundane than the rest of the complex, though oddly arranged like a mirror image of the sanctuary beyond the Moon Gate where they had met Akara. Instead of a tree sitting in a central fountain, there stood a pale marble slate. Its texture was much like the stones in the mirror plane. Upon its surface was carved an altered, yet familiar, image of a tree composed of both root and canopy connected by a central trunk. Around this figure an emblem was etched; one which might be of a possible solution to their plight. Billowing clouds were artistically woven into a torrent of rain. This was a clue which gave the young sorceress an unusual idea.

"Water is the elemental counterforce of fire, which is why it may be so weak in this realm," Medusa surmised as Kali listened, "the fountain that held the seed tree and the blanket of clouds that layered its sanctuary may be the solution!"

"How so?" Kali asked her companion, still perplexed.

"You mentioned that these realms, both ours and countless others, are tethered by connecting roots from each of the living seeds," the half-elf asserted.

"In an ethereal state, yes," she replied, "if you can imagine the tangle of all the roots in the forest soil if they were exposed to be seen. Naturally, many roots touch and intertwine," the queen motioned with her fingers touching tips.

"If we cannot cauterize this interfering rift by way of fire, then another way to kill a root is to drown it!" Medusa offered. The Queen thought for a moment on her plan, for the rift had invaded this world at the valley floor but how could they possibly find the volume of water they would need to suffocate the fissure and barricade it from the invading wraiths?

"The clouds are made of it," her young companion suggested.

Granted, her plan made sense but there were no lakes nor

oceans present to purge into the rift. However, Medusa had learned a great deal from Shandi, the gnome who instructed her on Elemental magic. The lands of Trinity were held in a perpetual mist of low-lying clouds, which allowed the plants a stable supply of moisture to grow so lush. This enveloping fog was the source of their strength and vitality.

Unfortunately, this evolved vegetation had no natural defense against the spectral forces of the Craven, whose touch was poison and cause them to wither. They had to choke off the source of the Anatari and eradicate their presence, lest they find another rift and migrate to another realm. This land of rainforests was entirely overcast by an envelope of thick fog. These plants survived not only by the ambient light but consumed all other animals that dared trespass upon its garden. Regrettably, the invading phantoms were not of flesh and blood.

The minions of the Craven were immune from harm among the carnivorous jungle foliage and met no resistance as they roamed. That was about to change. Medusa devised a plan to combine her sorcery with the Queen's in an attempt to forge the weapon they needed to close the fissure from which the specters flowed. Together they divined the elements they would need, though resources were thin with only the pair of them to stand against an entire horde of twisted phantoms.

More than once, Kali had to intervene and dispatch an errant shade that wandered upon them as they made their way through the valley. Spying a vantage point high atop the tallest temple roof, they prepared their sorcery.

With her ether vision, Medusa could read the invisible trails of the wind and coaxed them into forming a spiraling vortex which intensified into a gale. With great effort, she directed the element of air from the valley peaks towards the breach from where the Anatari now flowed. Using the crystalline staff the guardian had given her, Medusa merged it with the flame from the Queen's mystic lantern. Kali was skeptical of this method of execution to release the water held in the clouds, but not as much as her companion was nervous about fusing enchanted relics, since her recollection of such rare instances cited that such folly usually ended with catastrophic results.

Kali held up her Lantern with a steady hand and opened the chamber to the mystical flame as the winds wove their way towards the purged rift below their perch. With nervous breath, Medusa struck forth the glowing end of Akara's staff into the heart of the lamp as the winds met the glowing fissure resting upon the valley floor. It took all her strength to fight the staff as it resisted entering the lamp. One slip could mean disaster, as the two alien elements would either merge by force or the infusion would rupture their binding magic.

A powerful wave of heat seeped from the lamp as crimson ribbons unfurled from its shell. The young sorceress had the privilege of having her blind eyes protected, unlike the Drow Queen who had to shield herself from the blazing bloom of light. Medusa held the staff steady as it began to splinter and crack within her grasp. Fearing the worst, she gripped onto the fractured shards to keep the rod whole, knowing this might be the last moment of her life.

The blaze transformed into a shockwave that spread beyond the sphere of light in all directions as the two warriors stumbled to regain their feet. Half blinded, Kali turned her red eyes towards the jungle valley to see the low lying clouds burst into droplets of water, which suddenly fell into a torrential sheet of rain. The half-elf girl winced in pain from her bleeding hands which had been lacerated by the sharp splinters of the staff when the two relics had merged.

The sudden downpour instantly flooded the shrine and rushed downhill along the jungle floor, washing away loose rubble and vegetation in its wake. The force of the water magnified to the point that sections of the ruins became unearthed from the soft soil and tumbled into the current below. Medusa watched in awe as her initial plan to direct the torrent exceeded their hopes and coursed towards the rift and the deformed shadows that stood in the path of the approaching tsunami of mud and debris.

They saw many of the specters washed up by the flood, their mouths agape in silent screams of anguish. It was their muted cries which made it so truly terrifying, for the Craven were but voiceless shades of the dead. A whirlpool of water and soil engulfed their ghostly forms and cleansed them from the surface. Warped and misshapen arms flailed wildly in the stew of debris; frantically grasping for a salvation that would never come as they were pulled into the void.

The elation the companions felt seeing that their strategy had worked was short-lived, for it soon became apparent that the volume of the floodwaters began to breach their banks. Water began to surge around the rift and coursed farther down the valley beyond, dragging many of the Craven along with it. Realizing their oversight, Medusa turned to the Drow Queen and beseeched her to take the staff from her grasp.

"Take this and hold it as firmly as you can, I need to stop the overspill before the waters are purged into the valley!" Medusa yelled over the roaring wind and pelting rain. Kali sheathed her weapons upon her belt and used a pair of arms to take the staff from the girls bleeding hands. It was a risky move since the energy grounded between two sorcerers could be redirected, but this created a dangerous loop that would surge through Kali herself, but they had no other option.

Kali gripped the staff where the half-elf had held hers to try to bind the splintering breaks and removed her hold while tiny shards snapped free as the powerful energies swelled. Wasting no time, Medusa turned towards the valley and used her casting to freeze the raging waters into an ever-growing wall of ice to funnel the deluge towards the fissure. The young sorceress had never used the powers she had learned to such a degree and felt suddenly weak from the effort. Her face went flush as she turned towards her colleague after directing the spell, only to see the Drow Queen fighting the fusion of the lantern and the crystal staff in her hands as their energies exceeded her efforts to control them.

With a snap of light, the tip of the crystal rod broke free and the staff shattered in the Drow Mother's hands. The mystic lantern was flung from her grasp with a trail of flames marking its path as it spun into the air, tumbling into the valley below. The winds rose into the force of a cyclone as Medusa lost control of her spell and the world went dark while the elemental energies convulsed once and collapsed. She slipped on the wet stone of the temple roof and fell for what seemed like an eternity as the storm engulfed her limp body.

ഗ൪ൽ

Medusa heard a voice in the darkness that called to her. She wondered if this is what death was like, for she knew that her essence would never be reunited with the Evermore if she faded from life so far from the Faerylands. She wondered about that for a moment, considering if her life might be taken by another world tree amongst the cosmic void or if she would devolve into one of the Craven. That thought made her sad, and she felt a single tear shed from her blind eyes.

The voice called at her again and she tried to move, to see what form she might now have. It was a struggle at first, for the pain was intense. It was as if all of her veins had turned to glass, and that any small motion would shatter them. The sharp splinters pierced and bled, burning her from within.

Her senses felt dull, though she could smell a sweet fragrance like the morning dew after a storm. The wind held a certain sharpness, like a breeze flowing above the cliffs high above an open sea. She felt an ache like a lead weight holding her down, but yet again, there was that voice calling her name. There was an instant of confusion as she recognized the name as her own, for it sounded familiar, yet strangely alien.

She tried to touch her eyes to rub away the darkness; groaning in agony at even the slightest effort. Yet, again and again, the insistent voice continued hailing to her from some distant corner of her mind; pleading for her to rise. The ache she felt became increasingly familiar, belonging to a body she once knew. The voice was gentle, though a flooding brightness began to overtake her and the sorceress found herself lost in fog of confusion.

"What happened...?" Medusa breathed with a broken voice, now sounding much harsher than she remembered. Her throat was swollen and dry, and she felt a surging headache welling in the back of her mind as she propped herself up. The blurry illumination began to clear as she focused her vision. She felt displaced for a single second, seeing the curved moon chamber and the glossy fountain and its stark ash-white tree with its bare branches weaving in a spiral dance.

"Medusa, my beauty, you need to get up. Breathe deeply and clear your mind," the velvet voice of Akara petitioned the sleeping girl.

The pain was ever-present when the young sorceress strained to rise. Medusa looked around and recognized the surroundings of the sanctuary. Across from her sat the Queen in her formal armor, polishing a dagger she carried and tending her wounded hands. Looking to her own palms, she saw hers too were bandaged and recalled glimpses of memory when the crystal staff had shattered.

Seeing she was awake, Akara rose from Medusa's side and approached the Queen with a large silver lantern he had chosen lying among his collection.

"We choked off the route the Craven were using to traverse into this realm," Kali answered to the injured priestess, "you had fallen from the temple dome and I brought you here to recover," she informed Medusa in a sober tone just before she turned to their pale host who held the ornate lamp toward her.

"Please accept this gift," the masked guardian offered, "as a replacement for your lost relic," Akara nodded with approval for the dark elf to take the lantern.

The lamp was of an odd design, resembling a tall hourglass, yet, instead of sand, there were beads of light that sifted within its casing. A hefty ring adorned the top of the relic as its handle and the Drow Queen accepted this tribute with due grace. With a measure of curiosity, she wondered what strange magic it might hold within. Lingering in a daze, Medusa tried to gather her thoughts but felt as if she was going to be sick and began coughing, which quickly escalated into a dry heave.

"Come, young one," Kali spoke gently while using her extra set of arms to help the girl towards the fountain, "the energies of this world are unfamiliar and you have overextended yourself drawing from their source," the queen professed as she motioned the girl to drink from the water's edge. Taking a sip, Medusa suddenly felt dreary and lightheaded and fell back into the pile of furs. Within her mind's eye, the world began to swim with colors, washing away her ability to focus.

"Will she be alright?" Akara asked with a note of concern.

"It is easy to forget that her human half cannot handle the strain to which pure elves are accustomed. In time, she will be tempered to remedy her weaknesses and learn to use them to her advantage," the queen mentioned with a gaze of concern towards the girl, "It is unfortunate that your staff was destroyed in the process but we hope that you may be able to save this domain and repair the damage that was done," Kali afforded as an apology towards the pale guardian.

"It is not the fault of your kind, and any forthcoming atonement for our loss has been redeemed by your assistance, my Grace," Akara offered with a formal bow; his bone-white robes fluttering like fluid in the light, "the stray Anatari that had escaped the floodwaters will be dealt with."

"But it appears as though you are here alone. Will you be able to manage their removal on your own?" The queen inquired.

"Come, let me show you what has transpired since your battle with these wraiths ...these Craven, as you call them," Akara granted to the queen and her young assistant.

After Medusa recovered and was able to walk, they made their way from the sanctuary and through the bridge of light across the void, returning to the Moon Gate. There they stood in wonder as brilliant sunlight cast through the open portal upon the surface world of Trinity. Stepping through the pane, they were enveloped by a bright blue sky and towering trees. The entire jungle was vibrant with color amongst the bouquet of exotic plants and rich soil. It was an astounding transformation from the gloomy mists which had once shrouded this landscape for countless eons.

"It's ...it's so beautiful!" The half-elf exclaimed with excitement returning to her weakened voice, for the foliage was now no longer blurred to her without the aid of Akara's staff.

"What will you do now?" the queen inquired to their ivory-draped host, who stood like a smudge of purity encircled among the thick green overgrowth.

"This is a new beginning for our world and we look to this transition as a time of growth," Akara stated with hope as he raised his hands to the towering trees and its kingdom of green,

"With the aid of the plants we will hunt down the remaining Anatari and put them at peace," the guardian vowed, speaking of the forest itself, as his companion in this venture. The area where the rift had once been was now layered in mud and stone, having filled the void and suffocated the invading rift.

"Will we be able to return to the Faerylands?" The blind sorceress asked with a chill of despair, having learned that such ventures would always bear the risk of becoming marooned upon a strange and distant land.

"Yes, my beauty," Akara answered to the girl to settle her doubts, "the seed of life will make that sacrifice in your honor," he offered to his guests.

Preparing for their return took many days, so the two warriors took the opportunity to hunt for any stray specters which had survived the flood, and to study the temple ruins and the history of their long-forgotten people. The half-elf priestess explored the forest jungle alone in an effort to unravel her feelings about returning to her own world.

In all honesty, she had no one waiting for her. She had lost her human and elven family as an outcast of both races. Though Medusa had found a new home with the Drow, deep down, she still felt indentured to the Queen. As she walked alone among the giant trees of the silent forest with only her footsteps for company, Medusa had mixed feelings knowing that Kali had risked herself on this quest, which instilled a sense of shared sacrifice for the greater good. It was a lesson she would not soon forget.

In the end, Medusa began to question this invisible shackle by which she saw herself bound and wondered if the Queen saw her as an equal. If she viewed her as a possible successor, then surely it must be so. With renewed confidence, she made her way back to the ancient temple to help her queen to transcribe the hieroglyphs and history of this lost race while they awaited the next lunar conjunction for the opening of the Moon Gate. With mounting curiosity, Medusa marveled at the complexity of this dead civilization left etched upon the stones.

"Why is it that we are saving the creations of this lost tribe for our library?" The young sorceress inquired as she unrolled another scroll to etch upon its surface. A few steps away, Kali answered the girl without removing her attention from the ancient glyphs spread before her.

"In my years, I have learned that the universe is much older than most will ever realize," the queen revealed, "and there have been more civilizations as this one lost to the void than you can possibly imagine. However, don't be misguided by the Elves desire to dwell on the past, for it is in recognition that all lives matter, no matter how small," the queen mother deemed while drawing the girl's attention to a marking on a broken wall, "you see this symbol here ...it is quite similar to the lotus flower of our own world. It represents the impulse of life to grow and prosper."

"But these people are long dead," Medusa contended. The queen took a deep breath, citing patience for the naive youth from the ranks of the Coven.

"No, sister, they still live, and they speak to us through these records cast in stone at this very moment," Kali noted as she caressed the glyphs with her hands, revealing what the young half-elf had failed to see for herself.

Such a deep perspective had not occurred to her before, and Medusa saw a bigger picture beyond her blind eyes. The Elves had a proverb they practiced, that they believed there was neither good nor evil in the world but only a swath of shades between shadow and light. If one drifts too far towards the light, they could be just as blinded as if they had been cast into consuming darkness. It was this basic mantra she had learned from the elves as to why she viewed the Craven, not as evil, but to be regarded with a measure of sympathy.

The world of men, however, held no such philosophy and they became greatly divided among themselves. This is why they groped so desperately in the dirt for their forgotten past, as it was now their only tether to their lost immortality. Once the Evermore had withdrawn from their kind, the lives of the Elves extended while the days of Mankind withered away. When the natural life of an Elf and beings of the Fey comes to an end, they become one again with the Evermore which made them, and the Faerie to their given elements; and all is returned as it once was. For the Craven, however, were unnatural endings of life, lingering like a sickness. They had nowhere to go, and the Gaia did not want them.

"So, do you understand now why the Craven wander so, little sister?" Kali bade as she taught the young elfling.

"Because they are now orphans among the stars," Medusa conceded with a wrenching sadness to this revelation, but accepted the duty the Elves entrusted upon the sisterhood to cleanse this malady.

It was the blighted history of the Anatari since time began. There were consequences for beings that abused the gift of life and twisted it beyond all intentions. Their bitter legacy was to create harm upon itself and the world that birthed them. Medusa gazed into the sky above and felt her heart begin to ache as she wondered how many worlds there were scattered among the stars, where similar tragedies had yet to unfold. Kali advised her that in their past, the High Elves had once sent emissaries to distant realms in hopes to caution others of this blight, but it was a practice they dissolved over the eons as the noble Elves had become a dying race.

"You must understand, sister, that we once welcomed the brothers of Men into our fold in hopes they could meld with what was left of our fading race before we too, became lost to time," the queen relayed with a dry sadness lingering in her voice as she touched the carvings of the ancient stone, made by the hand of a long-dead artisan, "...which is how you came into being," she noted the obvious slant towards the half-elf girl, "but our hopes were dashed when the miracles we showed Mankind were misread and were in turn, sought to be exploited by their masses," the dark elf confessed.

This was the first time Medusa had learned of this buried truth and was warned not to spread its rumor. If the honorable and learned race of Elves were dying, the question begging to be asked, was why? The young outcast was not prepared for the answer.

"I understand why the Sisterhood must keep this disclosure a secret, but what is causing the Elves to perish?" Medusa asked with bated breath. The queen put down her etchings and came to sit beside the anguished girl whose covered eyes hid her welling tears.   Placing her many hands upon Medusa's shoulders and holding her head steady in a gentle embrace, the Drow Queen stared face to face with the girl.

"Time itself is also a living thing, for it is as the wind through the forest of stars above," she waved with one hand towards the night sky, "As the Evermore withdraws from Mankind, the world of Men hastens as equally as ours has diminished. In the short span of time you have been in the Eternal City and the Citadel of the Drow, centuries have passed in theirs," the dark queen revealed to the shocked elfling, "this prolonged lifespan we enjoy above others is not a blessing, but a curse."

The young half-elf had never considered the balance of energy that governed the world would also be tied between elves and men.   It sapped their vitality in exchange for an enhanced constitution, eventually leaving future generations of Elvenkind weakened and sterile.   It was the duty of the Sisterhood to correct this imbalance before permanent damage was done, for they could not dare leave their legacy to mankind.

"If the elves should die, who will carry on their teachings?" The young sorceress asked with a squeak of despair as the Drow Queen instilled the importance of their work and the ugly secret behind their struggle.

"That is in the hands of the Elven Lords who protect the Tree of Life in our realm; much in the way that the guardian Akara, is the sentinel in his own underworld, here in the forests of Trinity. They are doing what they can to save the Faerylands, as it is our duty to protect it," the queen acknowledged as she referred to the Coven of the Sisterhood, "We use the Elfire as the source of our powers while the Evermore itself dwindles, but there is another race birthed of creation..." Kali stated as she trailed off while Medusa finished her thought.

"You mean the Elvenborn, fathered by the Elves. I thought the first Fey were but a myth, merely stories told to little children?" Medusa caught herself in the sudden realization that all the legends she had heard were true.

"They are the most powerful of the Faerie to follow as our descendants, and you must swear to protect them at all cost

...for without them, we have no future," the Drow Queen bade to the girl with such emotional gravity while she grasped her shoulders that it caused the woven charms upon her headdress to jingle.

"...I will," was all that Medusa could muster to say, as she was almost breathless with the thought that their noble kind was fading from the Faerylands because mankind was killing their world. Little did the young sorceress realize that there would come a day when her solemn vow would be severely tested.

The Tower

It had already been many moons since Medusa and the Queen had returned from the forest realm called Trinity, leaving Akara to his tasks ahead. By this time, the warrior women had finished training the rest of the cadets in the Coven, having taught them the basic skills they would need in their duties to the Sisterhood in the times ahead. The young half-elf was still recovering from her exertion from her first encounter with the Craven; finding it a difficult lesson she had learned about tapping energies from other realms.

The Queen Mother resumed her duties to the Drow, residing back upon her throne poised above the rocky shores of Antilla. What Kali had taught the half-breed sorceress in their time together in that distant realm was something she would always carry with her. There were now only seven sisters left within the Coven, for those who had failed during their trials were infused into the Elfire at the central hearth of the sanctuary. Though it seemed like a cruel fate, their essence would be drawn upon in times of need; further serving their oath to the covenant, even in death.

The other students were excited to hear of Medusa's adventures and the tales of what they were to expect in their service to the Sisterhood, as they were bound by their blood oath to the Drow Queen. As a measure of their secret pact, they were forbidden to speak of what they had learned to the other Elven clans, and were kept in isolation from the main population that resided in the castle above. From an outside perspective, it might seem a cruel and lonely fate to spend their lives always hidden from the world above, but little did they know of the true nature of their Order and the wild and mysterious realms they would explore.

Each of the students found their own niche of magic they excelled in and mastered the weapons they would need in their tasks ahead. As the Evermore ebbed from Antilla, the seven houses of the Drow abandoned their cities as human raiders began to besiege their docks. Mankind had brought the blight of war to their island, and the race of dark elves withdrew into the underworld as their once great cities were ransacked by the hordes of human marauders.

The queen had always known that this day would come, and the population of the Drow was evacuated to the Citadel at the tip of the island as their last refuge. They could not risk direct war with the humans, for it would only quicken their demise. The Elves still had much work to do and the Queen was given the burden of facing this grave misfortune which had befallen their subjects. Magic itself dwindled from the island around them as mankind overran its shores, and there came a day of great sacrifice for the dark elves.

A great fortress was erected before the gates of the royal castle in the form of a mighty tower, standing alone before an open field. It was set with runes and glyphs upon every block and stone, mortared with earth and blood. The architects did not argue with the Queen on its exotic design or the esoteric ingredients required for its construction, nor why it was placed to stand detached beyond the protection of the castle gates. A vast hearth was built before it and its entry lined with standing stones, it was only then that the rumors of its true purpose began to rise in fearful whispers among the houses of the drow.

As their abandoned cities fell, one by one, human raiders began to approach upon the castle; requesting admittance for an audience with the Queen, only to be denied. Their appeals soon became demands, and there came a time when the Queen gazed upon the sea to find a fleet of warships approaching their shores. Among the race of Men were those of influence and greed, who had come to take the island for their own and craved the riches of the Citadel and aimed to depose its arrogant elven queen. However, within the castle walls were deposited many old and ancient secrets she could not allow to be plundered.

The very eve the soldiers of men had landed upon the ports and harbors of the seven cities, the fields beyond the gates of the Drow castle were alight with a thousand campfires. Men had claimed war upon the race of Elves and sought to conquer their stronghold. This lone isle was known as the last refuge to hold their secrets, and the greed of men would not be denied. Cornered with their backs to the cold and dreadful sea, the Drow had nowhere left to run.

Many of the elves now began to believe it had been folly to wait so long to follow their Elven kin beyond the reach of men and into obscurity. They had wasted countless years studying mankind and their weaknesses, only to become burdened by the very traits they sought to use against this enemy who had come knocking upon their door. The queen had foreseen this unfortunate possibility and was not caught unprepared. When the first light of dawn rose upon the tip of Antilla, it revealed an infantry of Dwarves standing guard before the last castle of the Drow in their defense.

Rays of sunlight glittered from their tipped pikes as long banners trailed in the morning wind. Among them stood Argona Shatterstone, who had personally beseeched her king to come to the aid of the Drow Queen. Dwarves were also quite reclusive, but even they had not failed to notice the mischief of men and the vandalism that they beset upon the soil of their own lands. Mankind also took and extracted from the earth as did the Dwarves, though far in excess than they could have ever dreamed.

The Dwarves had shied away from the race of Men and their strange infatuation with death and destruction. Dwarves had become accustomed to hiding within the earth but they found no honor cowering from this foe. When the armies of men saw the legions of stout warriors and their grim faces standing against them, they did not falter. Their numbers had grown so large that they cared not about the lives they would waste to achieve their goal, for they possessed a consuming ambition to conquer everything in their path.

A single envoy was sent to meet the captain who ruled the armies, standing against both Dwarves and Drow. Passing through the ranks of the stout dwarves heaving with defiance in their breath and coldness in their eyes, a single elf strode from the castle. Dressed in the finest silks embossed with silver threads, this sole emissary advanced like a divine being, trailing beads of light in her wake. She was beyond all beauty of what men desired; so much so that even their most staunch soldiers gaped in awe as if spellbound by her entrancing presence.

She approached entirely unarmed except for a single green sprig held delicately in her hands. Her shawl draped like wings, flowing behind her, and her steps were silent and graceful; it was as if she floated above an earth that dare not soil such perfection. Her head bowed, entwined in a golden weave of hair, she came to a halt as lesser men stepped away in reverence to this living transcendence standing before them. Finally, she arrived at their ranks and raised her eyes only to the man she was to address to be worthy of her presence.

"I am Autumn Bluesparrow, emissary of the Elven Lords and messenger to the Drow whose lands you now trespass upon," she uttered with a soothing voice that intoxicated the ears with underlying power, "I offer you this olive branch as a symbol of our sincerity that we wish to be at peace with the race of Men," the envoy bade as she held forth the green sprig.

"You offer peace, yet you greet us with an army," the captain voiced with a dismissive tone yet did not move to take the branch she offered forth.

"Heed my words well," Autumn declared with a tone of gravity seeping from her lips, "the world of men has encroached upon every elvish kingdom and sacred shore, and though to this day, the Elven Lords have not raised a hand against you; be warned not to misjudge this as a weakness. What you seek is not yours to possess," the glimmering emissary charged.

"We only ask your compliance in our laws and decrees, and sworn loyalty to our rule," The human officer answered in smugness to the wavering branch held before him. A resonance changed behind the emissary's eyes, for she could perceive his true intentions, which could not be disguised by painted words.

"Not so ...for you only seek blind obedience," as grief bit into her voice while she turned towards the armed soldiers standing before her to address them, "Whatever gods you have created to follow or whatever entitlement you think you are owed; within your short lives you should remember that the world your Masters would have you forge will throw all others out of balance," the Elven maiden asserted. Again, she stepped forward and held forth the branch, bidding a truce towards the Captain of the human troops who had trampled the grass and wildflowers into the soil beneath their heavy boots.

"So, you're telling me your pointed-eared Lords and this rogue Queen of yours, refuse to surrender the castle?" The Officer challenged with his hand moving upon the hilt of his sword.

"Be wary, for if you do not seek peace here today, you may never find it," Autumn granted with stern eyes that pierced through him. The Elves had a saying about the humans, as they had seen them as caterpillars that were given the chrysalis of knowledge with the opportunity to transform and prosper; though no winged beauty ever emerged from their shell, only the black moth of anger and hate, and all that was left behind was an empty husk in their place.

In one swift motion, within a flash the Captain's blade had struck out and gashed her throat, scarring her ivory perfection. For a brief moment, Autumn's piercing eyes widened, awash with anguish as she wavered to raise a bloodied hand from her neck. His men watched in shock as the angel of purity fell, breaking the spell of her beauty. The Dwarven warriors on the opposite side of the field were aghast in horror at such a callous and cowardly act; for striking down an unarmed messenger had proven that Mankind had no honor.

"We do not heed the bedeviled words of some elven witch who ventures to sway us from our destiny," the Captain spat aloud for all to hear.

The Captain raised his bloodied saber in hand in a rallied cry as the few soldiers standing beside him continued to stare for a moment in stunned dismay at the murdered elf as she slipped lifelessly to the ground at his feet; but still, they did nothing, for Men had not evolved into free thinkers, but as cowardly followers and obedient slaves. One by one, the soldiers fell into the fervor of his war cry, for they had traveled far to pillage this island on the promise of fame and fortune.

They had been groomed to see the Elves as pointy-eared demons that were to be hated and feared. Dwarven warriors raged as their spittle flew in anger, raising their heavy blades and jagged spears. Leather boots stampeded as armored foes clashed, even as the olive branch fell from Autumn's dead hands, its frail leaves tarnished with the first drop of blood to fall in the raging battle to come. As it struck the soil, the pounding of that crimson droplet resonated like the beat of a drum that grazed the skies above to the chaos and death that rained between men and the ancient races of the earth.

Elven arrows screamed through the air over the ramparts of the gate, striking down human soldiers as they advanced. This human foe had never seen such fierce berserkers as the angered Dwarves, whose skill in battle was only outmatched by the overwhelming number of their adversary. Mankind had stolen the craft of the Dwarves and used it against them, weapon to weapon, steel to steel. Upon this pristine island, the blood of many races mingled, finding common ground, not in diplomacy but instead, upon the trampled soil stained with their red hue.

The sky and the mountains cried with grief at the loss of so many lives as the two sides battled over reasons far divided. There is a specific horror to war, filled with bitterness and contempt. It is a dark place where a person's individual hopes and dreams come to a sudden and meaningless end, never to be realized. War is disharmony; a collision of mind and thoughts of those who take, and those who rebel.

There are those who live their entire lives on a code of ethics and honor, only to be tested in their final breath. The Elves and the Dwarves knew what they were fighting for but so very many of their enemies did not. Men did what they were told, not for themselves but on the empty promise of a better future, no matter whose lives they robbed in exchange.

The tide of the battle raged from dawn till dusk when the first stars began to glitter in the heavens. In the tug and sway of the assault, the fearless Dwarves slowly dwindled. Pressed by overwhelming numbers, they faltered and were forced to retreat back towards the castle and its high outer walls prickling with archers. Before they could reach the gates, a thundering rumble pierced the earth, knocking soldiers from their feet.

From the balcony at the highest point of the castle, the Queen had kept a vigilant eye on the course of the battle. In the eve before, the brood mother had met with the royal council of the Dwarves regarding the conflict to come, and they agreed to assist the Drow in their time of need. Their armored warriors arrived through a portal from their realm and advanced from the castle under the cover of night, where they had spread unto the field in the darkest hours before the dawn.

As the soldiers of men fell, legions upon legions took their place, and there seemed to be no end to their numbers. In their efforts to regroup, the fatigued dwarves were cut short by the crack of thunder that rolled beneath their feet. As they turned back towards the castle, the purpose of the strange tower erected before the walls soon became clear. At the edge of an open hearth stood a glowing gate, where there were lined many Drow who wore blackened robes as they marched single file towards a spiral of light emanating skyward from its base.

Both men and dwarves watched in horror as the dark elves in their black gowns stepped into the pane of light, and were engulfed by the fiery pit at the center of the hearth. With each sacrifice, an errant scream split the air as its cry was suddenly muffled into oblivion. Within this sphere, a massive flare roared in mesmerizing stillness as the blaze of the elfire rose in radiance with every life it absorbed. At the end of the line of druids stood the Queen Mother herself, who stopped short of the last of her subjects, who had offered themselves to the hungry flames.

Human soldiers stood in shock and gawked as they had never seen a creature such as the Drow Queen, who had raised her many arms from beneath the folds of her gown and closed the rift before the blazing pit of mystic fire. Within each of her hands, she held an orb that sparked and danced with an angry light. A great number of dark elves had sacrificed themselves to save their kin and kingdom for this final act. Fear swelled through the ranks of men who stumbled over one another in throes to escape this arcane menace, for the tales they had heard of the black magic by such demons had proven to be true.

A wild and angry glow poured from the blazing furnace towards these strange orbs the Queen held aloft, flowing around her body like liquid light. In a moment of realization, the

Dwarven warriors left upon the battlefield began to sprint on their stout little legs for the castle walls, perceiving what they expected what was to be a magical attack upon the legions of men to win the tide in their favor. The light from the elfire furnace grew to the brightness of the sun, casting long shadows of the standing stones and the queen which stood before it. A sudden flare exploded of such intensity that it blinded everyone upon the field as they held up their arms to shield their eyes.

Within a blink, the blaze was gone. Still blinded by the sudden brightness, warriors were flung into the air as the ground beneath them vanished. Dwarven troops stumbled over the edge of a vast void that had appeared before them, those in the rear coming to a sudden halt at the edge of a deep rift. Below them the hollow roar of rushing ocean waters came crashing inward to fill the void, the vacuum of air pulling in dwarves and men alike, including all lifeless bodies closest to the fissure, as they were drawn into the black swirling sea that consumed them.

The entire tip of the island had disappeared, from its bedrock to the castle's tallest spire. The last sanctuary of the elves left within the world of men had vanished without a trace. The few hardened soldiers of the dwarves that remained stood in grim silence, looking out at this hollowed shore as their long beards wavered in the ocean wind. They had been betrayed and left to die by the very ally they had come to protect.

For this treachery, the Dwarves would never forget. Their hearts turned to stone as they dwelled on this desertion by the Elves while they turned back toward the encroaching legions that swelled upon these last few pockets of survivors. Dwarves do not surrender; and to this day, it is unknown if any survived the onslaught of that fateful eve.

$$\text{\small ❧❦}$$

With a great heave, the entire castle swayed, and the Sisters within the coven below its foundation huddled in fear as dust and stone fell from the ceiling of their chamber. The entire castle rocked as it settled itself while the young sisters were left in shock over the sudden commotion. They had been secured in their quarters without having been informed of the encroaching battle. Their head priestess, Eden, had ordered them to remain confined without further comment.

The seven sisters sat worried and anxious within the dim light of the shrine as the creaking of the stone walls shifted in protest. Medusa was the first to venture to their locked door while clutching the shaft of the enchanted key that Ironbow had given her, which still hung around her neck. It had been too long without hearing from their head mistress, and the other girls agreed to venture outside their confines to see what had happened, despite the orders of the head priestess.

As she approached the great door, a blue aura emanated around its frame, warning that a glyph had been placed upon it. The half-elf thought this strange since her ether vision had not revealed such a ward prior, which could have meant it was only placed on the exterior of the door. Before she could take another step there was a flash of light only she could see, which was invisible to the other disciples waiting behind Medusa for her to use her mysterious key. The half-elf jumped with a start as the door creaked open just before she touched it; standing on the other side was the Head Priestess, looking at the group of startled girls crowded before her.

"Follow me!" Eden pressed with a sense of urgency towards the girls, and the disciples exchanged a worried glance before they fell in step behind her.

Once outside the protection of their chamber, the condition of the great hall told the sisters of the coven there was something seriously amiss. Great stones had broken through the high cathedral windows of the grand hall, which were not a part of its original architecture. Lit only by sparse torchlight, the group weaved through the maze of stairwells and bridges where massive stalactites had breached the ceiling above.

Making their way up to the central chamber for the first time since their arrival to the castle, they found the Drow Mother sitting upon a jagged throne bristling with massive horns and tusks. They were brought before the Queen and stood within their traditional half-moon circle before her in reverence. Her eyes, lightly veiled by a thorned crown encrusted with gemstones, the dark queen bade for them to raise their heads to her as she stood from her throne.

"A great plight has befallen us, sisters;" she breathed with tense resolve, "at the dawn of this day, soldiers of Men had breached our island and sought to overrun the citadel. We could not let this be," she raised her arms towards the assembly of onlookers who were left of her court, "...for we have a duty to fulfill as do the High Elves in the Eternal City."

Though the sisters of the coven were disturbed at this news, they managed to quell their dismay. Around them in the crowd, beyond the edge of the circle of the queen's court stood an array of drow from every walk of life. They were the last vestiges from the seven cities of Antilla. Looks of doubt and dread were etched upon their stark faces as they gazed upon the assembly of enchanters. Three to either side, Medusa stood dignified at their center, her red gown flowing gently in the torchlight.

"On this day your vows to the covenant are now called upon, my sisters," Eden declared to the bewildered girls, "You have been trained in sacred magic's to aid us in this time of need, and your duty towards that end starts upon this very moment," their head priestess affirmed as she bade them to take each other's hands, side by side.

The Queen mother strode directly towards the blind half-elf in her jeweled headdress lined with talismans, and placed a pair of hands upon her head, and the spare two upon her arms where she held tightly to the disciples standing at either side. Unseen to the others, the dark aura that only Medusa could perceive, flowed forth over her and across her arms as it spread its essence onto each consecutive sister of the coven. The sisters stood in a moment of silence as the queen had bowed her head, unable to see the enchantment the Drow Queen had bequeathed unto them through Medusa's touch.

Those present gasped in hushed awe as the blood-red stain of Medusa's curse began to seep among them as each of their pale gowns flowed with a creeping tint of deep crimson. The sisters became distressed by this change that befell them; though they began to sense the tingling power that coursed through their flesh and bones. Medusa's curse from the Elven Lords had become their symbol of honor; an emblem they would forever carry among their Sisterhood of Blood. Her forehead touching the young half-elf held before her, the Queen gently whispered a foreboding decree for only Medusa, alone, to hear.

"Fate has dealt a different path for us, sister Medusa, now we must take an alternate avenue in our lives. Yours will be much darker than mine, for I can not join you on the way now laid before you, but be assured that your day will come to ascend," the Drow Mother breathed quietly with a single kiss to her forehead, "I have bestowed upon you and your sisters a blessing to help you channel your skills ...though, as always, such gifts always come at a cost."

With those final words, the dark mother took a step back as a servant came forward and offered the queen a large relic by its ringed handle. Taking it in her grasp, the queen turned and handed Medusa the hourglass lantern she had been gifted by the guardian of Trinity. As the half-elf accepted the relic, its inner light pulsed brightly; accepting its new host. Without further ceremony, the dark mother took her throne and Eden Whitetail addressed the coven, bidding them to follow.

In a trance, the Sisterhood followed the head priestess towards the main entrance to the castle, but were astonished to see that the main gate was now obstructed by a wall of solid stone. Passing through an antechamber, they took a stairwell that led to the upper rampart and through a causeway littered with rubble, which had merged with the cavern that penetrated through the barriers of the outer wall. Through battered and broken sections, they emerged outside the confines of the castle where several armored guards awaited. The elven sentries bore torches and donned the emblem of the queen's guard, present to escort them to their final destination.

The disciples turned and saw that their exit from the high balcony was but a dark fissure of cracked and broken stone at the edge of a mountain, one in which the entire citadel had been embedded beneath it; buried from sight.

The night sky opened before them with a glitter of stars and a familiar crescent moon. The landscape, however, was foreign and unrecognizable. Before them stood a dark and brooding tower that lay perched on the precarious edge of a cliff. The walls of the city gate were left in broken shambles, leaving the Sisters of the coven distraught, wondering what had transpired.

"The last vestiges of the Drow have been evacuated to the citadel, which has now been displaced to another region within our own realm," Eden advised the sisters as they followed Medusa with her glowing lantern held aloft to light the way, while the armed guards followed them on either side until they reached the line of standing stones.

"We are no longer on Antilla?" Bella, one of the sisters, asked in shock as the other girls began to murmur among themselves with worry and despair.

"Antilla was lost, and the Drow were left with no other choice but to shift the castle to a sanctuary, not only for our people but to safeguard the living seeds we have procured, just as the High Elves protect our own Tree of Life," Eden replied with a measure of dignity, "and this fortress before you will become your new home."

The sisters approached the strange spire that emanated a sense of unease, a few of them turned to notice that the royal guard stayed behind at the edge of the stone-lined path; refusing to approach further. It made them wonder if the guards had been sent to escort them for their protection or merely to deliver them to this new cage.

"Why can't we stay below the castle where we were?" Inquired Asha, another disciple of the Sisterhood, just as they reached the large central cauldron filled with hot coals that lay in front of the tower entrance.

Raising her lantern, Medusa and the others could see that the embers within the bowled hearth were still smoldering. Tiny glowing sparks of deep red sputtered where they noticed with disturbing despair, several slender bones protruding through the thick ash. Hundreds of dark elves had sacrificed their lives to form the energy for the invocation to push the castle between spaces to reach this new sanctum. In the process, the fuel of the elfire had been consumed in its entirety. All those lives lost so that their lineage could be saved.

It was a heart-wrenching sight to behold, and the Sisters of the order were silent, finally realizing the true meaning of sacrifice and the dedication the dark elves shared. The head priestess ushered Medusa to light their way into the tower with the mystical lantern as the other sisters followed in step behind her. Once inside, they were perplexed to find that there was nothing but a dark void within as if the interior walls of the fortress were swallowed by a consuming shadow. Turning back, they only saw an open doorway standing isolated in the darkness where Eden Whitetail stood at the breach.

"I cannot follow you within, for this is your new domain, my sisters," Eden bade the coven through the open doorway, "Within the center of the chamber, Medusa, you will find the seed from Frostfall lying at the foot of a pedestal; only you, and you alone, can place it upon its rest, and above it is a ring to hang the lantern which you must never allow to be set down," the elder priestess instructed the blind half-elf.

Baffled by this chain of events, the sisters of the coven watched as Medusa took several steps forward with her lamp held aloft as its light pushed back the empty darkness where they found an iron ring hanging from a long chain that disappeared into the blackness above. With care, she raised the lamp onto the hook as the chain rattled with a sound that echoed into the eternity beyond. Once it was secured, they found a thick stone pedestal rising from the floor covered in archaic runes and spirals. At its base lay the obsidian seed, that Medusa herself had taken from the realm of Frostfall, nestled within the same wrapped cape she had released to the head priestess upon their arrival back at the coven those many moons ago.

She knelt and looked upon her blackened hands, having been transformed by this relic before and quietly followed Eden's instructions, knowing that she alone was immune to its touch. The sisters of the coven stood back as Medusa took the seed within her cupped hands and stood before the platform; staring in amazement as the seed began to glow. Ripples of magenta began to weave through its shell, while a radiance made of dark light flowed around it, as she placed it upon its rest at the tip of the column. Medusa felt the crackle of energy coursing through her as she released the relic and took a step back as the light from the lantern above melded with the dark aura.

There was a flash of darkness that befell them like a wave, leaving them dazed. All the girls, except for the blind half-elf, rubbed their eyes to look around in amazement as a vast chamber grew from the emptiness like a growing tendril. The walls, themselves, were much farther than the breach of the outer foundation, confusing their senses. A tall archway opened to a room beyond and they wandered through this new construct to explore its length. A short time later, they crossed an open window that viewed the valley under the moonlight and were amazed to find that they were now several flights higher up the tower, though they had never placed foot upon stair or step.

"A stairless tower," Eve whispered to herself, noting the same magic's she and Cynder had seen from the monolith in Frostfall.

There they found several more chambers and galleries of various designs and functions that unfolded into the higher levels of the tower and open balconies. The sisters were elated to be given the opportunity to see outside to the open world, only to have that small freedom snatched from them. Within the farthest chamber at the pinnacle, they found a single scroll lying upon the topmost balcony which read:

Sisters of the Coven,

This fortress is your new home, built from the last remnants of our ancestral enchantments.

I would bid you not to step foot beyond the standing stones that encircle this refuge, for the cost of this sanctuary is that you may never leave its boundaries, for the arts you have learned are far too dangerous to practice beyond the woven protections of this keep.

Though you will remain in confinement, while within these walls, you will continue your duties as guardians of the Evermore, and to protect our realm from the blight that has befallen our lands and those that lie among the great forest of stars.

The bottom of the parchment was stamped with the Queen's insignia of seven intertwining circles. So this tower of madness was to be their new prison, to be kept safe from contact even with they're own people. It sunk in at that moment, that their individual lives were no longer their own. They would remain in the protection of this tower to work their rituals to battle the Craven and end the withering of this realm. Wherever mankind went, its blight would follow; and they would take measures to cleanse the poisonous decay they left in their wake. Their legacy would be as the unseen warriors of the Faerylands, who would strive to regain the balance their world had lost.

The sisterhood of blood gathered on the chamber floor around the obsidian seed, which became the symbol of their Order. Their mood was dark as they contemplated their fate. Each of the warrior sisters specialized in warfare, both in sorcery and sword; the battle maidens trained to fight beyond the veil of the ether. Pooling their talents, they elected the half-elf as their head priestess for her ability of sight beyond sight, as was the mark of her powers.

Eve and Cynder had survived the trials of the coven, as did Bella and Luna along with Asha and Shira. The other disciples were not so fortunate to have fallen short in their studies; though new recruits would be trained in the time to come, to be initiated into the Order. The sisters began their quest by exploring the mystical tower and all it contained, to aid in their sorcery and martial talents by staff and blade. Medusa had learned well that they should moderate their skills with a measure of patience and wisdom in their art, for theirs was a forbidden practice banned among the elders for good reason.

Contemplating their new prison, the sisters welcomed the opportunity to explore strange and mysterious realms beyond their own for the sake of scholarly learning, and to act as sentinels to protect life wherever they may be called. Medusa frequently sat within her pillowed nook that overlooked the horizon, and took the time to weigh her life both past and present, though she was eventually moved to accept this strange fate separated from the world outside her window. The other sisters of the Order also met similar conflict with their own emotions, and sought balance within their hearts, for they also mourned for the world they had left behind.

They practiced their rituals and honed their arts within the accursed fortress of despair, and ventured out into the netherworlds beyond the doorways in the great gallery. In the flow of time, mankind and its blight became ever more aggressive and tormented the world outside the boundaries of their hidden realm. In a way, the sisters realized that all creatures of the Faerylands had become prisoners to this menace that called themselves Mankind. The noble Elves cloaked their kingdom to protect the World Tree from the poison of Man, while the Drow hid beyond the veil to shield innocent worlds from their encroaching rot.

Those envoys sent to sway mankind from their destructive path were never seen again, although the elven lords tried in vain. Men could not see beyond their religion of death and what it wrought to all beings in the world with which they shared. Their minds were as hollow as their hearts, and the world grieved for this failing. The sisters watched as the landscape outside their tower turned brown and withered, as once lush fields and valleys decayed. Around them, the oceans rose until their refuge became an island of solace, cut off from the rest of the world beyond their broken shores.

Though bleak, life was not without meaning for the Obsidian Order, for they learned the true definition of responsibility besides their individual lives and to care for the countless realms beyond their own. They would encounter creatures and beasts of legend and meet people of mythical lands; and in their maturity, they came to view the forest of stars as a whole. Not a single tree or grove, but as an entire valley that stretched beyond sight as a place where life could flourish,

One evening during her meditations, Medusa received a sending when a blackened butterfly flitted into her chamber. In the light of the tall candles, it came to rest upon the altar by her side. She held out her stained hand to let it climb upon her finger as it fluttered its wings gently, then took flight into the flame of the nearest candle and disintegrated into a sapphire blaze. The Drow Mother had a message of great importance.

Making her way to the outermost hall, she stepped through the single entrance to the tower and to the edge of the cauldron of ash. Along the path of stones approached a priest bearing a sealed scroll as the royal guards stayed behind far beyond its borders. Without a word, the servant of the queen handed the blind priestess the message with a formal bow and promptly returned to the castle below the mountain. With a pinch of ash from the hearth, she rubbed its soot upon the seal to dissolve the glyph that bound it and unrolled the parchment before her.

The contents were disturbing enough and would require the sisterhood to risk their own lives on a return quest to the rainforests of Trinity, at the pleading of their solitary guardian. The oracles had seen that a great tragedy had befallen Akara and his realm and that there was a danger of losing their Tree of Life. Heading this grievous news, Medusa marched back to the tower and convened a council to address this plight.

Shira Snowraven stepped forward with her frost spear to volunteer, followed by Luna Loathsome, with her enormous spiked flail. Eve Elmwood would stay behind to mind the fortress, though Cynder Firestorm with her flaming axe, would not be left behind. Asha Greymoon slowly took a stand to accept this appointment, bearing her twin crescent daggers. Lastly, Bella Bloodthorn strode into the circle with her jagged sickle, its vicious blade as nicked and blemished as her own scarred and bitter face. These five war maidens would accompany Medusa back to revisit the world that she and Kali had once freed of the Craven, or so they had thought.

Though they had battled the blight of the Anatari in the past, Medusa was apprehensive about returning to the realm of Trinity and the horde that had befallen them on their last encounter. All six women donned their armor and made haste to the gallery of gates, and opened a rift door to meet this new challenge. Stepping through the portal, they arrived upon a grim and sun-scorched valley the likes of which Medusa did not recognize. The once blue sky was now awash in red, and the stench of death lingered in the wind that stung her face. Akara's world had been incinerated.

Bloodmire

The bleak landscape was awash in a burnt and smoldering fog that drifted in columns from the valley below. It was a ghastly transformation from the lush jungle that had once thrived here. The blur of vegetation had been replaced by the haze of smoke that drifted over the landscape. The warrior sisters of the Order were noticeably confused as they had heard rumors of its impenetrable green forests and exotic flora.

"Did we open the portal to the correct realm?" Cynder asked, noting the vast damage cast across the scorched terrain. Her companions ventured down the ash-covered path towards the valley floor, while Medusa scanned the horizon with a worried expression creeping upon her face.

"This looks like the same valley, but it's not how we left it..." Medusa trailed off in thought as she spied the remnants of the toppled ruins she had explored during her previous stay.

With their weapons at the ready, they kept an eye out for any lingering wraiths of the Anatari that might be hidden among the blankets of smoke trailing in layers throughout the valley. The half-elf sorceress recognized parts of the landscape and several great trees, which were now but hollowed smoldering stumps. The party made their way through the charred remains of the jungle under the blood-red sky towards the site where the Moon Gate once stood. High above the haze, the three moons were far from entering their conjunction, which left Akara's hidden sanctuary beyond their grasp.

Communication between such distant realms was difficult at best, and they relied on the talents of the Elven seers and oracles to receive such visions and messages from afar. The ruins were coated with the dead brush and layers of soot from a previous inferno that had ravaged the landscape. Their footsteps left a trail in their wake across the burnt tundra, kicking up ash that caused them to choke and cough. Cinder investigated the charred remains from the blaze, as she was the most qualified among them to tell of its source.

"A fierce wildfire razed this valley but it was quick, which would mean that the plant life here had been long dead to be consumed so thoroughly," she noted while patting the haft of her flaming axe. This troubled Medusa even more as she knew the element of fire had been severely weakened in this domain. It was a mystery as to how such devastation could have happened here in this once wet and humid rainforest.

Finding the alcove where Medusa and the Drow Queen had discovered the tablet which described the ancient civilization that once dwelled upon this land, they were startled as they saw something move in the darkness of the chamber. Approaching with caution and her blades at the ready, Medusa saw a faint aura that she found remotely familiar. With a sudden flare, a ball of light erupted from the center of an oval lantern sitting upon the edge of a dry fountain. Beside it stood Akara, his former white purity, now sullied with ash.

"You have come..." he heaved with labored breath as Medusa stepped forward to steady him as he stumbled weakly. The other women lowered their weapons as they approached the wounded guardian, his pale robes tarnished and tattered.

"What caused this?" Medusa inquired with concern to the devastation, while Shira handed her a flask of water to the masked custodian. Taking the flask, he gave but a single sip from the decanter as a strange expression formed upon his lips.

"You did, my beautiful siren," he whispered back with a faint cough. Medusa was stunned by the accusation as her mind milled with the memory of their recent visit to save this realm from the invading Anatari. The guardian explained that the combined magics which had initially drained her had in turn destabilized the balance of the living energy of this realm. It was their act of sapping the water from its natural form of the clouds to wash away the Craven and seal the rift which had ignited a transformation that evaporated the elements from the sky and soil, and tipped their equilibrium towards disaster.

Over time, the rain ceased, the plants withered and died, and fire ravaged this once rich jungle world. The blind half-elf stood in shock, traumatized by his words. A dark shame befell

her as she stood among her sisters, realizing that she and the
queen were responsible for meddling with the delicate balances
of another realm. They had inadvertently destroyed what they
had sought to protect. She could not find the words to beg the
Guardian's forgiveness.

"And what of the living tree; did we...?" the blind sorceress
began to ask with guilt streaming into her voice. Noting the
pain beyond her covered eyes, Akara held on to her arm to help
him stand.

"The Tree of Life for the forests of Trinity has gone dormant,
but its seed must be rescued before the withering fully
consumes its essence, for it is helpless in its current state, which
is why I have requested your assistance once again," Akara
noted with a splinter of broken dignity. Overwhelmed with
regret, she bade the wounded sentinel that the responsibility
was theirs to correct. There was a great rot devouring the
World Tree in the mirror realm and they would need to secure
the seed before it was consumed.

The Moon Gate was out of alignment and Akara himself had
fled to the outside world to escape the decay of the withering.
However, there was another way to reach the tree, which was
through an ancient portal located within the axis of a great
temple built by the lost tribes many forgotten ages ago. It was
the original path from which their shamans drew their power of
this once-thriving world before they were overcome by the
plants and their people had faded from these lands. Beyond the
far reaches of the valley, they would have to track the path to
the remote city that had once been swallowed by the
unforgiving jungle.

Such a quest would have been a far greater challenge to find a
hidden metropolis within the former shroud of the vast
rainforest; however, their task now was beset by the dangers of
this charred and blistered landscape. Akara took what water
was left in the flask and poured it within the dusty fountain
beside them. There, under the light of his mystical lantern, the
water of life glowed with an inner radiance as it came to settle
within the basin. The priestess and her companions gathered
around to see the vision emerging within its shining waters.

"What you see within this scrying pool is called the Spirit Well, built over the sacred site of the living tree that first took root in this world," Akara struggled to say with labored breath, "it is from there that you must seek entry to the hidden sanctuary and retrieve the seed."

The masked guardian stumbled weakly at the edge of the fountain as one of the maiden's helped him rest against the pillars. Medusa tended to him as his breathing became shallow. He reached down into the glowing water of the pool and touched it gently, where droplets of water began to rise up his wrapped arms and weaved across his form, drop by drop. His body shimmered and became liquid as it transformed into water, which flowed back into the fountain as his ivory mask fell free and came to rest upon its rim.

Many of the sisters knew what the metamorphosis meant, for even the mystical fey in the Faerylands transmuted back into the elements from once they came. Upon this world, water was the essence of life for the rainforests that once flourished here. It only made sense that its custodian was one with the elements of this realm. Medusa touched a droplet of moisture upon the stone fountain and touched it to her lips, tasting the purity of the waters that was once their friend.

"We must hurry if we are to harvest the seed before it dies," the blind sorceress noted with urgency as she stood and headed out into the reddish light beyond the sanctuary. She had felt Akara's loss, but it was his sacrifice she understood well, for he had offered himself back to nourish the living seed to give them the time they needed. There was no turning back from this crusade to right this wrong. The war maidens fell in suit behind the half-elf as she made her way outside into the charred landscape and sought the highest peak at the edge of the valley shown within the vision of the ancient scrying pool, which would guide their path to the metropolis of this long lost civilization.

Through the smoldering scrub and shifting ash they wandered across the barren landscape towards the great city. Flecks of tinder floated through the air like red fireflies on a summer night as the scorched land dulled their sense of smell with its acrid stench. Soot clung to their feet and armor while they stood at the pinnacle of a great cliff overlooking the deep valley beyond. There among the enclosed walls stood the remnants of a vast metropolis, once covered in thick foliage of overgrown roots and vines but now lay exposed, littered with charred and smoldering embers left glowing within its dark crevices.

They had rarely seen such wonders, for here stood the remnant memories of a long-dead race. Medusa herself wondered if the palaces of the Elves might one day fall to this same fate should they fail in their quest to save the Faerylands. That thought struck a note with Medusa, who had ties to both worlds of Men and Elves. What they found so breathtaking was that the city itself was housed under a great cage of fossilized bones from the body of some ancient leviathan. As they scanned the frontier, their eyes made out many other such stone skeletons of what appeared to be remnants of mammoth finned beasts embedded within the landscape, revealing that this entire region had once been home to a great ocean.

This made Medusa realize that this world must not have been as young as she previously had been led to believe, or that her concept of time was limited in comparison to that of a living world. If such creatures once thrived in such a grand ocean which had dried out long ago, its elements must have transmuted into the mass of clouds which fed the rich rainforests that had recently grown here. The flourishing jungle, which had once covered the evidence of its ancient past, now lay razed by the fire that had swept across the land and reducing it to ash.

Burnt and decayed vines now hung between the ribs of the megalithic beast like dried sinew that fluttered in the harsh wind. The soft white clouds Medusa had once known were now replaced by blankets of soot that swept like dust storms across the horizon. She suddenly felt small in her meager skills compared to that of a living seed and all its creation; realizing it was far too easy to destroy what took countless eons to create. In hindsight, the Queen was likely correct in relocating their Order to the tower outlying the borders of her Citadel, for their practice of such forbidden magics could be treacherous and unpredictable to create such ruin.

They edged their way down the long path into the charred and broken city; the red sky overhead blooming with an atmosphere of death and despair. This was a cataclysm of their own making by recklessly manipulating elemental balances beyond their comprehension. It was a hard lesson, learned at a high cost.

"Look, the central shrine," Bella announced as she pointed ahead of them where the two cliffs met within the hidden valley. There, a towering spire stood like a giant before them within the cast of shadows, covered with the carved faces of strange and horrible beasts. Among the city ruins, they saw that these ancient architects utilized the hardened bones of these great leviathans in building their structures. All was quiet except for the hot wind whistling through the dead monuments of the forgotten city.

Dragging her scythe across the stone path, Bella disturbed the thick dust hanging from its surface. A soft rustle defined itself into a plume of soot as something sinister stirred behind them as she passed. Luna turned in shock to see a ghostly figure rise from the ash, coated in its flickering red coals. Rattling the chain of her flail, she called to the others to halt while the Sisters spun about towards the commotion.

"Craven!" Shira stamped aloud while lowering her polished spear, leaving a mist of frost drifting from its enchanted blade.

Medusa realized that some of the Anatari must have survived their last encounter and found their way to this distant shrine. More of the wraiths began to emerge from the dust and shadows, each infused with the glowing hot ash from the charred and broken land. They had encountered the Craven in remote areas of other realms before and observed the Anatari had the ability to meld with native elements in a state of flux.

Their touch could sap the life from the living, drawing its energy like a leech. Mankind, itself, had played with such forces before, creating the living dead through Necromancy and other dark arts in their pursuit of immortality. It was an obsession that created horrific mutations and monstrously unnatural creatures that the Elves and their kin were left to seek out and expel from their places of hiding within the secluded crevices of the earth. The Craven themselves were kindred spirits of these types of abominations; haunted by violence and death.

In a sudden attack, one of the smoldering phantoms lashed out at Shira from the length of her cold spear, sending a plume of baked ash towards the priestess, blinding her. Falling back to cover her eyes while choking on the thick soot, the ghostly creature leapt forward upon her drooping spear, using its shaft as a step to vault itself towards her. Coming within a breath of her face, the apparition was cleaved in half by one of Asha's crescent daggers as it spun through the air, embedding itself into the pillar beside them.

Luna entered the skirmish, whipping her flail; its oversized spiked head spinning before its snaking chain, which she flung at one of the ashen wraiths. Her strikes were thwarted as the smoldering shade sidestepped in the wink of an eye just before the massive flail came crashing down in the spot where it had stood. Irate that the phantasm was evading her attacks which shattered the stone ruins at every strike of her chain, the sorceress failed to see Cynder flip her blazing axe in her hand to spin and let it fly where the specter sidestepped the next blow; cutting it clean in half as the ash of its form flared into a blaze from the enchanted flame of her weapon.

Bella stood before a pair of wraiths, her jagged sickle twitching in her hand, with the other, she pulled up a dark orb forming within the cage of her cupped fingers and cast it at the walking shadows. The ball of black light hit one and bounced to the other before it came to rest between them; pulling at them with accelerated intensity. In climatic finality, it siphoned the very essence of the shades together into its vacuum. Bella seemed stunned when her spell dissipated prematurely; leaving what was left of the two specters, which had merged as a single misshapen shadow that lurched towards her on staggered feet.

A few steps behind her, Cynder was struggling to loosen her axe from where it had embedded into a toppled pillar, leaving her directly in the striking path of Luna's flail. Making wild slashes with her scythe to keep the encroaching revenant at bay, Bella tripped over a broken stone and fell while attempting another incantation with her free hand. The monstrous phantom was upon her in an instant, squirming in its grotesque malformation while its glowing cinders burned at her flesh where it clasped upon her shoulder. A horrible scream escaped her lips as black tendrils snaked across her bruised skin where the smoldering horror had struck her.

Upon hearing her companion's cry, Cynder abandoned her attempts to retrieve her axe, only to realize the proximity of the shade atop of Bella was too close for her to use her flame spells against the assailant.

"Cynder!" A voice called from behind her, and Cynder turned to see Asha toss her second crescent dagger for her to take. Catching the handle in mid-air, Cynder redirected its flight towards the wraith, cleaving its malformed head at its base in one spinning motion. The creature stood prone for but a brief moment, then dissipated into the hot wind. Medusa rushed to Bella's side as she lay there in agony, gripping her shoulder.

"Keep still, I'll do what I can to reverse the damage," the blind half-elf assured the injured woman as the other Sisters retrieved their weapons and stood guard, wary of any more wraiths in the area. A lonely wind sifted through the glowing ash, but no more Anatari rose to greet them.

"We should have brought Eve," Shira mentioned as she wiped the soot from her face to clear her eyes. Though they had learned a great many offensive skills, they had done little towards learning the arts of healing as much as Sister Eve had accomplished. Of course, they had no idea they would be walking into this nightmare and were woefully unprepared.

"Can you still walk?" Medusa asked her companion as she examined the horrific wound where a patch of bruised skin felt cold to her touch. Luckily, the contact had been short or it would have likely drained the life out of her entirely.

The half-elf could see with her altered vision that the mark left on Bella's body was pulsating as if it were a mass of ethereal worms writhing against her living aura. A physical tincture might not have any effect. Using better judgment, she had Cynder gently warm the area of the wound, which helped decrease her pain considerably. Though she could still use her scythe, the twitching pain reduced her ability to utilize incantations; though noting that her particular set of skills using void magic seemed to be fairly weak within this realm.

"This domain is in a state of flux and its energies are not what we would expect them to be in our own lands," Medusa warned the others, "we should try to keep primarily to using our martial skills as much as possible until we figure out what is going on," she noted with a frown while realizing she should have at least brought a weapon from their vast armory within their tower before departing upon this quest.

With added caution, they continued their way towards the central citadel which had been carved into the sides of the cliffs where their walls met. The backbone of the mammoth beast passed straight overhead, marked by its ridged vertebra as it curved far beyond the tall spire. Before the entrance was a familiar tiled circle, similar in design to the ruins in the lower valley. What they could not see was the enormous etching of a tree surrounded by clouds marked within the stones upon which they walked, being only visible from above.

On either side of the main entrance, strange mobiles made of bones and skulls of various aquatic beasts hung from dried and tattered ropes. Symbols of death such as these were either placed as warnings or as bordered signposts to sacred grounds. Medusa summoned an orb of light which floated above them as they made their way into the darkened chamber, ever vigilant should they cross any more specters within this shadowy grotto. The ceiling of the passage opened up above, revealing a lattice of giant bones tied upon one another in a grand work of art that resembled a wind chime.

"I hope those strands weren't weakened by the fire," Shira mentioned as she stared up past the tip of her spear to the immense tons of cartilage wavering high above. Precarious as it was, their hollow rattle only mimicked the smaller talismans made of bones that lined the great hall.

"Who were these people?" Luna dared to ask Medusa who was leading their party into this forgotten temple, hoping she would tender an answer.

"We could only decipher what was left behind in their art and images," the blind half-elf related to her last visit to the realm in the company of the Drow Queen, "they were called 'the Gobe' as we might pronounce it, and they too, honored the world tree and the sky. However, it appears this realm once belonged to giants of the sea, if in fact this land was once a domain to a great ocean," she finished to Luna's unsatisfied curiosity.

"I find it interesting that they did not fall prey to worshiping these great sea creatures of their ancient past," Asha proclaimed in reflection, noting that the multiple carvings lining the stone halls gave no reference to such aquatic beasts. Only their bones were left as relics from the past. Her companions realized she was referring to the deities of Mankind.

"Considering their great achievements in building such grand monuments, it appears they did not lose themselves to such illusions. The Gobe chose not to turn their back on the path of life, even if it meant their ultimate demise," Medusa answered, having spent much time recording their history for the Elven scholars, "...a dead god is not much of an immortal deity after all," she proclaimed as she motioned towards the remnants of great skeletons, now used as mere decor.

A world once saturated by water, its richness fed the living seed, and thus, had bloomed many forms of breathing energy. Here life evolved as the waters receded and were transformed into billowing clouds, which gave balance to land and sky; the air and soil becoming one with the rainfall. From this primal state, the plants bloomed as the Gobe enjoyed a time of learning and exploration of this plane. Eventually, they were overrun by the flora until another era had passed and their world was thrown into chaos and unbalance by the meddling of magics. This same analogy was being suffered in their own world by the hands of the humans and their hunger for power.

Entering the rearmost chamber, they came across a great statue, one that represented the branches of their world tree and its curled and twisted canopy. It was a mesmerizing work of art. Flecked with gold, and crystals, and precious stones, it was a centerpiece encapsulated within the six-sided platform that surrounded it from all sides. From its branches hung thousands of talismans representing a hope or prayer from the dream that was once the Gobe people. It was both beautiful and inspiring to view such a monument to life.

"I do not recall this chamber from the scrying which the white guardian had shown us," Cynder remarked as she looked about the room while using her flaming axe as a torch to illuminate the dark crevices. It was a disturbing fact that they were led here but could not find the entrance they were expecting to find. Thinking it could be somewhere at the base of the iconic tree, the Sisters of the coven searched everywhere but to no avail. The portal was nowhere to be found.

Even if they waited until the celestial convergence, there was no guarantee that the Moon Gate would open without the presence of the guardian Akara to guide their way over the bridge of mists, nor could they survive in this environment for long without sustenance or being able to draw strength from the elfire, which empowered their ability to use their mystical arts in such distant lands.

There were multiple antechambers, but they appeared to be nothing more than storage rooms that contained tattered and broken vases. For lack of a central alter within the shrine, the companions searched for clues as to where they should turn from here.

"Perhaps what we are looking for is in another section of the city or a smaller temple," Shira noted with a shrug, as they were not having any luck in their search.

Medusa disagreed with that opinion, since the vision from the fountain had revealed this particular temple and disclosed that there was a gate nearby. Assuming, of course, it was actually within the temple itself. It was that point that got her thinking. Surrounding the statue of the great tree was a shallow inset, which appeared similar in design to the fountain which had contained the ancient tablet. Was the element of water itself the missing key to this puzzle?

They carried a few flasks of water on them but they were of little volume to be of much use. Considering the idea, the half-elf followed a shallow channel that led from the inset rim surrounding the stone tree. She had manipulated the elements before to invoke a torrential rain, but there was an absence of clouds for her to perform such a feat again. It appears they should have had Eve along after all, since she alone had mastered the element of water. This did not bode well for their mission.

"Follow these grooves back to their origin and see what you find!" Medusa proposed to her companions as they set out to find the source of the snaking channels.

She had relied upon her ether vision to be able to see what the others could not, though she did note that a great many of the talismans hanging from the branches of the great tree gave off a strange aura as if they had been enchanted. The gnarled bark etched within the stone tree was deep enough to get a handhold, so she decided to take a climb. The glowing orb of light flitted through the curled boughs to illuminate her way as she climbed higher up the structure until she reached the first of numerous charms hanging as ornaments among its many branches.

Upon closer inspection, they appeared to be engraved discs and cylinders that had been fabricated into resembling oddly shaped leaves. Semi-precious gems and knotted twine were made from the sinew of vines, some woven into patterns akin to dream catchers with bands of metals and bells decorating the canopy as far as she could see. She also noticed there was an absence of any bones used in the array of talismans upon the tree itself. If this was a clue, it still left her bewildered.

"I found something!" Asha called from the edge of the chamber near one of the many statues lining the outer wall. She stood before a tall sculpture of an unfriendly looking beast with fins; likely one of the types of mammoths that had once lived in their ancient past. From its distorted mouth hung a metal bar connected to a chain that disappeared within its gullet beyond the wall.

"So, should we pull it?" Bella asked weakly as they had all stood around for an awkward moment, not knowing what to do. The war maidens looked towards Medusa for direction. She alone would have the ability to see if something was out of place or if there was a curse of sorcery that might expose a hidden danger. Though looking, she saw nothing out of the ordinary. Pulling the chain might open up a chamber and release a horrific beast that might slaughter them all or a poisoned device against which they would have no defense; they had seen many such diabolical traps engineered into sacred temples before. Then again, it might do nothing at all, but if they failed to take the risk they would never know. Determining it was worth the gamble, the half-elf nodded in approval as she climbed down to join them.

"I will trigger the device, but stay by me, Cynder," she noted to the maiden with the flaming axe, "two of you should take a defensive position back by the tree, and another pair near the entrance. We've had enough nasty surprises for one day," Medusa advised.

Shira and Luna took their position at the entrance to the chamber, while Asha and Bella stood by the tree to get a clear view of the room in case they needed to make a hasty escape to the door. The half-elf wanted Cynder by her for her flames in case something unpleasant should rear its ugly head. One could never bee too cautious.

Once they were all sufficiently separated, Medusa took a deep breath and gripped the bar with both blackened hands, giving it a hard pull. The metal chain clanked and rattled as the priestess gave another try, tugging harder than the last as she pulled with all her might. Behind the wall, a faint grinding of stone and metal could be heard echoing from the mysterious cavities beyond the mechanism. When the chain finally gave way, Medusa nearly fell on her rump before the strange statue as she released the handle from its sudden slack.

Cynder looked up and over to the wall to try to hear what was happening to get a clue what they might have triggered. Medusa had been hoping it was a floodgate to a hidden chamber of water or to release a flow from an underground well. What she hadn't expected was the floor to open up beneath her very feet to drop the sorceress into a deep pit. Cynder reached out in despair as she watched in horror as the half-elf tumbled out of sight down the dark shaft. Medusa's screech of surprise was quickly silenced by the consuming darkness below.

The other sisters sprinted to her aid as they warily approached the edge of the deep well, calling after her. The drop down the chute was too rapid for Medusa to cast any spell that might have slowed her descent as she saw the dim light above her disappear in a heartbeat. She had not been prepared for this dilemma and realized this might be her final moment. Instead of the sudden thud of death, Medusa found herself expelled from a crack in the ceiling of an enormous subterranean chamber.

A glowing pool of blue water rushed up to greet her as her body plunged into the wet abyss. Deep below the waters, she held her breath as she glanced around in frantic flashes to find the source of the illumination radiating from a distant source. Even more disturbing was the sight of dark silhouettes of hundreds of creatures, from strange and monstrous fish to bodies that resembled people, suspended in stasis floating beneath the eerie waters. Medusa clawed her way to the surface of the lake in panic, gasping for air.

Her shock of still being alive after such a great fall was replaced by the horror of the countless bodies that floated around her, bobbing across the surface; their skin dark and chaffed. She pushed the corpses away from her in terror as she made her way towards the nearest shore. Climbing out of the waters, she stumbled upon the sight of a vast city in ruins constructed in the familiar design of the ancient temples that lay upon the surface above.

She turned to see something quite out of the ordinary as a raging fire burned at the edge of one of the broken ruins. It hung there, not slowly dancing like the elfire but completely still, as if frozen in time. With curious wonder, she reached out to test its flame but felt no heat. That was when she realized that she felt no chill from the cold waters where she had been dunked, and slowly became aware that she felt no sense of temperature at all. A sudden fright overcame the half-elf that she might now be dead and trapped in a state of purgatory.

Her mind raced to wild conclusions as she replayed the last few moments in her mind. The half-elf wandered the edge of the ruins and into a shattered courtyard, where she discovered several more frozen fires ablaze in dreadful stillness. Smoke hung in the air like a stationary mist, disturbed only by her passing. High above, the ceiling of the cavern was hidden by a dull haze that lit the scene around her with an eerie glow as though she were caught in a nightmare.

Anxiety began to set in as Medusa realized she was likely dead, and would now forever remain in this foreign limbo. It was a horrible thought that gripped her mind with fear. Taking a long moment to settle herself, she thought back on her lessons and to face this challenge with a measure of dignity, for it was all she had left of herself. She looked out over the vast cold sapphire lake filled with the remains of creatures, wondering if they had initially survived as she, only to have drowned themselves as a final escape from this strange and timeless hell.

A great pounding could be felt at her feet that grew in strength as the source of these tremors shambled into view. She was not alone in this accursed place after all. An enormous figure came into focus over the broken walls that surrounded the lone sorceress. A great horned beast strode before her on two legs, it appeared to resemble either a Djinn or a Demon she had studied from the ancient texts.

The being was as tall as a stone giant but had reddish skin and clawed hands; most disturbing of all, was that atop of its head it wore a battle helm that seemed to shift and transform into different designs. It came to a halt several paces before her and knelt down upon one knee to get a better look at the small girl.

"Nom... nomas-tu?" She blurted out with an uncontrolled stutter as she shivered with fear; though trying as she might to retain her composure in this unprecedented situation. The demon just gave a chortled laugh with its impossibly deep voice and chose to remind her where she was rather than answer her summons.

"*Ah-hah*, tiny one, such childish incantations do not work here," he bade the stunned girl who took a faltered step back, "it has been a long time since I've had a guest, and a Ritualist no less..." it seemed to grin behind its armored mask which appeared to change on queue depending on its given mood. Medusa regained her stance and gathered her courage after hearing his remark. Regardless, she still hadn't tested her spells to see if her magics worked within this frozen realm.

"Who ...or what, are you, and what is this place?" The blind half-elf demanded of her monstrous host. The goliath turned to look in either direction as if to chastise her predicament.

"It seems you have entered the Bloodmire, although I don't believe you belong in this place, little witch," he responded coldly with a hint of mirth. The creature was correct about its assumption but the sorceress had little knowledge of this 'Bloodmire' realm. Medusa muttered to herself in deep thought, trying to recall any legends or lore from her studies about such a place. This momentary distraction of her concentration did not go unnoticed by the brooding monstrosity.

"I am head priestess of the Obsidian Order and I demand that you tell me your name, great beast!" Medusa turned with fresh courage.

"What I am, has many names, child of the snake," the creature stood as its war helm changed to a more menacing design with horns and sharp edges, though Medusa seemed a bit shocked that this being knew about her condition. Observing this, the demon continued to press the matter, "Yes, I can see everything that you are, my little viper."

The scarlet-draped priestess suddenly knew she had lost control of the conversation since this ancient being perceived more about her persona than she did of its intentions.

"I need to return to my companions..." Medusa added weakly as she became overwhelmed with confusion while she saw the great steel helm upon its head morph yet again while its red glowing eyes peered from behind its dark slits; its mysterious enchantment forever hiding the face behind the mask.

"That is an easy matter, if you know what to ask," the helmed demon answered to test her character. Medusa could see that this required an offer of service for release out of this accursed place. Looking around, she had never seen such a nightmarish landscape. Smoldering ruins as far as she could see, marred by vast plains and mountains that resembled intertwined bodies.

"What charge do you require for my release from ...from this domain?" The half-elf pleaded as she scanned the horrid image of a civilization locked in its moment of death, as though it were an eternal reminder of its failures. It didn't matter who or what the creatures and people floating in the lake once were; only that they were no longer. It was a scene that smothered her with dread and foreboding.

"A simple task, I would ask in exchange," the beast answered with a puffing of his muscled chest, "I am thirsty, and all you have to do is fill my chalice, and you will be free to go," it challenged.

"I agree," Medusa blurted out before realizing she should have designed her words a bit more carefully, especially so when making a bargain with such a fiend.

"Very good! *Ah-ha-ha*," the demon laughed aloud as the sky rumbled. Reaching beyond her line of sight, it stretched its arm before her, holding an enormous brass vessel that reached much taller than she stood. Medusa immediately regretted her blunt words, "You will now need to fill this cup with the nectar of your crops, which you must grow on your own without aid of enchantments, and when you fill this vessel to its brim, only then will you be set free," the demon offered as he pointed her towards a distant field to begin the burden of her task.

As Medusa tread through the broken path where she was led, a barren field unfolded before her. This deal she had made to regain her freedom went from bad to worse, as she was told she would have to retrieve the seeds of the blistered plants littering the landscape to sow and water on her own.

The sad half-elf had no idea how to be a farmer and cultivate crops, and her burden was further thwarted by the lack of available magics. The creature shambled off into the distance beyond the dark fog, leaving Medusa to her task with neither tools, nor any idea as to how long this venture would take. She gazed out upon the desolate landscape and realized she had failed her sisters in their task to save the realm she had destroyed. Tears streaked down her face as a wave of misery crept over the blind elfling as she considered her fate, and felt the heavy guilt of what she had left behind ...and it took all of her will not to let it consume her.

The Shroud

There were neither stars nor moons to track the skies, nor any sense of day or night within this bleak world as she was trapped within its frozen limbo. Medusa toiled endlessly and gave up long ago on a make-shift calendar. She had cycled dozens of crops, using the pale grapes that grew upon the vines to be crushed and filtered into wine that she poured by the bucketfuls into the enormous brass container that served as the demon's chalice. To her surprise, there came a time when a small child, devoid of its face, arrived upon the doorstep at the shack she had built from the ruins and debris.

It was always never enough, but the level inside the enormous goblet rose ever higher. At first, the half-elf needed to be exceptionally careful not to fall within the chalice, or she would have been forever trapped, for its edges rose far beyond her grasp. The child-like creature was an imp of some kind, though its faceless appearance made it more of a horror to look upon than anything else. Medusa considered that this minion which was so unsettling to look upon, was likely a gestured gift by the helmed demon to act as either a servant, or as a spy, to keep a tab on her progress. Either way, she had this eerie blank-faced serf to help her with menial tasks, though the imp was formed of a strange malady so as to not be able to offer any manner of companionship nor conversation as a relief from the bitter tedium of her toils.

There came a time when she looked into the bucket of wine she had just pressed and saw her covered face through her mind's eye. Her skin was now old and wrinkled and Medusa almost dared to remove the bandages from her eyes to see herself uncovered. A deep sadness overwhelmed her, that her youth was now lost; being only half-elven blood and thus removed from the Evermore, the ravages of age had caught up with her.

She felt old and tired, and even the taint upon her stained

hands had faded. Her magic had failed her long ago and she finally gave in to depression, that with the delivery of this one last pail to the chalice, she would surrender to her fate and end this eternal agony at the bottom of the lake of the dead. With tired bones, she took up her pail and gently patted the small imp to shoo out of her way, but it chose to stand and stare at her with its blank eyes as if sensing her despondence. With labored breath, the old sorceress climbed the ladder she had built to reach its lip and tipped the contents within.

The wine sloshed across its glossy surface, and for the first time, a single drop spilled over its rim to drip down the side of the enormous cup and came to rest upon the dusty soil. With a startle, Medusa looked up as she felt the ground quake and heard the stomping of familiar steps among the forgotten ruins. The great beast approached yet again to the same place where they had made their bargain so long ago. Finally, it arrived, the gleaming war helm of the demon ever-shifting, ever-changing.

"You have done as I asked?" The red-skinned fiend demanded of the withered woman before him, now humbled and broken.

"I have filled your cup, beast. Now I bid that you set me free," Medusa answered with parched breath, dry and weak from her many years of toil.

"It has been nearly one hundred years in the time of your world since you began this task, let us savor your efforts," the great demon spouted as the priestess stood away just as the giant swept up the enormous wine-filled cup. She watched as he brought it towards his lips hidden beneath the helmet, while carelessly sloshing several years' worth of its contents as it came spilling out from his unsteady hand, splashing to the ground. With a single gulp, the entirety of it was gone. The demon stood there for a moment in silence and gave a sigh of satisfaction before casually tossing down the giant urn as it clattered to the ground and reverberated like a giant bell upon the broken ruins.

"And now you will keep your bargain?" The sorceress remarked with a sour tone upon her wrinkled lips, for Medusa had thought long and hard about what kind of life she would be returning to. Was she merely to be left abandoned at the temple on a distant scorched world with no way to return to her realm with the Drow, or was she merely a forgotten memory lost to the ages? She wondered if the Sisterhood survived and if the Craven had been hunted out and eradicated, or if their scourge had overrun and decimated their realm.

It was a harsh reality she would have to face. Without the elfire or the Evermore of the Faerylands to draw her powers from its life-stream, she would be left a weak old woman with nothing but a skillset of meager parlor tricks left to roam a lonely existence. Time had softened her mind, though she kept up her art in combat training, refining her moves and tactics as much as her aged body could handle. With measured grace, the demon answered the elderly half-elf in her tattered red rags.

"I will do so, as promised in our bargain, though I would also offer you a hint of advice in your war against the Dybbuk," the crimson titan granted to the venerable priestess. Medusa was at a loss to this reference, for she had never heard of such a word.

"I'm not sure what you are referring to ...to this, this Dybbuk thing you speak of," the old elfling stuttered with a shrug of confusion.

"Ah, you may not know them by their primal names, for they are the vengeful revenants that spread amongst the realms," the hulking fiend answered as his helm changed into another design less menacing than the last.

"The Craven!" Medusa whispered to herself, the sight of them she had almost forgotten over this past century while lost in this purgatory.

"An odd choice of name for an apparition that knows no fear," the giant responded with an inquisitive tone, "but they are a menace among the realms and a poisonous threat even to my own domain, so I will leave you with this advice to consider; that you should fight one bane with another," the beast granted.

Medusa had heard of the term of fighting fire with fire but countering their blight with yet another made little sense to the half breed but she acknowledged his suggestion nonetheless. With weary impatience, the half-elf charged the demon to continue with her extradition from this realm.

"You have stolen enough of my life, Demon; it is time to

release me from this place!" She bantered with furled lips. Noting her impatience, the helmet of the brute changed as if every phase denoted a certain personality, though each design she had seen it convert to was never repeated. It was a strange mark indeed that this brute bore upon its shoulders.

"Come to the waters edge, little one, lay within its shallows and I shall grant your release," the monster bade as she made her way to the edge of the lake of the dead where she had first come ashore, whereupon Medusa obeyed and slowly waded into its blue waters, "now lie upon your back until you are lifted by nothing but the touch of the waters," he instructed as the great beast followed her a few steps behind.

The old priestess obeyed, but not without a gleam of suspicion; considering the countless number of corpses which lay afloat within the dreadful lagoon. At this point, she would try anything to be released from this limbo, so she waded out until she lost her footing and let herself drift into the ghastly pool. Following the demon's commands, she could barely hear his booming voice through the water which now filled her ears.

"As you are blind, you cannot close your eyes, so I must show you what true death is in order to release you from this place," the muffled voice relayed, and with a worrisome twitch, she was suddenly pulled under as everything around her went as black as pitch.

At first, she wasn't surprised, as such portals experience a delay as their energies collide but the darkness continued to linger. Not knowing what the demon meant by 'true death' – but as the moments stretched on she began to realize to her horror that she was now beyond the realm of purgatory and somewhere far worse. She felt neither heat nor cold, and even her enhanced vision was filled with nothing but suffocating darkness. She had been left in a void deprived of all senses from her body. There was neither light, nor sound, just a blankness with only her thoughts as company. There was nothing left of her but a memory floating in a sea of oblivion, nor could she hear her own screams drowning in anguish.

∞

With a shake, Medusa felt slender arms around her and a strange surge of gratefulness for the touch of a cold stone floor beneath her back. Voices of women, muffled yet familiar, coursed through her thin veil as she coughed up water from her lungs; though unpleasant but still gratified that she could breathe. Her mystic vision returned, slowly illuminating from the smothering void that had once swallowed her. Around her, she could see the blurred forms of her fellow Sisters coming into focus, and Medusa gave a strange smile of relief as she coughed up another spout of water.

"Can you hear me?" Cynder shouted into her face.

"What is she smiling about, she nearly died!" Asha proclaimed as the other war maidens approached the funnel where their head priestess had fallen into the well.

Cynder set her axe close to her and placed an incantation of warming light in the form of dancing flames beside the prone half-elf as she lay there shivering. Giving her room to breathe, it took several worrying moments for the Sisters to get Medusa to sit up and respond. Shaking her head as her talismans jingled, the sorceress checked herself over, noting they were back in the great temple with the stone tree and that her red robes were no longer in tatters. She could see that water was now freely flowing from the base of the statue of the sea serpent where she had once stood.

"What happened, how did you...?" Medusa stuttered incoherently for another moment until she could get back up on her feet. The sisters stood by and steadied her as the blind sorceress regained her strength.

Water was now pouring freely from the well into which she had fallen, and was being funneled through an elaborate labyrinth cut within the stone tiles where it eventually drained into the base of the great tree. Dragging herself over to the flow of water, Medusa gazed into the reflection and saw that her face and arms were no longer withered with age. Her mind spun at the thought of what had happened to her in that frozen world of Bloodmire, wondering if time there did not exist as it pertained to the outer realms. Had it even been real, or had the century she spent in toil been nothing but a prophetic dream? If so, she was muddled and confused about what it all might have meant.

"You fell into the pit below the statue when the floor beneath you gave way," Asha mentioned as Medusa followed the flow of water towards the stone tree, "we thought we had lost you but after several moments the level of the well rose to the surface, and you along with it," she noted towards the blind elfling.

After regaining her senses, Medusa and her war maidens approached the great marble tree and watched with interest as the basin around the immense statue filled with water from the hidden spring. Small pins of light began to glow within the liquid, though their illumination was weak. Apparently, there was still a trickle of magic left in this world.

"What now?" Luna asked, "This doesn't seem to be doing anything," she added with aggravation. There was a sweet ring in the air as they stood in silence, but still no gate or portal opened for them to enter the mirror-realm beyond which Akara had shown to them.

This dilemma got them to consider what they had learned from their teachings during their years with the Coven and of the legends and lore they had studied. Before them stood an effigy of a world tree and its many branches that represented the channels of life, existing together under a single canopy. Soil and water were vital conditions but so was air and light. They looked up towards the high ceiling and the many open breaks constructed in the dome, but the world outside had changed dramatically to mask the sunlight with its acrid haze. This got one of them thinking about the purpose of the great bone mobiles strung above the main hall.

"Maybe those hanging bones are more than just ceremonial decorations," Bella noted as she pointed her scythe towards the entry. That got them to consider that the countless talismans attached to the limbs of the tree might also serve the same purpose. They needed a way to move them.

"Can anyone else besides Eve summon a storm?" Shira asked among them as her own skills were limited to ice and frost. Medusa thought of the time she had used the staff and the Queen's lantern that created a tempest, but they had no such enchanted relics to use in this situation.

"I might be able to help," Cynder offered, "hot air rises the more intense the flame. Eve and I used to practice our spells together when we were training," she mentioned.

"It's worth a try, if you think you can do it," Medusa granted, "attempt to create a wind to get the talismans upon the tree to stir without harming them," she bade the fire sorceress towards the canopy above where they stood.

With a mark of caution, Cynder took a step around the tree and bade the others to back away. With a single incantation, she drew a sigil in the air before her which separated into tiny flaming dragonflies that began to weave through the air. With a motion, she guided them into a swarm that slowly encircled the base of the tree as they sped faster and faster until they appeared to be a single roaring flame. A circle of fire encased the base of the tree as the war maidens felt the cool air rushing up behind them at their feet, feeding the flames before them.

The rising warm air caused the metal talismans to dance and sway until they began ringing like chimes in a summer wind. The sound they made was like a chorus of bells; it was a beautiful hum, like the tinkle and patter of a morning rain in a crystal forest. The force of air became even more violent as the spell reached its climax, and the air in the temple spun up dust and debris as the immense bone chimes in the great hall began to sway. With a thundering clatter, the huge bones knocked against one another with deep resound.

The walls, themselves, felt as if they were moving from their resonance and the statue of the tree itself began to sway. To their amazement, the glittering lights within the basin began to multiply and gathered in brilliance. Cynder eased off her spell as the fireflies dissipated, leaving the tree shaking from the resounding chimes echoing from the hall. The glow at its base became blinding, and with a surge of light it swept up the tree through the grooves of its bark.

Hidden symbols etched within its shell were now exposed by their illumination. It was a dazzling array of light and sound that touched each of them with its entrancing beauty. They stepped back from the platform in alarm as the ground at their feet shifted. The maze of channels where the water flowed began to change as the tiles realigned. When they met in their ordered sequence, a symbol appeared in the base of the platform that glowed with an inner radiance, and to their amazement, the stone tree began to grow taller.

The base of the statue rose as the trunk of the tree extended, revealing a doorway hidden beneath. Medusa smiled to herself, realizing the connection from the myths and legends of many worlds held such similarity to one another. By combining the four elements they had opened the fifth as they saw a void of light open within the hollow of the tree. This was the image Akara had shown them in his scrying pool.

One by one, they entered the gate set within the tree, and as the last of the war maidens passed through the portal, the breeze within the outer chamber returned to its previous calm. The massive chimes hushed their call as did the ring of the talismans upon the canopy of the great tree, and all became still once again within the ancient temple. The chain set within the statue of the sea serpent withdrew with a dull clatter and the water from its spring ceased to flow. The lights in the pool slowly faded and the ivory tree sank once again to its former height, sealing the portal behind them.

Medusa led the way into the netherworld but she did not recognize the realm that greeted them on the other side. The floating islands piercing through the velvet fog were now replaced by a searing blackness of ooze. Rot and decay had replaced the purity that once thrived here. Looming through the haze was the tangle of roots from the inverted tree, no longer a color of pearl but cast in gloom by marred streaks of grey.

The taint of the darkness had writhed up its trunk and into the canopy above, dripping like black rain from the tips of its branches. There was no guardian here to allow them passage over the bridge of light, but they had to find a way to cross the chasm to reach the central fountain where the seed lay in waiting. They had come all this way but there was still one obstacle to pass. Reaching the twin stones at the edge of the gorge, the Sisters of the Order weighed their options.

In their own realm, they could have used the art of summoning to create a passage but their magics here were weakened and obscured. Akara's death had forged more obstacles than they could have imagined. Every spell they tried sputtered and dissolved here in this mirror plane; further thwarted by the decay engulfing this sacred sanctuary.

Medusa placed her hands upon each anchor stone on either side, the way she remembered Kali had done before. However, she had failed to consider the taint she bore from the Frostfall seed that coursed through her touch. Within a foreign realm where such energies were at their most vulnerable, after Medusa had called forth the bridge and placed her palm on each stone to either side, she found that she could not remove them. Struggling to withdraw her hands, the Sisters noticed her plight.

"I can't seem to remove myself from the stones," Medusa pleaded as the blackness from her hands began to bleed its way across the surface of the rock and fill the runes etched within. Luna tried to help her by grabbing Medusa's trapped wrists but lurched back in fear when the taint began to lash at her touch.

"It would be too dangerous to try to remove her," Asha offered to the others, as she had mastered the dark magics and was wary of its ways, "I suggest you let whatever energies have bound you to the stones to run their course, or it may kill you," the war maiden warned.

The half-elf didn't enjoy the idea of risking death twice in one day so she ceased to struggle, even though it pained her greatly to endure this process that felt like the skin was peeling from her arms. Her companions stood helplessly beside her as she blocked the only entrance to the bridge stones across the putrid swamp before them. The level of discomfort she suffered rose to become excruciating as Medusa twitched and spasmed until she could stand it no longer and finally cried out in agony.

Asha held the other war maidens away as she knew that interfering could lead to disaster. There was a melding of energies from two different living seeds, one dying and another that was but a shadow within its host. They had to trust in their training and face the outcome even if it came at the cost of losing their head priestess. Medusa gave a horrible cry as arcane energies leeched from her and coursed into the pillars, being withdrawn against its will. Suddenly, there was a shake of her body and she stood erect as her hands detached from the stones. Unseen underneath her veils that masked her face, her eyes had turned stark white.

A bridge of black light grew out of the stones towards the great tree, snaking its way like growing roots as they wove into one another and grasped onto its trunk. The Sisters stood in awe, not knowing if Medusa had manifested this passage for them in their hour of need or if it was some other force that merely used her as a channel for its own purpose.

"We must cross quickly!" Was all the blind priestess said in earnest, in a voice that was strangely not her own.

Her companions looked at her oddly but agreed that there was no time to waste since the magic of this dying world faded quickly. With swift resolve, they rushed across the narrow bridge while Medusa kept ahead, a black plasma seeped from her hands to the base of the catwalk as she progressed, appearing that the platform of their passage was materializing from her presence. In a trance, Medusa ambled forward to cross the length of the black swamp bubbling beneath them.

They came to a halt halfway across the rift when a primal cry could be heard echoing from across the emptiness. With horrible speed, a great black serpent loomed above the foul waters and disappeared in a heartbeat. It snaked its way closer to the trespassers upon their fragile bridge with added momentum as it dived beneath the clouded waters to arise within reach of the party of warriors. It had an almost beak-like mouth with tentacles stringing from the back of its sleek head; its ebony body was covered with an oily sheen.

Bella was still too weak to cast her void magic to thwart the creature from attacking, for they were still in a precarious spot across the putrid lake. Shira placed her spear to lance the creature should it strike but it was Cynder who had battled a similar creature in Frostfall on their first expedition to another realm. She raised her fiery axe and held out her left hand to guide a fireball at the beast.

The entire length of the creature was hidden under the muck until a large coil suddenly arose and smashed down upon the catwalk behind them, severing its connection with the anchor stones. The walkway jolted but did not fall as the ethereal tendrils continued to weave from Medusa's hands to support their passage. They turned in alarm to make haste towards the base of the great tree but were perplexed as to why the blind half-elf seemed despondent and wouldn't increase her pace. Turning to see Cynder casting her incantation, Asha tried to shout a warning to her, but she couldn't be heard over the shrieks of the monstrous beast.

"No! Don't!" Asha shouted, but the fire maiden hadn't heard her over the commotion of the collapsing bridge and screeches of the swamp serpent.

As her companions rushed ahead, Cynder stayed behind to guard Medusa as she shuffled forward in her trance. Cynder realized that she must protect her since the half-elf priestess was manifesting the bridge, and if she fell, they too, would follow. A ball of glowing flames spun and danced within the cage of her fingers and she thrust the brilliant orb with the flip of her palm towards the black beast. The serpent anticipated the fiery attack and began to sink below the surface with amazing speed.

Cynder had increased her skills as a fire mage and was able to guide the flaming orb towards its escaping target. It nearly connected with the beasts head as it slunk beneath the dark waters just as the fireball hit. Instead of fizzling out, the mystical flame exploded on impact and fanned across the entire lake, fueled by the putrid oil and gasses that bubbled up from below. Asha jumped back, seeing the eruption of flames racing towards her as the other Sisters strode headlong towards the open chamber at the end of the bridge.

The result was far from what she had expected, and her eyes widened as the fire mushroomed out of control. Cynder was attuned to her elemental skills and was immune to such mystical flames; however, Medusa was not. Realizing her mistake, she rushed beside the blind sorceress to form a barrier between her and the firestorm she had created.

Making the situation worse, the foulness dripping from the countless branches of the central tree ignited and migrated from the bog, setting the canopy overhead aflame. As the fire raced through its branches, Cynder erected a shield of heat to counter the engulfing flames with its blowback. She was puzzled why Medusa was in a daze, seemingly unconcerned about this dire turn of events; it was as if something had taken over her mind. Cynder kept pace with the blind half-elf as she made her way steadily towards the other side.

At the base of the trunk, Bella, Shira and Luna made their way to the relative safety of the platform, while Asha tried to return through the flames to help their two comrades left behind. Her powers of summoning were greatly diminished by the sudden unbalance of energies in this netherworld, and Asha Greymoon found herself suddenly stripped of the powers she so relied upon. Tucking her crescent daggers into the belt behind her back, she made a sprint towards the protective bubble which Cynder had formed around their head priestess who was helpless while affected by the hex she was suffering.

"Medusa, can you hear me?" Asha pleaded with the half-elf as she plodded along without concern for the havoc unfolding around them, though she was unable to read any emotion from her masked face.

"I didn't mean to do this!" Cynder began to wail in apology as she kept the heat shield up to protect the three of them.

"There's no use arguing about that now," Asha responded to Cynder over her shoulder, "but we have to get her to move faster without compromising the walkway emanating from her hands," she motioned to the dark energies pouring from Medusa's fingers.

"I have an idea..." Cynder exclaimed over the roaring fire coursing below and raining down upon them. Cynder felt a surge in her elemental powers and enveloped the shield around them and cast this screen to tilt towards the edge of the bridge. The heat, being repelled, thrust them forward along the bridge that was no longer tethered to the base of the stones from which they had entered.

The searing heat from the flames glided them across the bridge which dissolved behind them in their wake, and the sisters helped Medusa as she collapsed once she was separated from the bridge and the dark-ether radiating from her hands dissolved away. Outside of the open platform was a scene of hell itself. If the world topside had been razed, this was a living example of what had devastated Akara's world.

"I understand now..." the blind half-elf muttered aloud to the surprise of the others as she emerged from her trance.

"What happened to you?" Bella asked while the others converged as Medusa gathered her senses.

"It was the residual marking from the world seed which had tainted me when I handled it," Medusa began as she looked at her blackened palms before her, "it felt as if that energy was speaking through me ...somehow communicating with the living seed of this realm that was in distress," she revealed with a discerning twist of her lips.

"That is what I thought might be happening to you," Asha elaborated as to why she tried to stop Cynder from attacking the black serpent, "I actually didn't realize the place would go up in flames as it did," she explained, "but I recognized that blackened creature was not our foe."

"What do you mean?" Shira inquired with a furrowed brow, seeming quite confused at her statement, as were the others.

"This realm is the sanctuary of Trinity's living tree, its system of roots that feed this growing world," Medusa cut in to elaborate, "that serpent was a wurm ...a form of primal dragon that helps to nourish and sustain the elemental balance," she offered as an explanation.

"You mean like earthworms crawling through the soil?" Luna granted as she dragged her flail behind her.

"Much so, just as there are numerous legends from other realms which include such effigies and representations of serpents linked to the Tree of Life from other lost cultures we've studied," Asha declared, "that creature wasn't trying to harm us but to help guide us."

"Then why did it crush the bridge?" Cynder countered to her logic, though she did recall such accounts in her studies of ancient tomes from many such lost civilizations among those recorded in the great library of the Elves.

"It didn't attack us directly, but merely severed the energies from the bridge stones that were sapping its strength to maintain itself," Medusa answered to the stunned group. Turning from their conversation, she suddenly realized that the situation was far worse than they had realized and she made her way towards the central hollow where they had first met Akara and the refuge of Trinity's living seed.

Rushing to the central chamber, they found several toppled lanterns and discovered that the fountain which held the seed was now dry. There the tree sat barren and brittle, its baked roots exposed. Its central roots at its stem were now pulled away from the small egg-shaped seed that rested within its hollow cavity, nearly dead. The sisters felt their shame, for they had meddled in energies beyond their comprehension trying to cure the blight that spread from their world, only to end up destroying what they were sworn to protect. Here, the circle of life was broken.

Reaching into the crevice between the brittle roots, Medusa cradled the seed within her hands, feeling the life from it ebb away. Within moments of removing it from its resting place, the walls of the chamber began to erupt with pustules of strange matter and putrid boils that scarred the surface of all it touched. Gathering close, they awaited the transference back to their tower, but with encroaching dread, nothing happened, and they began to realize that something was terribly wrong.

"The tether is gone!" Shira spouted with distress as they all turned to see the flames churning into the chamber from the opening. The once bleached shrine became blemished with the reeking foulness of the withering.

Something spoke within the half-elf at that moment that no one else could hear, a reminder of the life she had wrought in service to a faceless demon over a century that passed in but a moment. She didn't understand the words but felt in her heart what needed to be done.

"Burn the tree," Medusa ordered towards Cynder, who turned to face the blind elfling, who was visibly perplexed by her statement. She seemed just as confused by the other war maidens by the sudden outburst as to what she was suggesting; considering that within their Order, a World Tree was the most sacred of symbols.

Cynder took but a moment of hesitation, realizing the direness of their situation and the sacrilege she was about to commit. With a spin of her axe, she felt a surge writhe through her body as she cast a magical flame upon the small tree resting within the empty basin. The branches blackened and curled as its core collapsed into a vapor that pooled at the bottom of the dry fountain. With an unearthly cry, the companions turned to see the black serpent crawl in through the opening of the sanctum, its body aflame from the enchanted fire wrought by Cynder's magic.

The Sisters backed away in panic, all except Medusa who stood with the seed held high above her head; cradled gently within her cupped hands before the fiery beast as it loomed before her. It perched there for a brief moment as it reared before the red-clad elfling. The war maidens gasped as it lurched forward towards Medusa, as the flames licking its sleek body grazed past her face. The great wurm abruptly turned and dove headlong into the basin of vapor left by the dead tree, its body transforming into a pool of water. Suddenly rising from the fountain, a circle of light emanated about the room, causing the encroaching stigma around them to withdraw.

"It will only last a moment, step into the light," their half-elf priestess ordered towards the rest of the sisters as they followed in kind. Medusa stepped through last, taking a paused breath to gaze upon the carnage their regretful actions had brought upon this doomed world. A deep sorrow overcame her to see just how fragile such balance was in any realm, and how it could become so readily undone by such utter recklessness; even if committed with good intent.

The sisters of the Obsidian Order fell through the portal, one by one, into the great hall of doors within their tower of madness. There was a somber mood drifting among the warrior women of the Coven as the blazing portal dissolved behind them and finally blinked from existence; the world of Trinity was no more. Medusa left to secure the dying seed within the sanctuary, where it would remain dormant until they could cure the blight of the Anatari from their midst.

She ascended through the stairless tower to the depository

where they kept these relics sealed. The Sisterhood of Blood cleansed themselves from their quest and returned to the central chamber where they convened to discuss the matters at hand. The shroud of silence was broken by the half-elf, who could feel the regret and disgrace lapping between them like a black tide.

"We have secured the relic, though there is another matter at hand that deems further discussion," Medusa bade her fellow companions, "it was regrettable that our interference was the cause of such misfortune to the realm of Trinity and its guardian but the price they paid would have been as dire should the Craven be allowed to spread," the half-elf announced.

Medusa assured Cynder that there was no guilt in her actions, but of those of herself and their own Queen, whose initial misdeeds were the catalyst which led to what had transpired.

"What do we do now?" Bella asked, still recovering from her wound suffered by her contact with the wraith, "By our own hands are we not guilty of being as detrimental as these Craven we seek to purge, if not worse?"

The other sisters nodded as if agreeing to the weight of the accusation. It was a valid question. In a broader picture, were the Elves merely pruning other seed worlds merely to cover their own shame and lack of responsibility for having failed to address the scourge which mankind represented? It was a rumor among the Elves, spoken in hushed breaths, that a war with the race of Men was unavoidable and that they should end their species for the sake of saving, not only our world, but others across the forest of stars. Medusa considered her words with gravity, for it was a thought they could not afford.

"The withering is a state from which these Anatari are but offspring and we cannot presume to influence every realm to act as their saviors. The dream of life comes and goes, but unfortunately, the likes of the Anatari are an unavoidable blight that besieges domains far beyond our own," the blind half-elf denoted to the congregation before her, "having joined with these living seeds myself, their message is that it would be far worse to add to the withering of life, than to curtail it. For of all things, it is the intention of the Elven Lords that we do not wish to become like Mankind, itself," she stated with finality.

Understanding that view, the Sisterhood slowly retreated back to their chambers to recoup from their recent quest. Each of them grieving in their own way for their failure but also learning from their experience and vowed never to repeat such flaws. When the once green world of Trinity tipped out of balance, one element became dominant above the others. This blunder led to the failure of their crusade. In the future, they would have to be more mindful in their tampering with such energies and overextending their self-righteous sense of responsibility.

It was difficult to retain such arcane powers, and they came to recognize why these teachings were forbidden among their people and guarded so preciously. The Sisterhood of Blood were willing outcasts; charged with a burden few would wish to bear. Most Elves came to see Mankind itself, as their enemy, but the sisters of the Obsidian Order, who resided in their tower of solitude, knew wiser. This blight would emerge in any realm or culture wherever there was an absence of kindness and compassion for others, or even the very world on which they lived; for lack of such virtues only breeds war and strife. The Elves did not wish to stumble down such a path, for they would rather die out and fade away into oblivion, rather than diminish into the likes of the accursed Craven.

Tormentor

In the days that followed, the Drow Queen called an audience with Medusa at the steps of their infernal tower, for they were not allowed to leave its grounds within their own realm. Standing at the edge of the guide stones, the Queen mother looked upon Medusa and saw how she had changed and could sense the regrets of maturity weighing upon her shoulders.

"The seers have informed me of the loss of Trinity and its guardian," the queen began with a flat tone, which neither harbored remorse nor blame upon the Sisterhood, "I take it you were able to retrieve the seed?" The dark elf inquired as Medusa sauntered towards the great hearth where the bones and ashes of elves filled its wide pit.

"Yes, the relic was retrieved," the blind priestess began, "...though regrettably, it was our combined attempt to sever the flood of Craven released upon that realm that was the cause of its ultimate demise," Medusa pressed under the stern gaze of the Drow Mother. In consideration of recent events, the blind half-elf scratched away random symbols in the soot layered upon the rim of the pit where she sat, "Many of the sisters are beginning to question the wisdom of removing these living seeds and the right of the Elves to intrude upon the grand forest," she mentioned while waving a hand towards the open sky in her reference to the stars hidden beyond the clouds.

"Our task is the result of many struggles over the countless centuries, sister Medusa," the queen mother cut harshly to remind the half-elf of her relatively young age, "the Craven would kill any world tree and consume its seed as readily as Mankind would abuse its powers," the dark elf clarified.

Still, this noble task placed upon their shoulders did not quell their suspicions that there was some other purpose to securing these relics under the protection of the Elves. An object of such power as creation itself was not theirs to own, even as self-appointed sentinels to preserve them. This was a moment that the Drow Mother had foreseen might come to pass. The seeds of life which had been rescued could also be used as leverage by whoever retained them. Clearly, the Sisterhood had become aware of that fact.

These warrior women had been trained in forbidden arts and drew on powers only written about in legends, and if they turned upon their Elven Lords, there would be little they could do to stop them; though one thing was assured, that the cost of their rebellion would be very high. Elves fighting elves was not the way of their world nor of their standing principles. Considering the current leaning of their conversation, the Queen chose her words wisely in response.

"What right do we have to covet these relics?" Medusa asked bluntly, which was the question the Queen expected.

"We are not the first race to bear this burden, my sister, and fate willing, we will not be the last," the queen offered with solemn grace, "our realm here in the Faerylands is but a small glimmer in time, but it is our duty nonetheless to carry that torch for as long as we are able," the drow mother answered, trying to convey the magnitude of their obligations.

"Before my induction to the Sisterhood, I spoke with the Gaia of our world and was witness to the consciousness of the realms of both the Frostfall and Trinity seedlings," Medusa informed the dark elf who was notably surprised but not entirely shocked at her words, "and I have come to an understanding that these energies ...these very powers we manipulate, will someday be our undoing if we do not reconsider our attunement with nature," the veiled priestess expressed with an aura of warning. This caught the queen off guard, for as far as she was concerned the Drow and the Elven Lords had devoted their lives to living in harmony with nature, not against it.

Kali was not used to being caught unprepared but had to weigh such a claim by the elfling with a measure of regard. The tradition of the Elves was to remain in balance with nature and to follow a creed of benevolence, although admittedly, their sense of mercy had crystallized over the millennia as their race became progressively self-centered and solitary. Their large almond eyes had become blind to their own vanity while treating other races with a sense of loftiness that could be read as conceit.

This turn of the conversation set the Drow Queen aback since the leverage fell on the side of the Sisterhood she had not only trusted but had also placed in control of these sacred relics. The only solace she found was that the crimson-draped priestess she had inducted for her role into the Obsidian Order, spoke not of power but of renouncing its use. Perhaps she had not given the young elfling enough credit in her foresight to see the world in its simplest of forms without the complexity of politics or commanding authority. Elvenkind could return to a simpler way of life, be they in the mountains, or oceans, or fields and live out their days pursuing their true doctrine for living as one with nature, instead of trying to enforce their lofty ideology upon others.

"I will speak with the High Elves about this matter and would ask you to consider the plight our world has fallen into, Sister," the queen responded, "the Craven are an abomination to be driven from this realm and all others that they have tainted. In time, these seedlings will be sown once again when the season comes," she answered prophetically.

"I read a particular tome in the dark library back in the Eternal City before we met," Medusa admitted, regarding the incident that led to her banishment from the hidden refuge of the High Elves, "it was a statement by our Elders that proclaimed: *If you strip human life from this world, you remove sadness*," the half-elf mentioned with concern towards the tall queen standing poised before her, "do you agree with such a concept as its suggests their genocide, my Queen?" Medusa inquired with a tilt of her head as though to exaggerate her concerns regarding the offhanded question. Again, the Drow Mother found herself searching for words she was unprepared to share with a level of candor, but she answered regardless.

"The words of our forefathers help us to navigate our future, not to be anchored by them," Kali offered in retort, "the world of Men place value not on one another but on objects, and thus, would wear their wealth as a badge of superiority over one another. However, poverty breeds despair, because they lived in a world where mere trinkets and possessions defined who they were."

The queen's words struck a note with Medusa, who, unlike most Elves, had lived in the world of men and saw how the destitute were treated so poorly. She had seen how they denoted the idea of property and applied its title to everything possible. The ugly truth was, they found it necessary to do so simply because Man was prone to be selfish and had no sense of equality. They would try to own something that could not be possessed. This sickness was beyond mere greed or vanity, it was an emptiness they had within them, and while they refused to recognize this, it became an empty void they could not hope to fill.

Every elf had food to eat and a place to lay their head, toil was not contributed for payment or for trade but provided through recognition of need, nothing more. Possessions come and go and common respect did not falter where Elves resided. What mattered was their connection to one another and recognition for the gift of life. Medusa had seen so much death and strife in her travels to other lands and she understood well the dilemma that faced both Elves and Men ...and knew they could not coexist as was once hoped.

It was this fundamental difference that placed both the worlds of Men and Elves on vastly different slopes; for what one saw as positions of power, the other merely viewed as roles of responsibility. What Mankind saw as a blurred line, the Elves found clearly defined. If Elves faded and the likes of Mankind conquered the world it would create a stranglehold that would choke the breath from the Gaia. Elves not only fought for themselves but for all life in plant, flesh, or stone; but did this make them some sort of whimsical defenders of the light, or something as equally dangerous? The Sisterhood witnessed the breadth of these arcane powers they tapped unbridled and it terrified them.

The Queen departed back to her citadel, realizing that she could no longer make any request upon the Obsidian Order that would go unquestioned, and this left their field of diplomacy lying on precarious ground. Sense of duty was a double-edged sword when soldiers began to question their cause. The Drow Mother wasn't truly worried that the Sisterhood of Blood would abuse their arts against their own kind, but it was unavoidable to grasp that the warriors she had trained had been tempered into a dangerous weapon rather than a mere tool.

Medusa returned to the tower and sat in solitude for many moons while the sisters of her coven continued their studies and refined their arts. Their last mission had placed far too many of them at risk at one time, and it became clear that their meddling in these raw energies began to take its toll. Separated from the Evermore and refusing further sacrifices from the Drow to refill the Elfire, the Sisters began to age. As their powers grew, their bodies waned at an equal cost.

The High Elves had not lived their long reign without making enemies of their own among the Faerylands. The Dwarven Kingdom viewed their actions during the battle on the isle of Antilla as an unforgivable act of betrayal, one for which all Elves would suffer. Though Dwarves were gruff and short-tempered, their memories were keen and long-lived. In the deep caverns where the Drow had bred their tainted fey known as the races of Orcs and Goblins, they faced ever-increasing resistance against their rule.

The Orcish soldiers were consigned to battle the armies of Men in place of the Elves, and sought their own caves and crevices in which to flourish beyond the reach of their pointed-eared masters. They could not be faulted for seeking their own freedom, for it was the nature of the Fey to resist bondage but its ideology found a different meaning in the chaotic minds of their twisted brethren. Within their brutal circle, it was strength and might that won respect between their clans. Soon thereafter, the races of Goblins and their kindred viewed the Faerie and Elves as weak, which only bred disdain.

The Elven Lords learned too late that their darker children were deserting and proliferating beyond control until the night finally came when the Orcs rebelled. The Elves had conceived a new enemy that resisted the shackles of their authority and there was little they could do to contain them. The Faerie were left to balance what was left of the light, while the Orcish ruled the dark, with the Elves trapped in between their extremes.

This created even greater bitterness between the Dwarves who saw the incursions of the Orcish menace into their underground domains. Soon tensions rose between the factions until the animosity forced a clash between the races. Orcs and Dwarves became embattled to rule the under-earth, and both species turned their hateful eyes towards the Elves with equal contempt. As the High Elves tried to quell the dissent, it became ever clear that their actions had only added fuel to the fire that was consuming their realm.

The Faerylands had fallen into an era of chaos where Mankind had become a lesser pawn in the conflict to restore balance. As Medusa sat in solitary within her tower, so did the Drow Queen who came to realize the margin of her mistakes. In their effort to regain balance, the Elves had furthered its instability. Her only hope was that the Obsidian Order would remain neutral in this epic struggle.

There came a day when one of the Sisters called upon the chamber of their head priestess and laid a cylindrical tube upon an altar behind which Medusa sat.

"We received this object from a messenger beyond the Isle," Eve announced as she addressed Medusa.

The item Eve set before her was a brass container gilded with the bold runes of the Dwarves. This was an interesting twist to relations, considering no word of this came from the Drow Queen herself. The half-elf sorceress took the hammered metal tube and inspected its shell, but saw no residue of harmful magic placed upon it. With curiosity, she snapped open the lid to find naught but a single shimmering candle within.

Dismissing Eve from her chambers, the red-clad elfling closed the thick door to her apartment and turned towards this strange gift she had been presented. Self-evident to its use, she set the butt end of the candle into the center of the stone slab and lit its tapered wick. The wax was embedded with rich flecks of gold and copper that sparkled from within under the light of the dancing flame. It was then that a voice emerged from the flame which grew ever brighter; radiating its words.

"I am Talis Nar from the longhouse of Shatterstone," the deep male voice commanded as the half-elf priestess recognized the family name of Argona, the Dwarven battlemage who had trained her during her trials, "though our grievance over the events upon the isle of Antilla has caused a rift between our peoples, we have considered the rumors that the Obsidian Order is a separate sovereignty and not responsible for the actions of the Elven Lords or their Drow kin," the voice of Talis Nar boomed through the flames as the candled burned fiercely, "your Sisterhood possess the talents to sway the Orcish invaders who have overrun our realm, to depart from our domain and save the lower kingdom from their onslaught. We call upon you and your Order to the gates of Orindale, the wellspring of Kar Nage," and with his last words, the entirety of the candle was consumed.

Medusa sat in silence for a long moment after the last sparks of the candle died out into a thin wisp of smoke, weighing what she had heard. The realm of Kar Nage was at the borders of the Faerylands where the Cliffs of Chaos rose from a vast silver swamp. The lands were ancient and untouched except where the Dwarven race had burrowed into the earth. A plea for help could not be ignored and presented a chance to corral the menace of the Orcs back into seclusion.

The maidens of her Order were no longer under the control of the Elves, who withdrew their prospects to assume such folly. Medusa and her sisters were free to choose their own pursuits towards any ends they ordained worthwhile, though accepting allowances from the Oracles of the Drow. A visit to Orindale would help to relieve the tensions between their factions which had forged a disruption in their crusade against the Craven. However, traveling there presented certain challenges.

Medusa spent the next day roaming the edge of the standing stones bordering the tower, determining what forms of magic were woven into its lattice. This tower of madness was tethered to the netherworld and those beyond but still bound to this realm by fragile strings of which Medusa could see with her altered vision. Those bonds stood as a barrier to the Sisterhood and were attuned to the frequencies of the portals infused within the tower. After many days, Medusa finally returned back to the Tower with a large urn clasped within her blackened hands.

"Eve and Asha, I require your assistance in a private matter," the half-elf requested of her fellow war maidens. The other sisters of their coven were curious as to the cause but knew better than to question the masked priestess openly.

In one of the more extraordinary chambers buried deep within the labyrinth of the tower, the three sisters convened; dressed in their red robes. A great pyre burned within a hearth against a far wall that circled on either side to meet at the doorway. Above them hung several crystal orbs, each aglow and pulsating with their own slow heartbeat. The infusion altar that lay within was used only on rare occasions when battle magic was enchanted into weaponry such as Shira's spear of frost or used to identify strange relics returned from alternate realms. Upon the carved altar, Medusa placed the heavy urn she had ferried through the many twisting corridors and halls.

"I have received a summons from the house of Shatterstone, to travel to the Dwarven realm of Kar Nage," Medusa began with a flat tone. The other two women looked at one another, knowing this was an impossible request.

"There is little we can do," Asha answered first, "for they are likely unaware that we cannot travel within the dimension of these lands," she related with a shrug of apathy.

Medusa, however, turned and tipped the urn onto the great altar where a cloud of fine gray dust glittered with a puff upon its cold stone surface. Both sisters looked upon the powder and were confused as to the composition of the material.

"I believe that we can, with this..." the blind half-elf motioned towards the spill and took a pinch of the soot between her fingers as she let it drift back into the pile, "this is the ash from the central hearth of the elfire," she noted as the two maidens in her presence gave a startle look of distress.

Removing the ash of the former elves who had sacrificed themselves bordered on sacrilege. Though, it was an interesting concept for this powder had never been analyzed for uses in alchemy in all these centuries they had dwelt within these walls. Within the chamber of the Coven beneath the Citadel, they would never have been able to commit such desecration, but now residing within their own tower of solitude far beyond the reach of the Drow, that was another matter entirely.

"What are you suggesting we do with this?" Eve granted with a tone of objection creeping into her voice. However, she was not so unschooled as to realize the possibilities this element presented and its potential uses.

"You excel in the healing arts with the mastery of air and water," Medusa nodded towards Eve Elmwood, "and your talents of a summoner and notable skills in the darker arts will be of relevance in this task," the masked elfling motioned back towards Asha Greymoon.

Nodding in approval of their assignment, the two warriors set to their duties without hesitation. Time was of the essence since they had little time to answer Talis Nar's desperate plea. Many days passed as they worked on the forbidden alchemy to bring a solution to life. Through the study of ancient text and exotic potions, the pair of war maidens eventually called upon their head priestess to rejoin them in the room of enchantments.

"Greetings Medusa," Eve welcomed the masked half-elf as she entered the chamber, where they lay about a great many mortar bowls filled with the remnants of strange concoctions and fragile scrolls that lay scattered upon the floor around the edge of the cell, "I believe we have concocted a solution that will serve your needs," she finished while motioning towards a wide-rimmed bowl filled with a swirling marbled black and grey mixture which excreted the fragrance of sulphur. Beside this bowl sat a pair of unfriendly looking needles.

"You may have heard of a by-gone myth of a spring that welled up from the earth, though it was touched by a single root of the tree of life," Asha granted towards the strange brew.

"So, I am to drink this remedy for its effects to manifest?" Medusa bade her two companions who had worked so diligently to create this tonic.

"Not quite so," Eve interjected.

"As the fable goes, this hidden wellspring was considered the fountain of youth, a well which would reverse the years of age of any being that partook of its waters, thereby a source of immortal life," Asha continued for Eve, "as the legend went, adventurers from many kingdoms across the realms sought out this mystical spring to gain everlasting life. Kings and knights and wizards of old fought their way through dangers to procure this magical substance, only to be thwarted at the very end of their quest by making one fatal mistake..."

"Those who drank from its sacred waters were drained of all life, and so they came to a horrible end knowing not the folly of their ways," Eve interjected to continue the fable.

"So the waters were poisoned and quickened their life cycle," Medusa considered the remnants of the tale she was told, "and I would assume there is a closure to this tale?"

"Yes, head priestess," Eve answered as she gently touched the rim of the bowl while she ran her finger along its edge, causing it to reverberate with a gentle hum, "the waters from the mystic spring were not to be consumed, but rather bathed in."

"*Ah* ...I do recall of another tale where such a feat was accomplished by a warrior who bathed in the blood of a dragon to become invincible," Medusa elaborated to her two Sisters.

"Rightly so," Asha granted, "however, these ashes are but remnants from the elfire, our surrogate replacement for the energies of the Evermore from which we once drew our powers before it faded beyond our reach. What you see before you is a blend of both legends."

"This amount seems a bit small to bathe in," the head priestess concluded with a sign of ambiguity showing upon her tight lips.

"There are particular glyphs that must be affixed to this medicine and woven into its tonic," Asha added as she walked up beside Eve where she stood next to the edged needles.

"This blend will need to be mixed with your blood and used to tattoo the protective symbols upon your body," Asha stated.

The blind priestess paced around the chamber in deep thought as her cohorts waited, for it was not a decision to be taken lightly. Glyphs and wards placed upon one's body were permanent and could affect her control of mystic energies and natural magics in a number of unknown ways that could forever harm or hinder her powers. Once done, there would be no turning back.

Without further word, the masked half-elf removed her robes

and laid down upon the alter, showing full trust to her Sisters of the Order. With great care they began the ritual, drawing the blood from the masked priestess with small incisions to her blackened hands. A small copper bowl etched with runes glowed brightly as a ration of her blood was being drained. Upon withdrawing the chalice, a single drop of Medusa's blood fell upon the altar where it sizzled into a noxious wisp and vaporized.

"Most interesting," Eve whispered to herself as the half-elf lay upon her back, unaware of the reaction.

Utilizing her powers, Eve blended the liquids while keeping the bowl chilled and set upon her task at embedding the intricate runes upon Medusa's body while Asha presented the sacred symbols from their ancient texts recorded among the many parchments and relics within their possession. Eve embroidered the weaving lines and bold forms that channeled up both her arms to merge around her neck. The cryptic writing was interlaced as if it were a shadow of embedded jewelry flowing in its graceful arcane language.

When Eve's work was complete, the marks were dried with the refined ash of the elfire, whereupon Medusa felt a surge of energy swirl within her. Feeling as if she was going to be sick, she suddenly sat up, knocking the ink bowl from the alter onto the floor. The head priestess shuddered as she cramped with hot flashes that snapped in spasms with cold chills. The tattooed runes upon her body glowed as the energies mingled, moving and reconnecting to form new designs. Eve rushed to catch her as she saw the half-elf begin to collapse, yet it was Asha that spoke out.

"Don't touch her!" She warned.

With a final gasp of air, Medusa fainted and fell to the floor in a heap as the glowing runes upon her body faded, now infused into her being. Eve was left distraught, not having predicted such a violent reaction, but it was the essence of the Frostfall seed which blended the mixture and reorganized the arcane text into unexpected scripts.

"The transformation is complete, help me get her up," Asha requested towards Eve as they placed the blind half-elf upon the altar once again and draped her clothes back upon her limp body. Eve placed healing incantations upon her, as Medusa was at first unresponsive. All they could do now, was wait. Asha placed an array of three black candles within the room to absorb any dark energies that lingered, lest they escape into the corridors of the tower to wreak havoc.

"From what we know, the Queen's augers cannot see within the tower but it is best that we conceal what we have done here," Asha suggested to her compatriot.

"I agree, and we should wait until Medusa revives before we reveal this rite we have performed to the other sisters," Eve granted. Asha nodded in approval that she concurred with this precaution before taking further action.

The two sisters secretly tended to their head priestess over the next three nights and bound her body with cloth in a way to hide the markings made by the inked enchantments. It wasn't until the last day when the black candles had fully expired that Medusa came to and was strained from thirst. The real question was if the charms which had been placed upon her would hold up outside of the barriers of the tower. Realizing there was no way to test their theory without risk of being spotted by the royal guard or the Queen's seers, Medusa chose to make her assessment when she reached Orindale.

After instructing her two trusted sisters to clean up and conceal any evidence of the forbidden ritual, Medusa retired back to her chambers to recoup. That evening under the light of a full moon, she stepped out upon the highest balcony, and with a stem of light she gently pinched from a candle, a cocoon formed within her hand. Slowly, it writhed and cracked open as a bright crimson butterfly, as red as the sunset, emerged from its shell. Holding it close, she softly whispered to it and held it aloft before her where the fragile creature fluttered off into the starlit night.

Withdrawing back to her bed, Medusa slept. Her dreams were filled with ecstasy and anguish as she felt herself drifting through turbulent waters, always unable to reach the surface as she struggled for breath. Unable to resist the strain as her body fought for life, her mouth instinctively opened, swallowing in the ethereal waters. Though she choked and convulsed, Medusa found that she needed not the air she so desperately sought in her fight for survival. It was then she discovered that the struggle itself was an illusion.

The piercing pain she had felt was merely caused by her resistance to giving in. She saw her body apart from herself as the inked runes across her body began to glow with a rhythmic heartbeat. She suddenly awoke, feeling a strange unease. Medusa stood and slipped into her sandals before rushing back to the open balcony.

As she gazed out upon the stars and moonlit clouds, a great black shadow lingered that began to grow; the approaching shade widening across the heavens, blotting out the stars. Ever nearer the gloom advanced, threatening to consume her and the tower itself. With a pause, the dark shadow began to take form as glints of light shined across the structure which glided towards her. With a gentle creak, the mast of a great ship came to rest a mere breath from the rail of her terrace.

Lanterns lit one by one across a large vessel that came to moor upon the high tower. A lone figure approached her over the tip of the mast, securing his grasp by a woven rope. A Dwarven emissary wearing chain mail swaggered his way to the edge of her balcony.

"Ay, we received your response, Milady, and here to provide you passage to meet with Talis Nar," the stocky dwarf declared as he offered out his stubby hand.

With a lingering thought back to her dream, Medusa hesitated for but a moment before she took his hand and boarded the floating ship. It was a time to test if the mystic glyphs would allow her to leave the tower once and for all. As she stepped out onto the deck of the great barge lined with ropes and sails, far below them, wards lining the edge of the great Tower glowed hotly before they eventually subsided. For the protective runes dictated that the Sisters may not step from the grounds of the dark tower but they mentioned nothing about flying.

Under the cover of night, the great ark cast off and they sailed through the evening sky to the lands of the Dwarven kingdom at the edge of Kar Nage.

"Can I get you some ale, Lassie?" The dwarf offered while many of his kin manned the flying ship, "just a nip to bide the time until we arrive in Orindale," he proposed with a smile shining through his thick beard.

"No thank you," the blind half-elf responded, "but perhaps you could offer a few details of this venture?"

"Ah, well that be something you need to speak with Talis about, Mistress," he answered as he slowly waved a stubby hand in front of her masked face while wondering how she could see. Medusa learned to ignore such gestures, having become accustomed to her apparent handicap.

"I'm glad he received my sending," the red-draped elfling conveyed out of politeness to carry the conversation.

"Ah, ho, yes, that wee butterfly as red as rubies. You elves and your fanciful magic," he bade, "though if you don't mind me saying so, you don't quite smell like an Elvish," he finished with an awkward sniff at her robes. Though uncouth, the half-elf tried not to be insulted by the tacky gesture.

"And you would be correct," Medusa offered in response, "and what a keen and noble nose you must have," she bade to her short escort, remembering that Dwarves were fond of receiving compliments. The dwarf grinned back at her and rubbed his nose as if to polish it and conceded that it was quite bulbous and magnificent.

The Dwarven emissary directed his tall guest into the main cabin where there awaited a grand display of meats and wine crowded upon an oaken table. Poised upright before her was a knife and fork, each stabbed directly into the wood of the table as her dining cutlery.

"Help yourself, lass," the Dwarf offered with a wave towards the banquet, "Talis spared no expense. You have glazed mutton and pickled pheasant, some pearled crab from the Secret Sea," he mentioned while grabbing a morsel here and there while stuffing them into his mouth, "marbled goose and horned rabbit. Oh, and tigers eyes with almond basted harpy breast, some wonderful opal berries, and smoked centaur rump!" he gleamed back at the sorceress, "It's not actually centaur meat, just a breed of wild boar really," he winked back to her with a whisper through the cup of his pudgy hand, as if he were sharing a secret.

There were mounds of grapes and fruits that were piled among the table but the presentation was mostly focused upon the assortment of meats, which was typical of the Dwarven diet. Though an impressive display of hospitality, her hosts were rather centered on their own views and forgot that Faeries and Elves were mostly vegetarian by nature, except for the wild woodland elves which lived by the hunt. Being half-elf and raised among tribes of Men, Medusa had no such qualms to prevent her from enjoying such a savory display.

Medusa pried her utensils from the wooden table and began to relish the meal set before her, accompanied by her cheery host who helped himself to the delicacies with noted vigor. Declining the barrels of spiced rum and malted ales, she could only manage to get a cup of the lightest of lilac wine since the Dwarves had never considered bringing mere water along as drink. They dined under the warm lamplight as the floating ship sailed through the starry sky and into the furious clouds toward the distant lands of Kar Nage.

"After the unfortunate events at Antilla, you don't seem too upset at me for being an elfling," Medusa dared to raise the question to her benevolent host. The dwarf turned to her as he wiped away a smear of grease and brandy from his lips to answer her while missing several bits of meat left lingering in his thick beard.

"Aye, word has spread of the betrayal those infernal dark elves doled upon our honored brothers and sisters on Antilla, but we don't blame the witches to whom their queen bred and exiled to that accursed tower," he began while downing several gulps of brandy from his tall cup, "Talis is a wise leader and would not shake us wrong to trust you, lass," he gleamed.

It was good to hear that the Obsidian Order was not being held accountable for the actions by the dark elves and could make use of such newfound friends. After eating her fill, the half-elf made her way to the deck of the ship and looked out upon the horizon towards which they were heading. They were sailing directly into a dark swirling cloud that made they're bearing precarious at best.

"Is there any way to avoid that storm?" Medusa asked one of the deckhands who was furiously strapping down the yards. The dwarf yelled back to her over the rising howl of the wind.

"Nay, that be the only way to go," the sailor conceded.

Her red robes fluttered in the approaching gale as she looked into the eye of the storm, noting that instead of reducing the sails, the dwarves were raising them to take full advantage of the wind. Surely, they would be torn asunder if they persisted on this route, and she was bewildered to their course of action.

"Come, we should wait inside," her host approached and took Medusa by her blackened hand to escort her back into the main cabin, "Besides, we still have a course of desserts being served!" He managed to spout with a piggish smile before she fought her way through the breeze and shut the door behind them. Several more dwarves wearing smocks rushed in and unceremoniously carted the platters of meats away, and returned with several trays of candied treats and other bits more questionable.

"Thank you, but I really don't think I could eat another bite," the half-elf pleaded as the dwarf shooed her into her seat while her belly grumbled uncomfortably in defiance.

"*Ah*, hogglewash!" He gleamed while wriggling his little fat fingers before him, indecisive of which morsel he should try first, "*ooh*, rot grubs baked in honey," he cheered as he smacked one of the fat worms into his cheeks, "chocolate bat wings dipped in peppered ooze. Ho-ho! Looky here; toasted griffon toes and sour serpent hair," he paused to savor the tuft of fur as if it was a fine vintage, '*Mmh-mh*, oh my, and a dainty array of butter balls," he finally mentioned while fingering through the sweets.

"Maybe I'll try one of those, what do these butter balls consist of?" Medusa asked cautiously as she plucked one up by her fork while attempting to be polite.

"Oh, they're just balls of butter, in case you get constipated and need a little help to make the meal go down," he remarked while edging up his leg to fart, "...and out!" He grinned for a brief second before diving back into the pile of aromatic snacks.

Medusa pretended to nibble on her sphere of butter while flashing a forced smile back at her host, who was mostly interested in partaking of the bounty at hand. She could have sworn she had already seen him eat his own weight in food, and wondered where he put it all.

The blasting wind buffeted the ship as the lanterns within the cabin rocked upon their hooks. Her host advised that she give it no mind and that they were soon to arrive at their destination. The rolling of the ship got worse until everything seemed to go still all at once as the vessel settled into a sudden calm. Curious as to what was happening outside, Medusa jumped off her short stool and unbolted the door to the cabin. She was greeted with warm sunlight and a cascade of billowing clouds surrounding their golden ship. It was a magnificent vessel bolted of wood and steel adorned with busts of Dwarven kings and other strange beasties.

Looking down over the edge of the rail, she could see that they were descending into a chasm that was encircled by high stone cliffs. The cloud cover touched their peaks as it blocked all view of the horizon. The ship gently spiraled as it plummeted below the rim of the chasm and finally came to rest. Dwarves wearing goggles and bearing elaborate contraptions helped secure the ship with several grappling hooks that came crashing upon the rail; one of which came dangerously close to where Medusa had stood.

"Aye, don't be startled, lass," her host waddled out of the cabin while rubbing his portly belly, "the dock hands know what they're doing," he assured her.

The mooring roped pulled taught and a giant anchor dropped from the bow to land upon the ground with a crash, though its purpose seemed to be nothing more than an absurd amount of overkill. The ship was secured to the harbor while a set of steps unfolded from the ground up towards her, the mechanics of which were fascinating to watch.

"What wonderful magic," the half-elf applauded towards her host as a compliment.

"Ah, not magic, lass, just good old fashion tinkering," he

remarked back while he stepped forward to lead her down the flight of stairs.

Several gruff guards, carrying immensely bulky armor and oversized spears, saluted the emissary and his guest as they departed the pier while they left the sunlight behind and entered a monstrous door as thick as she was tall. Beyond the entry, there were many dwarves in bright robes and soiled aprons running about on various tasks. They were promptly saluted several more times by sentries poised like stone statues at their posts until they reached a central court lined by blazing torches. There, at the middle, stood a gray-haired Dwarf bearing an iron circlet and a worn look in his eyes. He was accompanied by several other stern dwarves surrounding a table and obsessing over several maps stretched upon it.

"*Hm-hm*," the emissary began as he cleared his throat, "Sir Talis Nar, your requested guest has arrived," he bade with a formal bow while he nudged the elfling forward with his spare hand. The elder dwarf with the circlet turned and laid his sight upon the blind half-elf with a note of surprise sparking in his aged eyes.

"I am Medusa, head priestess of the Obsidian Order. How may the Sisterhood of Blood be of service, my liege?" She offered with a curt bow.

Talis approached the sorceress with noted caution, taking in this vision of dangerous delicacy. A woman whose eyes were masked but yet could see, the wrapping of her arms like a mummy yet draped with the suppleness of youth. Her robes seared like burnt rubies and adorned with enough talismans and charms that would make any Magi wet themselves with envy. Yet, she came unarmed, which raised his curiosity.

"Greetings Priestess," he bowed with acknowledged chivalry before offering the elfling to join him at the table, "thank you for accepting our request, I hope you had a pleasant journey to our realm."

"My apologies for the delay, Talis," the blind sorceress answered politely, "there were certain ...preparations to be made before my departure," she finished with mild hesitation.

Looking down upon the maps were several crude drawings on

parchment and pelts that had been pieced together to compile into one master image. Upon this diagram sat several miniature carvings of beasts and dwarves, all aligned at tactical points along a vast system of caves and hollows. Pointing to one side of the map, Talis began his introduction to their dilemma.

"If you could forgive the pleasantries at the moment, Sorceress, we are short of time," he began, "We are here at the outer borders of Orindale, where we have recently suffered an incursion of Orcish troops razing our mines and hamlets scattered throughout this section of our domain. We are here," he motioned to the farthest edge of the map, "and this is where the Orcish have installed their recent camp," he pointed to the opposite side of the make-shift map, "and between us is a tributary where we have had suffered great losses trying to fend off their ranks from breaching the sanctum of Orindale."

"Our casualties have been many and we have little defense against these vicious creatures," one of the soldiers at the war table sighed with heavy heart.

"We have learned that it was the Elves who spawned these vile beasts to embattle the tribes of Men," another weary soldier spat, "can you tell us why they now attack us if not to ignite a war between Elves and Dwarves?" The fat dwarf heaved with passionate disdain in his breath.

"Forgive them for their anger, Priestess, for the slight the Dark Elves branded upon us at Antilla is still felt through our homes across the Dwarven kingdom," Talis conceded, "but there has been a great increase of rogue Orcs turning upon all tribes of the lands beside the humans. It appears the Elves no longer have control of these ...these abominations," Talis seethed as he toppled several of the figurines upon the map with a crass swipe of his hand, "and their numbers are too great; can you help us stop their advance?"

As Talis heaved with a somber tone, a messenger arrived carrying a rolled fur bound by a strip of leather tied with bits of teeth and feathers. With a curt bow, he offered it to Talis.

"A message from the front, sire," the messenger bade before running off to disappear among the countless corridors of the keep. With a thick knife, Talis cut the binding and unrolled the skin upon the table.

"What in blazes is that! It stinks like a mire rat?" The soldier next to him covered his nose as the raw rodent skin flapped open upon the table. The Orcish symbols written within were crude and barely readable.

"They send a challenge," Talis read as he wiped the slime from the freshly peeled skin from his hands, "their leader has called a contest of might to settle this skirmish and demands that we choose a champion for a battle to the death; winner takes all. If we refuse, they will flood through the caverns and end every Dwarf, whether they be man, woman, or child in their wake," he voiced aloud, "signed, the Tormentor."

Battle Magic

Talis set about conferring with his council to this new development and how they should respond, while Medusa was escorted to her guest chambers residing along the outer boundaries of Orindale. The accommodations were adequate, though thankfully, not as cramped as she might have expected as she was much taller than her hosts. Luckily, dwarves had a sense of grandeur in their architecture. Everything about them spoke volumes of a no-nonsense scheme of sturdiness.

 Thick beams and riveted joints were common adornments to their general engineering. This ideology also applied to their weaponry and armor, all of which were forged to take a beating under the most rigorous circumstances. Though stout in stature, they had a tireless energy about them no matter what task they were put at hand. Dwarves were builders and they took pride in their work.

Looking out across the deck of her plush accommodations, the half-elf was pleased to see it had a pleasant view of a small underground river that twisted through its linear course under the spotlight of sunbeams shining through from the narrow cliffs high above. Such openings to the sky were scattered among the underground township of Orindale where homes were half-built into the heart of the stone cliffs. Their blocky design was far removed from the graceful architecture of the Elves, which in itself, told tales of the attitude and manners of the two races. The average Dwarve incorporated reliability in their construction, which was mirrored in their sense of honor.

Even below ground, there was lush greenery where oversized mushrooms and other fungi grew in abundance beside clear springs that twisted through the underground cavern. She could see how they could be happy here, being one with the soil. The earth held riches in the form of ore and their city was rife with such mines, which was how Orindale derived its name. It was, however, a far lesser province compared to the great Dwarven

Kingdom, which was rumored to be an immense floating castle beyond one's wildest imagination.

After debating most of the afternoon, a messenger finally arrived to guide Medusa to the banquet hall where she was to dine with Talis and his crew. Again, the priestess was astounded by the hospitality centered on their cuisine. Clearly, Dwarves worked hard, drank harder, and ate much. There were several taverns within Orindale but these hearty little people chose to eat together in both abundance and a state of festivity.

"Ah, here is our honored guest, come, come!" Talis sparked as he stood from his chair among the countless number of Dwarves. Barmaids and servers carried giant mugs and chalices splashing with every kind of ale under the sun. Fruits and breads and grains were piled beside literal stacks of meats of every aroma. The emissary who had accompanied her on her journey here spotted the priestess from the crowd and made his way over to her table as she sat down.

"Glad you could make it, lass!" He beamed while knocking cups in a cheerful greeting with a nearby dinner guest.

"Why thank you, sir..." Medusa responded respectfully, though she didn't know his name since he had never officially introduced himself. Catching this slight of etiquette, Talis intervened on her behalf.

"You remember Calan Chainbeard, who escorted you on your journey," Talis Nar smiled towards the red sorceress.

"Aye, that be, but he should be called 'Leadbottom' for what he can eat in one setting!" One of his cohorts across the table added, to which everyone chortled in agreement.

"...Or Granitefork," Medusa spouted as she picked up a utensil from the table as if wielding a weapon. The dwarves just gazed at her as if baffled for a brief moment by her comment while the priestess felt the shadow of embarrassment graze upon her; then just as suddenly, all the guests in earshot roared in laughter at her outlandish sense of humor. Cups clattered and brew spilled upon the tables and floors as they smiled as if they were merry simply to have lived another day, to eat another meal, and chug another pint of ale.

"They certainly seem to be in good spirits, considering the

circumstances," the priestess mentioned to Talis, who sat beside her at the banquet hall.

"Ah, that be true," he mentioned with a grin that quickly cooled as he turned his attention, "there have been times of strife set upon us by the infestation of Orcs into these caverns, but the will of our people is strong. Their forces have been committing raids upon our mines and thieving our tools and raw ore but what started off as larceny soon escalated into violence when we sent armed soldiers to stand our ground," Talis filled her in while they dined, "these forays made by but a few of their ilk was answered by swarms of hundreds when we attempted to defend our quarries."

"Have they made any demands before this formal challenge they offered?" Medusa inquired while picking at mere tidbits of food since she was still stuffed from her trip.

"A moon cycle ago, before I sent for your assistance, there was a confrontation at the tributary between both factions while we were on the retreat," Talis answered in a grim tone accompanied by a fistful of mutton, "our guards were escorting our workers from the mines to safety when they were ambushed by a horde of orcs that outflanked them, which resulted in many casualties," he spat.

"What was it they wanted, besides the mines they have already taken?" The priestess added to her query.

"From what we know, the Orcish clans may be burrowers but their skills in smelting and metalwork is crude at best, so we don't think it was the mines they were actually after but the source of water that feeds these underground rivers," Talis answered, "every Dwarf is equal to ten Orcs in a fight, but our sentries were eventually outnumbered."

With that information presented, Talis and his crew continued to eat and drink heartily as they toasted their fallen comrades who were no longer among them. They cursed the foul orcs and their kin, including the Elves who conceived them. Medusa left the hall and retired to her chambers, wishing she could wash off the smell of food and ale from her garments. She suspected there was another motive at hand, which had yet to be revealed as to the reason why these dark fey would covet the estuary. She would wait until morning to discuss her thoughts with Talis, and hopefully, she could introduce a measure of diplomacy to both sides without a further outbreak of violence.

Medusa awoke the following morning which arrived sooner than she would have welcomed. A light breeze drifted through the upper canyon as a light rain began to sprinkle in through the gaps between the high cliff walls. Without prompt, Medusa hurried to meet with Talis and his advisors to address this formal challenge they had received the previous day. As the Dwarves convened, a pair of guards bustled into the meeting as they were escorting a most peculiar guest.

A small round creature with green-tinted skin appeared to be a humorous looking ball of flesh with spindly twigs for arms and legs, and apparently, possessed no neck to speak of. It was an ugly little thing with crooked teeth and beady eyes, and stood smaller than the Dwarves themselves. This was Medusa's first sight of a goblin in person, and she could honestly say that she wasn't impressed. The repugnant creature was ushered forward into the crowd of angry looking dwarves. Talis made a show of his displeasure.

"You leader?" The freakish creature spat with its irritating high-pitched voice.

"Aye, I am," Talis barked back. It wasn't often Dwarves looked downward upon an enemy, and the gesture was more than a tad awkward for them.

"We send challenge, you answer now!" The whiney little imp demanded as its oversized necklace made of teeth rattled while it scratched itself under its soiled loincloth. Medusa admitted that if a Faerie were meant as beautiful and majestic, this creature certainly was the opposite of such regal qualities in every aspect.

Talis looked disgruntled and did not appreciate being told what to do by such a little cretin. He entertained grabbing the nearest axe and cleaving this loathsome creature in two, but that would be a dishonorable breach in protocol, for one never kills the messenger as that was the law of parley. Even so, by the looks of this wretched fellow it was easy to surmise that the Orcish tribes had sent their most expendable member to push their demand upon the lap of their Dwarven neighbors.

"Priestess, if I may ask if you would accompany us to this encounter to help bring a measure of diplomacy to this affair?" Talis inquired to the red draped sorceress. Medusa nodded her approval in response and they assigned a few more guards to accompany them on their trek back to the central estuary.

Talis and his handful of guards followed the green imp as it waddled along through the passages and side routes until they breached the central river. A great roar could be heard flooding through the halls until they strode into the daylight seeping in from the massive gap in the cliffs above. A small field of green sat in the midst of an island of shale covered with thick moss and giant mushrooms that towered overhead. From nearly all sides of the great chamber were drapes of waterfalls that poured into the grotto, cascading down the moss-drenched walls.

The brook it formed bled out into several more underground channels, however, the largest of them opened to one side at the tip of the small clearing where the torrents rushed over the edge to drop into a deep chasm that lay beyond. Flocks of birds could be seen flitting overhead as swarms of dragonflies darted between the mushrooms and sparkling waters. It was truly a beautiful sight, though its vision was left marred by the presence of hundreds of twisted orcs and goblins as they stood perched upon every ledge on the far side of the cavern. Upon entering into their line of sight, they erupted into a loud chant as they banged the butts of their wood spears and clubs against the ground.

"You meet Scorn, you present Challenger. Fight, fight!" The little imp spat with fervent glee as it waddled off ahead of them, bouncing across the stones in the brook and over the moss-filled meadow back to its own kin.

The chanting continued to inflamed levels until a single horn resounded from the cliffs high above. Stepping forward through the crowd of irate Orcs passed a single Elder of their kind draped in coarse cloth and bearing a staff encrusted with jagged spikes. The others stepped out of its way, and those not paying attention were roughly kicked aside by the array of burly armored bodyguards that surrounded him. The Elder crossed the river and entered the green pasture and stood waiting while the tiny imp scurried up to its chieftain.

"Great Scorn, I bring Dwarf! Dwarf come ...I did good, yes?" the wretched gobling cried aloud as it bounced up to the chief and began tugging on his tunic for attention.

With a bitter glare, the Orc Elder snorted in approval as it turned its gaze towards the party of dwarves with their red-draped maiden just as he spun his spiked staff in front of him and bunted the little imp into the air and over the edge of the chasm, as its reward for having become a mild annoyance.

"I am Scorn, Chieftain of the clans of the Black Claw," the elder spat as he opened his robes to expose a chest filled with beaded necklaces and talismans filled with hooked talons from numerous beasts, "Come Dwarf, let us end this," he bade.

His voice was deep and heaved as if struggling for breath, his face covered with black streaks of war paint, seen imitated in its design across the crowd of Orcs and their clansmen which lined the cliffside. His guards wore the crudest of armor, seemingly pieced together from bits of leather, steel, and fur for the purpose of functionality. Answering his call, Talis took a stride forward to address this challenge but Medusa stepped in front of him to block his way.

"I will take things from here," the blind priestess bade as she gestured calmly. Talis looked as if he was about to protest but realized he had surrendered his pride the moment he had beseeched the Obsidian Order for their assistance in this matter. It was time for Medusa to live up to her reputation.

The red-draped priestess stepped forward into the sunlight drifting into the canyon and across the river to face the Orc chieftain. A hush fell over the crowd of orcs as she glided towards the elder and their rattling weapons slowly ceased. Among the Orcs, the color red was sacred and the priestess was flush head to toe in its shade. A murmur arose from their ranks as they watched this single female approach, her eyes covered and apparently blind to their presence.

Scorn, himself, was unmoved, though he did take note of being unable to read her eyes. He saw that this strange priestess bore no weapons, and was irked that the Dwarves would offend him by sending a mere unarmed female to answer his challenge. He snorted in contempt and promised to make short work of this crimson wench after hearing her words. The clamor from his minions faded as Scorn rose his hand to address this challenger to his tribe.

"You accept this challenge in the name of all the Dwarves of Orindale?" He spat while rubbing the sticky filth dripping from a thick gold ring pierced through his fat nose.

"I am the High Priestess of the Obsidian Order, head mother of the Sisterhood of Blood," the blind half-elf responded as the Orc elder looked her up and down, wondering how she could see without eyes, "you have brought grief and strife to these lands and killed Dwarves without cause, and I am here for answers," she bade with a cool tone. With that, the chieftain glared even harder at the sorceress with his beady little eyes, sniffing the air with his oversized nose.

"Hmm, you smell of elf, but not of elf..." he grumbled, seemingly irate at that suggestion, "we do not answer to your kind. We are here to fight for these lands, so Dwarves move away and we take, or they die!" Scorn answered in kind. His bluntness was clear, for it seemed there was no negotiating with this egotistical chieftain. At the mention of the sorceress possibly being an Elf, the crowd of goblins, orcs, and ogres were riled into a fit.

"I do not represent the High Elves, nor do I answer to them either," Medusa answered, which cut Scorn's hateful speech short at the nib, "I am here to discuss this matter how your two tribes might find common ground and let peace prevail," the blind sorceress granted as she motioned towards the Dwarves and Orcs standing to either side of the grotto.

Scorn became miffed that he was attempted to be talked down from a fight by a mere woman as he rolled his shoulders in anger and unwrapped a chain from around his waist. Both ends of the chain were adorned by wicked spiked bars. It was a savage weapon he wielded but slow and clumsy in use. Medusa recognized its tactical faults when she saw it, recalling such from her extensive martial training. The Orc elder stretched out the length of chain before him and grunted in disgust.

"No talk of common ground, this ground belongs to us now," he voiced aloud for all his troops to hear, "Elves bind Orcs in chains; this very chain once shackled Scorn, but now it is a symbol of Scorn's might!" The chieftain barked, speaking of himself in the third person. That being said, the Orc troops began rattling their weapons and banging their shields once again.

This encounter was not turning out as Medusa would have hoped. It was clear that the Orcs wanted a battle, and by damn, they were going to have one. They also held an acute disdain for the Elves, so it was useless to try to sway them in any manner. The High Elves had created Orcs and their kind to be used as fodder for the ensuing conflict against Mankind, being, therefore, quite warlike by nature. Medusa had always wondered at the logic of the elven elders and what they had planned to do with these mercenary Orcish races once they were no longer needed for addressing their hostilities.

"Can you not share these tunnels and lands above and below with our Dwarven brothers?" Medusa pleaded once again towards a course of mediation. Her incessant attempts to downplay the Orcs contest for these caverns apparently riled the chieftain even more, for he began to growl in anger. In turn, he flipped the spiked chain in his hand and struck it into the ground a mere foot from where the priestess stood. However, she did not flinch, which angered him even more.

"Now time for Tormentor, now we end pointless talking!" Scorn shouted in rage. Medusa had almost forgotten that the decree of challenge the Orcs had submitted was signed by this supposed *Tormentor*, and had passed it off as merely their lack of possessing an articulate language. Scorn turned and signaled to the goblins behind him upon the high wall, who in turn, sounded a mighty horn. That was when she realized her mistake in underestimating how devious these Orcs could be.

Several tribesmen quickly stood aside to make an opening at the passage nearest Scorn, and from the darkness beyond several large eyes appeared from the shadows. Tromping into the light of the estuary was a great shambling beast. If one could imagine breeding a wild boar with an immense spider and a hill giant, this ugly monstrosity would be the result of such a union. The creature lumbered across the river on all fours and into the sunlight where it shook the water from its mane, snorting as it sniffed the air.

Medusa was taken aback, having never seen nor heard of such a creature in all of her years of study. Its appearance was that of a giant warthog covered in ritual war paint with a chain wrapped around its neck and torso. Where one might expect its tusks might be, instead, two sharp fangs breached its maw, even more disturbing were the half a dozen eyes placed about its deformed head. It was a grotesque creature that reeked of festering offal mixed with the dank smell of putrid soil as if it had crawled from a rotting tomb.

Its eyes wandered separately until they finally centered upon the blind sorceress. It glanced down at Scorn's chain, which had been used against the vile pet as its training whip, signaling what to attack. There was a clear absence of intelligence in its hollow eyes, being nothing more than a brutish monster of extraordinary size.

This was the Tormentor, the praised champion of the Orcish clans. The beast was battle-scarred and wore the skulls of its vanquished strapped upon its collar as grisly decor. The creature snorted to acquire Medusa's scent, her smell seeming to enrage the creature in the same way it had the Orc Chieftain. Stamping upon the moss-covered stones, it crushed their delicate beauty beneath its massive hooves which had been embellished with bindings of several sharpened tusks and antlers strapped upon its legs, designed so as to inflict vicious wounds upon anyone who got in its way.

The dwarves on the opposite side of the cavern gasped in terror upon the sight of this hellish creature, for it had certainly been armored thus for the purpose to create as much carnage in battle against opponents of their short stature. They had never dreamed such a monstrosity could exist, yet here it was, like a living horror from the depths of the darkest pits.

The priestess knew that faltering now could be the end of her and that the time for conversation was over. The beast lunged at her, and with the tap of her crystal rings, the Priestess flitted backward out of harms way in the blink of an eye like a wisp. The Tormentor came crashing down where she had stood the moment before, shaking its head from dazing itself upon the hard stone beneath the carpet of greenery. The fight had almost been over before it began, and a grim frown formed upon Medusa's lips.

She had never trained to fight such a demon, and she quickly scanned the monstrosity for any type of weakness. It had several eyes, allowing it a wide range of vision. Its body was massive and would likely survive several deep wounds, and its sharp fangs were as long as swords. She was at risk of being gored by the array of bones and antlers tied upon its appendages, its acrid breath was so vile that it could cause her to become overwhelmed by its stench.

Surrounding the river and cliffs above, the mob of Orcs and Goblins watched in glee with wide eyes and cheered at the creature's every move as it trampled a path of destruction across the moss-covered arena. Medusa could not retreat to safety where her Dwarven host stood, for doing so would forfeit the challenge and prompt a deadly raid by these savage tribes. She would have to stop this creature and force their clans to retreat back into the earth. Medusa bolted for the cover of a giant mushroom to collect a moment of respite in order to prepare a defensive spell. The Tormentor rushed once again and slid past her upon the slippery moss as she changed the direction of her lunge towards the canopy of fungus.

Hooting and hollering to have the challenger on the run, the Orcs laughed in chorus. Nearly smashing clean through the fragile mushrooms, the beast came to a halt at a particularly hardened stump and the cluster of pods exploded into a cloud of spores after being rammed by the beast. The Tormentor cringed and pinched its lids as the fog of spores stung its many eyes. Shaking itself free of the momentary haze, it backed away to gain momentum for another charge when the red-draped priestess stepped out from behind the giant stem.

Fire was always a good first offense, and a spray of fireflies fanned from Medusa's left hand as she guided them with the other. The glowing swarm fell upon the beast, blinding it with their flaming wings. Diving into its face, tiny wisps of smoke erupted where they burned into its putrid flesh. The Tormentor grunted in annoyance and backed away momentarily as it was dazzled by the attack but appeared to be mostly uninjured by the small balls of fire as it turned its hateful glare back towards its antagonist.

With surprising speed, the giant beast bolted once again at the bloom of mushrooms she had used for cover, smashing them to pieces. Medusa had barely dived out of the way into the soft moss as thick chunks of fungus came raining down around her. She could smell the beast's fetid breath and it made her feel instantly sick to her stomach. With an incantation, she dug her fingers into the moss before her and a ripple erupted through the field of green; tracing its way towards the monstrosity as it turned to attack once again.

Creeping up through its hooves, the moss grew thicker upon its legs, writhing through the tangle of bones and antlers tightly strapped upon its limbs. This armor only served to assist the greenery to secure its prey within its living vines that penetrated into their mass. The beast, discerning that its legs were now stuck, became agitated and bucked its hindquarters. Unseen by the creature, many smaller goblins ran forward from the edge of the river to assist their champion, helping to cut away at the encroaching vines and moss. Those bold few goblings aiding the wretched beast were either knocked asunder or gored upon its spiked tusks during its antics to free itself as reward for their noble efforts.

Ripping away at the soft flora, Medusa saw that the moss was neither strong nor thick enough to hold such an enormous brute. Water would be her next line of attack, and there was plenty available within this cavern. Looking upon the surrounding cliffs, she noted several waterfalls cascading into the central chamber. Preparing a spell, she fused the energies within the air and was ready to cast them upon the river that curved around them when a wall of flesh came crashing upon her.

Unnoticed during her incantations, the beast had torn itself free of the tangle and rushed the Priestess while she was distracted by her magics. With a bunt of its head, it had flung her far across the field towards the outer edges. Talis and his companions gasped as the horde of Orcs cheered at the spectacle of the red-draped sorceress tumbling through the air. The strike wasn't as painful as the landing itself when Medusa came crashing into the thin layer of moss which covered the loose stone slate lying beneath its fragile padding.

The monstrosity seemed to savor the moment as it honed in on the spot where the priestess had fallen and gathered its strength to make another dash towards its quarry, using its mass like a battering ram. The beast made a horrid sound as it trumpeted a hideous grating whine in victory and lowered its head once again like a stampeding bull marking its prey. Medusa had recovered well from the attack; poising herself to finish her incantation as she spoke to the frequency of the surging waters. Without a relic to concentrate her energies, she felt her power being sapped by the spell that pierced through the flowing waters, which crackled and froze the cascading waterfalls beyond the enraged beast.

Silence rippled through the cheering crowd of Orcs as they saw the river ice-over as the waterfalls solidified. Many of the savages nearest the falls slipped and fell on their rumps, while several more backed away in fear from the growing blanket of frost. The flow of water glazed over to the top of the falls until the force of the incoming deluge overpowered the frozen shafts from above. A thundering boom echoed through the cavern followed by a spray of cold spring water as great chunks broke away from the frozen falls and snapped loose from the cliff walls as they collapsed.

These icy boulders toppled upon the back of the Tormentor as it had prepared to make its rush; crushing it into the ground at its feet. The force snapped several bindings upon its legs and the clumsily-strapped tusks and antlers broke loose from their ties; goring the creature in its soft underbelly. The monstrosity howled with a freakish chatter in its cry of pain and glared back towards the red-draped priestess who stood at the edge of the precipice, where there was no escape for her to turn. As the ice shattered upon it, the creature shook free the frozen shards as the Tormentor fumed and honed its anger towards the half-elf.

The beast charged at her, centering the lone girl in its focus. Like a tsunami of stampeding flesh, the beast fell upon the sorceress. Medusa had no time left to cast a spell, for no incantation could overpower the kinetics of it advance, so she knelt there to face it head-on. As the brute barreled upon her, Medusa faked a lunge in one direction, though her hand, buried deep within the living moss, yanked a tether from her previous spell, launching her out of its path in the opposite direction.

The creature's inertia was too great to compensate for the misdirection as the sorceress dodged the charging behemoth. Its eyes centered on where Medusa had sidestepped and its body spun as its hooves cut through the thin layer of moss resting upon the slippery piles of slate at the edge of the falls. The antlers upon its quarters which had snapped loose from their bindings caught upon themselves, entangling its legs; and the beast fumbled. Tripping upon itself, an eerie chattering howl erupted from its maw as the Tormentor went tumbling over the edge of the chasm and into the dark mists below.

The wild hails and applause spewing from the Orc tribes came to a sudden halt as they watched in disbelief when their champion beast fell into the abyss. The looks upon their twisted little faces were one of dumbfounded confusion as if they weren't quite sure as to what they had just witnessed. Scorn himself looked stunned, his expression was ever more contorted in a state of fluster and turmoil; and with a single spark of realization, he uttered an angered shrill and rushed the priestess who had stepped to the edge of the chasm to look over the edge at the demise of her monstrous foe.

Wailing like a deranged banshee, Scorn strode forward in leaps and bounds across the slippery moss, swinging his spiked chain above his head. When he got within range of the red sorceress, she lashed out with her hand and caught the chain in its spin just above the spiked tip. With a tug of her arm, she snapped the chain towards her. If Scorn had let go of his death-like grip upon the weapon, he wouldn't have been yanked off his feet to skid across the bare muddy slate to follow in the same path of his former champion. As he passed over the edge and into the air, Scorn finally released the chain in shock; an undeniably poor decision which caused him to freefall into the churning mists below.

Back at the edge of the cliffs, Talis issued a deep sigh; realizing that he had been holding his breath the entire battle. The tribe of Orcs muttered among themselves as some wailed in despair at the loss of their chieftain. The code of the Orcs was that might was right, that the strongest rule, and that challenges be honored. Finally, a lone Orcish mage strolled forward as Medusa made her way back to the center of the clearing with their former Elder's spiked chain still wrapped within her grasp.

"You win challenge, you winner; what say you?" The green-skinned imp inquired to the vanquisher. Medusa felt bruised and sapped of all energy but she didn't want to give such an impression to the Orc tribesmen lest they take advantage of her current state of exhaustion.

"It is my wish that you remove your people from the outer edges of Orindale and return the territory and mines you have taken, and that no further harm will come to the Dwarves. Do you accept this truce?" The blind half-elf demanded towards the magi and the crowd assembled behind him. They all nodded in agreement as they respected those more powerful than they.

"Agreed," the stunted magi grumbled, "you must come with us to accept the challengers bounty and formal truce," he marked, though noticing her reluctance, "no harm will befall you, it is code of Orc," he stated with conviction.

Medusa made her way over to Talis and conferred that she must accompany the Orcs back to their camp to accept their rule of honor as the conqueror of their previous chief and to guarantee that they will keep their end of the bargain. Without shame, Talis approached and hugged Medusa with tearful joy, thanking the sorceress for saving his people. Striding off back towards Orindale, he began spouting off preparations for a grand feast in celebration. Before he departed, she handed Talis the spiked chain as a token of their triumph to show his people.

By the time they were done speaking, most of the Orcs had withdrawn to the upper cliffs and only a mere handful remained to escort Medusa back to their camp. She was a little wary of their intentions, but she couldn't appear to be afraid or distrustful and risk toppling the truce she had so precariously won. Making their way through the opposite tunnels, Medusa now retained the previous Chieftains bodyguards as her own chaperones. This was turning out to be an interesting day and she was looking forward to seeing a real Orc campsite. It was a wish she would soon regret.

Through many twists and turns they traveled, it was clear that Orcs had an unusually keen sense of direction underground. They could weave their way through labyrinths and endless mazes of corridors without skipping a beat. Medusa was interested to learn how these creatures had managed to break away from under the oppressive thumb of the High Elves, as it was a single matter of commonality between her and these vile brutes. It would help her Order immensely if she could determine the strengths and weaknesses of these dark fey; especially if they could be won over as allies in their fight against the Craven.

Bypassing several abandoned mines, she saw goblins heaving chunks of ore they had stolen from their previous raids. The Orc camp was a trellis of intertwined ladders and bridges between baked clay pods that were strung throughout the cavern. High upon the walls, many holes had been bored to create rooms and galleries. There was a mash of crudely made baskets filled with bits of bone and metal being crafted into various designs of armor. She wanted to say it was a form of art, though it was anything but artisan.

Through this foul maze they wandered, as the half-naked creatures milled about in self-important duties to keep their quarters in an apparent measure of disarray. At the far end of the encampment, they finally arrived at a hastily built rotunda which was designated for such formal meetings. It was becoming increasingly clear that these Orcish tribes cared not for quality of their food, clothing, or construction, but that such items were merely disposable in their view of life. It made her wonder why the Elves would conceive these creatures with such a lack of insight unless they were truly created to be disposable themselves.

"You sit, you wait," the magi spat towards Medusa, then

quickly waddled away in regret at his own audacity to order her around after she calmly turned her blind gaze towards the little imp. From a ragged tent stepped forth a diminutive sage wearing several talismans who bore a twisted staff. He sauntered with a limp towards the priestess who sat cross-legged on the matted floor, now as tall while seated as was the feeble sage who stood before her.

"You slay our leader, and now you shall take his place as our chief," the sage ordained. This was a turn of events Medusa had not foreseen. She understood that there were certain cultures which allowed such internal advancements but she was neither of Orcish blood, nor could she fathom ruling such vile and lowly beasts.

"I merely answered a challenge to settle a regional dispute between your tribes and the Dwarves whose domain you have invaded without cause," the blind half-elf answered after a moment of choosing her words, "As the victor of this contest, by your own decree, it is my wish that you relinquish the territories you have stolen from the Dwarves and remove your tribes from the borders of Orindale," she finished but the aged and wrinkled sage before her stood poised, leaning upon his staff as if mulling her words and awaiting her to continue. After an awkward moment of silence, she finally had to make the matter at hand clear to the tribal guide, "I have no desire to rule your clan, for I am not of your kind nor do I know of your ways," Medusa embellished, though she didn't fail to see this as a rare opportunity to mold a future alliance, "I would, however, be swayed to appoint a representative in my place ...to say, if perhaps *you* might care to accept this honorable position as the standing Chief?" She gestured to the old crone.

The sage stood there a long while in silence but the dull look in his eyes slowly grew brighter as a hint of a smile, no matter how hideous it appeared through his many broken and rotted teeth, began to wash across his face. The Orcish tribes had a raw, if not fundamental, political structure that had been built on those who were opportunistic. Medusa had opened a way to break that tradition by being a powerful and dangerous sorceress who ordained her own commander in her stead. The sage worked his mind more so than most of his kindred, and was conniving enough to understand what this meant, and how it could elevate his position and control. Orcs and goblins were petty and selfish; in this respect, they weren't so different than the race of Humans.

It took some prying on her part; however, Medusa established why the Orcs had invaded this segment of Kar Nage after having escaped the rule of the Elves. Their battles with the Humans had gone badly, and as they had fought force against force, mankind had evolved its tactics to the disadvantage of the Orcs and their kin. It was when she brought up the threat of the Craven that the old sage withdrew from the discussion; for such phantoms were seen as a pox upon those that opposed the race of Men.

It was a fear which had lingered in the back of her mind for quite some time that was now realized, for the Elves had made the matters worse by spawning a disposable offensive force to fight their battles for them, which only furthered to spread the blight of the Anatari. As the High Elves had birthed the Faerie to heal the lands, so had they created the Orcs as a tool of harm. But weapons can be turned and used against their wielders, and as such, the Orcish became aware of their shackles and chose to revolt against their masters.

To Medusa, this would only be expected as the races of Fey were offended by the very idea of slavery and the Elves had become victims of their own desperation. It was an example of how the Elven Lords had become far too isolated in their view of the world as they pretended to invoke the will of the Gaia at their whim. The priestess of the Obsidian Order did see an inherent need for guardians of these realms, but they needed to take measures not to overstep their self-appointed authority. Such corruption was only a crime if you recognized such a mistake but failed to correct it.

The Orcs and their ilk had the right to be their own people and seek prosperity and freedom by their own hand, but the danger was that in their breeding into violence, one had to suspect that they would be inclined to follow the soiled path of mankind. This fear was also shared in secret by the Elders of the Eternal

City, for they had also realized their folly far too late. So they hid, not only from the likes of Men, but from their own creation. Medusa promised herself that the Sisterhood of Blood would not meet their fate by repeating the same blunders.

In response to awarding the Orc sage as her right-hand and surrogate commander of the Goblin tribes, Medusa was treated to a ceremony of interesting appeal. Female tribal dancers gathered around the platform where torches were lit and a circle of drummers added to the festivities. They wore radical streaks of paint that were woven across their bodies as they moved in rhythm to the dancing flames. A feast of strange meats and fungus was served in her honor as the great warrior who defeated the Tormentor; and near the end of the ceremony, she was presented with a skin-wrapped bundle as a gift.

Medusa parted ways with the Orcs and their Sage, who promised to retreat back into the depths of the realms outside of the high cliffs of Kar Nage, and beyond the domain of the Dwarves. Hoping this would create the lasting peace that Talis sought, the priestess was guided back to Orindale with a procession of Orcs that carried her in a handborne chariot. She let them know this was entirely unnecessary but it would have been an insult to refuse the honor.

Along the way back through the tunnels, several Orc concubines attended to Medusa to mend any wounds she had received from the battle, and adorned her headdress with additional talismans and charms so she may be recognized as nobility among the many Orcish clans across the realm. Taking a bundle of her long hair hanging from beneath her headdress; they wove an intricate braid of wire and beads into its fibers, finally attaching a vicious blade onto the end of her ponytail as a sign of her royalty as a warrior. Inspecting it with interest, the sorceress could see how such a unique weapon could be of use in battle, so she kept the blade as a token.

Arriving back at Orindale, the Dwarves were astonished to see the procession that arrived at their doorstep. Confused guards raised their spears in defense as Talis came running to greet them. Lowering the tribal chariot to the ground, Medusa removed herself from the platform and bade her hosts a safe return, but pressed that they were to be gone by the next new moon that darkened the skies. Assuring the red priestess that her will would be done, the Orcs scampered back through the dark caverns and out of sight; leaving the stunned gaze of the Dwarves washing upon the half-elf as she brushed off her crimson gown.

"The Orcs have promised to return the caverns by the next full moon and never to return," she granted towards Talis, who appeared just as astonished to the ceremonial return of his guest by the pack of decorated Orcs.

"...*Ah*, well, that's great to hear!" He bade towards Medusa and the rest of the surrounding dwarves after the initial shock faded, "now come, let us celebrate with a feast in your honor!" Talis chimed as the dwarves erupted with applause and laughter. Medusa, however, gave a scowl of discomfort as her belly gurgled with the strange cuisine she had been fed earlier by the Orcs hospitality during their ceremony.

All the food and dancing and ale soon became overwhelming, and the blind priestess began to miss the silence and solitude of her tower. Bringing forth the bundled gift she had received from the Orcs, the packaged was laid open to the company of Dwarves at the revival. Lying there within the folds of leather where a pair of enormous fangs, retrieved from the corpse of the great beast known as the Tormentor, which lay broken and battered at the base of the waterfall. These ivory tusks were held aloft in the light and inspected by Talis and his companions in admiration; noted as a trophy of honor.

"Ah, let me give these ornaments to our smithy to be properly cleaned for you before your return!" Talis offered as he rewrapped the bladed tusks and handed them to a courier who rushed off into the maze of halls, which were now alive with the preparations for her feast.

"There really is no need, sir," Medusa answered, "you can keep them if you like."

"Nonsense, you have certainly earned them as souvenirs from your spectacular battle with that savage beast," Talis insisted, "and from this day forward your name will be forever remembered among the Dwarves!" He gleamed, "Come, let us enjoy the festivities and you will be returned to your temple on the morrow," Talis promised with a wide grin that swept across his bearded face. Medusa felt nauseous at the thought of more food, but it might help wash down the odd assortment of hairy fungus and pickled grubs the Orcs had urged her to dine upon in the hours prior. With a weary shrug and a sigh of surrender, the priestess submitted and headed towards the feasting hall where the clatter of drinking horns filled the air. Clearly, this was going to be a long night.

Solitude

Medusa kept quiet as the scene of the banquet unfolded around her while Talis and his men retold the account of her heroic battle with the Tormentor over and over again to the captivated crowd. Half feigning exhaustion, she made an excuse to retire early while the Dwarves pulled an all-nighter at the feasting hall. In the morning, she found dozens of colorful flowers and fungus blooms lying upon her doorstep as a token of the Dwarves appreciation for her valiant efforts against the Orcish intruders. The blind half-elf washed up and gathered her gifts as she made her way to the central courtyard where she met a pair of sentries who escorted her to the dwelling of her host.

Talis greeted her in his welcome room and bade her to have a seat on one of his stoutly built, if not undersized, chairs. With a snap of his fingers, he sent off a guard to retrieve a package from their blacksmiths who had worked through the night at their forge. Addressing her with the pleasantries bestowed by his people, Medusa admitted she was overwhelmed by the gracious gifts left for her as the guardsman returned shortly with a long parcel wrapped in white furs. Laying this gently upon the broad oaken table, he unrolled the pelt to reveal what lay veiled within.

Talis presented to her the pair of blade-like tusks from the Tormentor that she had defeated, which had now been grafted with ornamental handles richly embossed with polished rubies and golden filigree. The tusks had been given a keen edge to them and engraved with scrollwork of bold runes set into its ivory. They were beautiful works of art.

"In honor of your defeat of the Orcs, I had our smiths forge you these exquisite weapons, which are not merely ornamental, mind you," Talis embellished, "for each ivory blade has been infused with silver and iron alloys, which are useful against a range of enchanted creatures and aid in strengthening the full tang from the tip down through the pommel," he gleamed as he took up both swords and scraped the edges together until they sung with a vibrant ring.

"Do these blades also glow to warn when there are Orcs nearby?" Medusa inquired as she tried to read the strange Dwarven runes carved upon the ivory.

"Oh, *ah*, no ...not at all," Talis answered with a perplexed expression to the inquiry, "that would seem a bit impractical as a glowing blade would only bring unwanted attention to you in the dark," he cautioned with a furrowed brow of bewilderment to the absurdity of her question.

"*Hmm*, good point," the half-elf answered as she graciously accepted the gilded sabers from Talis Nar.

With a test of the blades in her hands, she felt the weight and gave each one a flip in the air with an agile spin as Talis stood back with a worrisome grin. With a practiced routine, she had learned from her Blood Elf blademaster, Medusa used the length of the room to dance through a set of deadly moves as the razor-sharp blades flashed around her, finished by a whip of the dagger blade woven into her hair which she used to pluck a fruit from the bowl on the table and flung it into the air before her. Slashing with both blades at eye level, the scissor motion cleaved the soft fruit cleanly in two while the pair of blades rung in the still air. After a silent moment of shock and awe, Talis and the guards nearby applauded with glee; though notably nervous in the presence of the apparently blind elfling who displayed such deadly skills in swordsmanship.

Thin lines lingered in the room which faded in the light as if she had wounded the very air around her. The weapons were longer than daggers, yet shy of being the length of a proper sword; still, they felt good in her hands. Folding the blades across her chest, she bowed with respect towards Talis for this most elegant gift.

"Oh, I'm so glad you like them. They are of the finest quality of our craftsmen," Talis smiled as he reached back into the folds of the white pelt, pulling out a gleaming chain, "and here is the souvenir from the Orc Chieftain, which we had polished and imbued with moonstone dust so as to be weightless in the hands of the wielder," he granted to the Priestess.

Medusa accepted the silvery chain and could see the matrix of webbing infused upon it with her ether vision. It felt as light as a scarf yet the clank of the spiked ends rattled upon the stone floor with an intimidating rumble. She wrapped this upon her waist as the former owner had adorned them and laid the twin blades back within the bleached furs. She then turned to address Talis with the concerns at hand.

"The Orcish tribes will be leaving your realm soon, and I would expect that you will reach me if any future problems arise as I left one of their Magi to act in charge in my stead. It is my hope that their mage doesn't overstep his authority to honor my commands in my absence," Medusa noted.

"I understand you were appointed their new leader according to their tribal law?" Talis inquired as to her transition of authority to the Orc Magi.

"It was merely a diplomatic formality, I assure you," the half-elf answered to be dismissive of her so-called title, "I have no desire to be a Chieftain or Champion, or even an Orc Queen for that matter," she smiled back at him in jest.

"Did you determine why they were invading Orindale to begin with, priestess?" Talis asked for he had an obligation to give answers to his people, for the invasion of the Orcish tribes had been swift and merciless. His fear was that there may be other clans of these cretins beyond her control that may choose to swarm upon these lands, which was a valid concern.

"The truth is, the High Elves conceived the Orcish races as an effort to fight their battles and stave the encroachment of Mankind into the Faerylands, but they had lost control of these wayward children," Medusa offered as an alibi, "now they roam free without restraints and the Elves see them as a new problem in their battle to preserve our future. Currently, orcs and goblins do not directly fight against the Elven races but I fear that neutrality may not last."

"Aye, my people share the Orcs loathing for the Elven Lords, and being birthed as indentured servants to a higher race is no way to live out your years," Talis mumbled with a note of despair, "but those brutish animals have become a scourge upon the Dwarven lands and it is the obligation of the high and mighty Elves to clean up their mess!" Talis barked with contempt; just short of forfeiting his own sense of dignity.

As the priestess wore a full headdress, it also concealed the length of her pointed ears, and no one else was the wiser that she was of half-elven blood. Not that it would have truly mattered to the Dwarves, but they too were prone to heated discrimination between the enchanted races if given the slightest of reasons. Fortunately for everyone, they frequently quelled their pride with barrels of mead and wine to dull their temperament. It was an effective tactic that worked for them as a distraction from dwelling upon their over-bloated sense of honor, while redirecting their energies towards more prosperous endeavors, such as gratifying their hearty appetites.

"The Drow do not share the vision of the High Elves, but we must still keep a vigilant eye on the greater threat of the Craven, which is a menace to all beings which dwell in the Faerylands; whether they be Orcs, or Dwarves, or Elves," Medusa yielded towards Talis to correct his posture, "please share word among your people that the Drow were forced to retreat from the lost battle of Antilla to safeguard the Sisters of our Order who were charged to protect something far more precious than our own small lives, and would be the downfall of all of us throughout the lands if Men and their kin were ever to attain it."

Her words got the attention of the Dwarf, for he began to wonder what this relic might be that hinted upon such power.

"Then perhaps the Dwarves can help you share this burden you bear, should you wish to spare yourselves," Talis offered, but the Priestess could see that the Dwarves had a weakness in character that would eventually lure them into abusing such powers which the living seeds contained.

"I thank you for your generous offer, Talis Nar, but as you can see for your own eyes that the price would be too great and I would forever bear the dishonor of laying such a curse upon your people," the blind half-elf warned with a dire tone lingering in her voice as she motioned to her concealed eyes and disfigured hands.

A silent shudder chilled the stout dwarf as he looked upon her deformation and scars of dark magic, and conceded that he had indeed asked too much. His own honor would be blemished if his people were ever to become marked as she. Though her powers were great, the cost was so dreadful that he dare not pry any further into subjects that were beyond his comprehension or willingness to sacrifice. Dwarves held an instinctual fear for dark magics and their black sorcery, and his arrogant pride quickly withered as he looked upon Medusa and felt a needle in his heart as he pitied her.

"I, I understand, Milady," Talis conceded, "then perhaps it is time to return you back to your manor on the isle of Tyre," he offered. Medusa was enwrapped by his words, for she had not known to what lands upon which the Drow Queen had delivered her citadel; for this is the first time the Priestess had stepped foot beyond the shackles of their forbidden tower.

"Tyre?" She muttered gently with mild interest.

"Why yes, your tower was situated upon the outer keys of a vast chain of islands beyond the cliffs of chaos along the outer frontier," he mentioned as he waddled over to a shelf littered with many scrolls and picked through them in a frenzy until he found the one he was looking for. Placing it upon the table, he unfurled it and weighted down the ends to show the map to the red sorceress.

"It was a great distance our ship traveled to retrieve you from the outer peninsula upon an island we had thought was uninhabited," he admitted to the elfling, "there is a great barrier reef strung along the atoll that trails upon the white sands of the northern savage shores," he pointed to the section of the rough map, "there lurk dangerous beasties in those waters among the moonlit isles," Talis noted with a stubby finger towards the crescent stretch of islands off the jagged coast, "Here, take this with you and the ship's captain will mark down the location of your fortress for you," Talis offered as he rolled up the map for her to take as she accepted the scroll.

"My most gracious appreciation for your gifts," Medusa offered as she took up the ruby-encrusted swords in the wrapped fur, "I express great sorrow for having to part company and to leave the gracious hospitality of Orindale and its people, and having to return to my Order on the lonely isle of Tyre," Medusa offered with a girlish sigh and turned her attention back towards the table where she quickly bound the blades within its soft pelt and took a step towards the doorway.

"...And so your sorrow shall be known and honored amongst our people, Milady," Talis smiled, though the priestess was clueless as to what he meant by that cordial interjection.

Several guards led the way as Talis joined her on her short trek through the grand halls towards the floating ship that moored outside the caverns. These people were lively and pleasant, Medusa admitted, but she had become accustomed to spending a majority of her time alone in her studies while submerged in a sense of serenity and the fragrance of incense, and longed to escape from the chatter of people and the heavy odors of food and ale. As they reached the dock, she was greeted by a crowd of Dwarves that were there to lavish her with exotic flowers and blooms wrapped in ceremonial white and yellow ribbons that slowly turned a shade of crimson by her touch. Talis stepped ahead upon the deck and addressed the crowd below them as the Priestess found herself burdened with several bundles of floral arrangements, and came to stand beside him.

"Our lady Sorrow, master of blades, will be returning to her Order, and we the people of Orindale will always be grateful to our Champion who saved us from the Orcish blight!" Talis shouted to the cheering crowd standing below who replied with excited applause.

He motioned over towards the priestess for her to say a few words but the blind half-elf, with her hands full of flowers and gifts which began to turn a shade of deep magenta was puzzled by the strange title bestowed upon her, so she merely bowed to the dwarves with an awkward smile, while not wishing to insult their customs, and quietly made her way onto the awaiting ship. Her curtness didn't disparage the audience in the slightest, who continued to clap and hoot aloud their goodbyes to the ruby priestess who had saved their people.

Medusa got the chance to lay down her gifts within the cabin, along with a troubled grimace towards the beautiful snow-white wolf pelt, which had also begun to turn a shade of burgundy where she had held it in her overstuffed arms. After the anchor was released, the floating ship began to rise gently through the column of clouds and the captain of the vessel came to inform her of their departure. Handing him the map Talis had given her, he took a quill and ink and charted down the placement of her tower upon the map. In a small way, she felt a little relieved that Calan Chainbeard was not among the original crew to escort her back home to the desolate isle of Tyre, lest he coerce her into yet another banquet of indulgence.

"Thank you, Captain," Medusa addressed the firmed-faced dwarf as he handed back the map, "and I would like to confirm that we will only return under the guise of darkness?" She bade.

"Most certainly, I will make it so," the captain remarked with a click of his heels as he turned towards the cabin door, "is there anything else you need, Milady Sorrow?"

"Why do you address me by that name?" Medusa inquired in a perplexed tone.

"Our lord regent has decreed it so," he answered with a dry tone, though he could tell she was still unclear to the purpose, "it is a matter of tradition, Milady."

"Of course, of course..." Medusa returned with a sigh as she nodded towards the Captain whom let himself out the door.

The tired half-elf wondered how many names she would accumulate over the years from one race or another that she would have to remember; although thinking back to her childhood, she found it oddly distressing that she had somehow forgotten her birth name ...and as she sat in the wood-worn cabin of the ship, that regrettable thought began to worry her so. Had she truly let go of her past so completely that she couldn't recall something so fundamental as her own childhood or was this disturbing condition a result of the intense magics which had been infused into her being? There was a brittle moment of comprehension that lingered within her as she sat there in the light of the glowing lanterns, with the stark and lonely silence only broken by the creak of the ship as it sailed through the clouds. The sorceress wondered if she had been stripped of her identity through all these tests and trials, or was she only coming to the realization that she had none to begin with as her life filled with alternate layers of responsibility and regret.

The voyage back to her tower seemed the longest time she had spent contemplating her past. Without her studies and charms or the sisters of her coven to help pass the time, the solitude she felt grinding upon her felt like an ache that wouldn't subside. Medusa considered the complexity of their dilemma; between the Dwarves, the Orcs, and their amplified animosity towards the Elves, when they should have all been united in facing the common enemy which Mankind had become. The surge of the Anatari, which fed this blight they called the Craven, had grown so far out of proportion that all the races within the Faerylands were at risk of vanishing from this realm.

Even humans, themselves, had carved a mortal wound into their own people, which only furthered to feed this pestilence they had wrought upon the world. The duty of Medusa and her sisters was to prevent this malignancy from its expansion across the realms. She considered the words of the demon which had enslaved her mind during that stint when she was left marooned in that timeless dimension called Bloodmire. How was she to use one bane against another?

At least Demons and Elves had something in common, as both had an annoying knack for speaking in riddles. The grievances held against them by the other races were proving to be justified and only served to dissolve what little was left of these fragile alliances. The Sisters of the Obsidian Order were the outsiders and misfits of Elven society, who could find no real peace nor measure of fulfillment in what could be called a normal life for themselves. They were condemned to an existence without love or companionship, without children or family. When seen from a different perspective, it was certainly a strange and dreadful decision to dedicate ones life to such a miserable existence. In a sudden epiphany, Medusa realized that the deep sorrow she felt by straying from an ordinary and happy life she would never know, was indeed a proper title to bear.

Medusa, the warrior priestess of the Obsidian Order as she was known to her coven, had relinquished her past to serve the Sisterhood of Blood. Sorrow, the blade master, as the champion of the countless mystical races of the Faerylands, would prove her worth to the kin of both Elves and Men. She unwrapped the twin swords she had been given and placed them crossed upon the table before her. Christening one blade as the Race of Elves, strong in their virtues to protect nature, while naming the other saber as the power of Men in their restless dream to be equals among the elves.

Unwinding the enchanted chain from her waist, she laid them between both hilts and contemplated this symbol of herself and these two races as joined. With a crackle of magic, she fused the spiked tips to the pommels of both swords, binding the two ends between a single chain. Two races, always opposed, now forever bound. The blind half-elf considered this unique weapon and held it before her in the light. Medusa realized that with such a weapon she could wield one bane against the other ...a riddle to answer a riddle.

Medusa was startled by a knock at her cabin door and she quickly covered the swords within the cherry-stained pelt.

"Come in," she bade as the captain of the vessel popped open the door.

"Lady Sorrow, we will be arriving at your destination shortly; upon the cover of night as you have bid," the Dwarven sailor bowed to her as she did in kind.

"Thank you, sir," the priestess granted in return, astonished that the time she had spent in contemplation had passed far quicker than she had realized. She would be glad to find herself in familiar settings once again, even if her fortress home had been dubbed by rumor as the Tower of Madness among the people of the Drow.

Stepping out into the cool night sky, the stars twinkled down upon her in welcome. The shipmates tackled the lines and lowered the sails as the craft came to moor and its bow came to rest but an arms-length from her balcony at the summit of the tower. Under the shimmering moonlight, the half-elf carefully stepped across an extended plank with her weapons wrapped in hand. Plopping down onto the balcony floor, she waived at the captain and his crew as they silently launched away and disappeared into the night. The full sails trimming the masts once again, the silhouette of their mystical flying ship cut into the light of the full moon.

Retiring back to her chambers, with a flick of her fingers, the priestess lit the candles and lantern set across the many nooks and shelves lining the walls. Laying down her gifts upon the central table within her cell, the half-elf fell exhausted into her red-draped bed and dreamt the kind of dreams you can only dream about. Her mind was filled with dancing goblins, and giant beasts, and waterfalls as blue as sapphires, of laughing Dwarves and clashing mugs that showered ale. There entered a serene tune of music she could not identify as she flew beneath the twinkling stars and into the moon as a black moth eclipsed the light to smother her in a blanket of darkness.

Medusa awoke with a start and looked about the room in her mind's eye with unease. Daylight now coursed in through the etched windows as a soft breeze touched the bright curtains upon her balcony to bid the passing of the evening into dawn. She had suffered a restless night and felt the weight of the calling of her dreams still heavy upon her shoulders. Upon the rude awakening, the sorceress found resting upon the balcony rail a single black butterfly; it was a calling from the Queen.

A tinge of worry crossed the half-elf's face as she approached this dark sending, knowing that she must answer the hail placed upon her stoop. The Queen knew the workings of the mystical fortress and could be its undoing should she put her mind to it. This could put the entire sisterhood in danger. Medusa had stood up to the Drow Queen before on the measure that the Obsidian Order was a power to be reckoned with, but there was always the matter of their reliance upon the elfire for their preservation and their powers.

Medusa made her way through the tower to meet with Eve Elmwood to inform her of the calling and wanted to know if it might possibly be as a response to her recent absence. Eve realized the consequences of such a confrontation and what it could mean to their future should the Queen Mother choose to resist further cooperation. The Queen needed their Order to perform their duties as sentries against the Craven, but she might also have a limit to her patience should the coven violate the perimeters she had forged towards this venture. If she ever got the impression that the Sisterhood had gone rogue, she might be persuaded to dismantle the tower and sacrifice every sorceress within to the cauldron of the Elfire. It was a substantial risk she had taken on their behalf.

"As far as I know, Sister, the runes tattooed upon you and the incantations woven into their design, that any efforts by a Scry or Seer will become blurred should they attempt to pursue or expose your location," Eve granted to the head priestess in the privacy of their chamber, "I have called upon Asha to assist in this dilemma."

Waiting upon their companion to join them, Eve reexamined the symbols that had been placed upon Medusa's body. With a mark of concern, she noted that several of the runes had changed, which had gone unnoticed by Medusa, as they were hidden beneath the bindings. It wasn't long until sister Greymoon appeared in the chamber and was apprised of the situation they now faced.

"The enchantments placed upon you were designed to camouflage your presence in the outer realm but not within the tower itself," Asha informed the half-elf, "I would assume she noted your return, but might become suspicious if there was no mission to attend to through the portal gates," the sorceress concluded to their head priestess.

"We still don't fully know what arcane weaving's it took to create this structure," Eve concluded as she motioned to the chamber surrounding them, "and we can only hope that she was not aware of the forbidden ritual we performed upon you."

"Regardless, I still have to meet with her to quell any misgivings, and we will cross that bridge when the time comes," Medusa conceded with a heavy sigh, "Thank you sisters, for your guidance," the half-elf offered in gratitude.

"Hopefully, your path will not lead to that crossroad," Eve granted as she and Asha both bowed and departed the chamber.

This led Medusa to make a decisive move and returned back to her chambers, where she accepted the calling by approaching the rail and taking the ebony butterfly into her hands. She redressed herself, making sure that the symbols etched upon her were thoroughly hidden from view. Marching through the tower, she made her way to the ground floor where she sat outside on the edge of the giant hearth, awaiting the arrival of the Drow Queen.

From behind a rocky outcropping, a small procession of royal guards approached, bearing tall lances adorned with banners which fluttered in the wind as the dark queen herself stood in the lead. The sentries took a position at a respectful distance from the standing stones that surrounded the tower as Kali strolled up the walkway to meet Medusa face to face. She had a look about her that was out of character, one of distress which Medusa found disconcerting. Even her posture revealed a sense of agitation, which was difficult to read.

"Good morrow, Priestess," the Queen Mother offered as an open greeting, presenting a measure of courtesy uncommon for her usual character.

"My Queen..." the red-draped sorceress offered in kind with a bow of respect. It was a tense relationship that the two women had fallen into after the sisters of the coven had been condemned to their mystical fortress, far from the subterranean city of the Drow.

"I appreciate you accepting my calling," the Queen granted again with undue politeness, "for we have a matter of urgency to discuss..." she led on with an ever so noticeable shake to her many hands which were clasp upon one another in flustered insecurity. In an attempt to hide this, the Queen quickly folded her pairs of arms in an attempt to conceal the sense of anguish bleeding from her. Medusa had never seen Kali so out of character, which began to fester an aura of uncertainty in the back of her mind. With a nod of agreement for her to continue, the head priestess offered the queen a seat beside her on the thick stone wall which encompassed the great hearth.

"What is this matter of import, Sister?" The blind half-elf pressed while attempting to keep from being lured into a verbal trap that might reveal her recent absence from the tower.

"I have recently traveled through Greymoore to the Eternal City upon the plea of the Elven Lords," she began with noted distraction as if she was searching for the words, "whereupon I was personally censured about the Obsidian Order without the approval of the elven council," the dark queen turned as her red eyes lingered upon the falling sunlight cast across the bleak landscape. One could almost read in her posture that she was unsettled how this island sanctuary had transformed from a once lush enclave towards its current dreary atmosphere. Even the climate here had turned unseasonably chilly over the years.

"The Elven Lords were unaware of the Sisterhood of Blood?" Medusa inquired with a raised brow hidden beneath her mask; which didn't strike her as such a shock.

"The High Elves hold no control over the society of the Drow, but it would be a conflict of strategy to oppose our common goals," she admitted, referring to their protection of the Tree of Life and their battle against the Craven, "but they have voiced their concerns over the dissolution of adjacent realms within the forest of stars and learned of our gathering of these world seeds beyond their sanction," she revealed with a gesture towards the sky, and it was then that Medusa realized that their coven had been forged under the veil of a secret occult among the many clans of Elves.

"The sisters are aware that we practice forbidden witchcraft, but it was our understanding that any impact of our acts within the Faerylands are limited within the protected confines of this fortress," Medusa noted while realizing after she mentioned it that she had been guilty of breaching this shield, by utilizing the banned sorcery during her recent stint in Orindale.

"It has come to their attention that the divergence of our realm has led to a further imbalance of the ether worlds; not only from the intrusion of the Anatari from our domain but that by our interference and uprooting the seeds of these distant realms we were only causing further harm," she confessed. This was a difficult consequence for the Queen Mother to follow, as it was her ambition to protect the living seeds from the Craven, but had in turn, made it appear she was merely withholding these powerful relics for her own ends. The exploitation of the Frostfall seed to create the mystical fortress for the Sisterhood was one such damning example, which no Drow could deny.

"So ...what are you saying, and what does this mean for our Order?" Medusa inquired, not wishing to hear the answer that fell from the Queen's lips.

"They were demanding that the Sisterhood be dissolved," the Drow Mother admitted with a heavy heart.

Covenant

The words the High Elves had chosen were most distressing, for if they deemed the Order of the coven was too dangerous to exist, they would likely call for the execution of every member of the Sisterhood to be fed into the Elfire. The warrior women who had trained them were themselves dangerous adversaries as it was, but as a Priestess of the Obsidian Order, each of the maidens had been taught an assortment of skills and sorcery which were forbidden to practice. The Elven Lords had good reason to hold such a heavy hand, for if any Sister of the Order might decide to turn upon the Elves and their kin, they could become a serious threat to the peace of the realm.

Accounts of such mischievous witches and warlocks were not unheard of, who quickly became a menace when they turned mad with power, and it always came to a messy end. This was why such dangerous spellcraft was retained within the Dark Library in the Eternal City; a brand of which the Drow Queen had illicitly kept secreted within her citadel. As a practitioner of magic, it was a natural urge to be curious about learning the mysteries of the arcane and explore the weavings of the world, but there were those who sought to use such knowledge solely for selfish reasons in their grasp for power. It was this very shade of thinking why the elves were currently at odds with the human race.

The argument to be had, was that the Sisterhood of Blood was the most effective weapon they possessed against the Craven, and the Drow Mother was currently teaching additional recruits to add to the strength of their Order, and as replacements when a sovereign priestess might meet her untimely demise. The forbidden magics the Sisters utilized slowly poisoned them in ways they had not foreseen. This was where the wisdom of the Elders took precedence for the sealing of their hidden library.

Medusa did not wish to expose that she and her sisters had already violated that strict covenant by tampering with magics they had sworn not to exploit. If the Drow Queen or the Elven Lords learned the Sisterhood had found a way to breach the protective wards of the tower, they would certainly be put to death. Soldier or not, the Elven Elders practiced a doctrine that was ingrained into their culture to never abuse power. Those that did were swiftly disciplined and penalized depending on the degree of their transgressions.

To kill an Elf within the living aura of the Evermore was not considered as true death, for their essence would return to the Gaia and be remolded into the world, but dying outside of its reach would either mean the Elfire or dissolution into nothingness. The very idea of such waste is was what the Elves feared most; to live a life without meaning was abhorrent in itself, but to die without rebirth in the Evermore was a genuine terror in their philosophy. True life in a living world was always full of second chances, to always be a part of everything in one form or another, but to be cut from its cycle entirely was a nightmare to be dreaded.

The sisterhood dedicated a great deal of time to the study of the Craven so as to know the face of their enemy and how the Anatari are spawned. In retrospect, the race of the Djinn had abused their natural affinity with magic, which was a circumstance the High Elves did not wish to repeat. The plight of the Craven was another matter, as they were the absence of life, like a cold stone that sucks the heat from a fire. The danger comes from the combination of this dark void and a conscience, one which lingers where none should be and exists without purpose. Nature will always attempt to balance itself when something goes awry, but the Craven were a persistent stigma and it was the Drow Mother who enlightened the blind half-elf to the cause of this recent inquisition.

"We had escaped the clutches of the armies of men who invaded Antilla, but even here on the ragged edge of the world, the Evermore has finally withdrawn," the Drow Mother informed her, "In their realm, centuries have passed and there has finally come a great cataclysm and total decimation of their world of the likes we have so desperately sought to avoid," the dark queen shuddered with the dire knowledge she had learned from her meeting with the High Elves, "by their own hand, Mankind has been blotted out by a great catastrophe and has left a dark storm in their wake.

"What do you mean," Medusa responded in confusion, "wasn't that the conclusion the Elves have been pursuing all this time; a permanent end to the human threat?" She asked.

"No..." the queen answered in a hollow tone that sent a shiver up Medusa's spine, "not like this ...*not like this*," she breathed with a hollow stare towards the cold horizon.

"If the race of Men are no longer a threat, this should spell an end to the conflict and the Sisters of the Order can be released from our bond and be free to pursue our own lives," Medusa contended in a plea to her sensibilities.

"You cannot imagine, child; the situation is now much worse," the queen gestured with a hand to Medusa's shoulder as she turned her eyes towards the mountain that hid her castle below its impregnable granite facade, "Mankind had relentlessly pursued knowledge they were far too immature to handle. They drifted in an existence where the greed of the few outweighed the good of the many, and they brought a tide of death upon themselves and everything they touched," the queen spoke though there was no joy in her breath, only a listless shudder of realizing the precarious future which had now been wrought for them all.

"I ...I am uncertain as to what you are saying," Medusa sauntered on the matter, still naive as to what it all meant.

"You were being trained in the sisterhood to hunt the Craven and to stifle the harm they have done in small checks and balances but now a torrent is coming, a great storm none can escape..." the queen trailed off again with concerning pause, "a sea of these phantoms swirl within the aftermath of this tsunami and I fear we have little chance of surviving this fight," she finished as she attempted to enlighten the half-elf as to the scope of the tragedy.

The Elven Lords had called upon Kali, the warrior queen of the Drow, to inform her of this holocaust and to address the contingency they must face to protect the Tree of Life and the Faerylands from annihilation. Mystical creatures large and small were being evacuated to sanctuaries beneath the earth. Even the High Elves, themselves, were facing having to abandon the Eternal City; it was a time of great despair. Even here, the Drow must find harbor within their sunken castle while the Sisterhood would be left to fend for themselves, relying solely on the very wards that imprisoned them to protect them from this encroaching scourge.

"Why would the Elven Lords wish to diminish our ranks by surrendering their greatest warriors in this battle?" Medusa demanded to know.

"It may be an overreaction on their part, by witnessing the dangers of such powers and what it can do in the hands of but a few. They fear the Craven, but they may fear the Sisterhood even more," the queen granted with a sigh, "it is their deepest dread that the plight that has fallen upon the world of Men might also consume ours. If elf ever turned against elf, it would be the end of the Faerylands and all that we've known."

Medusa finally understood their perspective and felt a wave of guilt for having violated the trust of the Elders and abused the magics for her own ends. The Sisterhood could have very well ignored the plea of Talis Nar and the people of Orindale, and left them to their own devices against the tribes of Orcs, but there was the burden of disgrace they bore towards the slight the Drow had served upon the Dwarves and the Orcish races that were regarded as disposable servants by the almighty Elves; which seemed not only cynical but contradictory to their philosophy. It was this weight of responsibility Medusa and her Sisters would have to balance and choose wisely which appeals from future endeavors they should answer.

Doing good for others was not always right, for there was always unforeseen consequences to answer for. It was a stroke of maturity that Medusa felt strike upon her heart, for she had always believed that if one has the ability to help someone, then why would you not do so? Now there encroached a looming darkness that imperiled every living being in the lands of the Faery, and it would take those who were willing to face the struggle to persevere, rather than those who merely draft others to face their hardships for them.

The two women parted, one back to her castle and the other to her prison fortress; each wondering what the future would hold. The Drow Queen promised to debate the desperate need for the Obsidian Order in spite of the fears the Elven Lords had displayed but warned that any future endeavors to acquire relics from other realms and upset the balance of the universal forest was to cease. For the moment, their coven had been shackled to battling the Craven within the ethereal domains, for their interference in other lands had proven to be as deadly as the Anatari itself.

Medusa understood this condition, for she and the Drow Mother had both been at fault for the collapse of Trinity and the Sisterhoods meddling in other worlds by manipulating energies they could not fully comprehend. The forest of stars would continue to exist with or without them, and the time had come to take care of their own.

৪০৫৪

Dawn sat with her mouth agape, her bright eyes looking upward to their queen mother as Nyx finished her tale.

"...And that's all?" She pleaded with a pout of disbelief while the other faeries both large and small congregated within the room became flustered with expectation, "But what happened to the Sisterhood, and the tower, and the fat Dwarves, and the funny Orcs, and the sneaky Drow, and the snotty Elves, and the scary Craven, and the...?" The small fairy went on an on, until Nyx raised her wooden hand to interrupt the eager sprite.

"All will be answered, little one, but you must have patience," the tree mother offered to the crowd of fey gathered before her throne, and with a grimace etched upon her cheeks, Dawn glowered in her silence. The other beings from the rivers and woodlands muttered among themselves about the context of the elaborate fable but instead, chose to let the outspoken morning fairy address their queries with the forest mother.

"Okay, okay..." Dawn began as she waved her arms to shush the other fey from harping her with questions, "Did the High Elves make the Drow Queen abandon their tower and their practice of *dark sorcery*?" She added with a sinister inflection in her tone for dramatic flare.

"Well, yes ...and no," Nyx answered with a mere hint of a smile as if to tease her audience, "Remember, that the main concern of the Elven Lords was that the Sisterhood of Blood, as they were called, might follow in the footsteps of Men. A concentration of unnatural power in the hands of a few was at the woeful cost of the many," Nyx bade as a justifiable answer. This gathered a thriving round of commotion around the fey, for they, of all the creatures in the world, understood the dangers of abusing magics beyond what was naturally allotted.

"What happened to the warrior women of the tower?" Dawn edged in after prodding by the fey whispering questions in her pointy little ears.

"There came a time when a phantom storm swept the realms, which even reached the remote shores of Tyre," the forest mother answered, "and the half-elf, Venusa, who had given up her old name to join the Sisterhood, was now renowned as 'Medusa Sorrowblade' beyond the diminishing world of the Elves. In this most dreadful time, the Drow had called upon the races of Elves from the mountains, forests, and sea to aid them in their battle against this encroachment upon the Faerylands; and Medusa herself encouraged the Dwarves to come to their aid," she finished with a look of guilt washing upon her face.

"The Dwarves?" Dawn spouted in disbelief, "I thought they hated the dark elves," she stated solemnly as the other faerie in the chamber nodded in agreement.

"They had come to understand the reasons behind their betrayal on the island of Antilla, and do recall that Medusa had become their champion at Orindale and was a legendary hero in their eyes," Nyx reminded the crowd, "the Tower of Madness protected the sisters from the Anatari in all forms, although this still left the Drow hidden within their sunken castle vulnerable. Thus, the Sisterhood could not sacrifice their own, for the Drow were the source of the Elfire from which they drew their mystic powers," she bade. With a nod of a few forest creatures, they understood this dilemma.

"And what happened when the Craven arrived on their tiny island?" Dawn dared to ask. Nyx sat forward and rested her arms upon her knees as she leaned into the group of fey at her feet as if to whisper the outcome of that fateful day.

"The honorable Dwarven armies traveled many leagues to answer the calling of their champion priestess which they had named Lady Sorrow. The Elves from the far corners of the realms were also beseeched for their aide but never arrived, for their numbers had dwindled to an alarming point. It wasn't that they would not help, it was that they *could* not!" Nyx stated with a jolt as she regained her posture, "The Obsidian Order fought with the storm of Craven that descended upon them, protecting the submerged kingdom of the Drow. It was a spectacular battle of magic against the consuming blight; the Dwarves, however, did not fare so well at the end of the day. Nearly all had either died or been devoured by the Craven, and there was little forgiveness for the failure of their Elven allies who abandoned them to fight alone with the Sisterhood trapped in their accursed tower. From that day, the Elves were marked as cowards in their furry-browed eyes," the forest mother related.

"The Elves turned their backs on them twice?" A tiny fey sitting behind Dawn spouted out in shock.

"Not intentionally, mind you, but their absence only managed to open old wounds. A dwarven sacrifice is not to be taken lightly, for they are a proud people," Nyx responded, "The war maidens won a narrow victory that day as the Craven scattered and their remnants surged onward to other corners of the realm to spread their decay; however, the Sisterhood paid a dear price as well in that assault. What fragments were left of the Dwarven people withdrew into the crevices of the earth and their kingdom, away from the reaches of all other races that might do them harm. Their trust had been shattered, and few could blame them."

"Do the orcs and goblins still slither in the darkness?" Another fey spoke out of turn while addressing the forest mother. The question touched upon their fear of the dark fey, for each had heard tales of the Orcs seething hatred for the Faerie.

"They had freed themselves from the Elves to pursue their own lives and their own realm, so I have been told. The elves that were left faded into the mountains, forests and seas, and hidden places unknown; and as for the dark elves, to this day I know not their fate," Nyx answered with a soft tone.

"But, but ...where are the Craven now, these An-ah-tar-ee?" Dawn struggled with the name they were called as she and the others were excited to know where these wraiths, these moving shadows of nightmares, might still linger. Nyx could see several of the innocent fey grasping one another in fright as if they really didn't want to hear the answer.

"The specters that were known as the Craven that continued to haunt the Faerylands were actually the collection of not only Men but of all living beings that had become a casualty of mankind's brutality and the unbalance they had created, which cascaded across this realm," Nyx mentioned to the astonishment of the fey whose voices began to erupt with worried gossip.

"You mean the Craven were not just the blighted shadows of the humans?" Dawn gasped in bewilderment.

"No, my child," the forest mother affirmed, "brutality is not the way of nature and those creatures, be they man or beast, whose lives find an end in such regrettable circumstance, risk becoming such lonely apparitions if they are unable to return to the spirit of the world to find peace."

The faeries all mumbled in agreement at the logic of this potent philosophy, as a flower or tree or bush that expired, would return to the forest soil from whence it came, so did the Faeries return to their selective elements; all of which was born of the Evermore, the thread from which was woven the essence of life. After the children of the forest calmed down, Dawn turned back to Nyx and asked what had happened to the dark archer Ironbow, and his giant wolf; and what of the enchanted key he had given to the half-elf priestess.

Nyx smiled and released more seeds of light from her palm which formed together to take on the likeness of the bowman, his dire wolf, and the amulet Dawn spoke of.

"Ironbow and Medusa remained friends to the ends of their days, he even helped her from time to time on many adventures; and it was then the blind half-elf had learned that the dark archer too had been trained by Druanna, the shimmering knight, which is why his arrows were made of glass," Nyx swayed the dancing lights to show the bowman shooting volleys of arrows at unnamable beasts from distant lands to the excitement and glee of the crowd of faeries, "and as for the key ...that mystical relic he had given her, which she had many opportunities to use but never did," the wooden mother explained before Dawn interrupted.

"What? She had a magic key that could open any lock and she never made use of it, wasn't that a waste of a gift?" Dawn exclaimed as others in the crowd wondered aloud.

"No, little one, for you misunderstand the principle of the gift her friend, the archer, had offered her," Nyx smiled softly, "you see, it matters not if she ever used the magic key, for what he had truly granted her was the notion that no door would ever be locked to her, nor any barriers she could not surpass. It was that small token which revealed to her a stepping stone she had not recognized that allowed the young girl to aspire towards a new level of self-confidence and courage," the forest mother gleamed while the rest of the fey smiled to one another as they shared in her honored wisdom.

"Mother Nyx, what became of the sorceress, Medusa?" Another fey asked from across the room as the soft glow of daybreak began to glisten through the branches of the great tree, and the fey folk were surprised that they had spent the entire evening enthralled by her colorful tale.

"As the Drow Queen had revealed to the half-elf Priestess; to protect the Tree of Life from the withering, the High Elves were forced to abandon the Eternal City as they fled the blight of the Craven. And so their numbers dwindled until the Elves, too, became lost in the mists of time," Nyx answered to the crowd as all eyes were glued upon her, "however," the forest mother announced with a dramatic pause as the morning light began to illuminate the heavens, and the stars above faded into the silky blue sky, "they're firstborn Faerie children, the Elvenborn, replaced them as the guardians of the Fey and protectors of the Faerylands. Many of the Elvenborn were as naive as a newborn sprout, but they too had to learn of responsibility and sacrifice. They learned to pity what Men had done to themselves and strived to help remove the blemish their race had left upon the world," Nyx, the elder tree sprite, revealed to her captive audience, "and they discovered what is truly important in life is showing kindness, compassion, and consideration for others so that we may all share this world together," the forest mother granted to answering the question at hand, "as for Medusa herself, I may have heard a rumor or two that she became a legend among the mystics and found her own destiny upon a long and lonely path now shrouded by the winds of time," Mother Nyx offered as consolation.

Her green eyes drifted into the brightening sky as the young fey, in all their different forms, who flew, or skittered, or crawled, saw the coming of the new day and dispersed from the grand chamber in the giant tree and made their way back into the forest. As she watched her fey children depart into the wild, the elder forest mother recalled a time long ago when, she too, was known by another name, in an era when she was but a curious young wood sprite who sought answers in this strange and mysterious world.

Ivy Elvenborn didn't grieve the loss of her raven black hair, nor her silken body and tender wings as she had grown with maturity into the ancient tree spirit she now was.   The Forest Mother looked down upon the aged bark of her wooden palm to the tiny glowing leaf embedded there, as a reminder of her pursuit of the Elves and the Tree of Life, and the valuable lessons she had learned along the way.

Focusing beyond her hands, Mother Nyx noticed that among all the clusters of Fey who had sat through the long night to listen to her fable and departed into the encroaching day, that only Dawn, herself, was left sitting alone in the center of the room; her hands folded upon her chin as she gazed upon the Forest Mother while she sat upon her mighty throne ...as though she knew something was left unsaid. Dawn was a stubborn little fairy, who quaintly reminded Nyx of herself in a time long past.   With a look in her sunny eyes, the tree spirit was compelled to answer the little fairy's unanswered question before she left on her duties to attend the sunrise. With a stretch and a yawn, the morning fairy glimmered with a beat of her wings as the first rays of sunlight began to dance across the sky; glittering upon the forest canopy and the sparkling dew gracing the fields of wildflowers.

"When can we hear another tale, maybe one that tells us what became of the warrior women of the secret sisterhood?" Dawn asked with curiosity as she peered over her shoulder out through the doorway; for the little fairy stood upon her tiny feet with a hint of expectation upon the call of daybreak.

With her own ancient eyes, Nyx had seen how the Faeries had healed the world, allowing the Evermore to return to these lands so it may flourish once again. She looked out over her peaceful sanctuary of the forest, feeling warm and content.

"Maybe tonight, little one, or perhaps tomorrow ...but know that not all stories truly have an ending, for their tales will continue in the lives of others, as does your own," Mother Nyx offered on a kind note; and with that, Dawn gave a quirky little smile of satisfaction and flitted off into the morning light.

ಬಂಡ

About the Author

Michel Savage has been devoted to writing throughout his career. If one reads between the lines, they will find his novels revolve around the reminder that we are only borrowing our small place on this planet but for a brief period of time, and to take responsibility for the environment, for one another and all other living creatures with which we share this world. And in doing so, hopefully planting a seed in our conscience of the importance to preserve what is left of the wilds, our untainted woodlands, and ever-dwindling rain forests.

He has shared his stories and artwork around the globe, and would encourage others not to waste too much of their lives chasing someone else's dreams but to follow their own.

One of the most valuable lessons he has learned is that there are far more important things in life than power and money, such as kindness, compassion, and consideration towards others.

...share that thought if you will.

World of the Elvenborn
Artwork from the Faerylands Fantasy Art Series
available online

www.GreyForest.com

Faerylands novels
The Grey Forest
Soulstorm Keep
Sorrowblade
Ivory

Faerylands I

The Grey Forest

Long, long ago the Faerie had roamed free, but for countless centuries now the fey themselves have remained unseen; hidden and withdrawn, shrouded within the boundaries of the Evermore. But just how they became imprisoned there was a mystery their own elders had forgotten or refused to speak of, and a subject of taboo among the ancients.

The Elvenborn had become a dying race, and now a strange and dreadful blight was encroaching upon their sanctuary. Ivy knew there was something terribly wrong with her world, something unspeakable her kind was hiding from. The Faerylands were vanishing, and she had to find out why.

Faerylands II

Soulstorm Keep

Many centuries after the passing of mankind, the blight known as the Craven still lingered, lurking within the shadows, a dark hunger awaiting its chance to consume what little was left of their ravaged world. Only one among the Elves knew the true face of their enemy, with the knowledge to awaken the Undying and save the Faerylands before the living veil of the Evermore was forever lost.

Ivy Elvenborn was presented with an impossible quest, one that would take her on a perilous journey to the steps of an ancient tower guarded by the secretive Sisterhood of the Drow, in her search for a mystical relic held within its walls.

Ivy knew that if she failed in her task, the entire race of Faerie would be the last of their kind.

Faerylands
Ivory
The Dreamkeepers

The Elvenborn were bestowed the task of healing their realm, a land left in chaos by the hands of men.

Limerick was but a simple bard who stumbled upon an epic quest, one that would test his courage and take him beyond the edges of the Faerylands. High in the mountains sat the ruins of Aldana, where the spirits of the forest gathered to bring balance to the world and end the dreadful blight of the Craven.

Along this journey, the young bard would learn that everything is not as it seems, and that dreams are but a shadow of something real.

Witchwood
The Harvesting

Every day around the world hundreds of people go missing without a trace. Year after year, their numbers add up to millions of lost souls who are never to be seen again; and their numbers keep climbing ...this is where many of them went.

Hellbot – Battle Planet

Tranquility was one of those out of the way planets in a system far out of reach from the normal space lanes. Loners, dreamers ...whoever they were, chose to colonize this world. Thirty cycles ago something went terribly wrong. It was rumored their terraformer reactor went critical, and few escaped the chain reaction that clouded the atmosphere with a planet-wide sand storm. A decade of hard labor evaporated overnight. What wasn't buried under the ocean of sand was left to fry under the twin suns.

Human explorers began to wander back into the forgotten zone. No one knew of the machines that had evolved, or the war that raged beyond the edge of the universe ...where mankind did not belong.

The Shadoworld Series
Shadow of the Sun

On a distant, slowly rotating world, Bronze Age tribes must migrate throughout their lives to avoid the long cold death of nightfall. As of late, strange events have been deeply troubling the tribal elders; revealing evidence perhaps, that something is lurking on the dark side.

As for a pair of young misfits, the ancient mystery is about to unfold; to reveal their peoples forgotten past, buried deep within the underworld, shrouded in the shadow of the sun.

Shadoworld
Veil of Shadows

Ash was an orphaned street urchin who grew up in the gutters of a desolate medieval city; his bitter youth spent picking pockets and snatching trinkets from the wealthy to survive. Over the years his art for stealth and sharpened skills had drawn the attention of the Thieves Guild who took him into their folds. Little did they know that the boys tragic past would one day find itself woven within the treacherous schemes of a mysterious spider cult.

As of late, a series of chilling murders had befallen several nobles within the privileged upper districts. Their gruesome deaths had appeared to be centered upon an ancient skull, a cursed relic which had recently found its way into the hands of a rich collector. There were few who would trespass upon the strange realms of witchcraft and dark magic ...but a master thief does not fear those who dwell in darkness, for he is one with the shadows.

Shadoworld
Shadows Gate

Asra found himself alone in the middle of the barren sands, unable to remember who he was or how he had gotten there. Saved by a caravan of traveling gypsies, he entered into an exotic world of dancing acrobats, fortune tellers, and mystics who performed their skills for cheering crowds across the desert empires.

However, his destiny would change the day he stumbled upon a forbidden shrine to find a mythical creature entombed beneath its shattered ruins. Promises were whispered and a dark pact was made with the ancient demon; a bond of magic that would lead him on a perilous journey to reveal his forgotten past.

Project EVE

In the late 1940s after the 2nd World War, a classified government program was created in order to explore the military use of psychics to gain an advantage for their soldiers during armed conflict. At a remote laboratory in the mountains, a secret compound comprised of several hundred test subjects were trained to enhance their abilities with the goal of achieving the skills of telepathy and mind control.

Assigned to investigate this covert project, Walter Grant found himself entangled in a web of conspiracy and deceit when he discovered that the residents of the colony were being held captive by the scientists who had hidden the ugly truth behind their dangerous experiments.

At the heart of the project was a girl named Eve, whose extraordinary mind held the key, a child who would prove to them why humanity could not handle such power.

Broken Mirror
Apophis 2029

Hurtling through space was an enormous tumbling rock known as MN4 our astronomers affectionately named after an ancient Egyptian god of destruction. Asteroid Apophis was the talk of the year that every scientific community on Earth was aware of, though its flyby in April 2029 was to be nothing more than a spectacular celestial event; but as warring nations were locked in global conflict, our civilization was unprepared for the devastation that followed in its wake.

Several years after governments fell and society dissolved a ragged pack of survivors stumble upon the buried truth, revealing what circumstances had led to the aftermath that ensued; leaving them to question their struggle to salvage what few splintered shards were left of our world that would forever define our bitter legacy.

Forgotten Future

At the edge of the world an impossible relic from the fables of antiquity has risen from the frozen wastelands of Antarctica. Professor Logan and his exploration team rush to investigate this historic find, but this unique discovery puts their lives in peril when they unearth the remnants of a long forgotten civilization left buried beneath the ice.

Within the twisting labyrinths below the melting glaciers they uncover an ancient culture which had perished from a mysterious cataclysm. They soon realize it was a polar shift which had caused their destruction, and our world was presently facing the same fate.

World of the Elvenborn
www.Faerylands.com